Dwight Whitney Marsh

The Tennesseean in Persia and Koordistan

Scenes and Incidents in the Life of Samuel Audley Rhea

Dwight Whitney Marsh

The Tennesseean in Persia and Koordistan
Scenes and Incidents in the Life of Samuel Audley Rhea

ISBN/EAN: 9783337294526

Printed in Europe, USA, Canada, Australia, Japan

Cover: Foto ©Raphael Reischuk / pixelio.de

More available books at **www.hansebooks.com**

THE TENNESSEEAN

IN

PERSIA AND KOORDISTAN.

BEING

SCENES AND INCIDENTS

IN THE LIFE OF

SAMUEL AUDLEY RHEA.

BY

REV. DWIGHT W. MARSH,

FOR TEN YEARS MISSIONARY IN MOSUL.

PHILADELPHIA:

PRESBYTERIAN PUBLICATION COMMITTEE,

1334 CHESTNUT STREET.

NEW YORK: A. D. F. RANDOLPH, 770 BROADWAY.

LIST OF ILLUSTRATIONS.

CONTENTS.

1 *   5

6 CONTENTS.

PREFACE.

Tennessee gave us a President—Andrew Jackson—who said, "The Union must and shall be preserved." Many have sealed those words with blood.

Tennessee has given to Persia a life and death which say, "*The knowledge of Christ must and shall be given to every creature.*" Many will die to make these words good.

Various persons in Asia and America, noting an example so worthy of grateful remembrance, have for two years past given much time to provide materials for this work. The reader may now follow this young Tennesseean to the inner fastnesses of almost pathless mountains. Adventures among robber chiefs in border wars will attract the young. The more thoughtful will ponder the fate of empires and vanity of life, as they follow the track of Xenophon, Alexander and Cyrus, or muse in the hollow tomb of Nineveh.

Christians, it is believed, will catch fresh inspiration from a soul so capable of responding to the call, "Come up higher." They will never weary of looking into the struggles, pangs, joys, agonizing wrestlings and glorious victories of this fellow-soul.

The name Rhea is already written upon the map of East Tennessee. It is written on hearts in Persia, and shall yet be written on the banners of many of God's embattled hosts.

These pages, as the reader will readily see, have caught intense interest from friends in Tennessee and Persia, and especially

7

from Dr. Justin Perkins, of Oroomiah, and from the one who was nearest Mr. Rhea in life and in the thrilling scenes of his death. The omission of a profusion of valuable matter has been the most difficult and trying part of their preparation.

Only in this sentence can the author disclose how very much the work owes for delicate revision and unwearied care in its embellishment to Rev. J. W. Dulles, of Philadelphia.

That Jesus may own it in the progress of his cause is our prayer. How can we forget the blessed foreign work! In this far land, our dear native land, we sometimes feel as the exiles felt at Babylon.

D. W. M.

ROCHESTER, February 22, 1869.

THE

TENNESSEEAN IN PERSIA.

CHAPTER I.

A GLIMPSE, GEOGRAPHICAL AND BIRD'S-EYE, OF MR.
RHEA'S FUTURE HOME.

COME with the swift-winged ships out of New York harbor, past Gulf Stream and Azores, between Europe and
Africa, through the Gates of Hercules. Linger not along
vineclad shores of Spain and Southern France; tarry not
for Italy or Barbary States; forget Carthage and Rome.
Come past Etna and Malta and classic Greece, and from
the eastern end of the Mediterranean, look up at goodly
Lebanon, more grand with every mile of approach. How
its snowy peaks catch roseate tints from the flush of morning! Take wings and fly right up to its cool summit, ten
thousand feet high, and look eastward. At your right,
beyond Hermon, lies Palestine; but across the Baalbec
valley, over Anti-Lebanon, beyond Palmyra and Damascus, for centuries Arabia has pressed its entering wedge
into Turkey, and, notwithstanding the Turkish shadow on
our maps, Arabia holds possession of all Central Mesopotamia. Wandering Bedouins threaten alternately the gates
of the bordering cities; i. e., Jerusalem, Damascus and
Aleppo on the West; Orfa and Mardin on the North;
Mosul and Bagdad on the East. You cannot leave the

9

gates of one of these cities on the Arab side without, as Layard wrote of Bagdad, running some "risk of making a triumphal re-entry in your shirt." Look across this Northern Arabia, and then at one flight pass over Euphrates and Arab tribes, and come four hundred miles to the Tigris, lighting on the towers of Mosul at the very gates of old Nineveh.

On Lebanon you were ten thousand feet above the level of the sea; at Nineveh, only three hundred feet. On Lebanon you were by the "Great Sea;" at Nineveh, at the central point, far inland, equidistant from the Black Sea and Persian Gulf, the Caspian and Mediterranean, four hundred miles from the two latter, and almost on the level of their waters.

. All Arab Mesopotamia south of Mardin, except the sharp mountain-ridge Sinjar and the mountain-peak Koukab (Star), is hardly higher than Nineveh; indeed, the Bedouins *never live*, and *rarely go*, where they cannot sweep at a gallop over the plains on their fleet mares. The broad basin has hardly a tree, and consequently, in its removal from any large body of water, during the rainless months of summer becomes intensely heated and parched. But there is no sandy desert, for, in winter and spring, grass is knee-deep, and nomad Koords (called Cochers,) and Arabs with countless flocks, roam over the wide expanse, whilst their sheep and dogs stain their feet and sides with the dyes of myriad flowers.

No fairer pastoral scene can be conceived than an Arab encampment in spring east of Sinjar. No house or tree is there for miles and miles, but scattered tents on every side. A hundred miles away east and north, the snowy mountain ranges form a rim of silver to the scene, and on the swelling slopes at hand, are flocks of sheep, camels wandering at will, Arab mares tethered to the long spears thrust

ARAB ENCAMPMENT.

into the ground at the tent doors. Patriarchal forms like Abraham or Job, in brilliant costumes and snowy beards, sit in the tent shade, while, with pitchers to the spring like Rachel and Rebecca, gentle forms glide here and there, from tent to tent, or among the lambs of the flock.

Would that I could make you see it! Once seen, these Oriental views remain a joy for ever. The West has nothing just like it, although the visions of Pike's Peak, from the plains of Colorado, have some of its features.

Stand, then, on the north-west angle of the wall of Mosul, where the tower is more than a hundred feet high, and look eastward. If it is late winter or early spring, you have behind you four hundred miles of Arab verdure on the great plain stretching to Hermon and Lebanon. At your right the Tigris stretches south to what was the garden of Eden, thence flowing among palms and groves of orange to the Persian Gulf, seven hundred miles away.

Just across the Tigris, not a mile distant, lies Nineveh and Nebby Yonas, like a chain of mounds and hills, sleeping for ever. Beyond, at eighteen miles' distance, towers Jebal Makloub (Overturned Mountain); and still beyond rise mountain ranges forty, fifty, seventy, and even one hundred miles, tier above tier, yet still in sight. Winter and summer here ever strive, summer never yielding the plains, and winter ever holding the hills. So it was when Cyrus issued from these mountain-gates of Persia to drop down a conqueror on Babylon. So the Tigris flowed when Alexander, a few miles at your left, bade his soldiers strip on the bank, bear their bundles of clothing aloft on their spears, grasp each two the same spear, and wade in rank by rank, some to perish, but most to reach the eastern shore. Alexander passed right by Nineveh, and there, just back of Makloub, fell upon Darius and his million. The Tigris flows on just as when Xenophon passed, right

2

here, with his ten thousand. Here Jonah came when the glory of Nineveh was at its height.

Take the wings of morning once more and fly up from Nineveh to the eastern hills. Strike out north-east across the Tigris and Zab rivers and nearer ranges, and finally pass the deep gorges and precipices and passes of the highest mountains, and there, high above the highest peak, you can look off to the Oroomiah lake in Persia, seventy or eighty miles away. But only a hundred miles from Mosul, just over the Jeloo crest, and seven or eight thousand feet above the level of the sea, lies the valley of Gawar, the future home of Mr. Rhea.

From your high post let your eye now take a circuit of forty miles north and south, and fifteen or twenty east and west, and you look down upon the Gawar mountain plain. The stream that gathers the icy waters flows north through the valley, then turns west and joins the Zab, and finally, through gorges and chasms, flows down to the Nineveh plain, into the Tigris, and on to the Persian Gulf. Here, at the top of the world, the snows often linger in the Gawar valley till late in April, and, in midwinter, mercury sometimes congeals. Snow sometimes falls two-and-a-half feet in a single storm, and collects during the long winter to almost incredible depths.

Jonah, even when the fierce sun of Nineveh "smote upon his head so that he fainted and wished in himself to die," could look eastward and see the peaks where snow still lingered. The writer left Mosul for Persia in July, and after a few days, within a hundred miles of Nineveh, passed over acres of snow. It never leaves the higher peaks of the Koordish mountains, although at times it becomes almost black. The highest peak, that of Jeloo, is within a hundred miles, and sometimes discernible from Mosul.

Take your position under the great Jeloo peak (the highest), on a mountain spur jutting from the west on to this Gawar plain, just over the village of Memikan. You are in the wild heart of Koordistan. Fierce Koords, and Nestorians hardly less fierce, occupy the villages in sight from your mountain-top, and Koordish chiefs look down, ready to swoop from their robber eyries on the traveler.

In 1850, Dr. Perkins, of Oroomiah, led a large party—among them the writer—out from Persia into this upper creation. There was Rev. Mr. Bowen of the English Church, afterward Bishop Bowen, now in heaven; there was Judith, the "Persian Flower;" there was Rev. Mr. Stocking, ascended now to the mount of God, and Miss Fiske the heavenly-minded, also worshiping above; Miss Rice was there, still in charge of that blessed Oroomiah Female Seminary, and Mr. Sandretzki, serving still the Church Missionary Society in Jerusalem. There also were Rev. Geo. W. Coan and Mrs. Coan, the latter (with her husband and Mr. Rhea) to be the first Frank lady to brave a winter in Gawar. The singers of the party ascended the crag overhanging the village and overlooking the plain, and with full hearts sung out heartily in God's name:

> "On the mountain-top appearing,
>   Lo, the sacred herald stands!
> Welcome news to Zion bearing—
> Zion long in captive bands."

And thus over Mr. Rhea's future home, one year before he saw it, the gospel banner was unfurled, and we took possession in the name of the Lord.

Let us from this eastern height turn back to America, and look into the home in Tennessee which he left for his solitary and dangerous post in Koordistan.

CHAPTER II.

HIGHLAND TENNESSEE.

LOOKOUT MOUNTAIN, EAST TENNESSEE.

O F the many beautiful regions from which the waters of the Mississippi flow, none is more beautiful than the great valley of East Tennessee, in the heart of the Alleghanics. There you may find Blountville, halfway between the Cumberland Mountains of Kentucky and the Blue Ridge in North Carolina, where Virginia and Tennessee overlap each other, thrust in between Kentucky and Carolina.

Bald Mountain, the highest point east of the Rocky Mountains, is not fifty miles away. Chestnut Ridge and Blue Ridge, Cumberland Range and Cumberland Gap, are close by, in a region, since the war, for ever memorable. Waters pure as crystal flow from hill-top and mountain, fed by a thousand springs in groves of oak, chestnut, pine, maple and beech. The beautiful rivers Clinch and Holston, each longer than the Thames, yet mere twigs on the vast trunk of the Mississippi, unite not far from Knoxville and form the Tennessee, flowing on by Chattanooga and the bold, picturesque and historic Lookout Mountain. After gathering its waters from Virginia and North Carolina, the Tennessee flows on through Alabama and Mississippi, and then north, through West Tennessee and Kentucky, into the Ohio, through which it reaches the Father of Waters.

The beautiful highlands along the great valley of East Tennessee, already the home of thousands, will soon become the resort of poets and artists, and a health-retreat for savannas inhabited by millions of men.

There, in 1826, the daughter of a general of the Army of the Revolution was received as a bride by a successful young merchant. Happy hours passed on golden wings. But, one month after she saw her first-born, whose adventures in distant lands we shall now trace, they followed the beautiful mother, early dead, to the village graveyard.

God supplied a gentle friend, who writes: "I can look back on the dear little motherless babe whom I so tenderly loved and carried around the town to be nursed by different persons, more especially by a dear aunt, a sister of his

2 *   B

mother, who always seemed to feel it a privilege to give to the little helpless one."

The pastor's wife next gives us a mere passing glimpse of a little boy of five, at the hour of family worship, with his little chair always near his father, his little hand loving best that manly clasp as they two walked to the evening meeting for prayer, sometimes sadly to the dear grave, and regularly to Sabbath-school and village worship.

So far as pure air, clear waters to swim or fish in, beautiful groves for nutting and climbing, and grand mountains around can elevate, he had from mother earth the high privilege of being well born.   A classmate of academy days has told us how they sported and studied together, of noble oaks on Blountville Academy Hill, not only for sharp knives to carve immortal names, but where they constructed rude seats among the strong boughs screened by canopy of oak leaves—very kings.

While yet in the academy at Blountville, seated in the academy attic, he one day laid down his Euclid, turned to one of two friends seated by him, and told him that he had been deeply pondering questions of duty that extend over all this life and into eternity.   He asked and received the revelation of the other's soul.   Shortly after, aged fifteen, he united with the Presbyterian Church, of which his father had long been ruling elder.

Newly consecrated to the service of the Captain of Salvation, when he passed thoughtfully into the yard where he expected some day to lie by his mother's side, and read the maiden and married name of the one who loved him on earth for one month as no other in all the earth could love, he received a life-long impression.   Ever after, by sea and land, in the Old World as the New, he cherished his mother's memory.   Her maiden name was Anna Rutledge. Close by her grave he read the following inscription:

SACRED

TO THE MEMORY OF

GEN. GEORGE RUTLEDGE,

WHO DEPARTED THIS LIFE ON THE 1ST OF JULY, 1815,

AGED 53 YEARS.

Gen. Rutledge, the grandfather of Mr. Rhea, served with honor to himself and usefulness to his country in the Army of the Revolution, was member of the convention that formed the Constitution of Tennessee in 1796, and for many years thereafter was a representative from Sullivan county, Tennessee, in the State Legislature.

The married name of Anna Rutledge was Anna Rutledge Rhea. She married Samuel Rhea, Esq., and the name given to their soon motherless boy was Samuel Audley. The father, Samuel Rhea, was a merchant of sterling integrity and eminent piety. He was for more than forty years a ruling elder in the Presbyterian church of Blountville, and indeed may be called its founder. He gave liberally of his time, money and influence for its support through life, and took an abiding interest in all the churches of the Synod of Tennessee. He often attended the meetings of his Presbytery and of the Synod, and occasionally of the General Assembly. By his wise counsels and liberal heart he did much for the prosperity of all the churches of East Tennessee. No layman in that region took a deeper interest in the welfare of the Presbyterian Church than did this good man.

The general operations of benevolence had his hearty co-operation and support. Early did he enter into the Temperance Reform, and he did good service in helping it forward. His annual contributions to the cause of Foreign and Home Missions were generous, and at one time he gave to the American Bible Society one thousand dollars. He died peacefully in 1863, in the midst of our civil war.

Mr. Rhea was of Scotch-Irish ancestry. His great-grandfather, Rev. Joseph Rhea, a Presbyterian minister of the parish of Langhorn, Ireland, married Elizabeth McIlwaine, of county Donegal, near Londonderry. He came to America in 1770, lived in Philadelphia, Octorara, and then near Taneytown, Maryland. In 1776 he accompanied a military expedition to Tennessee, and decided to settle in the region afterward the home of his descendants. He returned to Maryland and sold his property, but, while preparing to move, died in 1777. The widow and family reached their home in Sullivan county, East Tennessee, in February, 1779, and here their descendants still dwell.

As Mrs. Rhea died shortly after the birth of her son, he was deprived of the affectionate care of a mother's love; but that want was supplied by the nurture and tender training of a most estimable aunt, Mrs. Elizabeth Fain, whose lovely Christian character was duly appreciated by her foster-son.

After a widowhood of five years, his father was married a second time, to Miss Martha Lynn, a lady of mature Christian character, and well qualified to assume the delicate responsibilities of a step-mother. She discharged these duties with great fidelity, and secured the affection as well as respect of her step-son.

The house in which the boyhood of Mr. Rhea was passed was most comfortable. It was of brick, two full stories, with a front of forty feet, and an L back. It was situated on a slight eminence rising from a small stream which flows through the town. The view was beautiful up and down the valley, and the majestic hills, which shut in the view in other directions, were covered with large forest trees.

In September, 1863, amid the horrors of war, about half the town of Blountville was destroyed by fire; this cheerful homestead among the rest, with all its contents.

His college days were spent in the University of Tennessee, at Knoxville. Here he took a high stand as a student, and gained the love as well as the esteem of his companions and of his instructors.

CHAPTER III.

IN NEW YORK AND ON THE WING.

FOR the following brief and interesting sketch the reader is indebted to Rev. R. P. Wells, well known as a clergyman in Jonesboro', East Tennessee, and more recently at Gilbertville, Massachusetts:

There lies before me a letter from Samuel Rhea, Esq., the father of the missionary, making inquiries relative to Union Theological Seminary, New York, with a view of sending his son Samuel thither to pursue a course of study. After having written full answers to each inquiry, I gave him to understand that sending his son to that school of the prophets involved the question of his sacrifice to the cause of foreign missions; that a missionary spirit was quite prevalent among the students, and that many of them were consecrating themselves to the foreign field; that this spirit was contagious, and his son might yield to its influence. Thank God! the father did not falter.

I knew well under what influences the son had been reared, and that the good seed sown so diligently and prayerfully would bear fruit in toils and sacrifices for the world's salvation.

No stranger could pass the night in that home of genuine hospitality and not be charmed with the spirit that there prevailed. Esquire Rhea was a rare man. He had an excellent heart; and the goodness of his nature, vastly enriched by the grace of God, shone in his genial face, gleamed in his eye and spoke in the tones of his voice. Gifted with a large share of good sense and native sagacity, and familiar with human nature in business relations, he could read men. Scrupulously exact and just in all worldly transactions, he had great weight of character in the com-

22

munity. Being known as a public-spirited, energetic, Christian man, his personal influence was by no means confined to his own county, but his name was quite familiar throughout the Presbyterian churches in East Tennessee.

He loved the Bible and the duty of prayer; and morning and evening he called around the family altar his large household, not excusing the clerks in his store, even when business was pressing, nor the servants in the kitchen. On all occasions his systematic, clockwork plans gave time for family devotion. A short portion of the Scriptures was read in an easy, spirited manner, a hymn was sung by the whole family, and all knelt around the throne of grace, uniting in a brief, fervent, earnest prayer. These devotions were not tedious, lifeless nor commonplace, but the youngest of the flock seemed to take an interest in them. And so, on the night of the weekly prayer-meeting, nearly every member of that circle was sure to be in the place of prayer. Often might you have heard this good man remark that prayers on such occasions should be short and to the point.

Pre-eminently did a spirit of love reign in that family group, and the smile of heaven rest upon that home. The roar of thundering artillery has since broken its quiet, and the fiery wave of war has swept over it; and when I last looked upon it, the blackened, crumbling walls stood in the midst of surrounding desolations; but the memory of its inmates—their words, their kindness of manner—will not soon pass out of mind.

To a young man going forth from such home influences, I felt that the question of personal duty as to the last command of the Redeemer would come with emphasis.

His course of study in the seminary was completed in June, 1850. By his classmates and friends he is remembered as a modest, diligent, thorough student, as a genial, warm-hearted friend, and as a living, working, zealous Christian. Under the influence of Drs. White, Robinson and Skinner, a foundation was laid for his subsequent high attainments in the ancient and modern Syriac, the Koordish and the dialects of the Tartar Turkish.

Having been accepted as a missionary of the American Board, and designated to the Nestorians of Persia, it was decided that he should spend the autumn and winter in extending his acquaintance and awakening an interest

among the churches of East Tennessee and the South-west,
and be ready to sail as early in the spring as the snows on
the mountains near Ararat would admit of a passage over
from the Black Sea into Persia. `These visits to the
churches made him many warm friends, and the pleasant
impressions left behind are by no means effaced.

His sermons were well written, and, delivered in his modest, unassuming manner, commanded the undivided attention of his audiences. Long will he be remembered as an
agreeable, impressive, faithful preacher.

It was a rare privilege to enjoy his friendship and share
his confidence. The sunshine of his countenance, the tones
of his voice, the urbanity of his manners, will dwell long in
the memory. Especially was he beloved and trusted by
the young. We wonder not that the simple Nestorians
loved him, confided in him and wept over his grave.

His ordination as an evangelist was by Holston Presbytery, in the old church on the hill, by the graveyard of his
native town (Blountville), Rev. Frederick A. Ross preaching
the sermon, and the writer giving the charge.

But a short time before this, having fallen in with Rev.
D. T. Stoddard, with whom he subsequently traveled to
Persia and was pleasantly associated in missionary labor,
his views were somewhat modified as to going out unmarried. It had seemed to him that he could serve Christ
more efficiently to be unencumbered with family cares, and
such a life appeared to be more apostolic and more in the
spirit of primitive consecration to Christ. These views he
had adopted deliberately and prayerfully, and nothing but
the decided opinion of an experienced Christian brother,
who had been on the ground before him, could have shaken
his purpose in the least. His choice had been made from
pure love to Christ and an ardent desire to advance his
cause, and at that late hour he did not think it wise to
change his plan, but he went to his distant field remaining
even as Paul.

As fellow-student at Union for two years, the Author
ventures to add the following recollections of Mr. Rhea.
When he entered Union Theological Seminary, in New
York city, in 1847, he joined a band of young men conse-

crated to the noblest work that can summon the energies
of the human heart.

White and Robinson and Skinner—names that live on
earth and in heaven—and the devoted Halsey, were instructors.

At that date those consecrated walls were like cedar and
spice and sandalwood, redolent with the blessed graces of
living saints just gone in Christ's name to Christ's work.
Of these, one (who was never seen by Mr. Rhea nor the
writer, who first met there) had left a most precious fragrance. He had given a new impulse to the love of souls.
Up to manhood an infidel, a wonderful conversion had
made of him another Paul. Like Paul, he cared not to
marry. Like Paul, he sought to labor in regions *beyond*,
where Christ had not been named. Like Paul, sometimes
he would be at no man's charges, but in India, independent
of missionary aid, wrought with his own hand to give his
life as a more personal gift. Like Paul, he sent his epistles
to all parts of the world, urging his brethren to higher life.
This one young man wrought a great work in Union Theological Seminary. I need not mention his name—better
known in heaven than on earth, better loved of saints and
angels than of men—as he still lives to seek the honor that
cometh from God only.

I allude to him because, during the days in which Mr.
Rhea was in New York, his memory was more potent than
that of any other student, and he made upon Mr. Rhea his
mark; an influence doubtless swerving a little in the direction of asceticism, and therefore to decrease as the presence
and power of Christ increased.

Even on the other shore, for ever memorable is Union ·
Seminary to Mr. Rhea, because there he learned so much
of Christ and of God's word and doctrine. There he began
to love that Hebrew Bible which to lose finally on the

3

Koordish mountains by Koordish robbers was worse than loss of gold.

There, resisting manifold temptations to neglect the literary society for city attractions, he was faithful to culture in debates and essays. None who have not tried it know how very difficult it is in a great city to sustain efficiently an entirely voluntary literary society. The writer remembers well Mr. Rhea as one of the "faithful among the faithless found." That faithfulness to literary as well as every other duty was characteristic, and a key to subsequent remarkable success.

But far more than poet, orator, historian could teach him, or even any human interpreter of God's word, he learned in the wrestle with God's Angel of the Covenant to wring from him a blessing in choosing a field of labor from Jesus direct. Nor did his Saviour leave him without *human* sympathy; for, while the power of city temptations, multiplied by the aggregated force of young fellowship, sympathetic and captivating, to break away from all restraint, human and divine, seems *almost* irresistible, on the other hand, the restraining power of a praying student band in Union Theological Seminary generally calls down the mighty presence of God's Spirit in a measure that is really omnipotent.

It is unquestioned that few men ever went through deeper struggles, going to the foundation of being, than did Mr. Rhea in the Seminary. It is believed that he touched bottom and built upon the rock, and that he built not of hay, chaff, stubble, but almost entirely of gold and silver and precious stones. The character of his manhood was there determined, and his subsequent career was but the glorious shaping in the Master's hand of a life then fully given up to Jesus.

He entered Union Seminary a youth, he left it altogether

a man; he entered provincial, he left it for ever cosmopolitan; he entered a Southerner, he left it an American; he entered it a citizen of the Union, he left wholly a pilgrim and a stranger in this world; he entered it expecting in future life a happy home near beloved parents and friends in his own sunny South; he left it expecting a Koordish mountain hut for his dwelling-place, and looking for no home but heaven. Was Christ better or worse to him than he promised? We shall see.

We append a closing sketch of Mr. Rhea's early life in Tennessee, a fragment from the pen of one whose eyes even then seem to have rested on him with some complacency:

"When Mr. Rhea was at college in Knoxville, Tennessee, his careful father took pains to procure an excellent boarding-place for him in the family of Mr. Joseph King, an elder in the Old School Presbyterian church, who lived up town a long distance from College Hill. In going to meals he passed a small white house with green blinds and rose-covered portico, in which portico he often saw the only child of the widow lady who lived there. The child remembers him slightly from that time, and particularly as belonging to the small number of young men then in college, members of the Church, and exhibiting Christ's spirit before the world by a pure walk and holy conversation.

"Afterward that little family became incorporated in another, and removed to Jonesboro'. Mr. Rhea had meantime finished his collegiate and theological studies, and had come to the *rare*, and, to many, unaccountable decision to leave home, friends and native land for the self-denying life of a foreign missionary; and it happened that a meeting of synod convened in Jonesboro', in the beautiful church, then freshly painted, and solemnly dedicated, like the young missionary, to the service of Jehovah.

"The two most conspicuous persons at the synod, observed by all observers with emotions of mingled love and admiration, were Dr. Coffin and Mr. Rhea—one an aged man, ripened for heaven by a lifelong service of faith and good works in the gospel ministry, approved of God and man, reverenced in the churches as one who had fought the good fight, kept the faith, and was now only waiting the Master's signal to exchange the cross for the crown. He was a beautiful man to look upon, bearing the impress of benignity upon his furrowed yet glowing features, and wearing a crown of silver hair.

"The youthful candidate for mission life appeared in charming contrast, taking up the implements of spiritual warfare, for he was 'but a youth, and ruddy and of a fair countenance,' like David, when, alone and single-handed, he went out before the hosts to combat with the giant who defied the living God.

"After the service, Dr. Coffin and Mr. Rhea were invited to supper at Dr. Cunningham's. His Knoxville observer was here at her mother's table, and received, for her father's sake, whom Dr. Coffin had loved, much attention from the doctor, but not a word or look from the diffident young minister. During the meal, Dr. Coffin said, in his cheerful yet impressive way, 'Are you sure, Brother Rhea, that you have counted the cost?' The youthful features were lighted up a moment by a smile of seraphic meaning, a sublime and holy purpose, as he looked up across the table into Dr. Coffin's face, and said, simply but satisfactorily, 'I think I have counted it; I have tried to.'

"The young girl at Dr. Coffin's side encountered the look, which impressed her in a manner which she could never forget; and the thrill of sympathy and attraction it awakened left its permanent record upon her memory.

"During the following days of his final preparations and farewell visits, many hearts went out toward him in tender

and admiring love. Motherly ones expressed their sorrow
that he should go unmarried and alone. Some thought
that his going was a lamentable sacrifice, while others
thanked God for such grace, and thought it noble and
sublime that he had heart and courage to count it joy to
follow the Master so. And thus he left his native land."

3 *

CHAPTER IV.

OCEAN LIFE AND LETTERS.

THE bark Osmanli has left Boston Harbor, crossed the stormy Atlantic, has passed Gibraltar, is gliding in the blue Mediterranean. She has our friend on board. Let him speak for himself in his first ocean letter to his parents:

MEDITERRANEAN SEA, }
Bark Osmanli, April 1, 1851. }

MY DEAR FATHER AND MOTHER—I have been waiting several days for a smooth sea, when I could sit down and quietly write the many things I have in my heart to say to you. In giving you a faint picture of our voyage, I will refer to a brief journal which I have kept, and will go back to the day of embarkation. At ten o'clock the secretaries and the friends of the missionaries met on board to sing with us the last hymn, and seek God's protecting presence across the deep waters. At two our sails were unfurled to catch the favoring breeze, and soon all that was dear to me on earth was fast receding from view. I stood on deck and watched object after object becoming dimmer and still more dim in the distance, until at last evening threw over us her dark mantle and the last object faded away. And then, as my thoughts began to cluster around my dear home, and as I began to realize that I was separating myself from you, an air of sadness crept over me, which I could not bid away. Nor would I, for it was a relief to give vent, though in tears, to all those tender emotions linked to country, friends, kindred and home. Still

30

I felt it sweet to give up father and mother, and sisters and brothers, for One whose claims upon me were still more tender.

From the day that we started until we reached Gibraltar we literally rode upon mountain billows. Not a day without rain and a constantly rolling sea, and scarcely a day without a strong, steady breeze. We were confined closely to the cabin; the decks being constantly wet with rain or spray, the winds heavy and cold, we seldom found it pleasant to walk on deck.

I have spent the greater part of my time in studying Syriac with Mr. Stoddard, Mrs. Stoddard being my classmate. We have learned two hundred words, and can read the Syriac characters with some ease.

We reached Gibraltar in nineteen days—a very quick passage. How anxiously did we all wait for the sight of land; although our three weeks passed rapidly and pleasantly, it seemed a long time to see nothing but a waste of waters. We were hoping for several days that we might pass Gibraltar in the day-time. In this our wishes were gratified. Early on Monday morning, March 24, we saw the coasts of Africa and Spain. Through a spy-glass we could see the green wheat-fields on the Spanish coast, and far in the distance the dim outline of the mountains of Africa. I mourned within me when I remembered that I looked upon the home of sixty millions of benighted Africans and deluded Musselmen. On my left, the continent of Europe with its millions, though far in advance of the other in the arts of civilized life, but little better prepared for the judgment-seat of Christ. And yet I rejoiced when I thought that, as the navigator in the name of his sovereign takes possession of the newly-discovered continent or island, so, in the name of my King, I could say to Africa and Europe, "Ye belong to Jesus, and though the night sit

heavy upon you, it will flee apace before the beams of the
Sun of Righteousness. Your valleys and mountains will
echo and re-echo the praises of our triumphant Saviour.
Even so. Come, Lord Jesus, and come quickly!"

At twelve we passed the Rock of Gibraltar and entered
the Mediterranean. I had looked forward with some
interest to the Rock, celebrated in olden time as the pillar
of Hercules, beyond which the timid mariner did not dare
to plough the deep; and in modern times as the strong
fortress—the key to the Mediterranean—for which England and France and Spain have fought so fiercely and
wasted so much life and treasure. The fortress is a rock
extending three miles into the sea, and connected with the
main land by a low, narrow strip. It is from a half to
three-fourths of a mile in breadth, and towers more than
fifteen hundred feet in the air. Its north, south and east
sides are steep and rugged, and forbid all approach. The
west slopes gradually to the sea, and the town of Gibraltar
stretches along its base. This side, lined with strong forti-
fications from base to summit, is made as inaccessible by
art as the other is by nature. Vast galleries have been
excavated, and are mounted with heavy cannon. This
garrison, well manned and victualed, is impregnable.

For many miles after we passed through the Straits we
could see the snow-capped mountains of Grenada on our
left, distant not far from a hundred miles. They seem to
be bare rocks entirely destitute of vegetation. They run
frequently into numerous sharp points, like so many sugar
loaves.

Yesterday was the Sabbath—the sweet day of rest. The
sky was almost cloudless, the sea was so calm that we
could have service on deck. All on board were present.
Mr. Stoddard preached. I tried to sing, one or two sailors
helping me. We felt it sweet to lift up our voices upon the

lonely air of that solitude of waters, and think of the love of Jesus.

God has given us some access to the sailors; we have given each of them a Bible, but two having Bibles. Every other night we read and pray with them in the forecastle. They seem to be gratified. Of all men they are, as a class, the most abandoned. But we do not despair, for we know there is One who can touch their hearts and call them from the dead. For our captain we have felt much interest. He is a kind man, attentive as he can be to all our wants. Unceasing prayer is made for him in our little circle.

April 7.—We passed Malta on the night of the fifth. We are now in Adria, through which Paul was tossed many days and nights. Yesterday we had service on deck. I attempted to speak a word from 1 Timothy, i. 16: "Howbeit, for this cause I obtained mercy, that in me first Jesus Christ might show forth all long-sufferings, for a pattern to them which should hereafter believe on him to life everlasting."

April 15, Monday.—This is the sixth day we have struggled against head winds, while we have beat about in the Gulf of Greece. Our captain, finding it impossible to force his passage through the Straits of Doro, thought he would go up the Gulf and give us a view of Athens. My emotions were indescribable when I gazed upon the land of Homer, Plato and Demosthenes—a land once world-renowned for all that was noble in philosophy, eloquence, poetry, arms, painting and sculpture. The captain did indeed give us a view of Athens. We saw the Acropolis. The Parthenon still remains, splendid in its ruins. Seventeen of the old columns, six feet in diameter and thirty-four in height, are still standing. But by far the most interesting thought suggested was, that just over those hills which line the shores of the sea near that same summit, and with

C

his eye fixed upon those splendid temples, stood the Apostle Paul, and uttered his thrilling oration on Mars' Hill.

We can now look into Mr. Rhea's soul through his own pencil-marks upon fragmentary sheets, evidently designed only for God's eye and his own. Thoughtfully notice some of the work of God's Spirit upon his thoughts, emotions and will:

March 31, 1851, *Sabbath.*—Rose by sunrise, a clear sky, pure air, mild sun and favoring breeze—a pleasant Sabbath. Oh when shall the cravings of my soul be realized? I have visions of what I desire to be, to feel, to know; but I do not realize them. My unceasing prayer is for God's Spirit, that I may realize to the full the yearnings of my soul after my Saviour. Oh that I might see that face all resplendent, so that my cold affections might be kindled to an intensely burning flame! O my Father, holiness, spotless and pure, is the craving of my soul.

Prayed for my dear brothers and sisters out of Christ, for several of my godless kindred, and my townsmen who have for many years stood out against the truth.

Monday.—Rose early—had an hour for prayer and the study of God's Word. For several days my hungerings after holiness have increased. I have longed especially for soul-satisfying views of God, but he has given them only in gentle drops. But God has evidently heard my prayer. He has led me to the Bible. Oh may I not hope that if God gives me hungering for that bread which he puts in my hands, I shall grow in all the graces of the Christian character? But, instead of revealing to me in subduing power his holiness and love, he showed me my own vileness. Only lead me to thyself, gracious Saviour! I deposit my poor soul with all its imperfections. Do thou choose the method of its sanctification.

Spent a short time with the sailors. O Father, let no one of them perish!

April 4, 1851.—Rose pretty early, earnestly wishing that the day might be for God, but I can only talk of regrets and disappointments. I have before me the ideal of the complete Christian. Why is it not realized? Must the experience of each remaining day be like this? Divine Saviour, undertake for me, or all will be disaster and shipwreck.

April 5.—Passed Malta last night; visited the sailors, read and prayed with them. My heart yearns for them. Oh that they might find Jesus!

April 6, *Sabbath.*—Rose early. Beautiful Sabbath morning! Jesus, the altogether lovely, revealed himself to me. Wonderful condescension! oh how little I know of him! It will not be so alway; I will, by his grace, know more of Jesus before he takes me home. Let this inspire me; yes, it shall quicken me. Preached on deck.

Here is the complete fragment of a day just as it stands in pencil-marks upon the scrap. Reader, have you had such a day?

April 7.—Rose early. My thoughts were with Jesus, my Saviour, my all. My first desire was to walk this day with Jesus, and he heard my groan; he had compassion. I washed my body, and prayed that Jesus would cleanse my heart, so that body and spirit should be pure for his dwelling. I clothed myself, and he put in my heart the prayer to be clothed with his righteousness, not as a garment, but to drink in his purity and holiness; and as I ate my food I prayed for bread and water for my hungry, thirsty soul; and as I walked abroad upon deck I prayed that I might walk in the spirit with God as Enoch, and that Jesus might walk with me and make my heart burn with his words of love. Thus Jesus was with me. Oh that I might carry Jesus with me, and make everything I do fragrant with his Spirit! My soul rests sweetly in Jesus.

April 8.—Cold and rainy. Came in sight of Greece: the name awakens thrilling associations, but to see her mountains! the brow of Taygetus white with snow, five thousand feet high, rising far above its fellows, her valleys, her plains, all themes of her poets, the land of poets and statesmen and orators and philosophers and painters and sculptors! Greece, once almost the solitary light that beamed upon our darkness; Greece, whose soil was pressed by the foot of the great Apostle to the Gentiles! At Mars' Hill, in Athens, in Corinth, the mart of luxury and pride, he hesitated not boldly to preach Jesus. Alas, how changed! Where once primitive churches, in the glow of youthful love, flourished, now churches called after Christ flourish; but alas! churches whose ministers are as vicious as they are ignorant, and whose superstitions are as burdensome as they are fatal.

April 9.—Disappointed with myself. Oh that at the close of each day I might say I have walked with Jesus! My soul will never rest until Jesus is all and in all.

April 14.—This day God gave me to see something of my heart's vileness. How deep-seated, how dreadful the disease of sin! Pride! Envy! Malice! And yet he did not leave me to despair. Oh, if there is any feeling beyond all others excruciating, it is to witness the occasional upheaving and outbursting of these hidden fires, which are checked, but not extinguished. I was humbled. I was amazed that God should permit me to speak to him. And still I was comforted; for before the day closed, I was enabled to rejoice in God's pardoning love.

April 15.—God lifted upon me the light of his countenance. Rose and sung with a glad heart, "Come, thou fount of every blessing." Felt well both in body and in soul. Perhaps much of peace and joy of mind is often the result of the bodily condition. I have learned that there is a higher life than simple reliance on frames; that is, simple confidence in Jesus in the hour of desertion as well as spiritual prosperity. I *felt* the presence of my Saviour, and it was precious, *passing all* understanding.

He writes again to his parents from

SMYRNA, April 24.

God has brought us thus far safely, and permitted us to set our feet upon missionary ground after a passage of forty-five days. What shall I render to him for all his benefits? It has been a pleasant voyage, and I trust a very profitable one. I think I have been enabled to live nearer to my Saviour. There have been times when I felt that I was receiving an answer to prayers offered in my native land. Jesus has taken me by the hand and said to me, I will be thy father and mother and sister and brother; I will strengthen thee for thy work. It was but a short time after we cast anchor that we saw the little boat, with Mr. Riggs, one of the missionaries, making for our vessel. It was pleasant and refreshing to meet warm-hearted Christian friends in this spiritual wilderness. I have much to say about Smyrna, but must defer it till I reach Constantinople. To-day we take the steamer, and will reach there in a day and a half.

TREBIZOND, TURKEY, May, 1851.

MY DEAR PARENTS: If you had seen what I have seen of the desolations which reign here, and felt what I have felt, never would you regret my leaving you. From the time that I first trod upon missionary soil, at every step I have taken I have rejoiced that I have been sent to these benighted lands; and if Christians in America felt as I believe they should feel, hundreds and thousands would

4

make an offering of time and property and talents to give them the bread of life.

I cannot express to you the surprise and joy I felt when, in Constantinople, I received your letter. We were widely separated, but your letter followed me so rapidly it seemed to bring us quite near. Our visits at Smyrna, at Constantinople and Trebizond have been very agreeable and profitable. Our friends have given us hearty welcomes. They say they never have regretted their coming to this land of darkness and death. I think I never saw more interesting groups of little children. During the few days we have been here we have been busy in preparing for our journey over the mountains to Oroomiah, and to-day we expect to set out. We think the road is passable, the snow having melted. On the plains it is now quite warm. We shall be on the way about four weeks. I have a huge pair of saddle-bags made of thick, heavy leather, so as to be secure against rain. They are hung one on each side of the large wooden pack-saddles, which are used upon beasts of burden. In one I put a small mattress for my bed. In the other, two or three quilts, my India-rubber suit for the rain, and a few changes of raiment, etc. Mr. Stoddard has a traveling chest in which he carries plates, knives and forks, a little tea, sugar, salt, etc. Our friends have put up for us a boiled ham, a few dried tongues, some light crackers. We will buy a few things along the way—milk, butter, etc.—and we have a tent to shield us from the cold and rain and dews. We have all that we could wish to make our journey a pleasant one so far as it can be made so.

Two Nestorian Christians came to be our guides over the mountains. I was glad to see the representatives of the people among whom I am to spend my life, and to stammer a few broken sentences in their language. I hope to make considerable progress in speaking the language by having

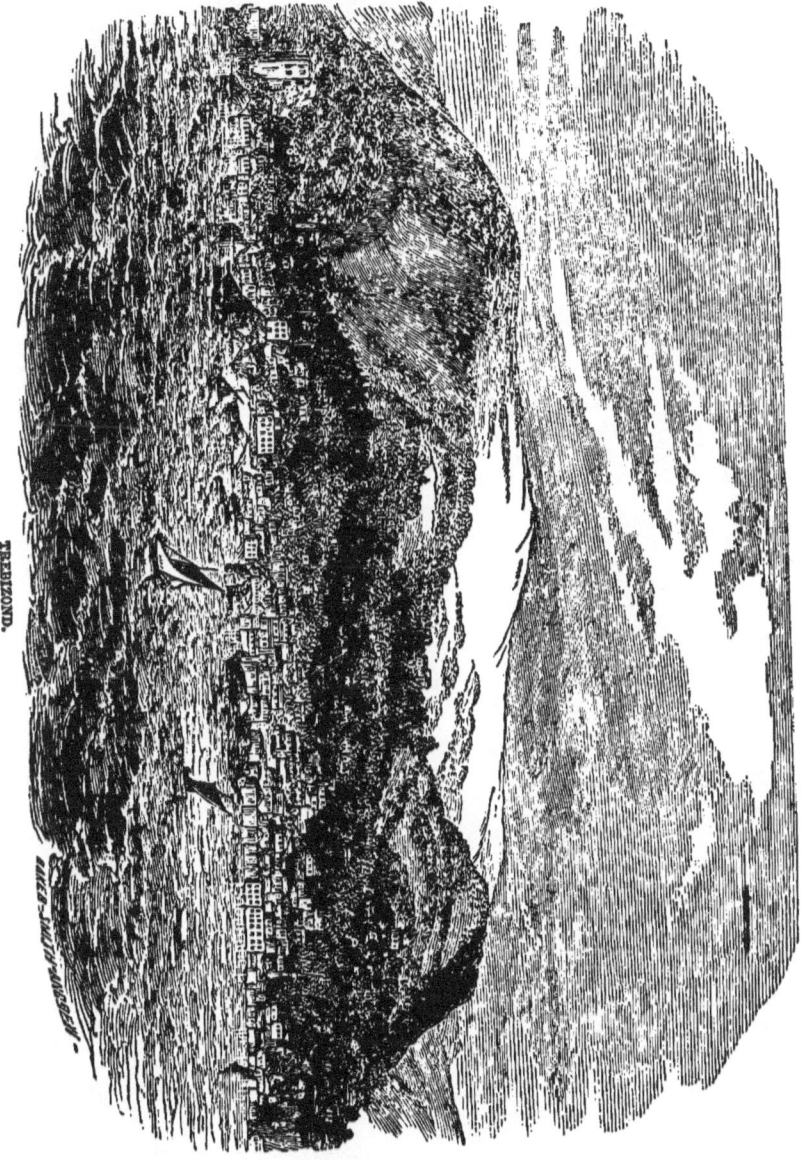

TREBIZOND.

them with us. They are both Christians, and last night Mr. Stoddard had a little prayer-meeting with them. One of them seemed much affected when he prayed for his poor people, and thanked God that we were going to them. If we can only go with hearts burning with love for dying souls, our going will not be in vain.

Trebizond, from which the previous letter is dated, is a large and ancient seaport, built on ground rising from the shores of the Black Sea. It is famous for the retreat to it of the ten thousand Greeks under Xenophon. Its houses stand tier above tier on the hillside, and look out upon the sail-studded but often angry sea. In the background are forest-clad mountains, in winter capped with snow. Erzeroom, from which the next letter is written, lies inland among the mountains, at the head waters of the Euphrates and on the road toward Persia, but still in Turkey.

ERZEROOM, *May* 30, 1851.

God has brought our little company thus far. We have been kept in the hollow of his hand, whether on the stormy sea, or on the burning plain, or climbing rugged mountains.

We are at the extreme eastern missionary station among the Armenians. On our way to the Nestorian field we have stopped at four stations, mingled with missionary brethren, heard and seen something of the wonderful movements of God's providences, something of the results of their labors in these dark lands. Some of them have toiled here for nearly thirty years. Their heads have grown white in the service of their Master. They came a band of defenceless men, looking only to the God of missions for protection and success. They dropped the precious seed and watered it with tears; and now they cherish the glad hope that when the Lord of harvest shall say, It is enough, rest from

4 *

your labors, they shall come again, their arms filled with sheaves.

The Armenians, numbering three millions, are scattered throughout the extent of the Turkish Empire. They bear the Christian name, but it is a name to live, while they are dead. Slaves of the grossest superstitions, their spiritual leaders as blind as they, and, if possible, more depraved, they have no true notions of God, of sin, of Christ, of the new birth or the way of salvation. They know that their crimes are flagrant, and the doom of the transgressor is terrible; but ask them the ground of their hope, and it is in the prayers of some departed saint, in the strict observance of their fast-days, in confessions to their priests or in a pilgrimage to Jerusalem. They know not Jesus, their Sin-offering, their complete and all-sufficient Saviour.

Ask them what it is to be holy and the reply is retire from the world, go to a monastery, to the wilderness, or a lonely cave, put on sackcloth, live upon dry bread, torture your body, and thus become meet for the purity of heaven. And when called suddenly to a bed of sickness and death, and they feel that soon they will stand before a holy Judge, if they can but receive from the priest the bread dipped in the wine, their fears are relieved and eternal life secured. They are utter strangers to the truth that there is to be a change in the heart of man before he can in peace behold the face of God.

Our tenderest sympathies must be awakened in behalf of a people upon whom the night hangs so heavily, whose errors are so gross and whose hopes of heaven are so false. But our hearts are gladdened by God's kind dealings with them.

Six or eight churches, numbering one hundred, fifty, twenty and ten members, at central points hundreds of miles apart, have been gathered. True, they may be small

compared with many American churches, but when we
remember that it was only a short time since when men
came tremblingly in the dark hour of night, to inquire of
the missionary what they must do to be saved, when they
were pelted with stones and cruelly beaten, when, their
property destroyed, they were cast into prison or driven
from their homes into lonely exile, and thus counted the
filth and offscouring of earth for simply confessing the
name of Jesus, and that now, although they are secured by
the government from personal violence, still they are insulted and reviled, treated as outcasts by their friends, and
many ruined in their worldly business—when, in a word,
we think how heavy is the cross he must bear who, in this
land, would follow Jesus—we will not despise the few who,
thus distressed but not in despair, stand up fearlessly and
hold forth the word of life in the midst of a crooked and
perverse people.

It was my privilege to celebrate our Saviour's love with
one of these little churches in an upper room in Constantinople. When I thought that in the midst of the darkness
which brooded over the empire, here were a band of men
whose affection for their Saviour had been tried in the furnace, some of whom for him had been beaten, imprisoned,
exiled and had suffered the loss of all things, I felt that if
American Christians could have witnessed the scene their
hearts would have overflowed with joy, and they would
have said we are far more than repaid, even if the work
should stop here.

But by the grace of God it will not stop. It will triumph.
Many of the converts here are earnest Christians; their
hearts burn in sympathy for their dying brethren. Through
their efforts, through the tours of devoted missionaries into
the interior and through the press at Smyrna, the light is
spreading far and wide.

Men have been found rejoicing in Christ and preaching
to all around them, who never saw the face of a missionary
or an evangelical Christian.   It was through the instrumentality of a Bible or tract, over which God watched as it left
the press at Smyrna until it reached their hearts that they
were enlightened.   A spirit of earnest inquiry is abroad;
intelligence of new awakenings is every few weeks greeting
the ears of God's servants, and the anxious cry, "Send us
missionaries," is coming up from many parts of this field.

ARMENIAN PATRIARCH.

This work among the Armenians has gone forward most

gloriously since the date of Mr. Rhea's letter, the attempt to bring them back to a pure Christianity having been crowned with a success that promises much greater progress in the future.

ARMENIAN PRIEST.

As might be expected, the resistance of their clergy is resolute, being sustained by every selfish motive.

There are nine orders of clergy in the Armenian church, the six lowest of which are porters, readers, exorcists, candle-lighters, sub-deacons and deacons. These perform the subordinate parts in all the services and ceremonies of the church. A candidate for the higher orders must first pass through all these lower, though they may all be passed in one day.

It matters little how ignorant a candidate for the priest-hood may be, provided he is able to read the church ser-vice; but two things are absolutely essential to his becom-ing a priest—that he discard razors and marry a wife.* As celibacy is enjoined on all the orders above the priesthood, by marrying the priest cuts himself off from all hope of promotion. This fact and the narrow and belittling nature of the priestly duties tend to fill the office with an unam-bitious, inferior class of men, whose ignorance and indolence are only equaled by their meanness and treachery. If the priest's wife dies, he is not permitted to marry again. He may, however, become a vartabed, and thus be thrown in the line of promotion. But it generally happens that a priest left a widower is more anxious to break over the rules of the church and marry again than to be promoted.

The *priest* in our illustration is seen in his bell-shaped cap and long broadcloth tunic with loose sleeves, which constitute his every-day street dress. While officiating in the church, his tunic and cap are removed, and over his shoulders is thrown a kind of cloak, which is pinned in front, and on his head he wears a close-fitting skull-cap—a far less tasteful arrangement than his out-door dress.

The priests are the most numerous of all the orders of ecclesiastics. They are found in large numbers in the cities, and every village has at least one, and more frequently two or three. Their support, often very meagre, is derived chiefly from fees which they receive for baptism, marriage, burial of the dead, prayers for the repose of souls, etc.

The order of *vartabeds* is by some reckoned collateral in rank with the priesthood, inasmuch as candidates are or-

* Says Rev. M. P. Parmelee, of the Armenian Mission.

dained to both, directly from the rank of deacon. By others
it is made a separate order, superior to the priesthood.
However this may be, it is certain the vartabeds are much
more intelligent than priests, and their position is invested
with far more dignity. The priests never preach; instruct-
ing the people forms no part of their duty. This work is
specially committed to the vartabeds.

ARMENIAN BISHOP.

Every considerable city has its *bishop*, whose diocese in-
cludes all the neighboring villages. He ordains all the
clergy below himself, receiving a fee for each ordination,

and if there be two applicants for the same place, not scrupling to give it to the highest bidder. The bishop has an important part not only in the management of the financial affairs of the Church, but also in the assessment of taxes demanded by the Turkish government, taking care that a fair margin remains in his own hands. He celebrates mass on all important occasions, and, while doing so, wears a most costly mitre and magnificent silken robes, and bears in one hand a silver mace of office (seen in the picture), and in the other a silver cross.

The *patriarch* is generally treated as merely a bishop with extraordinary jurisdiction and powers. For instance, the bishop of Constantinople is called patriarch, because, by virtue of his position, he is able, in great part, to control the appointment of all the bishops of the Empire, and is also the recognized civil representative of the Armenian nation in Turkey at the Sublime Porte. He owes his position more to political than religious considerations. The crosses and stars seen on his person (see illustration on page 44), as on that of the bishop, are badges of office and decorations granted by different civil and ecclesiastical authorities. The *Catholicos* is the highest of the ecclesiastical orders, and is the "Pope" in the Armenian Church, having his seat at Echmiadzin, near the Turkish border, in Russia, but having far less power than the Pope of Rome. He seems content with the honor of his position, together with its emoluments derived from the sale of bishoprics, the monopoly of the traffic in holy oil used in all important ceremonies of the church, and the offerings of the devout. All bishops are ordained by the Catholicos, while he in turn is ordained by a council of bishops.

The lack of vigor in the ecclesiastical domination of the Armenian Church, the people's profound though misdirected veneration for the Bible, and their native intelligence and love of investigation, have contributed largely to the success which has already attended the missionary work among them.

From Erzeroom Mr. Rhea writes again on June 30, to a friend: "We left Trebizond on the 20th of May, and reached the city of Erzeroom, distant one hundred and fifty miles, in eight days. They were very pleasant days to me, and I shall long remember our dwelling in tents. Our tent was large. We spread the ground with carpets and our mattresses upon them, and, although we had no chairs nor tables, we found it a pleasant mode of life. We rise by three, and are on our horses by half-past four in the morning. We generally ride from seven to nine hours. By that time the day becomes warm, and we pitch our tent. We were one whole day in ascending the lofty mountains of Armenia. In the plain the sun was burning hot; but at the summit unmelted snow-banks were all around. During our journey our eyes were charmed with scenes of surpassing beauty and grandeur.

"Four hundred miles of high mountains and burning plains are still before us. Thus far I can only sing of loving-kindness and tender mercy."

And thus, like a pilgrim, with a song he journeyed on the four hundred miles, past sublime Ararat over heated plain and snow-clad mountain to Persia.

5   D

CHAPTER V.

ARRIVAL IN PERSIA. FIRST IMPRESSIONS OF THE
VILLAGES, PEOPLE AND CITY OF OROOMIAH.

OROOMIAH, *July,* 1851.

OUR company reached Oroomiah, June 26, having been
on our way from America nearly three months, and
upon our land-journey about four weeks.

The scenes were as varied as the journey itself was long
and toilsome. Sometimes, for hour after hour, our road
was a narrow path winding up steep and rugged mountains, until, from some lofty point, we looked out upon
scenery unsurpassed in its grandeur and beauty; and sometimes we traveled day after day upon the broad plain,
spreading in one unbroken level far beyond the limit of
our vision. At one time our tent was pitched far up the
mountain side, surrounded by fields of unmelted snow; and
again it was upon the beautiful green by the murmuring
brook, its banks blooming with flowers of every hue; or
we were driven by the heavy rain into a caravansary—inn
and stable in one—and were lulled to sleep by the noise
of our horses chewing their barley within a few feet of our
beds. The thought that in just such a place the Lord of
glory was born, and in such a manger cradled, might well
reconcile us to all its inconveniences. At one time we
were traveling upon the banks of the Euphrates—here a
little stream, not yet worthy the name of the "great river;"
and now in silence we were gazing upon Ararat, lifting
serenely its snow-capped summit 17,000 feet in the air.

50

For some days we traveled over plains almost desolate, seeing here and there a lonely shepherd leading his flock in green pastures or by the still waters; and again we would be upon the plain, richly cultivated, with its fields of ripening grain, its gardens and orchards and smiling villages, or meeting the caravan of hundreds of horses and camels laden with the merchandise of Persia.

On the 25th of June we reached the village of Gavalan, thirty miles from Oroomiah. This is the home of Mar Yohannan, one of the prominent bishops. He visited America in 1843. His brother, Deacon Joseph, met us as we entered the village and urged us to come to his house. The father of the bishop, a venerable old man, came out to the gate leaning upon his staff, saluting us cordially with, "Peace be with you," "Peace be with you," "It is your house." We were brought into the best room. The walls inside were whitened, the hard earthen floor was spread with thick hair carpets. The natives use no chairs, bedsteads or tables, and consider it very impolite to bring in muddy or dusty shoes upon the carpets on which they sit.

The roof of the native house has joists of heavy unhewn timbers. Upon them are laid small sticks of wood, then a coarse straw mat; this is covered over with bunches of a thorny shrub which lasts for years without decaying, and last of all a layer of earth from one to two feet thick, made hard by tramping. By frequent repairing these roofs will last for many years.

Soon a large wooden tray was brought in, its edges covered with the long, thin cakes of native bread. Two or three bowls of milk, honey, eggs and a few wooden spoons completed our table.

We ate, sitting upon the floor, from the same dishes, without plates or cups, or knives and forks.

This is the first Nestorian village we have seen. Our

hearts were filled with gratitude, as, after a long and toil-some journey, we looked upon the remnants of a once flour-ishing but now sadly corrupt Church, among whom we are to live, and, if God is willing, make our graves.

We started early for the city of Oroomiah. Within eight or ten miles of the city our missionary friends had come out and pitched a tent, where they gave us a cordial welcome. Having spent a few pleasant hours with them, we set our faces toward our final resting-place.

Large numbers of Nestorians came out to welcome us. At one turn of the road we were met by a company of young men eager to grasp the hand of Mr. Stoddard, who had been their teacher, and now, after three years' absence, was returning to them. At one time we saw a man coming toward us with rapid step, dressed in large red trowsers, striped jacket and huge turban. I awaited his arrival with curiosity. He was Guergis, the mountain evangelist, once a bold and wicked ruffian, who climbs like a deer the cliffs of his native mountains, preaching to the dwellers in their fastnesses the unsearchable riches of Christ. We had not gone far before we met with the venerable bishops Mar Yohannan, Mar Joseph and Mar Elias, bidding us welcome to labor among their perishing people.

As we approached the city the throng increased until they filled the road, on foot, on horseback, old and young and middle-aged, each anxious to grasp our hands. I looked upon this scene with a full heart, and at times with overflowing eyes. I asked within myself, Who are these? Are they the people who a few years ago sat in darkness, without God and without hope? And will American Chris-tians regret that they prayed and gave that such a scene might be witnessed in the heart of a Mohammedan country? No, no! Pray on, Christian brethren. Continue to give as Jesus gave for you, and we will labor on until songs of

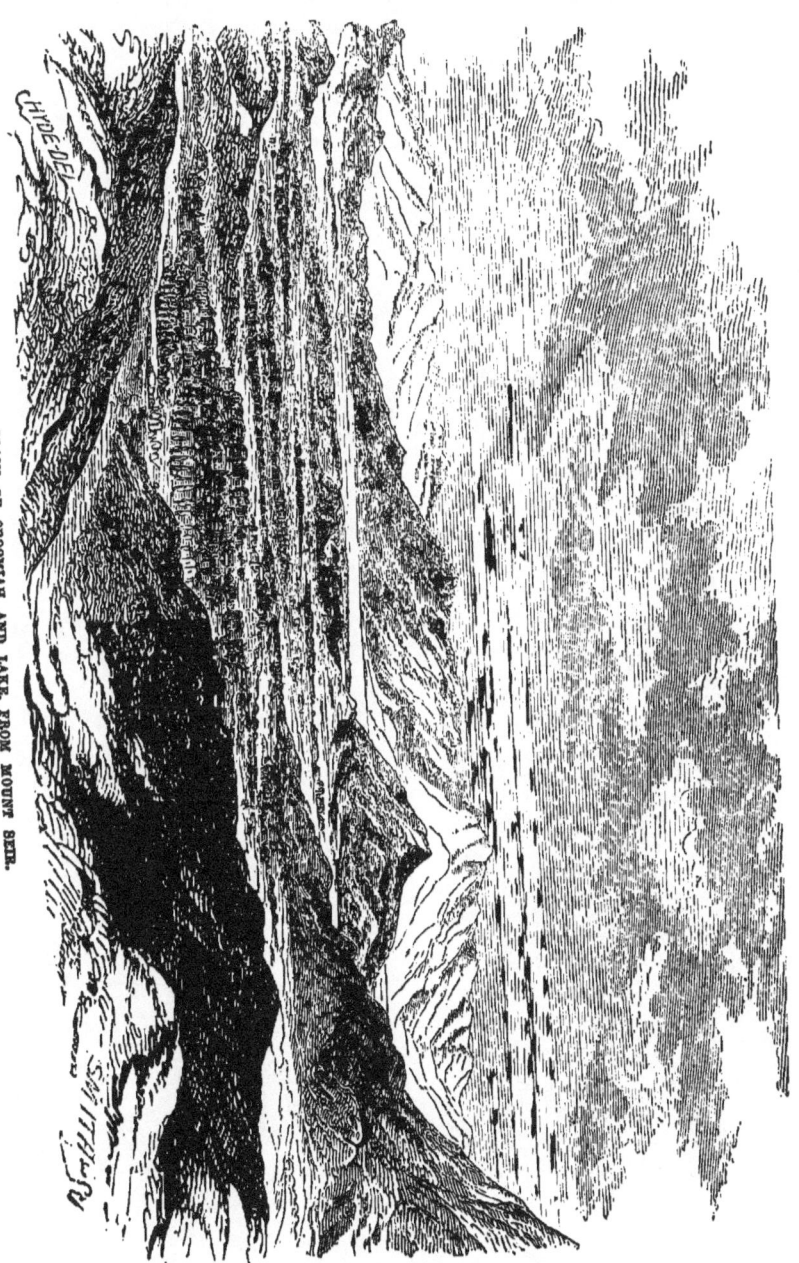

PLAIN OF OROOMIAH AND LAKE, FROM MOUNT SEIR.

joy go up from every village and hamlet on the plain and among the mountain Nestorians.

A HOME IN PERSIA.

OROOMIAH, PERSIA, *October* 8, 1851.

That I may give you a vivid picture of life in Persia, I will invite you in spirit to make me a visit; and what could be more delightful? I will imagine you just descending from the last mountain upon the plain of Oroomiah.

There on your left is the beautiful lake, but a few miles from your road. How calm the bosom of its dark blue waters! It has more than three hundred miles of shore, and is within twelve miles of the city.

Now your road winds among fields of rice, cotton, wheat and barley; now by a beautiful vineyard, its vines bending with rich clusters; now among orchards of fruit trees laden with the peach, apricot, pear, plum and nectarine; and now on either side of you are extensive melon-grounds, embracing many acres; and, finally, your road is leading through a beautiful avenue of trees planted along the banks of one of the water-courses. You see what a multitude of trees! They almost hide the villages scattered so thickly over the plain; for you must know that upon this great plain, stretching far beyond the limit of your eye, there are three hundred villages—two hundred Musselman and one hundred Nestorian.

This is Persian taste, for the Persians are very fond of shade, and take great pains to secure a refreshing retreat from their burning sun. Not one of these beautiful trees is spontaneous. All have been planted, and each is watered every few days. How forcible the description of the happy man! " He shall be like a tree planted by the (*channel*) of waters, his leaf shall not wither," etc. Every other tree here is fruitless, and soon withers away.

You see that small river in the distance? There is another, somewhat larger, upon the other side of the plain. From these two rivers many little channels carry the water to different parts of the plain and pour it upon the vineyards, melon-grounds and fields of grain; for no rain falls here for months.

Those villages among the trees, at this distance, you think very pleasant, but find the walls of mud, the houses low with flat roofs, the streets narrow and often far from clean.

SEIR GATE OF OROOMIAH.

Here we come to the city of Oroomiah. Its walls, you see, are built of mud, baked and made very hard in the sun. That deep moat all around the wall, twenty feet wide and perhaps as many deep, is the defence. It can be filled with water very readily, and cannot easily be crossed.

Your long journey is almost ended. There is one of the

gates, its folding-doors plated with heavy iron, through which we enter the city.

Ride in. As you pass on you see no house-doors, nor windows opening upon the street; only a narrow alley with walls rising blank on each side. Here is the entrance to the mission-yard. Pass through the wall. I welcome you to the hospitalities of a home in Persia.

You are now in a pleasant yard, square, and planted with plane-trees. The tall branches are full of singing-birds. The houses of the missionaries are built around this square yard. Ah! I see you are thinking them rather shabby-looking houses; but do not be too hasty. Our great Pattern, our blessed Lord, had not where to lay his head. These walls are of mud, but they are durable, very thick, and warm in winter and cool in summer.

But will you not step into my own room a moment? I welcome you with heartfelt joy. You see the walls are white and pleasant-looking. The square recesses are in Persian style. They are filled with my books. My bedstead is rough, but it is the best they can make. You admire the mode in which the Persians cover their floors; first the mat, and over it, in the centre of the room, the thick, strong carpet which will last a lifetime. Are not the colors neat and the figures arranged with much taste? These rugs around the carpet at the end and sides of the room, some three feet wide, are curious. "How are they made?" That groundwork of drab, of coarse wool, an inch in thickness, and those other colors in handsome figures, were beaten into the texture.

Are you ready to take a little walk? Excuse me for suggesting that you veil your face closely, for no lady walks unveiled in Persia. Let us follow this narrow street to the homes of the poor people among whom I am to live.

This is the Nestorian quarter. Each yard is surrounded by a high wall. Sometimes two or three families occupy one yard. We will enter the first door. The room is large, but how comfortless! The floor is mud, and *nothing* is spread upon it. Not a chair or table or bed is to be seen, and no windows, except two or three little holes in the walls.

That round hole in the centre of the room, two feet in diameter and from one to two feet deep, is the fireplace. In this they burn the native fuel. Here the cooking is done, and around this they spend the winter. That large opening above serves for a chimney; but until the fire is fully kindled, which frequently occupies more than an hour, the room is entirely filled with smoke.

Let us go outside and up a ladder. You have good courage to climb to this upper room. It is spread with coarse carpets. Those bundles are beds, which in winter they spread here, in summer upon the roofs. These little windows make it much more airy. It is pleasant in the summer season.

Wait a moment for the native meal. The wife (oftentimes little better than a slave) brings in a large wooden tray. Some have copper waiters. She places bread and one or two dishes. That dish, piled with rice which has been boiled in butter, is called "*Pilau.*" A little meat, some grapes and melons complete the course. Notice the husband sitting on the floor and eating with his fingers, the wife standing near, ready to obey his orders. Well, he has finished, and she is carrying the table away to the lower room, where she and the children can finish the meal.

Were we to enter a Persian house, you would find much more comfort, as many of them are wealthy, while the Nestorians are very poor.

Their spiritual condition is sad—it is deplorable. Were you to go often among them, your tenderest sympathies would be enlisted.

In your last note you close with the following line: "I wish I could go to Persia, but I am not good enough." Permit me, my dear cousin, kindly to correct your error. It is a common opinion, and your remark implies it, that a missionary is bound to be better than any one else. But is it true? What does God require of a missionary? To love him with a perfect love, and to spend all the powers of body and mind to his glory. Does he require any less of you or of any other Christian, in whatever occupation he may engage? And is not the one who is doing his or her duty in the ordinary walks of life good enough to be a missionary? God requires of every Christian perfect love and entire submission to his will. He requires no more of a missionary.

Mr. Rhea calls his letter-writing "a recreation from severer studies." All missionaries need untiring energy fully and suitably to acquire their new language, and Mr. Rhea was pre-eminently a student. The reader will bear in mind that these letters were only unstudied episodes from earnest work.

OROOMIAH, *August* 14, 1851.

MY DEAR PARENTS: To me it is a welcome hour, and I trust ever will be, when I can turn aside from my labor and studies to talk with you. I am well, and happy in my new home. Two weeks ago I went out with Mr. Cochran to spend two or three days in some of the near villages. I am at Seir, a little village six miles south-west of Oroomiah, with Mr. Stoddard. Three of the mission families live here, also the school for the young men is here. It is a pleasant little village, lying a mile and a half up the mountain-side, surrounded by shade trees, with pure air and a fine mountain spring.

Mr. Stoddard kindly invited me to be a member of his family while I remained at Seir. Mrs. Stoddard is very much like a sister to me; she is very attentive to my wardrobe, looking after many little things which, without a lady's attention, would be neglected. I do not think she will let me use my needles and thread with which mother so abundantly supplied me. But I shall not have such kind friends long, as probably my field will be among the mountains, away from the pleasant intercourse of friends. But the Lord, I know, will be with me there. All the mission families here seem to be very much like a band of brothers and sisters, sympathizing with each other in all their joys and sorrows.

I shall remain here until the hot months are past, and then go down to the city. The mission gave me a very good room, which I am preparing for my study. So far as earthly comforts are concerned, my wants are fully met. Missionaries here are not called to endure trials of that kind. Their houses, although of mud, are comfortable; the walls inside are whitened, and, being very thick, are cool in summer and warm in winter, and, although the roofs sometimes leak badly during the rainy season and drive the families out, still they are, perhaps, better houses than many poor ministers have in America. I have wished sometimes you could drop in and sit down with us around the table loaded with the fruits of the country—apricots, plums, apples, pears, melons and nectarines. Perhaps you might at first think it extravagant, but large watermelons and muskmelons are bought for a cent a-piece. The poorest people buy them. Fruit here is made a part of every meal; you will see upon the table for breakfast, dinner and supper three or four plates of fruit. I think it is at least half the living of the people at this season. I am now bending all my energies to get the language. It is a great work to become at home in a new language and speak it as the people do. God is helping me with it. By his gracious assistance I hope to overcome its difficulties, and in due time make known to this people the unsearchable riches of Christ.

One thing above all others I need—a baptism of the Holy Spirit. I feel that I cannot go forth to this people without it. "He shall baptize you with the Holy Ghost."

Is it presumption to expect it? Then pray with me and for me, that I may receive this indispensable qualification for the minister and the missionary.

It will be seen hereafter that he did "overcome the difficulties of the language." Our next chapter will be briefly devoted to the inquiry, Did he at *this time* receive "the baptism of the Holy Spirit," which he regarded as the "*indispensable qualification for the minister and the missionary?*"

6

CHAPTER VI.

RENEWED CONSECRATION. HE THAT IS HOLY LET HIM BE HOLY STILL.

THE writer is not singular in the impression that, among the thousands of Christians whom he has known, he has never met with one who walked more closely with God than Mr. Rhea. A missionary who crossed the ocean in his company said, "I never knew one who appeared so perfectly to reflect the holy image of our dear Saviour. His many rare qualities live in sweet memory, and we shall never behold their like again. The world produces but one such man in a generation, and it is enough for us that we knew him."

One in Eastern Turkey says, "I cannot express in words the high respect I had for him. He hungered and thirsted after righteousness. He longed to resemble Christ. He seemed fettered by the body."

Another missionary once associated with him in Persia, but come home to die, testifies: "The recollection of his prayers alone must strengthen you for all time to come. I imbibed from them strength for the future. How I have loved to recall his prayers—often making parts my own! When he has conducted our little meetings" (in Persia) "as his own soul seemed all aglow with the celestial fire, sometimes one spark has lodged in my heart for weeks, until a whole flame has shot forth, warming and enlightening the very corners of my soul."

Mr. Rhea had in the academy given himself to God to

be a Christian, in college to be a minister, in the seminary to go to Persia, and *now* in Persia to draw still nearer to God. He had been sick in August, and now, having recovered, is on Mt. Seir, in that house from which Mr. Stoddard in a few years will ascend to heaven.

Mr. Rhea is alone, and has pen and paper. He opens his Bible and reads and prays. See, his countenance glows! and Moses and Elias and Jesus seem truly to be here! After writing we see him take what he has written and kneel down again and read his written covenant aloud. It is dated September 16, 1851. He rises, comes to the table as to an altar, lays his covenant upon that altar, and signs his name in full—*Samuel Audley Rhea.*

He has given it to God, and God has accepted it and has taken it and given it to us. Let us take it reverently from God's hand and read and make every word our own. By God's grace, through the blessed Spirit, it will enable us to be more like Christ:

AN ACT OF SELF-CONSECRATION.

Our Father who art in heaven, in the name of thy dear Son, and in the strength of thy Holy Spirit, I come to thee. Deeply convinced that thou alone art my rightful Owner, that I have been bought with the precious blood of Jesus, I do solemnly surrender my entire being to thee; my body, with every organ and member; my soul, with every power to think, to feel, to will and act; every moment of my time; my property, my influence, my plans, prospects, interests for all coming time and under all circumstances, whether of joy or sorrow, adversity or prosperity; to be disposed of just as may please thee; to live or die, to be sick or well, to be despised or honored, to be joyful or sorrowful; my own will for ever to be sweetly and humbly lost in thine.

Upon thine altar I lay my all, because I know it is sacrilege any longer to withhold from thee that which is sacredly thine. I do solemnly renounce the dominion of Satan, and of sin in all its forms, and take thee for my Father, Protector, Preserver; the Lord Jesus for my Saviour, my sin-atoning Lamb, my Elder Brother, Shepherd and Friend; and the Holy Spirit for my Enlightener, Comforter and Sanctifier.

With feelings of deep penitence and self-loathing I mourn over years of the grossest and most aggravated sin, in view of which I cannot but feel that I am the chief of the chiefest sinners; and were it not for that precious word, "Jesus Christ came into the world to save the chief of sinners," I should die in despair. In view of these aggravated sins I do look away from myself and all human aid, and without one plea, direct my eyes to that dear, bleeding, suffering, dying Lamb of God, whose blood was freely shed for the remission of the sins of the world, and, if so, then for mine. Here I rest my only hope of acceptance with God, when, defenceless, I shall stand before his judgment-seat.

I am deeply convinced of my utter inability to begin or carry forward the life of God in my soul, and this work, which, O Lord, is thine, I do this day commit into the hands of thy Holy Spirit, and do resign my mind and heart to all his holy influences, to be enlightened, baptized, anointed, sealed and completely sanctified by him.

I rejoice this day that I have the hope that to me, the least of all saints, is this grace given, that I should preach among the Gentiles the unsearchable riches of Christ! To the work of the holy ministry I do now solemnly give myself, praying that I may be anointed by the Holy Spirit; be a vessel sanctified and meet for the Master's use; that I may make full proof of my ministry, endure hardness as a good soldier of Jesus Christ, be instant in season and out of season, and, so long as I have a voice to speak, plead with dying men to become reconciled to thee, only to the praise of the glory of thy grace.

I feel this to be the most solemn act of my life. I never can do a more solemn act. It is a personal transaction between my soul and God, and, though I tremble, I cannot shrink from it; and, though looking at my own sufficiency all is hopeless, I believe that thou, O Father, Son and Holy Spirit, wilt keep that which I have committed into thine hands.

And now, O Lord, seal to all eternity that which is and ever shall be only thine.

In the presence of God, the Father, Son and Holy Spirit, I make this dedication of myself to all eternity.

(Signed)   SAMUEL AUDLEY RHEA.
September 16, 1851.

Renewed upon the mountain near Memikan, June 4, 1857.

6 *   E

CHAPTER VII.

FIRST MOUNTAIN TOUR.

PERSIA is the Land of the Sun. There fire-worship began. Well does the writer remember mounting his horse very early one summer morning in 1850, and riding with Dr. Perkins and Mr. Coan to the summit of one of those eastern outlying ranges of the Koordish mountains to witness the sunrise over Persia, and to look westward at shadows in the gorges and glens as peak after peak in that sea of mountains caught the coming glory. Westward were cloud-capped, snow-capped mountains. Eastward, for full one hundred miles, lay Persia, its jewel, the lake of Oroomiah, visible in its full length of eighty miles, except where mountains near the centre seemed to cut it in two. On this side of the lake stretched groves and vineyards watered by silver streams, with orchards and fruitful fields. The lake itself reflected the glory above, while, in the east, colors bright and playful as dancing northern lights transfigured earth and sky into paradise and heaven. Beholding this glory, it was easy to know how heathen might linger in things created and seen, to worship fire and the sun.

Into these western mountains, from that sunny land, Mr. Rhea was now making his first tour:

Monday, Oct. 13, 1851.—We left Oroomiah about one o'clock for the mountains. Our road soon left the plain, and led over the high hills lying between Oroomiah and Tergawer.

We reached the village of Hakkie, on the plain of Tergawer, about seven, having ridden more than an hour in the dark. We providentially had a servant with us who knew the road winding up the valley to Hakkie. This is the village of Deacon Guergis (or George), the mountain evangelist. It was dark, and we could only see the faint outline of the few low stone huts. The deacon gave us a cordial reception, and we were soon ushered into the great room. The floor was covered with hay. At one end a coarse carpet was spread for our reception. The cold wind blew through one or two unglazed little holes left for light, but they were soon stuffed with hay. Our light beds, which we carried with us, were spread upon the rug, and there we slept.

The chief man of the village, the priest and several villagers came in and spent an hour. The universal topic was bitter complaint of government taxes. The evening closed with reading and exhortation by Dr. Wright and Mr. Coan.

Tuesday, Oct. 14.—We made an early start from the hospitable house of the deacon. He followed us out from the village, and left us asking the blessing of God on our way. We traveled all day in the rain. After ascending a high mountain and going down its steep and long descent, we came upon the banks of the wild, leaping river Nazloo, which finally waters the plain of Oroomiah. Hour after hour we followed its course, the rugged mountains with their bold cliffs rising far above us on either side. Frequently our road for miles was a narrow path, sometimes upon the very edge of the precipice. Once we found we could not proceed. We were fifteen or twenty feet above the river, and had no alternative but to dismount, hold our horses by the bridle and let them slide down the steep, which they did without injury. Through this wild valley we traveled for some hours, seeing no human habitation except the castle of a once-famed Koordish chief. It was

perched upon the top of a lofty rock, which rose perpendic-
ularly from the side of the mountain.

The loneliness of the road was relieved only by here and
there a little company of mountain Nestorians going down
to the plain. After hours in this wild gorge, we were
cheered by seeing occasionally a little green patch of wheat,
a few yards in circumference, upon the banks of the river,
marking our approach to the dwellings of men.

Suddenly, as we turned a corner, we saw, far up the
mountains, little clusters of trees and little fields of wheat
hanging upon the steep sides.

We soon reached the village of Mar Beshoo. Swarms
of little children came out upon the housetops. Around
the door of the priest's house I counted no less than fifty.
Mar Beshoo lies upon the side of the mountain, so steep
that the roof of one house is literally the yard for another.

The old priest, looking feeble, met us at the door. He
had sent for Dr. Wright, having a few days before had a
stroke of the palsy. We entered the family-room. Among
the Nestorians several families live in one house. Sometimes father and mother, sons and their wives and children
are all together. So it was in this house. And what a
busy family! In one corner two were sitting sewing a garment; others were standing, distaffs in hand, spinning; little
girls were drawing out the wool over three or four spikes
fastened to a piece of wood.

Some coarse rugs were spread around the great tandoor,
a hole two or three feet in diameter and three feet deep.
In this, in the morning, they build a great fire, and after
an hour or two the stones become thoroughly heated and
the fire dies away. The room will continue warm till the
next day. In the cold winter frequently a circle of mountaineers will let their feet hang down inside. This tandoor
is also their bake-oven, the dough being stuck in thin cakes

to the smooth side-stones.   In a porch outside our beds were spread; a fire was kindled on the floor, and we slept comfortably.

The church of Mar Beshoo is far-famed, taking its name from the holy saint whom their traditions make its builder. We went there in the evening.   It is built, as nearly all the mountain churches are, of rough stones.   The old priest had hobbled his way there, and, with two or three deacons, was going over the prayers in a sing-song tone, kissing the cross that was cut in stone, and bowing and kissing the floor of the church.   Very few of the villagers come at all to the church, except at Christmas or Easter, when the sacrament is administered.   After the sing-song was ended, Dr. Wright read the Lord's Prayer and addressed the few present.   The walls were tapestried from top to bottom with hangings of calico and coarse silk, and scores of old lamps and bells were strung upon cords from one side to the other.   These were offerings of those who wished the holy saint Mar Beshoo to pray for them.

In looking upon the small, low stone huts running up the mountain-side, one is astonished to learn that they hold more than fifteen hundred souls.   Their lot is a bitter one. Upon the mountain-side they sow a few turnips and a few patches of wheat, and plant a few potatoes.   Their priest, upon whom God has laid his hand, was overbearing and oppressive in his exactions, taking from them a tenth of all they raised.   This, with heavy taxes, rendered their lives oftentimes lives of sorrow.   Such is the character of many of their priests.   Instead of breaking to them the bread of life, they leave their souls utterly to starve; or, what is worse, stuff them with the most ridiculous fables, while they are robbing their bodies of all that a grasping, covetous, unsatisfied spirit would exact.

In the morning I followed a beaten path up the moun-

tain-side. It led to a beautiful spring, and in the side of
the towering cliff there was a door opening into a small
cave. This cave is most holy, having a tradition of a saint.

Wednesday, October 15, 1851.—Our road to-day was
through as wild a region as yesterday, and in some places,
to one at all timid, more fearful. I was overjoyed after
winding for several miles up a long valley and reaching
the top of the mountain, to see spread out

THE BEAUTIFUL PLAIN OF GAWAR.

It stretches for forty miles in length, and at the widest
point perhaps the same in breadth. It appears like a great
basin, and on all sides around, bold mountains rise to an
almost equal height, except the lofty Jeloo range, whose
summits, capped with snow, tower far above their fellows.

The villages can be distinctly marked for a great distance
by great stacks of straw, piles of wheat and chaff, and huge
mounds of native fuel* laid up for winter, which begins
early and lingers long upon this plain.

We soon descended to the plain, and after an hour's ride
reached the village of Cherdenar. In approaching, almost
the only signs of houses were the conical roofs rising above
ground. The house proper is dug out below the surface
and walled up a little above ground, and the roof is then
built by laying timbers or crooked branches of trees cross-
wise until they terminate in a point, where an opening is
left for a chimney. These branches are covered with earth,
forming the cone.

Cherdenar is the village of Priest Dunkha, one of the
oldest native helpers of the mission. We rode to his hut.
He was not at home, but his daughter, Sarnum, one of
Miss Fisk's best pupils, was overjoyed to see us. They had
lately moved to the village, and were in so poor a house

* Dried dung.

that they could not accommodate us. We went to the house of a neighbor.

It is difficult to give an adequate idea of the poverty and wretched nature of this house. We entered through a low, dark passage, and soon found ourselves in a stable, buffaloes and a donkey being the occupants. In a corner, a little elevated above the rest, was the platform, some ten feet square, where the family ate, slept and lived; the *tandoor* (pit for fire) was in the centre.

The family went to a neighbor's, and gave up this platform to us. Here our beds were spread out, and we laid down, indulging the fond hope that we might rest, although the buffaloes, cattle and horses were feeding and fighting all around us. I deposited myself in my bag, tightened the drawstring to my neck with secret delight, putting the fleas at defiance. But no! I was in new quarters, and was destined that night to pass through scenes of conflict which beggar all description.

We will omit the graphic and humorous description characteristic of lands over which the venerable Dr. Goodell said that many of the plagues of Egypt had crawled, and simply chronicle the result:

Sleep fled my eyes. The breath of buffaloes and horses came up like piping steam, and I thought myself in a furnace. Hour after hour I sat up looking at my watch, fairly conquered, and the sport of my companions. As morning approached, the moon shone brightly through a hole above. It was suggested that the snowy mountains of Jeloo would appear grandly under such a moon, and knowing that we could not fare worse, we emerged from the hot cellar into the cold open air.

After enjoying the grand scenery of bright heavens and snowy mountains, we proposed to lie down upon one of the large haystacks; but finding heavy dew, Mr. Coan brought

out a rubber blanket. Seeing a fire at a distance, we went
to it and found a Koord watching the grain, wearing away
the long night by heaping the flashing straw upon the fire
and puffing his pipe without intermission. While Mr. C.
tried to sleep, I amused myself in learning the language of
our Koordish friend. Soon the day dawned. I called him
a good teacher, thanked him for the fire, and we moved
toward our home.

This eagerness to learn was well repaid in after years by
his marked success in various languages, including the
Koordish.

On this tour he wrote his first missionary letter to his
seminary friend, the writer, then at Mosul on the Tigris,
and he kept up the correspondence thus commenced generally monthly for eight years. That letter affords all the
farther notice we have of this tour. It is dated twelve days
later from the opposite, or western side of the plain, at Memikan, Gawar, his future home, October 27, 1851. Only
extracts will be given:

More than once since my arrival in Oroomiah I have
attempted to write to you a line. To meet with you was
by no means the least pleasure anticipated by me in coming hither. For two weeks, in company with Dr. Wright
and Mr. Coan, I have been traveling among the mountain
Nestorians. With this brief tour I have been charmed,
and, I trust, profited.

Expecting that my lot would be cast among this people,
my first introduction was attended with especial interest.
My field of labor was not definitely determined when I left
America, although the committee thought it would be in
the mountains.

* * * My great anxiety is now to acquire the language

of this people. A field of labor, I doubt not, will be opened when I am ready to work.

You can almost see him put foot in stirrup up in Gawar as he adds, "Our missionaries are in haste to be away. My object in writing is, I confess, rather selfish, as I am anxious to receive a letter from you."

Very kind were the salutations, very cordial the sympathy of that first letter, and very precious in future the letters from that same village, now hallowed.

7

CHAPTER VIII.

AMERICANS AT HOME IN KOORDISTAN.

THE efforts of Dr. Grant, eighteen years earlier, to establish a permanent missionary station among the mountain Nestorians were completely thwarted; first, by the dreadful massacre at Asheetha and Lisan, in 1843; and later, by the death of Dr. Grant and several others at Mosul. Christians in America might well look upon the mountain field as bloody and dangerous. Yet it can hardly be conceived in America with what thrilling interest those whose privilege it had been in 1850 to resume the labors of Laurie and Grant, and to plant a church at Mosul, received Mr. Rhea's announcement that the gap between the missions of Turkey and Persia was being closed by a new advance into the mountains. The date is at

MEMIKAN, GAWAR, *December* 11, 1851.

I wrote you from Gawar some weeks ago. I again write to you from the same village and the same room, but under quite different circumstances. Then I was here on a transient tour; now I am permanently located for the winter.

We fondly hope that in the favoring providence attending the formation of the station we have token of the divine approval.

In November we had two weeks as mild and genial as spring; and it was not until the last blow was struck in fitting up our winter quarters, and we were ready to close our doors for the long, dreary winter, that the heavy snow-storm came, lasting three days and giving us two feet of

74

snow. But for those pleasant days our enterprise would have been entirely thwarted.

Mr. Coan and myself have just returned from accompanying Messrs. Stocking and Stoddard on their way to Oroomiah. They reached here with much difficulty, owing to the depth of the snow, having been strongly tempted several times to turn back. They spent but a single night with us. This we much regretted, but felt that it was running a risk for them to delay long. Our brethren at Oroomiah have voted to visit us monthly; but we fear we have had our last visit from them this winter.

This is a very small village, but there is no other on the plain so evangelical, and where we should feel so much among friends. God has been signally with us in his favoring providence; we long to see him present in the subduing and sanctifying influence of his Spirit. Oh, if we could see one poor thirsty soul longing for a new life in Christ, and if we could have the privilege of opening for that soul the wellspring of salvation, how it would gladden our lonely winter hours and make our hearts overflow with gratitude for the privilege of being here!

We are all happy in our new homes. We feel much nearer to you here, and we know that you will feel nearer to us. Let us not cease to bring near to a throne of grace our precious work.

During the August previous he wrote to Mr. Coan, then making a preaching tour in the mountains, and expressed his longings:

SEIR, *August 5*, 1851.

As I read your journal and letters, and thought of the opening prospects of that field, I longed to be with you. It is trying to have reached the field of labor, to witness the crying wants of the people, and yet to be unable to lend a helping hand in relieving them. Yet, for many reasons, it is well that it should be so. What a profitable season it furnishes for earnest prayer for a baptism of the Holy Spirit! Peter and John, though they had preached many times before, never really preached with divine power until the day of Pentecost. I believe there is for every Christian minister, and every Christian whose heart burns to labor for the Master, a Pentecostal day—a day in which God will, in mercy to our infirmities, in an unusual manner sanctify these frail vessels and make them meet for his use—when he will supply us with those spiritual gifts upon which success in winning souls almost entirely depends.

When we are called upon to plead with dying men to be reconciled to God, the work is so solemn, the consequences for weal or woe which hang upon every such attempt are so momentous, that God will not leave us alone, but has ordained that at such times, if we earnestly seek it, we shall be in an extraordinary manner under the divine influence. May we all thus be baptized from on high. Permit me to say that your good wife is very happy teaching.

And now that good wife with her husband and Mr. Rhea were housed in Gawar, snowed in under the great crest of Jeloo. All honor to the Christian lady, for Christ's sake glad to exchange a pleasant city of America on the Hudson, for the hut in the little village of six houses! All honor to the first American lady to brave a winter in the mountain field! Long may she still live to bless Nestorians, Persians, Turks and Koords!

We are now fortunate to be able, from a fragmentary journal, to give Mr. Rhea's own words:

MEMIKAN, KOORDISTAN, ⎱
Thursday, January 1, 1852. ⎰

The year just passed has been the most eventful one of my unprofitable life—the year in which I was ordained to

the holy ministry—the year in which I bade a final farewell to my country, my kindred, my dear father and mother
and brothers and sisters, crossed the stormy seas, looked
upon the Old World with all its thrilling associations, and
reached the field of my future labors.

Having remained five months in Oroomiah, the mission
then thought that the providence of God clearly pointed to
the occupation of Gawar this winter.   Accordingly, on the
19th of November, Mr. Coan, Mrs. Coan and myself left
Oroomiah, and reached Memikan Saturday, 22d.

Our journey was most delightful, and for ten days here
we had a bright sun and clear sky, and weather mild and
genial.   During that time we were busy fitting up two of
the native mud cabins, making them as comfortable as
possible for the long, severe winter before us.   And it was
not till the last blow was struck, and the last stick of wood
brought upon the backs of Koords from a point in the
neighboring mountains twenty miles distant, that the storm
came, covering the ground with two feet of snow.

Though we have been here shut in by the deep snow;
though we have been hampered for room, and for several
hours in the day have lived in the smoke and scent of the
native fuel; though our little village numbers but six
houses, and our only church has been a stable, and we have
sung the praise of God and knelt before his throne and
spoken his precious words among oxen and buffaloes, still
it has been an unspeakable privilege to be here.   For we
have seen the pillar of cloud by day and fire by night, the
token of the near presence of our covenant-keeping God.
He has gathered around us a little company of dying men,
and although they have been oppressed with enormous taxes
from the Turkish government, and have borne the heavier
burden of scorn and denunciation from some of their own
people for welcoming us to their village, still they sit at

7 *

our feet, and without a murmuring word drink in the words
of life.

Just here we may fitly favor our readers with the first in-
stallment of reminiscences that flow from the heart through
the pen of Rev. Dr. Perkins, the veteran missionary of
Persia, well known in Europe and America, as well as in
Western Asia:

"It was a hot June day in 1851 that I first met Mr.
Rhea on the beautiful plain of Salmas, about sixty miles
north of Oroomiah. The late Mr. Breath and myself had
started on a rapid journey to Erzeroom. We halted at
midday at a Persian village under the shade of some willow
trees to rest our horses and refresh ourselves. We were in
hourly expectation of meeting Mr. Stoddard on his return
from America with his family and Mr. Rhea. While thus
resting, our eyes detected, in a party of approaching travelers two or three miles distant, *open umbrellas,* and we immediately mounted and started at a rapid pace. My
younger associate soon left me in the rear, as John did
Peter; and when far in advance he halted for an instant,
wheeling his horse and crying, at the top of his voice, 'It is
they! It is they!' and then galloped onward. The sequel
can be imagined better than the joy of that meeting can be
described. After a few minutes' halt and mutual greeting,
Mr. Breath and myself returned with the party from America to our willow shade, and spent an hour with them in
delightful conversation. *They* were to halt there for the
coming night, while *we* had still full thirty miles to ride to
complete our stages for the day.

"Our impressions of Mr. Rhea in that first interview were
altogether agreeable, and a pleasant earnest of our long subsequent intercourse."

"And it is but fair to give also in this connection the young
missionary's first impression of his future associates whom

he met on the way, which he afterward playfully stated as being that of 'ancient men,' not unlike his conceptions of 'staid Moravians.'

"Mr. Breath and myself," says Dr. Perkins, "performed our journey of nine hundred miles, in going to Erzeroom and returning, in eleven days, using post-horses. On reaching Seir an hour after sunrise one morning, having ridden all the previous night, my ears were greeted by the well-known sound of my daughter's seraphine at family worship. But a new voice accompanied it, of singular sweetness, richness and power. I wondered whose voice it was, and on entering the house found that it was Mr. Rhea's. He had already, during the few previous days, won all hearts in our mission circle, and especially the hearts of the children."

"Mr. Rhea's first Persian home was in the family of Mr. Stoddard, on Mount Seir. It was a precious boon to him to accompany to his field that seraphic man, and to be initiated by him into a course of preparation for his work. Mr. Rhea could not have had a better guide.

"Our annual meeting for the review of our labors occurred that year a short time after the arrival of the party from America. To bring our youthful associate into the programme, we appointed him to preach the opening sermon. His discourse from the text, "Lengthen thy cords and strengthen thy stakes," Isaiah liv. 2, surprised and delighted us by the very marked ability evinced in its preparation, and the unction and power with which it was delivered. And while it most successfully struck the keynote of our annual meeting, and gave an unwonted tone to all the subsequent services, it also proved but the truthful earnest of his wonderful powers as a preacher both in English and in Syriac, which have so often thrilled us in subsequent years.

"His first study for three months was a humble room in

our male seminary on Mount Seir. In that quiet retreat he gave himself ardently to the study of the modern Syriac, which he had successfully commenced under the instruction of Mr. Stoddard. Deacon Joseph, of Seir, was his first teacher. His wonderful power over the children appeared in their often stealing away to his room for entertainment, a very common one being his playing his sweet flute in moments of relaxation to their unspeakable delight. Nor did his influence over those delighted children end with entertainment. It was during those three months that he commenced with them a juvenile monthly concert, which was successfully continued for several years.

"When the sickly season of summer had passed, Mr. Rhea fitted up the present library-room for his winter residence on the mission premises in the city of Oroomiah, where he would see more of the people and enjoy increased opportunities for acquiring their language and laboring among them. But scarcely was his room comfortably prepared when the mission decided that it was important that he embrace a providential opening for entering the Koordish mountains in company with Mr. and Mrs. Coan. That field had long been closed against us, and the favorable hour for entering it was not to be lost by delay.

"About the middle of November the little colony started cheerfully on their arduous enterprise, as much more self-denying than our work at Oroomiah as the latter is more self-denying than a comfortable residence in the United States.

"If possible to smooth their way, sufficiently rough at best, I preceded them some days with some doors and other fixtures, and did a little toward preparing a shelter for the threatening winter. They arrived on Saturday of the same week, and just before sunset the single window of four small panes was placed in the wall of the rough mud structure,

VILLAGE IN THE MOUNTAINS OF KOORDISTAN.

VAN INGEN & SNYDER

F

and the delighted party caught a glimpse of the last rays of the setting sun on the lofty, snow-capped mountains across the beautiful plain of Gawar as a bow of promise for their future quiet possession.

"The miserable character of the first dwelling of the missionaries in Gawar cannot well be conceived. It was dark from want of windows, smoky from its proximity to other native houses, and filled with uncomfortable odors from adjacent stables. Their two small rooms were separated by their common entrance, through which the huge, lubberly buffaloes of their neighbors of the adjacent house were driven daily to water.

"Soon after Mr. Rhea reached Oroomiah he was invited by a missionary associate to accompany him on the Sabbath to a Nestorian village for religious services. As he entered an uncleanly dwelling, shared by the family and various domestic animals, he remarked, 'I can hardly conceive of human nature more degraded.' Yet, on settling in his rude hovel in a village of Koordistan, he was soon heard to say, 'This is as much below the villages of Oroomiah as they are below villages in America.'

"Born and reared in the lap of affluence, endowed with the nicest natural sensibilities and refined by culture, we might have supposed that life amid such circumstances would have been to him little short of martyrdom. But the fact was far otherwise. The first letter which he wrote to his missionary brothers and sisters, on my return to Oroomiah, was cheerful and graphically playful, a fair earnest of the happy, heroic spirit with which he ever afterward endured hardness as a good soldier of Jesus Christ.

"The discomforts of their miserable dwelling were all greatly enhanced by their virtual imprisonment by deep snows during the long and dreary winter, eighteen feet falling that season, which rendered egress very difficult most of the time, and often engulfed the building till the snow was removed by shovels. But none of these things moved him, for he remembered who it was who, though rich, for our sakes became poor, that we, through his poverty, might be rich. The presence of Mrs. Coan as a brave and patient sharer of such self-denials also tended strongly to banish misgiving.

"The missionaries soon opened a school for the children of the village. Mrs. Coan had little girls and women several hours a day in her room, which served the various purposes of dining-room, kitchen, dormitory and school-room. They also had religious services daily with the villagers on the central platform of the largest stable in the place, the breath of the numerous buffaloes keeping the air at a high temperature, even in that almost Greenland climate.

"Added to Mr. Rhea's deep and ever-growing interest in his missionary work, his close application as a student yielded him ample occupation during his first winter in Koordistan. He usually 'prevented' the dawn by critical study of the Hebrew Bible, collated with the ancient Syriac. He also reviewed a considerable part of his college classics during that time, to acquire the greater general facility for mastering Oriental languages. He soon comprehended and well appreciated the advantage of his position and circumstances (shut up though he was in the wilds of Koordistan) among these ancient Christians, whose language is a modern dialect of the ancient Syriac (the latter being spoken by the Saviour while on earth), and who are eminently scriptural in their habits, thoughts and feelings. His teacher, Deacon Tamo, who had learned a little English, could even sit in judgment on the interesting notes of the able commentator, Mr. Barnes, where he suggests that there must have been *cows* in Job's country and time, because *cheese* is mentioned by him; the artless, yet discerning Nestorian claiming that this is a palpable *non sequitur*, inasmuch as cheese in the East is usually made of the milk of *sheep* more than of cows.

"It was to hard study that first winter that Mr. Rhea was greatly indebted for the foundation of his peerless gifts as a preacher in the modern Syriac, and for his general success as an Oriental scholar and missionary.

"Mr. Rhea's removal to Koordistan diminished not a whit his interest in his young friends in the mission at Oroomiah, nor theirs in him. Henceforth that interest was cultivated by letters, which were anticipated by our children with greater delight than any other earthly boon.

"On a visit subsequently made to Oroomiah he assisted the two eldest children to commence a juvenile monthly periodical, called *The Persian Star*, which was conducted by them and their successors for several years with very commendable zeal and success.

"As the senior member of our mission, I felt special interest in the success of the little colony which I had assisted to inaugurate in the wilds of Koordistan; and my desire to visit it during the winter was wellnigh uncontrollable. Accordingly, in February—our winter in Oroomiah being unusually mild, and the ground there still bare—I started for that purpose. On the second morning I mounted my strong horse at 2 A. M., in the bright moonlight, with an exultant assurance, the road being still bare and dry, that I should greet the missionary circle before evening. But day had scarcely dawned, as I was winding my way up the great mountain range, when I suddenly came upon snow, which increased in depth so rapidly that the powerful horse in which I had unduly 'trusted' was unable to proceed another step. With a saddened heart I committed the little store of comforts which I had carried with me, and had hoped to

8

deliver in person, to a hardy mountain Nestorian to convey on foot, and reluctantly headed my horse homeward.

"I did not venture to renew the attempt to visit Gawar till the last week in April, and then found it sufficiently difficult and hazardous both to the horse and his rider from deep snows and swollen streams, though I was by no means averse to a measure of adventure. As I approached the missionary residence, my horse floundering in the still deep snow, and myself dripping from an involuntary bath, I was recognized by Messrs. Coan and Rhea, who had for the first time that season taken their horses from their stable and made their way to a neighboring village, from which they were now returning. I need not say that waving hats soon testified to the joy of that recognition.

"My visit of a few days at the humble mountain-station was one of the most delightful that I ever enjoyed; while it was a standing marvel to me how the missionaries, and especially Mrs. Coan, had so cheerfully endured their self-denials and discomforts during the long winter."

CHAPTER IX.

FIRST WINTER IN GAWAR.

MEMIKAN, *Jan.* 1, 1852.

IF you were approaching our little village this morning, you would almost be puzzled to discover our premises, nothing appearing but a portion of our front wall and the top of the chimneys. As a sailor would say, we had "a stiff breeze" last night, sweeping and piling the snow all around us. The sky is now clear, and we look for cold weather. The villagers are all out this morning, opening roads from their doors. We have taken our turns in pitching snow from the roofs and around the walls. In Tennessee the snow is hardly ever more than six inches deep; and expressing surprise this morning at the depth here, they said, There has been no snow yet. One held up his long pole into the air to show how deep it sometimes falls. Another said it was sometimes level with the tops of the stacks of fuel. This clear, bright morning you would enjoy the magnificent scenery around us.

Few have come to us from other parts of the plain. Deacon Tamo has visited one of the neighboring villages every Sabbath except one, and has met with uniformly kind treatment. He is of great service; and if the seminary does not suffer, we shall rejoice that our brethren gave him to us.

The late oppression will rather further than retard our work. The people know why they suffer; they feel its injustice; they are every day becoming more and more enlightened, and convinced theoretically of the truth of

87

evangelical doctrine. Confined pretty much to their village, few passing, free from diverting cares of the busy season, they sit every night and three times every Sabbath under the truth. We long to see their slumbering consciences aroused.

Rose early this morning. Endeavored to get a lively sense of the tender mercies of God toward me the past year, and of my very unprofitable life. For the future I am not anxious. I have placed everything at the disposal of my Father, and I know that all will be well. Oh I long to walk with him all my remaining days in humility, in faith and entire self-renunciation.

Taught David and Khamis two hours. Talked with Deacon Tamo—he in English and I in Syriac. My progress in the language has seemed slow, but still I hope to acquire it. For two days and nights it has snowed incessantly to a depth of two and one-third feet. Spent two or three hours in pitching it from the roofs.

January 2, Friday.—This morning the mercury stood sixteen degrees below zero. My room has been cold and chilly all day. Felt very dull and stupid from my exposure and labor yesterday, having worked too vigorously. Have hardly been able to lift a clear thought to God, and have not been as cheerful as one who is professedly traveling to glory ought to be.

January 3, Saturday.—Felt unwell. Spent an hour or two in stopping the large cracks around my door and window. From morning till night my room is employed as a school-room for our native helpers, so that I find little time for devotion, except early in the morning and late at night. I must learn to walk with God in the tumult of life as well as its quiet hours.

4th, Sabbath.—To-day we three—a little band—remembered the dying love of our departed yet our ever-present Saviour. I did not meet my dear Lord as I had hoped and prayed, and I was in deep distress. With much desire and longing I had looked forward to this holy communion season; but when the hour came my heart seemed cold, a tide of worldly thoughts rushed upon me, and I could not get near the cross. I was much depressed. I tried to pray time after time, but it seemed as if a high wall were between me and the mercy-seat. The tempter came and pressed me sorely with the thought that I had prayed much preparatory to this feast, and that my prayers were not regarded. And why pray more? He would fain persuade me that it was the fault of God and not of my heart. I tried to meet this temptation and to feel humbled in view . of my great sin and my great loss.

5th, Monday.—This day we had appointed a day of prayer and fasting for the presence of the Holy Spirit. The day was sacredly consecrated to reading God's word, meditation and prayer. I found near access to a throne of grace, and the hour of prayer and praise was sweet.

6th, Tuesday.—To-day wrote to Dr. Anderson; my first mission letter.

7th, Wednesday.—Rose early. Nearly all day preparing for the post. If my letters are only written under the influence of the Spirit, it will not be lost time. "The chariot wheels draw heavily" to-day, because I did not seek God's blessing on each department of my day's labors. I long to speak the language of the Nestorians. Every hour given to anything else is given almost with regret.

8th, Thursday.—Khamis reports his little school increasing. He began with two, and has fourteen. Two to-day began the gospels who five weeks ago did not know their alphabet. Two girls came to read, making five of the females of the village. Thus the Lord smiles upon our little work.

8 *

9th, Friday.—Deacon Guergis left to-day. It snowed, and we were sorry to have him go alone. He is a tender-hearted Christian. Would that there were more of his simple-hearted piety! The ground is covered with three or four feet of snow—the roads hardly opened. When coming, he and his companions were overtaken in a storm upon the mountains; it became very dark; they could not see their road, and thought they should be lost. They knelt down in the deep snow and prayed. When they rose the sun came out, and their road was plain before them.

10th, Saturday.—To-day our long-expected messenger from Mosul arrived, bringing us letters from Brother Marsh.

11th, Sabbath.—A full attendance. They listen with much earnestness. Deacon Tamo went to Kardian. Many quarreled with him, charging that he was English, and wished to abolish their customs, fasts, prayers and sacraments. He spoke mildly, reasoned calmly and soberly until the principal persons present said his words were true. Eshoo came from Keat; says they threaten to kill our helpers if they go there. Odeeshoo and Khoshaba came from Kerpel, a Koordish village. They say they spoke much with the Koords of Christ, and they listened attentively. There is a very friendly relation existing between many Koordish and Nestorian villagers; many are warm personal friends of each other, and the Nestorians are not afraid to preach Christ among them. It would not be strange if the Koords should be the first Mohammedans moved upon. Oh what momentous interests are involved in the reawakening and reviving of this remnant of a once powerful Christian Church!

January 12, Monday.—About noon we were startled by a message that two of our brethren from Oroomiah were in a neighboring village, and wished us to send

them horses, theirs having given out. We mounted our
horses and at the village of Mar Slewa found Mr. Breath.
He had left his horse at Dizza, and walked through the
deep snow ten miles. Dr. Wright came with him to the
mountain pass, but seeing the depth of snow and fearing
detention in Gawar, as his family required his presence,
thought best to return. Mr. Breath seemed much exhausted. Brother C. and I gave him and his servant our
horses, and came on foot. We were much refreshed by the
presence of our good brother. After the last fall of snow
to a depth of three feet, we gave up all hope of seeing any
of our Oroomiah brethren.

13th, *Tuesday.*—Brother Coan and I accompanied Mr.
Breath on his return home some three hours. We were
sorry that he could spend but a night with us; but when
we remembered that by delay he might be shut in for
weeks, we could not detain him.

January 18, *Sabbath.*—The Lord is good. I felt an
earnest longing after holiness, perfect love, poverty of
spirit, utter self-renunciation. But oh how unstable in
all my ways! Felt that I must pray especially for fixed-
ness of purpose, singleness of aim, whole-souled consecrated-
ness to the work of personal holy-living—holy-living by
the moment, reaching to the minutest secular employment—
to every word and every thought. I can aim at nothing
short of this.

Began to read our Lord's sermon on the mount: "Blessed
are the poor in spirit." Here I stopped and found such a
depth of meaning, such heavenly wisdom, that I dwelt upon
it all the day. Poverty of spirit. What a jewel! How
precious in God's sight! How hard to gain! Blessed life
here, and yonder inheriting the kingdom. But it is one
thing to admire the brilliancy and richness of the gem, and
another to purchase it. Without price, and yet of untold

worth and beauty! O my Saviour, I no longer resolve—
I do *now* seek it, struggling to reach it.

My room was filled to-day with near fifty of the villagers,
listening earnestly, and yet apparently without any deep
impression. One cannot look upon them without intense
longings for the melting Spirit of God.

19th, Monday.—Read a Psalm in Hebrew; also Kitto's
Introduction to Solomon's Song. Can a more exquisite
picture be drawn of the life of the believer after he is once
married to the dear Redeemer in an everlasting covenant?
They twain shall be one. Oh what a life! One with Jesus
in love, in joy, in meekness, humility, poverty of spirit, in
tender sympathy for every fallen man and woman! One
with Jesus in purity and ceaseless self-renunciation, and
one with him in his glorious inheritance! Joint heir with
Christ! Blessed Redeemer, perfect now this heavenly
union, that I may sing, My Beloved is mine, and I am
his.

Deacon Tamo returned from Senawa. He no sooner entered the village on Saturday than a poor woman, with a
full, overflowing heart, made him welcome as a servant of
the Lord Jesus. On the Sabbath she went out and brought
in all her neighbors, fifty or sixty, nearly the whole village,
to hear the word of life.

20th, Tuesday.—Enjoyed sweet peace to-day. My mind
much on heavenly things. Never felt such longings after
communion with God. Read some passages from the life
of the holy Leighton.

21st, Wednesday.—Was enabled to cherish a sense of
God's presence in a feeble manner. Oh to live continually
in the presence of the Great King, and to hold uninterrupted communion with him! Before evening, by my poor
success in some writing I had undertaken, I was taught to
seek the Divine blessing upon everything.

January 21, 1852, to the author at Mosul:

The formation of your little church had a special interest. May it be watered with the dews of heaven! May it be the leaven which is silently but powerfully to permeate that whole mass of deluded, fallen mind!

Just at this time there seems to be in several villages a bitter hatred against us and our work. Mar Shimon (the Nestorian patriarch) has succeeded in infusing his own hostile spirit for a time into many hearts, and the universal cry is, that we are aiming to make away with their time-honored church and the loved customs of their fathers.

To a playful allusion to his choice of single life, he replies: I should be sorry indeed, my dear brother, if you should think me so ungenerous as not to bid you God-speed. Because I might prefer to spend the first years of my missionary life, and probably all of them, unmarried, is certainly no reason why I should not heartily approve of a brother's adopting any mode of life which will make him a stronger and happier armor-bearer in the army of our Immanuel. I will most gladly pray for the prosperous issue of your journey home.

22d.—This day twenty-five years ago I was born into this world. Upon many of my past years I look back with shuddering at my aggravated transgression. I look back upon all with deep regret and dissatisfaction. A poor, sickly life I have lived for Christ—the weakest of babes in Christ. I wonder that I am now living. I wonder that in the midst of my sins I did not go down quick to the pit. With deepest humility I bow before him and adore the riches of his grace.

Oh that this year might be the holiest of my pilgrimage! a year of walking upon the borders of the heavenly world! Resolved to live, by the grace of God, as holy, prayerful, watchful, exemplary as if I had been assured that this would be my last year.

23d, Friday.—Rose at six. Six inches of snow fell during the night. It still snows. Read Pilgrim's Progress in Syriac. Words of God and seasons of prayer refreshing. Found mingling God's Word constantly with prayer and turning it into petitions profitable.

Several young men have joined our school, and even after it closes they sit in the dekana and read for hours.

24th, Saturday.—I look back upon this week with mingled feelings of joy and sorrow—joy, because I have felt deeper longings than ever before after holiness—unblemished holiness, evidence to me that God's Spirit is with me, preparing me for a reception of that blessing; sorrow, because this week's experience shows me how desperate my case is without God's help. One day I felt strong in God; another, all my resolutions gave way. O Father, thou hast not left me altogether desolate; let me not be fretful because I have not received those spiritual blessings which I have sought. Thou knowest, O Father, when I am ready to receive these pearls—when I will not trample them under foot.

25th, Sabbath.—Sky clear, air mild. 40°–50°. Met this morning for Sabbath-school. Mr. Coan repeated the Lord's Prayer, and it was a touching scene to see all, from the old man of seventy to the lad of six or eight, repeating it after him until each one was able to say it alone. Every Sabbath we are cheered by the apparent earnestness with which they listen to the words of life.

January 26, Monday.—Rose early. Read a Psalm in Hebrew. Wrote a letter in Syriac to Joseph, my first teacher."

To Dr. Perkins, January 26, 1852:

I remember with delight the pleasant evenings spent in

your parlor, when we sung the sweet songs of Zion. We often sing, "And let this feeble body fail," and "How firm a foundation." They are favorite pieces with Mrs. Coan, as with us all. These dull walls have no sympathy with the melodies of sound. They will not even give an echo, and our flutes, feeling the slight, have become of the same mind.

We feel a longing to break over the walls of our confinement and sow broadcast the seeds of eternal life. And yet we know that the warmest sympathies of these poor hearts of ours are an iceberg to the warm beatings of that heart whose unknown depth of love and sympathy eternity only will reveal. We rejoice that Deacon Tamo goes as often as he can to the neighboring villages. He always leaves us begging our prayers, and when he comes back his face beams with smiles.

May I not say, if the Lord will, we shall see your face in February? We think you can reach Dizza, and, once there, we can help you over the plain should another fall of snow render it difficult. Our brethren have made us such short visits that we ply them as soon as they come, and cry, "Give, give!" till they leave us.

A GATHERING STORM.

The beloved Physician records the words of the Lord Jesus: "I send you forth as lambs among wolves." It is time for us to take some note of the powers on the dark mountains in and around Gawar that might be directed by the prince of this world against the little flock in the little village of six houses. This hamlet is hid in the wide dominions of the Sultan of Constantinople. The eye of sultan or vizier, or great pasha, never rested upon it. In a very feeble and precarious manner the Sultan makes show to govern Koordistan by a great dignitary of the Empire, a pasha stationed at Van. Van is a considerable city by

Lake Van, in Eastern Turkey. As the mountain roads wind, it is one hundred and fifty miles north by west of Gawar, and about equally distant from Russia and Persia. Under this pasha, nearer at hand in the mountains, at Bashkollah, sixty miles from Gawar, an inferior pasha holds an important fortress in the midst of almost independent Koordish chiefs. These in their mountain holds alternately treat with and receive salary from, or openly defy, the representative of the distant Sultan. Under this pasha at Bashkollah there are modirs, or governors—among them one at Dizza on the Gawar plain.

Over against these Moslem powers we may place Christian dignitaries. In Gawar the bishop of the Nestorians would in some degree approach in dignity the Turkish modir. Outside of Gawar the *Patriarch of all the Nestorians*, always called Mar Shimon, or Saint Simon, would hold rank with the pasha of Bashkollah. One step higher in influence, the consuls of England, France or Russia claim equal consideration with the pashas of Van, and consul-generals with the greatest pashas of the Empire, while at Constantinople the ambassadors of the great Christian powers approach the Sultan on such high terms as often to bend the councils and plans of the Empire.

Here, then, were three Americans, housed like their Master in a stable, unable to be hid in a little unwalled village of six houses on the Persian border, for they were ambassadors of the Great King. For human protection they must look to Koordish chiefs, Turkish governors and pashas, and the shadow of far-off America—that American influence acting by courtesy through English consuls more than a hundred miles away in Mosul, Turkey, or still farther off at Tabreez in Persia; or through the American minister at distant Constantinople.

Who shall protect that little band? Less than a year

before had seen the Rev. Dr. Bacon of New Haven, and his son, now the Rev. Leonard W. Bacon, of Brooklyn, and the writer, robbed and detained, in the power of fierce Koords, to the imminent peril of their lives, at a point a few miles south of Gawar. All previous attempts to locate a mission station among the mountain Nestorians had failed. Had God's time now come?

Would the Nestorian bishop in Gawar prove a friend to plead for them with the modir? Would the patriarch speak a kind word in the ear of the pasha of Bashkollah? Would both bishop and patriarch sympathize with them, or stir up Nestorians, Koords and Turks alike to hostility?

The second month of their stay was not complete before the villagers were forbidden by the Nestorian bishop to send their children to the school, and a tax of twenty dollars was imposed, simply because they had received the ambassadors of the Lord Jesus Christ. We proceed with Mr. Rhea's journal:

January 27.—The bishop has made a great wedding. On Saturday several of the villagers asked our advice; knowing the scenes of wickedness at such places, they hesitated. Deacon Tamo thought of going. We told them to go. Our Saviour went, not to revel, but to turn water into wine. They went, and had fine opportunities for preaching the gospel to Nestorians, Koords, Armenians and some Turks who had gathered from all parts of the plain. They spoke the truth fearlessly. Many reviled, but they blessed.

Tamo is everywhere respected for his learning and his piety. They all said to him, "Come to us. Leave the English. Be our priest. We will do you honor, for we love you much." He said, "I cannot leave those men, for they preach the truth." They replied, "Then do not preach to us." Tamo said, "I must preach; I will come to your villages and houses;" then appealing to the chief men : "Will

9   G

you drive me away?" "No, no; come to our houses and
we will welcome you."

At every little gathering the one topic at the houses of
chiefs or the bishop was our presence here this winter. On
Monday, a vile man, who had said, "*I love wickedness, and
will practice it,*" when reproved by Tamo, rose up and said,
"Let us drive these men from our country." He had been
around endeavoring to stir up opposition. A few called
them fools, but the proposition met with general favor.
Baso, the agitator, carried the day. They resolved to send
a delegation to the modir, petitioning that he would expel us. Poor deluded men! May God have mercy upon
them!.

29*th, Thursday.*—Two soldiers came from the modir;
would not tell why, but wished to see us. I called them in.
They said, "We come to present you the compliments of
the modir, and to do your service." We had no service,
and supposed them spies. They said they were ordered to
remain here one or two months.

We think the modir has listened to complaint against
us, and sent the petition for our expulsion to his pasha.
The villagers are very anxious to know why the two Turks
have come. Met to-night for prayer in Deacon Tamo's
house, as the Turks were in the dekana.

30*th, Friday.*—One of the soldiers said to-day that the
modir had sent a messenger to his pasha at Van, saying
that the people of Gawar, to a man, wish the English
driven from the country. We learn, too, that the Nestorian patriarch wrote to his bishop to take every measure
to have us driven out.

31*st, Saturday.*—Deacon Tamo feels rather downcast. He
stands alone. He knows that all his people are heaping
upon him reproach and scorn for welcoming us to his village. He is a brave spirit, and would go to the stake be-

fore he would flinch from the stand he has taken. We had a large meeting to-night in the dekana. The Turks were present. They will see that we are very quiet, and love the people and that they love us. They listened respectfully; one understood much that was said, and told his companion.

February 1, *Sabbath.*—Without, a bright day. A few faint beams from the Sun of Righteousness have found their way to my soul. Rose early. Felt the stirrings of a proud spirit, but God gave me the victory; felt willing to be counted as the offscouring of all things if it is his will. But I know this victory is only for a season; I know this easily-besetting sin is only asleep. Oh that I may be sober, and watch unto prayer! Poverty of spirit, utter self-renunciation, unfeigned humility—in these I am far behind. Our little meetings this morning and to-night were full and very attentive. Brother Coan spoke of faith. Deacon Tamo was not inclined to go out to preach, the opposition is so bitter.

2d, Monday.—Heard that the people of Gawar sent their chief men to the modir. When they entered his room they threw down their turbans at his feet, saying, "Shall we or the English stay here? One must leave." Report goes that the modir wrote out their complaint, and sent two of their number with it to the pasha of Bashkollah.

4th.—This morning we were almost buried in the snow. It was above our roof. The tempest has blown furiously all day. What matter, if our house is on the Rock? The storms of life will soon blow over, and we shall rest in the bosom of Jesus.

6th, Friday.—The storm has raged all day, one continued heavy wind darkening the air with whirls of snow.

I felt the stealing of despondency upon me, but God was with me and I did not yield. Felt a disposition to dwell upon the faults of others, but was enabled at once to banish all such thoughts and to pray for a kind and charitable spirit. Felt weary to-night—weary of my sins, weary of the world. O Father, may I have a burning desire to show thy power to this generation before I go hence!

7th, Saturday.—Calm and peaceful. One would not know that it has stormed so hard for three days and nights. Often sweet peace comes after the heavy conflict.

8th, Sabbath.—A beautiful Sabbath day. Our little company gathered around us as usual. When we see them so attentive, how our hearts yearn over them! Oh there is but one voice that can reach these poor wanderers, and every day they are getting farther away and that voice becoming more faint! O dear Saviour, call louder, that they may hear and live.

The two Turks left us to-day, as if for a neighboring Koordish village, but we hear they have gone out to the modir at Dizza. They said in the village, "The people there are all of one mind; very quiet, and so busy learning to read that they have not time to water their cattle."

11th, Wednesday.—Wrote to-day to my presbytery, hoping that it will reach America before their meeting in May. I want to do something in this way in advancing the interests of the Kingdom, but I feel deeply my weakness. How can one mind influence another spiritually unless that mind is eminently spiritual? To-day my one all-absorbing longing is to be filled with the Spirit; but to-morrow my heart may be cold and apparently destitute of all sympathy with holiness. Oh for more steadfastness!

Memikan, Gawar, February 14, 1852, to Dr. Perkins:

"I cannot express to you the deep regret we all felt when we learned that you were compelled to turn back from Bazan. Although we had had a heavy fall of snow, and for three days and nights heavy, drifting winds, still we felt pretty confident you would *start* from Oroomiah, and, once started, we knew you would reach us if it was in the bounds of a reasonable possibility. But we were deeply disappointed; and yet I think we had the grace of submission. How many times we said, 'We will talk this and that over with Mr. Perkins!' But although you did not reach us, from Zaia's account we know you did all you could, and we thank you with all our hearts.

"We have had several very mild and beautiful days, and we begin to hope the *cold* weather is over—I mean *eighteen or twenty degrees below zero.*

"This plain has at times presented scenes of rare beauty and grandeur. There is something almost terrible in the angry clouds, the thick, dark atmosphere and the howling winds. Then, after the storm is hushed, and we look up at the clear blue sky, and look out upon the plain lying in calm beauty like a silver sea, unruffled, and around upon the mountains standing like old watch-towers, their sternness all softened down and yet none the less grand, we begin to love our mountain home for its natural scenery. And we know it would have found an enthusiastic admirer if you could have gazed upon it this winter.

"We do most earnestly hope that the impressions of solemnity which seem to be taking hold of some hearts in the two seminaries will be deepened. I know the solicitude you all feel. We too are so bold as to hope that perhaps our dear Saviour will even visit us this winter.

*   *   *   *   *   *   *   *

"I have not a moment of sadness or sorrow *but on account of my sins.* This should not be sorrow without hope, for 'there is a fountain filled with blood.'

"*Sabbath, 15th February.*—To-day in our little Sabbath-school all repeated the first two commandments. It is affecting to see the parents come to the dekana (a raised platform in a stable), and, instead of spending their time

9 *

as formerly in idle talk, listen to the little boys committing the commandments and learn with them.

"*Saturday, February* 21.—I look back over this week with deep regret. My mind has been unusually taken up with modern and ancient Syriac and Hebrew; and, strange to tell, I found my heart growing cold and my hours of devotion irksome because my heart was unusually interested in the study of that language in which I long to preach Christ crucified!

Sabbath, 22*d.*—It is deeply interesting to see the people of this little village so unwearied in their attendance upon religious services. Every Saturday afternoon they meet in the dekana to learn the Sabbath-school lesson with the little boys. This morning all, young and old, repeated the third and fourth commandments. As yet we see no heart-work going on. That a very great change has taken place since our coming here is evident; but it is outward.

To-day we were much tried by the apparent slothfulness of our native helpers, being unwilling to go out on the Sabbath to preach to their dying people, urging their bitter opposition as a sufficient reason. Other little trials connected with our missionary work have saddened my heart to-day. I feel that I deeply need far larger supplies of grace for my work; and especially to be kind and forbearing toward our native brethren. O Lord, let me ever remember my many frailties.

29*th, Sabbath.*—Rose early, and enjoyed communion with my Father. I do thank him for this Sabbath. I was enabled to walk softly and carefully before him.

My room was filled with people of the village, and as usual they seemed much interested in hearing the truth. To-day *they repeated all the commandments.*

March 1, *Monday.*—A day of fasting and prayer in behalf of my own soul, my dear brothers and sisters out of

Christ, a world lying in wickedness, and especially the poor people among whom I live.

Read the Epistle to the Ephesians, pressing my own soul closely with practical questions; turning its petitions, its warnings, its promises, its rich disclosures of the Divine fullness into prayer and praise. I can in no other way get so much spiritual good out of the Bible as when I pray over it, verse by verse, and sentence by sentence. I charged and summoned my soul this morning to the holy duties of the day, and God did not leave me alone.

With but the faintest impressions of divine things, still the hours were precious. From necessity I could not be much alone, and had to hear my two lessons. Still I found my Saviour in some measure present. Now and then it seemed that I did get a faint impression of what it is to be an ambassador for Christ, an heir of glory, and what it is to rescue a soul from eternal burnings. But oh, often the feeling came over me how utterly short is this of the great realities! O my soul, wilt thou, canst thou rest until heaven and hell become more real? Canst thou be a trifler? Upon thy life, thy prayers, thy holy, heavenly walk, thy words, and thy hourly behavior may hang the eternal destiny of some kindred spirit! O my poor soul, I charge thee by all those tremendous realities among which thou wilt in a few days mingle, sleep no longer! Be to-night what Jesus bought thee to be. Be what heaven, just at hand, calls thee to be. Be what judgment, and the undying worm and quenchless fire, warn thee to be. Be what the grace of God is now ready to make thee. Be, oh be now what thou knowest thou canst be. O my soul, wilt thou go back to slumber? I know thy weakness. Come, O dear Jesus, come and give relief.

March 2.—Rose early. Read my usual Hebrew. A calm and peaceful day. Oh, it is sweet to get a faint glimpse of our glorious rest, even a *taste* of its joys. O my soul, thou hast nothing to boast of yet. Thou art poor, and blind, and naked, and thy greatest misery is that thou knowest nothing.

March 3, Wednesday.—I have frequently found it true that when I am striving with unusual watchfulness and earnestness to abide all the day in sight of God and eternity, I am suddenly surprised, thrown off my guard, and utter some word which does not seem like the meek spirit of my Lord; and which, I fear, gives him pain. Thus it was to-day. I look up with a deep sense of my weakness to that rich grace which, at all times, if yielded to, would quickly bring us to the calm, composed, spiritual and heavenly frame of mind so desirable for every Christian, and especially for a missionary.

Many rumors come to us about the exceeding bitterness of the people in other villages. Tamo has hesitated about going out to preach. His last visit was rather trying. His kindred refused to bring him a Testament, telling him to talk without preaching. They will do nothing to encourage his coming to them. The modir, we learn, has advised the people to keep aloof from us, that we may soon leave. That is good worldly policy, but he knows nothing of heavenly policy. It will be one of our greatest trials to keep ourselves shut up in this village till the opposition passes away, but we must not despise our little work.

Friday, March 5.—Yesterday, with several of the villagers, Deacon Tamo went to the village of Keeat. In the evening, perhaps half the village assembled. They said, "Your words are true. We have not heard these things before. How could we? We are as beasts upon the mountains."

Thursday, 11.—Messenger detained here on account of the fearful storm that has raged for three days. The wind has blown furiously; and this morning we found the snow drifted far above our roof, completely stopping up the door. All the villagers had to dig their way out.

Sabbath, 14.—Solemn, but joyful day. For several days my heart has been cold, and I know that I have grieved my Lord; and yet he did not cast me off, but stirred my poor, frozen heart to return to him. I felt deeply humbled. I have no confidence in myself. I am utter weakness. Felt deeply grieved that I had refused to walk with Jesus, or to entertain him in my heart. He wishes to enter. He knocks. And oh, can I drive him away? I have been trying to live in the sight of men. Oh, I fear this treacherous heart has longed to be holy because holiness is esteemed lovely. O Lord, help me to despise and thrust out from my heart every such motive, and to aim at holiness because it is pleasing to thee. Resolved, by the grace of God, never by looks or words or outward conduct to make an impression that there is more grace in my heart than there really is. O Lord, purify the fountain and pure streams will flow out.

A month elapses, bringing the next entry down to the middle of spring, but winter still lingered.

Friday, April 16.—For several days have been sick. Probably a slight attack of fever. Still feeble and unable to study much. Took a long walk with Mr. Coan. There is still much snow on the plain.

Thus ends the last record in the journal of the *first winter*. We give a few extracts from letters:

Under date of March 10, to Dr. Perkins: "The other day the rayis (chief) of Pirzalan came to our village. Mr. Coan and I went into the school, spent an hour or two hearing the boys spell, read and recite. The rayis seemed delighted with their progress, and *the fact that every youth in*

the village is now a reader must make an impression.   With
all the stir that has been made, I doubt not that we have
friends in every village who secretly desire the work to go
forward.   I have had to battle to-day with the leakage.
With my little table and writing apparatus I have been
dodging from corner to corner and side to side until here I
am in the middle, about dark, with my papers considerably
bespattered.   The boys came to the rescue, and have kept
up a great racket with their treading and pounding on the
roof.   *They say, 'It won't leak any more.'*   We have more
snow on the plain than we thought.   Brother Coan and I
measured it yesterday morning (March 9), and when we
got down into the holes which we dug, we found that *we
could not cleverly see our way out.*

"20*th.*—Violent S. E. wind.   Rain, snow and hail.

"Could you see the towering ramparts of snow and the
deep ditch with which we have entrenched ourselves, you
would think we feared being assailed with carnal weapons.
I think an inundation is more to be feared than all our
other foes put together.   We should rejoice to announce to
you that a highway is opened to our little village; but we
must be patient a little longer.   Though we are charmed
in the morning by the birds frisking and singing merrily,
and now and then the sun shines mildly and genially, these
are the only tokens that the spring has come.   Old Winter
still hesitates to let go his hold.   Since our messenger arrived we have had another foot of snow."

Even April 26 he says to Dr. Perkins at Oroomiah : " I
suppose when this reaches you, you will be on the eve of
your departure for Gawar.   So far as we can learn, you
will find the mountain pass difficult, and perhaps imprac-
ticable.   Callash spoke of it as impassable the day he came
over.   I suggested a delay of a few days as the safest.
Your long-expected visit has been the theme of many an

evening chit-chat, and our expectations we hope will soon be realized."

So soon ended their long winter siege the last of April. To their eyes beautiful upon the mountains were the feet of one of God's messengers of salvation joining them in publishing peace.

THE NESTORIANS.

Before going farther, let us turn aside from our story to answer the question, "Who are these Nestorians?" using materials furnished by Dr. Justin Perkins, the veteran missionary to this ancient Christian sect:

The Nestorians are a small remnant of a once great and actively missionary church, the oldest of Christian sects, and once numerous through all the regions of Asia, from Palestine to China. Of the Semitic stock, they claim to be of Israelitish lineage—a claim which can hardly be established. Nestorius, from whom they derive their name, was born in Syria. He was a presbyter at Antioch, where believers were first called Christians, and, in A. D. 428, was made bishop of Constantinople. His courage in resisting some popular superstitions, and perhaps his rashness in theological speculations, made him a mark for the hostility of contemporary bishops, particularly of the fiery Cyril of Alexandria. Summoned to a trial for alleged heresy before the third general council at Ephesus in 431, Nestorius was deposed and exiled to the desert of Lybia, where he died. His comparative purity in the general corruption which then prevailed was the real ground of the rigor with which he was treated. His refusal to apply the idolatrous epithet *mother of God* to the Virgin Mary was the brunt of his offending; and if he ventured into dangerous theories on the mysteries of the Trinity, they received at the hands of his enemies the harshest construction. In fact, Nestorius may with considerable reason be pronounced the first *Protestant.*

His cause rapidly gained adherents ; and possessing the vitality of comparatively simple belief and practice, the sect early took the character of a vigorous evangelizing organization, sending missionaries and planting churches through all Central Asia, while the rest of Christendom were slumbering in the profound torpor of the Middle Ages. The history of this Church has been a varied one, sometimes— as under the tolerant policy of the mighty Tartar conqueror Genghis Khân—being raised to high places in the camp and at the court, while subsequently—as under the bloody monster Timourlane—they were cut down and swept away by myriads, till scarcely a vestige of them remained save in the fastnesses of inaccessible mountains.

The present Nestorians are on the eastern borders of Turkey and the western borders of Persia, being thus in the very heart of Mohammedan dominion, and on the dividing line between the two great rival Mohammedan sects, the *Shiites* and the *Soonees;* the former embracing the Persians, and the latter the Turks and the Koords ; those sects being mutually almost as hostile to each other as they are in common toward Christians. About two-thirds of their country—the western portion—lies in Turkey, comprising much of Assyria, or modern Koordistan ; and the eastern third is in old Media, the north-western province of modern Persia, now called Azerbijân.

The former portion is physically one of the wildest and roughest regions on the globe, abounding in scenery of surpassing grandeur and sublimity, and is inhabited by the not less wild Koords, among whom many of the Nestorians dwell. The Persian part of their country is one of the most beautiful on which the sun ever shone, consisting of several of the most charming Persian plains, bounded on the east by the lake of Oroomiah, which is ninety miles long and thirty miles broad, while the towering ranges of Koordistan rear a lofty, snow-capped barrier on the west.

NESTORIANS.

The Nestorians stand in the relation of *oppressed tenants* toward the Mohammedans, among whom they dwell, being cultivators of the soil and artisans in the more common and useful mechanical trades. One continuous people, while living in the two contiguous empires of Turkey and Persia,

10

they partake much of the respective local peculiarities of the two parts of their country ; those in the Turkish portion, Koordistan, being rude, untutored, bold and defiant, and those in the mild and sunny clime of Persia possessing much of the blandness and suavity common to all classes in that genial country. Their language is a modern dialect of the ancient Syriac, the language used by the Saviour when on earth.

Their present number probably does not exceed one hundred and fifty thousand souls, about one-third of whom are found in Persia, and two-thirds scattered over a larger extent in Turkish Koordistan. They are a noble race of men ; manly and athletic, having fine forms and good complexions. They are also naturally a shrewd, active and intelligent people, yet remarkably artless, affable and hospitable, and peculiarly accessible for missionary purposes.

THE KOORDS.

Over a million of people, called Koords, speaking dialects of their own distinct languages, live wide-stretched through these same mountains of Turkey, from the north-east corner of the Mediterranean, along the Taurus mountains eastward, and from Russia down the vast ranges of Koordistan, that in Eastern Turkey form an almost impassable barrier between Turkey and Persia. This widespread mountain race separate the Arab-speaking populations of Mesopotamia and Syria from the Armenians and Turks north of Taurus, and from the Persians eastward. History connects them with the Karduchi of Xenophon ; some think with the Chaldeans. Their language is corrupted by Turkish and Persian, to which (and to the English) it is more allied than to the Arabic.

The Koords are almost all Moslems, of the Soonee sect, and are very superstitious and bigoted. They are divided into numerous petty tribes and sects. Like most mountain people, they are brave, passionate and rebellious, and often semi-independent. The Yezidee devil-worshipers speak Koordish, and belong to the same race. The Koords are profoundly ignorant, being almost without readers and writers. In ferocity and cruelty, when aroused by passion or in pursuit of plunder, they scarce fall below the savages of our American frontier.

KOORDS OF THE MOUNTAINS.

CHAPTER X.

THE STORM BURSTS.

WE continue from the journal of Mr. Rhea:

July 31, 1852.—Early in the spring we employed Deacon Tamo to build us a house. Timbers for the roof were purchased in the mountains, stones were drawn and workmen employed. The modir, to whom we had spoken freely, intimated no hindrance. We looked forward to a long, happy winter with our new associates in our new house.

Our masons reached here July 2d, and began to lay stone July 6th. As soon as the modir knew that they were at work he sent word to Deacon Tamo, "The people of Gawar have a quarrel with you; come and settle it." The deacon met the bishop and his people in the Turkish court. They were very violent, threatening to tear down as fast as he might build. The modir had no authority to prevent, but advised against his building. Tamo thought it would be wrong to yield to the unreasonable demands of an excited people; therefore he asked three days' time to consider his answer. It was granted.

Early on the morning of the third day two soldiers, with orders from the modir, rode up to the building after Tamo had gone to Dizza, and peremptorily ordered the masons to stop working, saying that a letter had come from the pasha forbidding the work. The work ceased. We had suspicions that this statement was false; and afterward learned from the modir himself that he had received no orders from his pasha, but that the whole thing was planned in the mejlis (Turkish court). As his only excuse for such summary procedure he stated the fear of bloodshed, or at least personal violence to us; a mere excuse, for two soldiers could have protected Tamo fully. But, recently in office, he was easily imposed upon by the bishop. The mejlis also, composed of an Armenian (the head of his village), a Koordish chief and a mollah, are our enemies. The poor villagers seemed deeply grieved, and urged us to obtain immediate redress. It was a heavy blow upon our hearts; but we were enabled to look behind the cloud.

Shortly afterward (July 14) I visited Oroomiah to take counsel. We concluded, with full statements of fact, to forward to our minister, Hon. G. P. Marsh, Constantinople, a paper signed by all the people of our village, requesting us to remain as their religious teachers; and also to complain to the pasha at Van of the conduct of the modir.

Another sad and apparently very unpropitious event happened a few days since (July 14). A Turkish soldier was spending the night in our village. He was once a Christian, but five years ago fleeing the country (Mosul) for murder, enlisted as a soldier. He attended our evening worship, and lay down before our door in the enclosure made by the newly-drawn timbers. He was urged to put his beautiful Arab mare in the stable; but he preferred to rest his head upon the halter, and thought he would be secure. About eleven o'clock, for the first time this summer, thieves came prowling around the village. The young soldier arose and fired upon them. They fled. About midnight they returned, stoned the shepherd of the village and came very near. Again the soldier rose, and, standing upon the timbers, fired upon them. The fire was returned. He fell, and died almost immediately, before Mr. Coan reached him.

10 *   H

The next morning very early two men were sent to inform the authorities. They were detained while five soldiers came and carried away the corpse. The next day the people of the village were all taken to Dizza, and the modir took their testimony and forwarded it to the pasha at Van.

Much excitement prevailed. Our enemies were busy. The young man falling just before our door necessarily brings us into undesirable connection with the affair in the minds of the Turks. The low soldiery even intimate that we were implicated in the murder.

Yesterday a soldier came and took the villagers to Dizza again to give their testimony, the pasha not being satisfied. On arrival at Dizza, they learned that they must go to Bashkollah, or even to Van. They were confined closely, and treated rather as prisoners than witnesses. Some threats were used by the soldiers.

When it was known that the men were to be taken to Bashkollah, the poor women seemed distracted. They gave vent to their grief in most lamentable cries, wringing their hands, smiting upon their breasts, uncovering their heads and pouring ashes upon them. We tried to comfort them, saying, Your husbands have only gone to Bashkollah to testify before the pasha. We hope they will soon return in safety. They almost refused to be comforted.

One poor mother, a widow, had an only son thus torn away. It was already dark, and the village of the bishop was some three hours' distant. She said, " I will go to the bishop; I will fall at his feet; I will seize the skirts of his robe and kiss them and beg for my son, my beloved, my only son. Let them not take him from me and I be left desolate."

I trust this grief may prove the result of ignorance, and that the poor villagers will not suffer. Yet the rude soldiers who had care of them in Dizza, keeping them closely confined and giving them little to eat, taunted them by saying, *Thus we treat murderers.*

We are in a wild region, the home of a savage race but lately subdued, and we are in a measure defenceless. We have no human end to serve here; only to help poor, bruised, downtrodden humanity around us, and we know that we have the sympathy of Him who bled for it, and we can calmly repose in the arms of his tender love.

August 3.—A dark day, but not too dark to rest calmly in the hands of God.

Late in the evening one of the Koords who was carried to Bashkollah returned and told us that Tamo, Eshoo, Zaia and Hoshaba were in prison and in chains.

At Bashkollah, on arrival, they were sent to the tent of the military pasha. He demanded of Tamo and his brothers and Hoshaba, "Why did you kill that soldier?" All at once replied, "We are innocent of his blood." "Did not those Englishmen (the missionaries) kill him?" With horror they spoke out, "They are men of peace. They own no weapons. All their teaching is to forbid murder, theft and lies." Of Deacon Tamo the pasha then demanded, "Why do not you and your village expel them?" Tamo said, in reply, "We cannot; we want them; they are good men, only doing us and our people good." The pasha asked, "Have you become English?" Tamo replied, "I am their friend, and can never withdraw my hand." At this the pasha became angry, and commanded that he and his brothers and Hoshaba be thrown into a narrow, loathsome prison, where were already more than twenty prisoners—that heavy chains be hung around each of their necks, and their feet confined in stocks.

As we feared, our enemies seem to take advantage of the unfortunate murder at our door to bring serious annoyance and suffering upon the poor people who receive us, attempt-

ing to expel us by persecuting them till they, or *we for their
sakes*, are forced to leave. When the wives and mothers
heard of the prison and chains, they set up the most distressing wails.

We were enabled in a measure to comfort them. Mr.
Coan left at 9 P. M. for Oroomiah, hoping to get a letter
from Colonel Williams, and with Dr. Wright to go speedily
to Bashkollah, perhaps to Van, to aid our friends in bonds.
God speed and crown their efforts with success.

August 4.—Last night, at 2 A. M., three soldiers came
to the village. I was sleeping on the roof, but they would
not allow any one to waken me. They ordered the watch-
man to tell the villagers to break every brick of ours upon
the floors, or they would be beaten. They themselves went
to the piles, and broke perhaps a hundred bricks. An hour
before dawn they left, taking Benjamin with them.

About ten o'clock two soldiers came for Guergis. He
slept by the side of the Turkish soldier when he was killed.
He has been sick for some time. All remonstrance in his
behalf was vain. My heart bled for the poor boy when I
saw the soldiers carry him forcibly away, pale, emaciated,
scarcely able to sit upon a horse, much less to travel a two
days' journey. I gave Guergis a few kerans to buy him
anything he might need, and sent my servant to help him
on the road to Dizza.

For two days we have been expecting our English friend
Mr. Loftus, the geologist and antiquarian of the English
commission for the survey of the boundary lines between
Turkey and Persia. There are four commissioners—English, Russian, Persian and Turkish. They have been engaged in the work for four years, and will complete it in
about six weeks. Colonel Williams, the queen's commissioner, and his party, together with the Russian and Persian parties, visited our friends at Seir. Colonel Williams

(afterward the famous Sir William Williams, of Kars), while there, became deeply interested in the evangelization of the mountain Nestorians, and entered into all our troubles here with whole-hearted sympathy, kindly consenting to throw all his influence to secure us a comfortable residence here. To this end he forwarded letters to the modir and bishop, and also gave a letter to the pasha at Van.

Friday, August 6.—A cavass came about twelve o'clock, bringing letters of introduction for Mr. Loftus, who with his party came in sight about two o'clock. I rode out, and had a very pleasant meeting with him and Mr. Cassalani. They pitched their very comfortable tents on the plot below our house, but they ate at our table and spent the time chiefly in our rooms. They make many inquiries, and are anxious to render us all the help they can. In fact, their leaving their company and visiting this plain is chiefly on our account, and is another testimony to the hearty interest Colonel Williams takes in our work. Mr. Loftus will deliver letters from Colonel W. to the modir and bishop, and call in person. We esteem it an unspeakable privilege to meet with gentlemen so intelligent and refined, and to enjoy their very agreeable society, in this wild region.

Saturday, August 7.—Early this morning Mr. Loftus sent Colonel W.'s letters to the modir and the bishop. Two or three hours afterward, an officer and two soldiers came from the modir, inviting Mr. L. to call upon him and dine with him. At 12 we started over to Dizza. About two miles from the village we met a number of officers and soldiers with renewed salutations from the modir, and another invitation to dine with him. As we approached Dizza we were met by the modir himself and the colonel of the regiment, who conducted us to their tents, pitched upon the flat below the village.

We had not been seated long before Mr. Loftus introduced the subject of our residence here. He told the modir that he had left his party and traveled out of his way three or four days only to see us, his friends and the friends of the English commissioner; and if he wished to show attention and respect to him, he could do it in no better way than by making our residence here comfortable and pleasant.

The modir expatiated upon the friendship that he had cherished for us.

When asked, "Why have you stopped their building?" he plead "orders from his pasha at Van;" pretended that no subject could build a house so large as Deacon Tamo was building, without permission from Constantinople.

Mr. L. was not disposed to press that point, for we knew he could give no liberty to build; and we only wished to impress on the modir's mind that we had friends willing and able to obtain redress when our rights were trampled under foot. That impression I think was deeply made.

The modir would not permit Mr. Loftus to leave without eating bread with him. While we were sitting, the modir having announced that the dinner would soon be ready, unexpectedly Mar Sleewa, the bishop, came in, shook hands with us all, and took his seat. Mr. Loftus told him that we had sent him Colonel Williams' letter and word that we would call upon him at his house. The old man said, "Here is the letter, its seals unbroken. I have come to see you and get my letter read."

Mr. Loftus interpreted the letter through his servant, who speaks a little broken Syriac, but the bishop, not understanding, requested me to explain the words of Mr. Loftus, and also had a Turk read the letter to him.

I had a pleasant interview with the bishop, telling him that he knew well the objects of our residence here—to raise up his downtrodden people, give them their own Scriptures, and declare their precious truths, of which they were now ignorant; that he knew our only object was to do good; and · still, for some reason, he was opposed to it; that we wanted his helping hand to save his dying people; but if he chose not to give it he must bear the responsibility; that we wished him to share the glorious work of evangelizing his people; but, as it is God's work, "if it does not go forward with your influence and approval, it certainly will without."

Dinner was now announced, and we walked up the hill to the room of the modir. A large platter was placed in the centre, upon a wooden frame, a foot and a half high. Little piles of bread were placed at the edge of the platter, and a dish in the centre. White napkins were spread upon the bread. Water was brought; we washed our hands, dried them with the napkins, and then spread them on our knees. We then put our fingers into the centre dish. It was soon taken away and replaced by ten or twelve, successively. Mr. L. complimented the dishes: "They must be prepared by a European cook." "No," said our host; "but modern Turks derive all their notions of cooking from the Europeans." The food was very well prepared, indeed, thanks to the queen's commissioner.

We soon took our leave; Mr. Loftus, in the name of Colonel Williams, commending us to the protection of the modir. He of course replied as one very anxious to please. We rode rapidly, and reached our village after dark.

Monday, August 9.—Much to our regret, our English friends felt bound to leave us on the Sabbath to fulfill their engagement with Colonel Williams. How often I felt during my intercouse with these amiable and worthy men, "*But one thing is needful,*" and lifted the silent prayer that they might be led to choose that good part!

About 3 P. M. I was surprised in looking out of my little window to see a horseman approaching our village rapidly.

It proved to be none other than Mr. Coan. His return was very unexpected.

On Wednesday morning, as he was descending upon the plain of Barodost, he descried the large assemblage of white tents of the boundary commissioners. (Nearly all the tents of Asia, of Arabia, of Koords and Turcomans alike, are *black*, being made of black goats' hair.) He could hardly believe his eyes. He was directed to the camp of Colonel Williams, and met with a warm reception. He soon made known his object.

The most noble-hearted Colonel Williams at once said, "I am commander-in-chief of this party, and you, as a soldier, must obey. We will go direct to Bashkollah, and secure the release of your poor villagers."

They were soon on the way; traveled one day fifteen hours; reached Bashkollah Thursday night late, and appeared before the pasha.

The pasha was thunderstruck when he learned that the queen's commissioner was before him. Colonel W. requested that the chains be loosed from the necks of those innocent men—innocent at least until proved guilty; that their feet should be taken from the stocks, and they be provided with a comfortable place until the legal investigations terminated.

This was promptly done. Our villagers were brought into the colonel's presence. They were worn down with fatigue, being compelled to labor in the burning sun with chains about their feet. They were deeply affected by the kindness of Colonel W.; *they crawled to him, kissed his hand and bathed it with their tears.*

Mr. Coan learned from Tamo the sad story of all their sufferings. When the pasha at Bashkollah told Colonel Williams that he was an inferior pasha, subject to orders from Van, Colonel W. at once requested a guard of five soldiers, saying, "I will go to Van in person and see that these men be released." He was unwilling that Mr. Coan should go with him, since he had left Mrs. Coan alone, and with much reluctance Mr. Coan consented to part with Colonel W. and return.

That most noble man has now gone to Van, leaving all his appropriate work, traveling long stages through the burning sun, that he may secure the release of our poor prisoners, and throw the entire weight of his influence to get for us the liberty of building.

May God bless him and make him yet a most distinguished soldier of the cross of Jesus, and give him the crown of gold and the white robe of triumph! Our hearts have been most deeply and tenderly affected by these providential occurrences. God rules in the heavens. Why then should we ever see a dark and frowning sky?

In July of this year (1852), Mr. Rhea broke away from his mountain home for the first time, and visited his fellow-laborers at Oroomiah. His intercourse with them for a few days was highly refreshing to him, and not less so to them, and especially delightful to his young friends. The sweet hymns were again sung, accompanied by the seraphine, played charmingly by the "Persian Flower," Dr. Perkins' daughter, Judith, then scarcely twelve years old. Little did our brother imagine that that was his last visit with Judith, who, a few weeks afterward, was suddenly cut down by cholera.

Mr. Rhea in Oroomiah again (on account of illness), writes thence to his parents:

October 4, 1852.

It is a long time since I have written you—nearly two months. Just when our post for August was leaving, I was taken with fever and confined to my bed two weeks. About three weeks after, when Mr. and Mrs. Coan left to

11

spend a few days in Oroomiah, I had not recovered my accustomed strength, but was able to ride out with them an
hour on their way. Shortly after I returned to the village
I was taken with chills and fever, which lasted ten days.
I was all alone, except Eshoo, a young man who stays with
me. The next day he was also taken with chills and fever.
The days which intervened between fever and ague I was able
to sit up and take care of Eshoo, as he was also able to take
care of me when he was not shaking. Dr. Wright very
kindly came to my relief. He at once advised me to return with him. The first day I could only ride two hours.
But I improved so rapidly that on the fourth and last day,
by resting a good deal, I was able to ride seven hours, and
reached Oroomiah. I have been here ten days, enjoying
the hospitalities of my dear friends. My health has improved every day since my arrival, and I hope to return in
a few days. I look back upon the past few weeks as the
most blessed of my life. I think I can thank our Father
in heaven for every pain I have felt—for every long, wearisome, feverish night. It is very sweet and blessed to learn
submission—quiet, joyful, submission—under his chastening
rod. There is no solid peace or bliss for our souls until we
can bring all our interests for time and eternity, and, without a single anxious thought, leave them at his disposal,
feeling perfectly assured that he will do all things well.
And I think one of the blessed fruits of sanctified afflictions
is to lie quietly in our Father's arms, willing to be in adversity or prosperity, sick or well, to live or die, just as
seemeth to him good. I said "I was all alone," but God
was never so near and precious. They were most joyful
days. I tremble for fear my heart will lose the impression God was pleased to give me of his wonderful tenderness, compassion and love.

October 13.—More than a week has passed. I have had

another chill, but am feeling much better, and hope to set out for my mountain home in the morning. When I last wrote to you, a number of our villagers were in prison. All have been released except Deacon Tamo. He is still retained, though not treated as a prisoner. We hope he may soon be released. God has raised up in the person of the English commissioner, Colonel Williams, one who we trust will rescue him from the clutches of a government still cruel and oppressive. The pasha of our district has lately visited Gawar, and although we have not yet received permission to build the house we commenced, he has given us the privilege of putting up two small storerooms. Brother Coan and I occupy the station alone this winter. Mrs. Coan will spend the winter in Oroomiah. It is not advisable for her to spend another winter alone in a region so inhospitable. Most gladly would she spend another dreary winter alone, without the society of a missionary sister, or even a pious Nestorian female, with but few more comforts than she had last year, were it not considered hazardous to her health.

We hope to-morrow to celebrate the Lord's Supper, and on Tuesday Mr. Coan, Mr. Crane and myself will return to Gawar.

If we can breast the mountain storms and find a path through the deep snow, we hope to make our way to every Nestorian village on the plain. We cannot longer leave these perishing souls in hopeless darkness.

The noble efforts of the Queen's commissioner for weeks, and months even, proved fruitless to release Tamo. Other trials were added. Mr. Rhea writes from

MEMIKAN, *Dec.* 15, 1852.

Within the last few weeks we have received a positive order from the Sublime Porte to remove from Gawar.

We were just on the eve of starting when we received the

order from the Turkish government, through Mr. Marsh, our Minister at Constantinople. He did not advise us either to remove or remain, but simply announced the fact, hoping that the charges made against us were false. We determined to write to him immediately, assuring him of their entire falsity, and in the mean time proceed to Gawar and quietly prosecute our labors. We may be compelled to abandon our work in these wild mountains. It would be the saddest day of my life, but I have no idea that God will permit the enemy to triumph.

Mar Shimon has lately made a tour of the mountain districts. You would naturally think of the venerable patriarch, in the spirit of one of the holy prophets or apostles, passing from village to village, gathering around him his simple-hearted people, lifting upon them holy hands, invoking the rich blessings of God's grace, and with a loving heart pointing them away from earth's tears and sighings and oppressions to a home in heaven. But in all his journeyings not a word of prayer in their behalf fell from his lips; not a word of tender warning and entreaty to his poor, lost, wandering sheep to seek the good Shepherd. Oh, our heart sickens to think how God's ambassadors among this people have fallen! I asked my good old friend, the crippled pipe-maker from Ishtazin, if Mar Shimon assembled the people to pray with them and tell them of the things of God and heaven. "What," said he, "does Mar Shimon care for our souls? Do you not know why he visits our villages? Is it for anything else than to get our presents— our mules and garments and money? No, no, not one poor soul did he point to the Lamb of God." Of one thing we are certain—and whenever I think of it my heart is filled with unutterable joy—that wherever there is light or conscience it is on our side. A few nights since a stranger was present at our regular evening service. I looked around upon the little group of forty immortal souls, and asked him if it was not pleasant thus to meet together to read God's Word and talk together of God and heaven. He replied,

"Yes."

"Why, then, do you not meet in your village?"

"We are afraid."

"Would God be angry with you were you to assemble thus to hear his truth?"

"No."

"Would your bishop?"

"Yes."

"Then are not God and your bishop disagreed about this matter, and ought you not to obey God rather than man?"

He was thoughtful for a moment, but at length shrugged his shoulders and said,

"What shall we do?—we are nothing but men."

While I was telling him that our errand to these dark lands was not, as some said, to take away their religion, but to save them from the coming wrath of God, soon to be revealed against all ungodliness, he broke out with some fierceness:

"Do you not know that we intend to drive you out of our country, and had you not better return home now, in time?"

I held up the New Testament from which I had been reading, and asked him what book it was. He replied:

"The word of God."

"Do the bishop and his priests preach it to the people?"

"No."

"Why?"

"I don't know."

"Is it not because this book is all light, and their deeds are all darkness?"

11 *

He looked around upon the villagers and said,
"It is true."

I continued, "Does God wish this word preached among your people?"

"Yes."

"Then is it not evident that this dispute is between God on one side, and the bishop and his priests on the other? Is not God on our side? Are you not fighting against him? Do you hope to measure arms with the Almighty and triumph? Can he not, and will he not, scatter to the winds all your counsels?"

He made no reply. After a few moments he apologized for what he had said about driving us from the country, and feared that he had offended me.

I said to him, "Oh, no. We love you, and we have made up our mind to keep in a good humor about this matter. If there are any angry words to be spoken, they shall all be on your side. While you revile us and threaten our expulsion, we will try and love you the more and pray for you the more fervently." He had a word to say to me in private, which amounted to about this:

"If Deacon Tamo were released, and it were evident that the Turks would not oppress us, more than half of Gawar are ready to welcome you to their villages, and hear from your lips the words of eternal life."

Poor Deacon Tamo! We have yet no good word with reference to his release from imprisonment. Nearly six months have passed since he was taken from his village. He bears manfully this heavy trial. We send him some money to buy his food, also some little comforts in the way of clothing.

Mar Shimon when he was here showed great hostility to our residence in Gawar, and demanded of his bishop why he had not expelled us before this. The bishop told him he had tried as hard as he could, but he couldn't do it. "Then," said the Patriarch, "I will drive them out."

We expect a hard-fought battle before we get firmly settled in the Koordish mountains. We are not in despair. I am very happy here in my little room, shut in again by the deep snows. I have had some chills and fever since my return, but I hope that a good deal of exercise in this bracing air and simple living will restore me to accustomed vigor. Bread, milk and rice form my diet, and I am grateful, I trust, for that.

The following letter from Mr. Rhea to Mrs. Coan gives us a cheerful picture of the home-life of the two missionaries, if home it may be called when deprived of the presence of the lady whose society had illumined the mountain hut and gilded the mud of its walls:

MEMIKAN, GAWAR, *January* 20, 1853.

First of all I will render my most hearty thanks for the beautiful velvet cap. When I held it up and its rich colors gleamed in the light of the lamp, my first thought was, This will never do for Gawar. But then I thought you made it, and you made it for *me*, and you made it for me to wear in Gawar; and it will not be in sympathy with your unostentatious spirit to bring it forth at set times and for special effect. I will give it at once its place, to be a continual remembrance of a dear friend. It seems to do Brother Coan so much good to see it on that I could not be induced to take it off. He has made me blush more than once by flattering my improved personal appearance; but I quietly think he means "the cap;" and now, ye dust and smoke of Gawar, lay not your unwashen hands upon this crown of glory, until she who made it shall have looked upon it and recognized her own fair work!

How pleasant beyond expression would it be were you now with us! But I know you bear with true womanly patience and fortitude this separation. Were I not afraid, I should say Brother C. is happier than last winter; at least (being less anxious) he appears as cheerful. Sometimes we keep close to our books and writing all day, and hardly see each other's faces until our evening meal, when we throw off dull care and "pour a hand" to each other's comfort. Separated during the day, we prize our evening visits.

When you hear that an armed troop, with fife and drum and other warlike insignia (until forbidden by the modir), were coming to carry us, with our effects, over the mountains, to deposit us quietly on the Persian side, perhaps you will be glad that you are already there. The mode of passage might not have been the most comfortable. Let me not speak lightly of the pitiable infatuation of our poor people. Oh no! It grieves me to the heart. They are fighting against God. Jesus weeps over them; so should we weep and pray.

The great mass of the people would not harm one hair of our heads were they not overawed, but would welcome us as guests and religious teachers.

Amid all this brightening and darkening of our skies, this beating and surging, and then lapsing of the billows, it is very soothing to rest in the arms of our Lord. Oh how often we say he is asleep! With trembling hearts and faces pale with fright we call the Master. With what shame we see him calmly rise and bid the waves, "Peace, be still;" and then we hear his mild rebuke: "O thou of little faith, wherefore didst thou doubt?"

A few days later Mr. Rhea writes:

Yesterday our mail brought us good news with reference to Deacon Tamo. The English ambassador at Constantinople presented his case before the Turkish government, and a promise was given that an order would be sent forthwith for his release.

This winter has not been so severe as the last, but the mercury fell several mornings to 15°, 20° and 24° *below zero.* Two weeks since we made a little tour of five or six days among the nearest Nestorian villages. We tried to become one with the people—traveled on foot, sat with them in their stables, ate of their coarse fare, and lay down at night on a pallet of clean hay. I never felt better; had a good appetite, slept soundly and sweetly, and was able to preach without fatigue day and night. In each village little groups of from forty to fifty persons gathered around us, and sat oftentimes from sunset until a late hour at night, listening to the truth. One night, after the younger part of the crowd had talked rather long and hard, contending for their long fasts and other vain superstitions, two venerable men, whose heads and flowing beards were white with the frosts of many winters, rose and said: "We are all wrong, we are all wrong. These, our friends, are right— they preach the truth; hearken unto them."

Mr. Rhea was left alone for some days whilst Mr. Coan visited Oroomiah. The following letter to Mrs. Coan depicts the eagerness of watch from the mountain height under the Jeloo cliff, and the delight of brotherly welcome to the mountain post:

"On Tuesday I pointed the telescope once or twice in the direction of Dizza, thinking that Mr. Coan might be on the way. On Wednesday I confidently expected him, and ordered our cook to make a good loaf of bread and a soup from the best part of our lamb, to take up the rugs and give them a thorough shaking, and make things look as bright and cheery as our limited resources would permit. About 1 P. M., as I was gazing at Dizza with my telescope, two horsemen suddenly came into the field of vision, and I

I

knew that Brother Coan was one of them. I turned to
Eshoo, and told him: "They will be here in two hours."
He was much astonished at the power of the instrument;
but sure enough in a little less than two hours your husband
was with us again, safe and sound. It was good to be
alone, that I might all the more heartily appreciate our
intercourse."

Here is an Oriental picture:

"I am sorry you cannot be here to mingle in the festive
scenes soon to be enacted in Memikan. Oraham the son
of Tulya is to take a wife from the house of Basso of Keeat.
A number of our villagers went on Friday to fix the price
and consummate the bargain. On Saturday the father of
the bride and others came, and yesterday were very attentive to all our religious services. During our walk this
morning we met them starting homeward with an ox and
six sheep, the price they had set upon the head of their
daughter. The nuptials will probably be celebrated in six
or eight days."

DEACON TAMO.

Thus the weeks and months rolled on, and during all
this time what of poor Tamo. Has the powerful influence
of the queen's commissioner been thwarted? Is it possible
for the responsibility for bitter persecution to be tossed back
and forth like a shuttlecock over the head of such a man
as the hero of Kars, the poor prisoner still wearing out
weary months while modir writes to pasha, and pasha awaits
instructions from the Sublime Porte at Constantinople, and
the Sublime Porte writes down to the extremities of the
languid Empire for fuller information, and letters take over
a month to go and come? Has "how not to do it" rusted
into the heavy bolts of the doors which never turn for one
wearing the garb of justice unless essence of gold be distilled

into smoothest oil and applied with free and silent hand to both bolt and hinge?

The queen's commissioner at first, and next Lord Stratford Canning, the most influential of ambassadors at Constantinople, have asked and received promises in behalf of innocent Deacon Tamo. Was a promise ever broken in the good land of the faithful who pray five times a day and fast the whole month of Ramadan? Was ever one of those smooth promises that slip so easily from the oily tongue of a pliant grand vizier into the delighted, trusting ear of the favored ambassador of the most favored nation, ever meant to be as crisp and well buttered and as brittle as, for hundreds of years in old empires, pie-crust has traditionally been?

Ask Lord Stratford. Ask Colonel Williams, the later "Williams pasha" of the Turkish Empire, and since major-general commanding all the queen's forces in Canada. Ask, if you ever see him, here or in glory, our noble friend, Christ's faithful disciple, suffering for Christ's sake, Deacon Tamo!

Unceasing efforts were made for the poor prisoner, but still in vain. Tamo yet languished in chains.

Mr. Rhea writes to Mr. Coan, March 14, 1853, after a short visit to Oroomiah: "We found the snow had melted from the road almost to the pass. By keeping on the sunny side of the mountain after crossing the pass, we had a fine road to Mero's Castle; there we met considerable snow, increasing in depth until we reached Bazirga. The last hour was very difficult for our horses. The next morning a few inches of fresh snow had made a fine crust, and the villagers all said that there would be no difficulty in crossing the plain. We, however, had gone only a few paces from the village when we found deep, stiff snow, impassable for horses. After floundering for a while we returned to the village, left our horses and traveling bags, and took up the line of march for Memikan on foot. The river was full, and only to be forded at Kerpil. Two Armenians became our pilots. The crust was pretty good, though we frequently broke through, and several times found ourselves nearly knee-deep in water. Then our waterproof boots did good service. From Kerpil to Memikan we had a hard time. At midday the crust would not bear us, and the old path had been filled in with snow. I despaired of reaching the village; but we tugged on, and at last arrived about sunset.

"A large company of the villagers, headed by the good old Eshoo, came out to meet us., I was unmanned by the tokens of their affection. The little girls smothered our hands with kisses, and the poor women were all out upon the roof to bid us welcome. Their first question was, 'How is hanum (the lady, Mrs. Coan)? How is hanum?'

"Eshoo and Khamis and the family were much rejoiced at the news from Tamo. They had been in great anxiety for several days. Evil-minded men had circulated another report that he was beheaded, and the family half believed it."

Two months more of Deacon Tamo's prison-life passed, and March 22 he writes to Dr. Perkins: "Poor old Eshoo came in this afternoon burdened with grief. Every few days his heart becomes too full, and he must come in to pour out his sorrows. He says he has no heart to go to the mountains to get timbers for his ploughs, or make any preparation for labor the coming summer, so long as his dear brother is in prison. I told him to be of good courage; God will deliver Tamo. He has raised up many friends; and, if necessary, some of our number will go even to Stamboul (Constantinople), and stay there till the news of Tamo's release reaches them. I told him, 'If we are so happy as to get to heaven, we will sit down together and talk over these days of sorrow, and praise that rich grace which brought us safely through to that happy land where the eye never fills with tears, the heart never throbs with anguish.' His face brightened with joy, the tears stole down his cheeks, and the poor old man's heart was comforted.

"Khamis (a younger brother) seems quite anxious to visit Tamo, and I have been disposed to favor his going, that he may be there when the order for release may come, to bring him home if it takes effect—if not, to know the reason.

"They have been sorely tried by all kinds of rumors. A few days since an old sheikh came from Bashkollah, and reported that the pasha was demanding of Tamo 600 tomans ($1200), and that he should renounce all connection with us; and if he did not meet these demands, he should lose his head, and his brothers would then be seized and confined until they were willing to expel us from their villages. These rumors, although they do not believe them, have naturally a depressing influence. I am glad that they feel that we are doing all that can be done. All the kindness we can show to Tamo will tell in years to come upon his attachment to us and our work in the mountains. He has much that is generous and noble in his temper, and a heart peculiarly sensitive to the approaches of sympathy and affection."

After nearly another month, April 12, sorely-tried Mr. Rhea writes to Dr. Perkins, of Tamo: "He is our brother in bonds. The more I think of it, the more and more it seems a case of most flagrant oppression. I have no hope in the last order. An inimical pasha, such as we know Mohammed Pasha to be, *will*, or in all probability *has*, slid the order under the cushions of his divan, saying 'The case is misapprehended in Stamboul.' There is a faint hope that the poor fellow will now be released."

12

Tamo's brother, Khamis, visited Van with high hopes, but returned disappointed. "The pasha kept him four days," says Mr. Rhea, and "at last told him that he could not release Tamo according to his promise; that he was just ready to do it, but he got a letter which showed that we had been complaining against him; it made him angry, and now he would not release him; but '*it was that letter which spoiled the whole affair !*'"

He talked to Khamis in a very angry manner, charged him with being an accomplice with us in making complaint. He made so strong an impression of hostility and deceitfulness that Khamis says he will never venture to trust him again. The deacon, he says, is as patient as we could expect him to be.

Would there be risk in attempting to build up our front wall, which is insecure, and the wall of our store-room, which tumbled down, or in attempting more effectually to keep out the smoke? Would it affect Deacon Tamo's cause unfavorably?

On July 12, 1853, he addressed to the writer, at Mosul, the following letter:

On last Saturday I had the pleasure of welcoming to our humble cabin in Gawar, Mr. and Mrs. Crane and Master Morris Crane, and Mr. and Mrs. Coan, from Oroomiah. Perhaps you will think it strange that ladies should be coming into Koordistan at this time of 'rumors of war,' but Dr. Wright immediately on its arrival at Oroomiah will send us the latest news from Constantinople, so that there will be time to retreat if the stay of our friends is perilous. About half of the soldiers here have left for points nearer the capital; and at any time heavier drafts may be made. With intense interest we watch the arrival of our next messenger from the West. How consoling the thought that God rides upon the storm, and can make its fearful elements usher in the reign of peace and love!

"Just before leaving America, in talking with Dr. Anderson about my probable sphere of labor, he gave me the liberty of circulating between Oroomiah and Mosul. As yet I am only thus far, and I am anxious to see other portions of my parish. Had Mr. Crane an associate, the two families would suffice for this region, and I would try and get a hold in the heart of the Nestorian mountains. For two long years I have nursed and cherished this longing of my heart, but I know not when it may be satisfied. God oftentimes tries our faith and patience and love by a comparatively insignificant sphere of labor, and if we are true and loyal in meeting those responsibilities, he will doubtless say, sooner or later, 'Come up higher.'"

For the past two weeks, during Mr. Crane's visit to Oroomiah, I have been making some repairs in our premises, and I think we shall succeed in getting the two rooms, which we have hitherto occupied, out of the ground, free from dampness, darkness and smoke. Khamis has built a small room, which we can occupy if necessary, and will probably build another this season. Thus little by little, year by year, we hope to get a home in Gawar, where our health will not be exposed.

Poor Tamo is still in prison, every effort for his release having signally failed. Mr. Stevens made a representation of the case to Lord Stratford, and we are in hopes now that every post will bring good tidings of liberty to the captive; but it would not be strange if, in the present disturbed state of things at the capital, poor Tamo should remain for weeks yet in confinement.

He writes from Gawar, August 10, 1853:

MY DEAR BROTHER MARSH: We rejoiced to hear that your apprehensions in regard to your safety have been in a great measure relieved. The news this side of the mountains to-day is scarcely more recent than you sent us three weeks since. We are in the dark as to the fact of war having been already begun, though you are probably now informed.

Mr. Stevens (English consul at Tabreez) has advised us to withdraw from the mountains; but we who are on the ground, and see and hear everything that is going on around us, are probably better able to judge of our security than our friends away. The soldiers, amounting to some two hundred, have, two or three weeks since, except thirty, left this district. But the pasha at Bashkollah sent for two or three old Koordish chiefs, from whom, if at all, danger was to be apprehended, authorized them to raise forty or fifty horsemen, and to them, with the officers and remaining soldiers, committed the country, requiring the damage of thefts and robberies at their hands. Our people say the country was never so quiet and secure; still, we do not know. Koords are treacherous, and wait a fitting time to do a dark deed.

Our friends in Oroomiah felt anxious, and advised Mrs. Crane to return to Oroomiah. She was just becoming acquainted with our people and interested in teaching the little girls, and to think of returning was a great trial. Still it was safest. Mr. Crane has come back, and we are alone again, working off these long summer days as we best can.

We have been very anxious to spend some time in the interior mountain districts, but until now have been prevented, waiting the issue of poor Tamo's case; but the prospect of his release grows darker.

Three months ago it was the opinion of a majority of our mission that Tamo would not be released until some one of our number went in person to Lord Stratford with all the necessary documents and facts in the case, and remained in

Constantinople until a strong order was given for Tamo's unconditional discharge. Mr. Stevens was consulted at the time, and he was requested to lay the case before Lord Stratford. He was confident that very soon he would bring him out. But I fear the great man is so absorbed in political affairs that, when the fate of an empire may be pending, the poor prisoner, from necessity almost, will be forgotten.*

Our position was never so embarrassing; but it is a position in which God's providences have placed us, and we only beg for the grace of entire and unreserved submission.

The deep feeling of Mr. Rhea for Tamo is still more earnestly and tenderly depicted in the following extracts from a letter to Mr. Coan: "Tamo is well, but I am afraid, poor man! is getting out of heart. I send you a few lines from him. Khamis says he has kept up nobly till now; but he thinks sufficient time has passed for some reply from Lord Stratford, and that his case is almost hopeless. The last day Khamis was there a poor fellow-prisoner was taken from Tamo's side to appear before the pasha. As he went out he threw his cloak over his shoulder, saying, 'I am going, Tamo, but God only knows if you will ever see me again.' That afternoon the poor fellow was beheaded. The murdered man was the only son of a widow, and she refused anything less than blood for blood. The tragical scene seemed to work strongly upon Tamo's feelings. Although he has the general belief that the pasha would not dare to harm him, still he has shown such determined hostility that Tamo does not know but that he might in an evil hour make way with *him* too. The *first* day Khamis saw the pasha he told him Tamo would never leave his prison till we left Memikan. The last day he swore three times that in twenty days he would send him home. He seems to take a fiendish delight in tormenting the poor sufferer,

* The Crimean war was coming on.

and tantalizing him by delusive hopes of relief. My dear brother, believe me, *winter* is coming, and we must do something for poor Tamo. For one entire year, day after day, and week after week, and month after month, through the long winter, and again through the long summer, we have put off his confiding friends by promises of help through letters.

Another month passes. September 13th he writes:

"From an interview Dr. Lobdell and myself had with the modir on last Wednesday, I had strong suspicion that there would be foul play in some way in reference to Tamo.

"On Thursday morning it was determined that Mr. Coan and myself go to Bashkollah and know definitely about Tamo's case. We left at half-past one, spent the night in Manis, rose before daylight, went on our way, and reached Bashkollah at half-past two o'clock. We called on Kamil Pasha a short time after reaching there. He told us that Mohammed Pasha had sent Tamo to him a week before, commanding him to see that the people of Gawar make no disturbance on Tamo's arrival. He wrote to the modir *here,* inquiring how it would be if Tamo should come home. The modir wrote back that the whole people were bitterly opposed to his return. Kamil Pasha then sent for the bishop and Meero Bey, intending to charge them to see that no disturbance was made on Tamo's return. These two dignitaries spent the night in Manis with us. We did not then know their business; but having strong suspicions that they were going on, if possible, to prevent Tamo's release, we left them the next morning two or three hours behind, feeling the importance of our seeing the pasha first. We asked Kamil Pasha, 'Is there any objection to Tamo's return with us?' He said, 'None whatever,' and added, 'I know Tamo is innocent. He has been persecuted by the bishop, whom I know to be his enemy.' He gave us a soldier to accompany us and to carry a letter to the modir, in which he charged him to see that no man 'moved his tongue against Tamo;' and if any man troubled Tamo, to inform him immediately, and he should receive merited punishment. He wished to know if he should remove this modir; for, said he, 'I fear he does not look after your interests.'"

We did not ask his removal, but that he would not permit himself to be used as a tool by a few wicked and designing men. The pasha said he would charge him to that effect, and particularly to rebuke the bishop, Aibkhan and Basso for the iniquitous part they have played in this affair.

He called in Tamo, gave him his hand, and asked God's blessing upon him. We left the pasha with hearts overflowing with gratitude that He had conducted us to Bashkollah just at that time.

Our party left Bashkollah at 7 P. M., and we reached Memikan at half-past five Saturday evening. It was an affecting scene to see Tamo embracing his little children and the crowd of kinsmen and friends who came out to meet him.

If we had not gone to Bashkollah, the bishop and Meero, without doubt, would have brought him with them. In fact, Meero said in Manis that he was going to bring him out for our sakes, and would bring him at the risk of his head. It would have been very unfortunate, after Tamo was released through the influence of the English ambassador, to have had the bishop and Meero Bey bring him home and make the impression that his final release was secured through their influence.

Blessed for evermore be the name of our God for all his gracious superintendence of this afflictive event. Tamo appears very well indeed—his spirit much chastened and humbled. He will probably visit Oroomiah before long.

I have written this very hasty line amidst the confusion and uproar of chavadars loading their animals, and also with unnumbered interruptions. It is to me a very unsatisfactory account of a journey the most pleasant I ever made. Kamil Pasha is a most affable, and *apparently* a most generous, humane and noble-hearted man.

I regret to be under the necessity of requesting you, as I cannot possibly find time for it, to address to Lord Stratford a letter expressing our most sincere thanks for his successful efforts in behalf of Tamo.

We leave in a few moments for Mosul.

CHAPTER XI.

VISITS MOSUL—EXPLORES THE MOUNTAINS.

IF Paul ever had hope and was enlarged "to preach the gospel in regions beyond," Mr. Rhea shared his burning zeal. The Master now took him by the hand, led him into the great mountains, showed him the lost sheep, shepherdless these many generations, yet under the Rock sheltered from utter destruction, that threatened from wily Persians, relentless Turks and cruel Koords.

Dr. Lobdell, more fortunate than the Mosul party two years before, had run the gauntlet of Koords from Mosul to Persia, and now, almost trembling to return alone, had asked company of the Oroomiah brethren. Rumors of war were floating. Doubts were felt of the propriety of risking a journey in the mountains. It was decided finally that Messrs. Rhea and Coan, accompanying Dr. Lobdell, should visit their brethren at Mosul, and explore not only the mountain districts between Persia and Nineveh, but also the Nestorian districts beyond, between Mosul and Diarbekir on the Tigris.

Thus Dr. Lobdell was at Gawar on his way home. As I write the name of the dear doctor, my most beloved physician, how do these thin paper letters before my eyes from so many Persian and Turkish fellow-missionaries recall a thousand Oriental scenes, of Constantinople, Smyrna and Beirut, of mountain and plain, of Tigris and Zab, of Koordistan and Persia! While by our own Mississippi I write now in sound of passing steamers upon this longest river in the world, that "ancient river" of Paradise seems nearer; and again, from Diarbekir to Nineveh, two hundred and ninety miles, I float down the Tigris on raft of goatskins to Dr. Lobdell's sick bed; again, at the bridge of boats, I crowd by the camels into Mosul gate, hasten through the familiar, narrow streets, enter my own court, softly greet the loved ones, ask hushed inquiries, gently pass into the doctor's sick room, stand by that iron bedstead, look into the hollow, joyful eyes, read my blessed welcome, feel the thin arms thrown around my neck, and hear my sick brother say, "Praise to God! Praise to God!" Even then my dear doctor was on the bank of the heavenly river, the clear river of paradise which flows from the throne of God!

Oh this is all so real! So is Gawar real. That great Gawar valley I see. I see the hamlet where I tented, a passing guest, three years before, in this very village of Deacon Tamo, where, with blessed self-denial, Mr. Rhea had now for two years made his home.

At this period Dr. Lobdell had in him such fullness of exuberant life as we might expect in a young angel. I know well what those expressive words mean which Prof. Tyler has from his journal placed in the doctor's memoir in regard to this Gawar abode: "Such a home!" Mr. Rhea was almost troubled that his home should seem to his most welcome guest so little like home. Each thought of the comfort of the other. Of this matter he writes:

September 6, 1853.—We are enjoying the doctor's visit as you might well suppose we would who see so few strangers, and especially missionary brethren. The sick have come in from all quarters. He seemed perfectly astounded to find American missionaries living in such a place. Contrasting our present accommodations with those of the first winter, I had begun to fancy them pretty comfortable; but the doctor has made so much sport of them that I have almost become ashamed of them."

Dr. Lobdell, with whatever of playfulness, had also a noble enthusiasm. These are his exultant words greeting Mr. Rhea's return from Bashkollah: "Deacon Tamo is free! And could you have seen the joy of all his fellow-villagers as he came home from his prison-house, and the kind salutations even of the Koords of the mountains—could you have witnessed the meek bearing of the man himself, and heard the eloquence with which the next day he spoke to his attentive audience of salvation by the Redeemer's blood—I think you would have felt that the truth is speedily to triumph even in those regions where now are wandering among the ignorant and superstitious Nestorians men of villainy and blood."

A few words from Prof. Tyler's admirable memoir will afford almost a photograph to the careful reader:

"They set out from Gawar on the 13th of September. The first night they spent without sleep in Ishtazin, at the foot of a frightful staircase, down which the mules, loaded with their bedding, had rolled into the river. The next day they wound among the gorges of Little Jeloo, creeping now along the face of almost perpendicular rocks by passages cut in the time of the Assyrian kings, and now reaching an elevation from which they could look around on an ocean of mountains rising wave beyond wave, sometimes eight parallel ridges at once, and with the storm-clouds ever and anon gathering and bursting over them, reminding one strongly of a storm at sea. Sometimes they came to low, circular depressions, in which were terraced grounds covered with millet, tobacco and vines, with here and there a green tree, while the houses are built above the arable ground, on the mountain-side, in tiers, perhaps a dozen or twenty rising one above another, and every roof being a

sort of door-yard for the house on the next terrace. Every
foot of ground is occupied, and is as valuable to the inhabitants as the ground along the wharves to the people of a
great city."

Dr. Lobdell says, " I have heard of the attachment of the
Laplander to his snows, the Scotch Highlander to his mountains, the Swiss to his Alpine glaciers, but I cannot conceive of a stronger love of country than these Nestorians
cherish for their little plots of ground far down amid the
volcanic peaks, among which their fathers were driven to
find a refuge from the fierce hordes of Tamerlane. The
two giant summits of Jeloo, with their precipitous sides
robed in white, were on our right. These two peaks are
said to be fifteen thousand feet high. They are the highest
in Koordistan, and are distinctly visible from Mosul."

Mr. Rhea and Mr. Coan delighted to linger with those
mountain Nestorians to whom they could in their Syriac
freely declare the unsearchable riches of Christ.

The travelers were ten days in reaching Mosul, whence
Mr. Rhea wrote to Dr. Perkins:

" With all the vexations we had from muleteers, and the
much sorer trial of not being able to have as much religious
intercourse with the people as we wished, still I enjoyed
beyond expression my first sight of the wild scenery of
Koordistan. For the first three days of our journey I was
oppressed by the idea of being so hemmed in by mountains
so lofty and so difficult, but this feeling was much relieved
as I entered the beautiful valley of T'khoma, and as the
mountains from that point diminished in height our road
became easier. The close and narrow ravines of Bass and
Jeloo and T'khoma widened into the more open but still
broken districts of Choll, the rolling plains of Amidiah,
until at last the great mountains of Koordistan had all
melted away into the immense plain of Assyria, stretching

out like a vast sea, having no visible beauty at this season, and impressive only in its *immensity*.

"As my mule slowly plodded on over the great plain of Assyria, once teeming with a mighty population that is now mingling with its dust, one idea filled my mind, and that was a vast desolation. O God, how mysterious and how mighty are the revolutions wrought by thy powerful arm!

"Blessed be his name for the lesson he taught me of his majesty and dominion; of man's insignificance and the vanity of all human glory!" He reached Mosul Sept. 22.

Prof. Tyler speaks of this blessed season of spiritual communion as "a missionary visit made useful and delightful, like those of the apostles, by frequent seasons of social and public worship." The native brethren, and especially the church members whom Mr. Rhea (with or without an Arab speaking brother) *visited every one and conversed with them in their homes*, "saw and felt as they had never done before, how sweet is the fellowship of real spiritual Christians. Though the churches were organized under different forms, and the missions (Assyrian and Nestorian) were conducted on different plans, they were manifestly one in spirit. Though separated by lofty mountains, they belonged to the same fold, and were under the care of the same Shepherd.

A month later, Mr. Rhea wrote, "The few days we spent with our dear friends at Mosul I shall remember as among the most pleasant days of my life." The Mosul circle was then an unbroken band—three happy homes, three young missionaries and their wives.

Of course Mr. Rhea must visit the ruins of Nineveh. It was our frequent luxury for years not only to visit ourselves, but to introduce our English friends, or, at rare intervals, fellow-missionaries to these wonders. Mr. Rhea says with regard to the memorials of the ancient Nineveh:

13   K

The ruins of Koyunjik, supposed to be one of the royal palaces and within the precincts of the great city lie but a short distance east of the Tigris. The ancient wall may still be traced distinctly, and at one corner, within the enclosure, is the large mound from which have been dug up remains of the "buried city."

We gave our horses into the hands of some Arabs, and entering an opening in the mound, and going down a short distance, we found ourselves among what are supposed to be the old Assyrian palaces. We entered the gateway of the palace, between two gigantic figures standing out in bold relief from the great marble slab, bearing the head of a man, the body of a bull, and the wings of an eagle. We met quite a number of these colossal figures during our walk through the ruins. They are supposed to be the emblem of the Assyrian deities, having the intelligence of a man, the strength of a bull, and the swiftness and energy of the eagle. Passing through this grand gateway, we now entered the halls of the palaces, whose sides were faced with sculptured slabs. Strange sensations came over me, as these walls gave back a hollow echo to our voices. Here kings and nobles once reveled; these walls once resounded to the song of the viol and the stamp of the dancers; eager eyes once looked upon these marble pictures, and read these now mysterious inscriptions, which record the triumph of proud Assyrian monarchs. Here were sculptured pictures of a besieged city, its strong walls and lofty towers, the invaders at one point scaling the walls with ladders, at another just ready to enter the breach made by the battering-rams, and at another repulsed and hurled back by the soldiers that man the walls. There were descriptions of a triumphal procession of the king returning from some foreign conquest, and in his train long lines of fettered and sorrowful-looking captives—perhaps the poor Israelites;

KOYUNJIK.

and again there were suppliants, each, with his present coming to acknowledge his new sovereign.   In other places were sculptures of chariots and horses and horsemen, cities and walled towns, battles and sieges, lion-hunts and varied representations of the chase, together with domestic scenes, such as bread-baking.

Thus we wandered on and on, hour after hour, looking at these strange antique devices, admiring the skill and taste with which they were executed more than twenty-four hundred years ago.

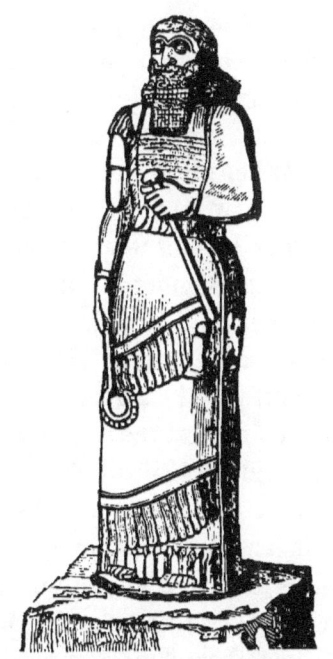

STATUE OF A KING—FROM TEMPLE AT NIMROOD.

Another day we went to Nimrood, supposed to be another palace, but still a part of the great city.   It is twenty miles south of Mosul.   The most prominent object that met our eyes as we approached the place was the high, conical mound which rose up from one corner of the ruins of the

13 *

palace, which Xenophon saw and described on his famous
retreat with the ten thousand. This lofty, conical mound
is supposed to mark the grave of some distinguished mon-
arch. At Nimrood we do not go underground, as at Koyunjik, but walk on the surface, and look down into the
palace halls which have been exposed to sight. These
walls are wainscoted with marble slabs, bearing figures
sculptured in relief, looking as fresh as if they had come
from the chisel but yesterday. There were some very fine
sculptures of men, and lions, and eagles. We spent an hour
or two strolling among the ruins, picking up here and there
a fragment of marble, bearing a part of an eagle's wing or
some of the arrow-headed inscriptions. The infidel might
walk over that vast plain, now the very picture of desolation,
and tauntingly ask, Where is Nineveh, a city of three days'
journey, and when and where are any of the monuments
of its greatness? and as he stumbles along over the dry and
arid desert, God, in his wonder-working providences, un-
covers under his feet her kingly palaces and ten thousand
insignia of her pomp and glory. How sublime Nahum's
description of her overthrow! I returned to my room, and
read with unspeakable interest the allusions and descriptions
of the great city written by God's holy prophets.

Mr. Layard has won a golden name by his great energy
and perseverance in the prosecution of one of the most
wonderful discoveries of this or any other age. Mr. Loftus,
the geologist in Colonel Williams' suite, whose visit to us
last summer you remember, is now exploring the ruins of
Babylon. There may be buried treasures there, which may
throw new light on the history of that famous city and empire, and add a new testimony to the truth of God's holy
word.

After spending about a fortnight at Mosul, on October
6, 1853, Mr. Williams and the author joined Mr. Coan

and Mr. Rhea, and spent another two weeks in a tour to
the Nestorian district of Botan, near Jezirah, where labors
for years afterward were generally carried on by native
Nestorian missionaries from Persia under the aid and comfort of our Mosul band. As three of us had been together
in the seminary at New York, the worship of our journey
revived the days when in New York we had often joined
in prayer and sung, "My faith looks up to Thee" and other
sweet songs of Zion. We passed up the Tigris for days in the
very track of Xenophon and the ten thousand, and where,
near Jezirah, he debated the routes to the Mediterranean
and Black Seas, and chose the latter. We too turned north,
and then, heart and soul, Brother Coan and Brother Rhea
gave themselves from village to village to the blessed privilege of preaching the gospel. Afterward we turned east,
up the fine valley of the Khabour—our brethren constantly
preaching—and so on by the crag-perched castle of Teiner
Bey, to Asheetha.

One evening at dusk, near the Khabour, an armed
Koord intercepted us. Our Mosul attendant gave him the
Moslem salutation. Soon the Koord, discovering that
Ablahad was a Christian, demanded, "Give me back *my
peace. Give me back *my peace,*" meaning to get back
whatever was pledged in the prayer, "Peace to you!" He
then, as we rode on, deliberately leveled his gun at us
and snapped the lock. It missed fire. I have seen many
brave deeds, but never one more cool and gravely amusing
than Mr. Williams then performed. He had not mounted,
but with bridle in one hand, he raised the butt of his riding-
whip, and walked rapidly up, shaking it closely before the
Koord's face, with eyes fixed upon the Koord's eyes, not
striking, but following him up as he stepped back farther
and farther, till he had backed him out of the way, and
thrown him completely off his guard, when suddenly Mr.

Williams whirled, mounted and joined our rapidly-moving party. A half hour brought us, with darkness, to friendly shelter.

At Asheetha, Mr. Williams and myself, with one attendant, left our brethren among friendly Nestorians, and I doubt if ever in that slower world much better time was made than we then made in *two days* to Mosul. On the way we learned incorrectly that war—the Crimean—was declared, and *that* news, added to the usual dangers of the way among somewhat unfriendly Koords, did not slacken our steps. At one point we were taken for the advance of the Russian army.

From Asheetha, Messrs. Rhea and Coan returned to the mountain home in Gawar, with steps somewhat hastened by war rumors. They reached Lizan, stopping at the villages as they advanced. Thence they passed through the districts of Tiary and T'khoma.

"In T'khoma," says Mr. Coan, "we met Mar Shimon (the Nestorian patriarch), and had two very pleasant interviews with him. He was surrounded by his great men, with decided appearance of state. Mar Shimon and all his great company rose when we entered, and we were treated with the utmost respect. He was anxious to hear the latest war intelligence, which we whispered in his ear for his own private benefit, and for which he appeared very grateful. He at once determined to winter in Tiary, rather than return to Kochamis. We passed two nights and a day in T'khoma, and had good opportunities of preaching the word. The heavy storm of rain we had in the valley was snow on the mountains around.

"A day brought us from T'khoma to Bass, where we passed a very pleasant Sabbath, but found the people becoming infected with the leaven of Papacy, imbibed during winter sojourns on the plain of Mosul. One day more took

us to Great Jeloo, where we passed two days pleasantly;
and Thursday morning, the 27th of October, we reached
our dear friends in Memikan, in season to breakfast with
them.   We found all well and expecting us that day; and
if we had been an hour later, Brother Crane would have
been off on another road to meet us.   We were none too
soon in getting over the mountains, for we crossed great
fields of fresh snow, and our path was drifted full in some
places, while the snow flew merrily about our ears."

Extracts from a letter from Mr. Rhea to Dr. Perkins,
will show the practical bearing of this journey.   It was
written October 27:

MEMIKAN, GAWAR.

I am happy to announce myself as once more safely at
home.   Our party reached here this morning in time to
breakfast with Mr. and Mrs. Crane.   I am compelled to
write so hurriedly that I can say but little of our tour.   It
has been to me a most delightful and I trust profitable
journey.   Every step seemed to bring with it new and
varied interest.   The few days we spent with our dear
friends at Mosul I shall remember as among the most
pleasant days of my life.   They are evidently deeply absorbed in their work and bear with fortitude their peculiar
trials.

I received a strong impression of a Mosul sun.   Our
brethren use the utmost care in avoiding its power.   Absolute necessity compels them to expend more than they
would otherwise desire to do in renting and fitting up
houses where they can in some measure protect themselves
from the inconceivable heat which they must endure or
abandon their field.   *I had the pleasure of meeting all the
members of their little church at their homes and conversing
with them.*

We had a very delightful visit in Botan, in company with

Messrs. Marsh and Williams, they going in part to accompany us, and in part to secure a health retreat during the summer months. We spent the Sabbath at Monsooriyeh, the extreme southern village of the district, one hour and a half west of Jezirah. We visited all the principal villages, meeting everywhere a kind reception, and having some precious interviews with the people. Our sympathies were drawn out in much tenderness toward that remote district; and indeed I may say I went through the mountains everywhere with a burdened heart, in vain inquiring, 'Who will break to these dying souls the bread of life?' I longed to stop in each district and cast in my lot with the people.

Something must be done for Botan, and for all the mountain Nestorians on the western side, and that speedily, or seed will be sown which will one day bring a harvest of tares to be rooted up.

(Mr. Rhea proceeds with most heartfelt earnestness, yearning over them, his soul saying of each, How shall I give thee up?)

The leaven of the Papacy is at work. Its silent, poisonous influences are spreading slowly but steadily toward the heart of the mountain Nestorian country. The tide of annual emigration which pours down from all the mountain districts and comes in contact with the ever-wakeful emisaries of Rome, returns more or less infected with the poison. I found poor, deluded Papists in Bass and in Jeloo, and they are not inactive.

I know of but one remedy, and that is a station at Asheetha, just as soon as the way is opened, even before the way is fully prepared for mission families. From that point Botan can be well superintended, as well as the villages of Amidiah. Is it possible to send two men immediately to Botan? Can two men be found who will stand fire? If so, they can do a good work.

He closes his letter, "I hope to be in Oroomiah next week." That visit to Oroomiah was full of earnest efforts for Botan and the western side of the mountains, and its influence was felt in the action of the Oroomiah mission in applying for laborers from America, and in the immediate sending of two native helpers to Botan, and the opening of a train of influences to extend far into the future.

Mr. Rhea's next letters to Mosul were full of plans for the progress of Christ's kingdom on that side of the mountains among the mountain Nestorians, the "Protestants of the East," yet, with all these aspirations for the greater glory of God, he did not forget considerate personal sympathy. To Mr. Williams he writes, "Let me venture to congratulate you upon your safe arrival at home, having escaped the bullets and blades of any prowling Koords you may have met with in Berwer." To the writer, "We thought much of you and Brother Williams after we left you—especially during the days you were passing through Berwer. I shall wait with much interest to hear of your safe return to your homes. I think we shall one day shake hands in the beautiful valley of Asheetha. Will you not help us to make a plea for help for the mountains? Having just been on the ground, you should have a strong voice in the matter."

After earnest discussion of various mission plans, he closes, "My apology, for so long a story is, that I felt you would be as much interested as we in the early occupation of the mountains. May God keep you in perfect peace, your minds stayed on him during these troublous times. We and you, I trust, look forward with much interest to our labors for the winter. May we long for the coming of the Lord, with the power of his Spirit."

CHAPTER XII.

MOUNTAIN LIFE WITH MR. CRANE.

UNDER date of November 15, 1853, Mr. Rhea writes: "I returned a few days ago from Oroomiah, having provided stores for our long winter. Mr. Crane and myself will spend the winter here. We should be glad indeed if Mrs. Crane and her boy (now with us) could remain. Our friends in Oroomiah feel strongly that, for the winter, it would be better for Mrs. Crane to return to Oroomiah. We hope to see Dr. Wright here in a few days, and then, probably, the question will be determined."

While the reader waits the decision, Dr. Perkins will lead us on in pleasant narrative:

"In the autumn of 1852, Mr. and Mrs. Crane joined the mission to reinforce the station in Koordistan. The heart of Mr. Crane had long been set on that rough and self-denying field. When a little boy in Utica, New York, seventeen years before, he had carried the valise of Dr. Grant to the canal-boat when that heroic man was setting off for the Nestorian mission. This incident was a nail fastened in a sure place, which fixed his purpose to follow in the footsteps of that devoted missionary.

"The rough field of his choice was in wide contrast to his character. Seldom have we seen a Nathaniel more artless, a more gentle and lovable man. He possessed many most amiable traits in common with Mr. Rhea, but, as yet, his beautiful, symmetrical character was much less developed and expanded. Seldom have missionaries been mutually better adapted to live and labor together in undisturbed harmony.

"The failing health of Mr. Stocking and the necessity of his return to America soon led to the recall of Mr. Coan to Oroomiah, and the primary responsibility of the arduous mountain enterprise devolved on Mr. Rhea, who was now a ripe and very able missionary. Most ardently did he and his younger associate, Mr. Crane, endure hardness in their difficult and self-denying field.

"A glimpse of that field is well given in a nutshell, in a hymn composed by Mr. Rhea (here somewhat revised) on his first visit to one of the deepest mountain gorges in Koordistan:

ISHTAZIN.

Wild leaps a dashing river,
   Whirls boiling, gurgling, roaring,
With foam and splash for ever,
   Down chasms and gorges rolling.

From up each side that river,
   Far down in madness wailing,
Vast mountain cliffs, in grandeur,
   The heights of heaven are scaling.

God's Koordish ramparts, towering,
   To passing man proclaim—
His eye and soul o'erpowering—
   The great Creator's name.

Five towns, like swallows nestling,
   Grip tight the storm-beat margins;
Shrub, tree and vine cling, wrestling
   For life, in wind-swept gardens.

There crumbling, ancient churches,
   On Living Rock once founded,
Lie desolate; dark ages
   Since gospel note resounded.

14

Poor blind lead blind, affrighted,
 To ditch and darkness there;
Blood-bought men, benighted,
 Are groping to despair.

How can Christ's flock be gathered,
 If none will guide their way?
How long shall they be scattered?
 How long left lost to stray?

"Often has the missionary scaled those mountain-heights and threaded their deepest gorges to search out the sheep of those long-forgotten folds and point them to the Good Shepherd. Sometimes he has crept along the steep and lofty cliff towering threateningly above him, where whispers, at particular seasons, must be his only method of communication, lest the echo of the human voice bring upon him an overwhelming avalanche, ever ready, at such seasons, to quit its bed at the slightest jar.

"A large part of the journey must be made on foot from the exceeding roughness of the country; and in doing this the traveler must often *creep* instead of walk, or rather make his way by carefully *balancing* himself; and after a few days of such experience I have actually found it difficult to stand still and erect on first reaching a level region.

"On the great plain of Gawar, too, journeying in the wintry season must be performed on foot, from the great depth of the snow, which is exceedingly laborious, except for a short time in spring, when the frozen crust bears the pedestrian.

"Mr. Rhea's labors in the mountains were, however, by no means simply itinerary. At his station, the village of Memikan, he usually superintended a school, doing much of the teaching himself. The pupils were promising young men and boys gathered from different parts of the mountain

field.   They there received very valuable training and deep
and lasting religious impressions, as we are now often reminded when individuals of their number join our seminary at Oroomiah, and gospel seed sown in Gawar springs
up here and bears precious fruit.   Such pupils never tire
in their expressions of admiration of their Gawar teacher
and guide.

"When thus occupied at his station, Mr. Rhea uniformly
visited on the Sabbath several villages on the great plain
of Gawar—two, three or even four in a day—some of them
ten or more miles distant, where he preached to the simple
villagers in their humble churches and dwellings or under
the shadow of a wall."

It was decided in December that Mr. Crane should accompany Mrs. Crane to Oroomiah, and leave her there with
her sister band of missionary ladies whilst he returned to
Gawar.

It was no doubt wise.   The great Crimean war was
lowering portentously, and clouds overhung these Koordish
mountains.   The modir had sent them soldiers professedly
to guard them, who were spies, demanding food and room
and attendance, like soldiers billeted in war.   Owing to
their presence in the delightful summer-time, when tent-life
is in some respects delicious, Mrs. Crane had found it wise
to retire from tent-life to the greater privacy and security
of the dreary house.   In November, Karaman Agha offered
to bring down an armed force and camp by them all winter.
Such a proposal indicated an excited state of the public
mind.   The field was not abandoned, but the husband felt
safer with his wife in Persia, across the border.

Thus the two brethren were left alone with their work,
but not without presence of feeble native friends and an
Almighty Helper.   In January a strict quarantine was established on the Persian frontier, with design to prevent any

Persian spies in the interest of Russia from penetrating the Turkish Empire. This new obstacle, where everything is ordinarily aggravatingly tedious in travel and interchange of thought by post or messenger, proved a serious hindrance. Their missionary work could not possibly avoid some suspicion of a secret political end.

A letter written to me on the 25th of that January has not a word of war or politics. Extracts will show what was both deepest and also broadest and constantly uppermost in Mr. Rhea's thoughts:

"My dear brother, I am happy in being able to renew a correspondence which has ever been delightful and profitable to me. Our sympathies were tenderly enlisted for the dear doctor when we heard of his illness. We are now in the midst of our winter, confined. Occasionally, with difficulty, we are able to visit a neighboring village. The villages, as you know, are few and scattered, with little communication, the people keeping closely housed; and after the storm, when the paths become somewhat trodden, we find it very tiresome to plod in them any great distance, they are so rough. A few days ago I went to Kerpil, an Armenian village, two hours' distant, to see a sick man, also to visit two or three nearer Nestorian villages. In Kerpil fifty persons gathered in, to whom we preached a free salvation, through the life and death of Jesus only—a salvation which no man can buy with fasts and alms. The doctrine was novel, but they received it and pronounced it good. We met a kind reception in the Nestorian village where we spent the night, conversing until a late hour about the great things of the eternal world. Over this plain, here and there, is an individual, thoughtful, earnest, inquiring, feeling after the truth, yearning for life in Christ Jesus. The *old* religion does not and cannot meet the felt craving. The *new* sounds strange, and yet carries with it in its appeals the conscience and the intellect. They know it is true; they tremble at the consequence of fearlessly espousing and openly embracing it.

"Your new house—may it be a holy house, and all who come in and go out feel its sanctifying influence. I have been thinking recently of those passages: 'Be ye filled with the Spirit,' 'Walk in the Spirit;' and have asked myself, Ought not faith to lay hold of God's promise, and believe that it is a privilege, *a really attainable thing*, to be habitually full of faith and the Holy Ghost, as Paul and Barnabas were? There are some passages which I fear I do not understand experimentally: "the unction of the Holy One,' 'that ye may be filled with all the fullness of God.' What do these mean?"

In February, Mr. Rhea gives a piercing picture of the snow and the cold; it makes one think of Keat's "limping hare and owl chilled in all his feathers." He tells of snow drifted fifteen feet deep—mercury gone down to 26° below zero (Fahrenheit), and of a terrible wind which the villagers said was unexampled in fierceness. He says in a letter to me, dated Gawar, February 23, 1854: "For the last twenty days we have had an almost incessant tempest, and with it heavy falls of snow and rain. This month has given me a much stronger impression of the inhospitality of our climate, and I can tell you, sir, it is no ordinary wind that sweeps down the gorge from Old Jeloo. It is a wind that makes a man wrestle hard for his breath, and cuts him right up with its keen, icy blades, and sends him home penitent enough for having made the encounter.

"We make it a point to keep pretty closely housed at such times. Now and then, Brother Crane, to give the natives an idea of Yankee pluck, will get on a pair of Gawar snow-shoes, circular in shape, about a foot in diameter, made of twigs twisted and platted together, in the centre of which the foot is placed and bound fast with thongs, and plunges around among the snow-drifts.

"We are now completely blockaded with bulwarks of snow. As we look up out of our window we are able to bring into the field of vision about a square yard of the heavens, and we are grateful for even so much of the clear blue sky. For several days the snow was heaped so high above us that in going out of our door we ascended seven steps to get out on the level of the drift. The poor villagers fare hard enough, having to water all their animals in their stables, by carrying water some distance day after day."

Mr. Crane succeeded in reaching Oroomiah on foot, thus leaving Mr. Rhea for four weeks with no American or European in a little Gawar village. He held on.

Hearing that his former beloved associate was very sick, Mr. Rhea sent a remarkable letter, revealing the workings of his own soul:

MEMIKAN, *February* 11, 1854.

MY DEAR BROTHER COAN: My heart has been sad all day in thinking that you are sick. Such tidings were as unexpected as painful. Would that I were with you. I know I could relieve Mrs. Coan—perhaps I could comfort you. I have been sick alone, and my heart goes out in yearning toward those who are afflicted, and especially a brother beloved, with whom I have spent many, many happy days, never to be forgotten. Some of the darkest days I ever passed through were on a sick bed. The darts of the adversary, tipped in his own fire, fell thick and fast upon me. I cried out in the bitterness of my heart, 'All thy waves and billows have gone over me.' In that dark hour memory and conscience and remorse were busy, and as the sins of past years rose up around me, under the temptations of the adversary, I was brought to the verge of despair. He said, Your sins are peculiar—too great to be

forgiven; and I, for a time, believed it; no, I did not believe it, but I could not disprove it. In the general promises of mercy I found no relief. I found at length much
comfort as I read Rev. xii. 10, 11, and Isaiah 1. 10, where-
in I found strength to use the shield of faith and the sword
of the Spirit, which is God's holy word. Then the enemy
left me.

Oh how blessed are all God's dispensations! If he
will only sanctify us, let him choose the means; if the
body of this death might only be slain, though it be by a
long and painful crucifixion! if we might only find *complete deliverance*, though it be through a process most hu-
miliating to pride and selfishness!

February 28.—I have just returned from a pleasant
excursion with Tamo among some of our villages for the
last three days. During the whole time, though we met
with different classes of men, from the bishop's brother to
the poorest peasant, and under very different circumstances,
now marriage and next funeral, and though we endeavored
to declare the whole counsel of God in its special adapta-
tion to the people we met, still we did not hear a whisper
of opposition; but, so far as kind treatment is evidence, we
had it most abundantly that we were welcome.

Tamo seemed to be in fine spirits and in a very good
mood for preaching. I never went out with the deacon
that he did not on his return express his great enjoyment
in such labors, however hard it may have been to get him
started; for, when asked to go out to preach, though he
assents, you feel it is not with heartiness. This morning,
as we left Pirzalan, after we had preached for an hour to a
crowded dekana, he said, "How pleasant it is thus to meet
the people!" "How well the people listened!" and "How
much encouragement we have to hope that there will be a
great awakening in Gawar before a great while!"

Yes; I never felt at any time more the preciousness of the privilege of inviting dying men to the life-giving cross.

In March he tells us that the faithful Mosul messenger, after vain attempts to get through the utterly impassable mountain snows, returned on the eighteenth day with account of numerous avalanches down the mountains, crushing many bridges and suspending communication. The same was to a degree true between Gawar and Oroomiah, so that, on March 22, Mr. Rhea records that he has been four weeks without hearing any word from any missionary friend or the great world outside the heart of Koordistan. But God was with him. His soul prospered. He speaks of there being no opposition; of Deacon Tamo as busy; of prospect of winning over Priest Guergis and his village to the truth. He anticipates a crust on the snow which will allow him to welcome Mr. Crane's return. He alludes to the political skies as growing darker and darker, and the question at times comes up, "Is-it safe to be in Gawar?" But he trusts in God. On March 29 we find that Mr. Crane has succeeded in walking back, and reports a blessed revival in Oroomiah. All effort to exclude them from Gawar seems to have died away; although, from a distance, the brother of the patriarch writes letters encouraging opposition. Early in May Mr. Rhea visits Oroomiah, after an absence from those friends, only some eighty miles away, of six months. What a joyful meeting! Words will not describe it.

Among the Koordish chiefs he had some warm friends. Mr. Rhea was always kind and polite to such chiefs, giving them coffee, and he was also faithful. He says: "We preached to them righteousness, temperance and a judgment to come." But now, for a time, nearly five weeks, he enjoyed the rest of comparatively polished Persia, and the society of the families of dear missionary friends.

THE TAKTREWAN IN THE KOORDISH MOUNTAINS.

Mr. Rhea returned to Gawar in company with Mr. and Mrs. Crane. Of this journey he writes: "We wound slowly over the hills, myriads of mountain flowers springing up along our path. We often turned to drink in the beauties of the plain and lake and mountains behind us. Having traveled eight hours and a half, our muleteers just as accommodating as could be, we pitched our tent on a grassy plot near a river, which went roaring by us all night.

"Occasionally, as on Wednesday, it was necessary for Mrs. Crane to mount her horse. The takterewan (a sedan chair borne by horses) made two or three narrow escapes from rolling down into the river, owing to the ignorance and carelessness of the Koords. They went blundering and staring along, apparently perfectly reckless as to their horses. We had to keep constantly near the takterewan, and frequently one of us rode on to reconnoitre. We crossed over a large snow-bank near the mountain pass. We intended to spend the night at Mero's castle, but when we halted, a man from the castle roof called out, forbidding us to pitch our tent, saying that it was meadow ground. We rode about nine hours and a half. Mero expressed great regret when he learned we had passed on.

"We made a short call on the modir at Dizza, and learned that the Neela was not fordable at Vazerawa, but that the ford was good at Pirzalan. For more than half the distance to Pirzalan we waded through water, much of the way two feet deep. Then we took a guide, who told us that it was perfectly dry till we reached the river. This was true, but *we had no idea that we should reach the river so soon*. It had spread over a large part of the plain this side of Pirzalan, and for hundreds of yards we were crossing over a marsh covered with water two and three feet deep. Our animals sank terribly in the mire, and for a time we despaired of ever getting our loads and takterewan over.

Mrs. Crane, of course, was on horseback. One of the horses sank down with his load, but finally recovered. Once the takterewan horses both stuck fast, and for a long time they struggled with their burden, still, however, keeping it above water, and at last bringing it out safe. Again Sheikhoo, who had little Morris Crane in his arms, went down so deep that only his horse's head and shoulders appeared above the water. He meantime had managed to get off safely into the water, and the rest of the way carried the little boy out in his arms.

" You may imagine our feelings of joy and gratitude as we saw our last load safely emerging from this slough of despond, and our Koords smiling with imperturbable good humor; and often exclaiming, ' Kanja, Kanja!' At this point I put whip for Memikan, met a hearty greeting, and had the fleas cleared out before the party arrived. For two days I have had a ' clearing-up time.' "

During this month of June the Turks had scarcely a shadow of authority in the mountains. The native Nestorian missionaries to Botan on the Tigris, upon their return to Oroomiah, were robbed between Gawar and Oroomiah. The Sultan was still calling for Koordish troops. The Koords were disturbed, and some in rebellion. Several of the rebel chiefs called upon Mr. Rhea, and were very free in abuse of the Turks and prayed for their defeat. He advised them that some power outside of Koordistan would surely always hold the mountains; and *then* he preached, "Repent ye," concluding with the thought that God would do with the Empire as he pleased. Ishmael Agha took off his turban and uttered a devout *Imshallah* (may it please God) that he give it to the English.

At that time the English consul in Tabreez was astonished that they should venture still to hold on to their dangerous post in Gawar. But in July they enjoyed the rare treat of seeing Mr. Cochran, of Oroomiah, with his wife and four charming little girls, making them a most welcome visit. All Orientals are charmed with children, and the novel sight of four little American girls under the crest of Jeloo touched many a wild Koord's heart with that quick and generous sympathy which often wells up from the breasts of the most rugged of men.

The little Americo-Persians came and went in perfect safety. But Callash, the Mosul messenger from Gawar, was again robbed, as he had been in the winter, and this time was stripped.

August 18, Mr. Rhea commences a letter to the writer by an extract from holy Bishop Leighton on the death of an infant, a soothing strain to sorrowing hearts, and closes the same letter with the picture of Koords, in large parties of horse, passing over the plain in retreat, spreading the wild alarm of war, Bayazeed taken, Kars soon to fall, the great Russian army pouring on, and perhaps the Russian flag soon not only (as it did) to fly over Kars, but even over all the mountains.

Such were the wild scenes in which the banner of Christ's gospel love was kept flying and his gracious call sounding to Turk, Nestorian, Armenian and Koord in Gawar. Hearts were in the work.

From Salmas, in Persia, Mr. Rhea writes, under date of September 29, 1854, to his father:

I am seated in the churchyard of an Armenian church in the old town of Salmas, two days' journey from Oroomiah. Since my arrival in Persia I have lost some of my dearest friends, among them my dear, dear aunt, who nurtured me and loved me with such tenderness. Though many months have come and gone since the tidings of her death reached me, still the wounds of my heart are not healed. They flow afresh as I think of her devoted affec-

15

tion. I never think of her without tears. Oh, how precious to me her precious memory! She was more like the Lord Jesus than any person I ever knew. Her life, how beautiful! It ever was in love, in meekness, in prayerfulness, and in all the sweet graces of the Divine Spirit. When I begin to speak or write of that dear aunt I forget myself. No words of mine can express the devoted esteem and affection I cherish for her.

My errand to Bashkollah is a sad one. But before telling you what it is, I have tidings still more sad to tell you. My dear associate, Brother Crane, has been taken from me. On Sabbath morning, August 27, he sweetly fell asleep in Jesus, and went immediately into his blissful presence, to be a holy, happy and blessed man for ever. On August 17 we rode over to Dizza together to see the governor, who was dangerously ill. In the evening Brother Crane complained of acute pains in the head; this continued for two days, and then passed away. But on Wednesday, August 23, his fever had increased; he seemed prostrated and decidedly worse, and sent for Dr. Wright. That day he took his bed, and his disease, typhus fever, made rapid strides. Mrs. Crane was with us. On Saturday evening we were much relieved by the prompt arrival of Dr. Wright from Oroomiah; but it was too late—the disease had done its dreadful work. That night I watched by his bed, but he was delirious all night long. In the morning he seemed to be sinking, and at half-past seven he most gently rested his head on the bosom of Jesus, and breathed his life out sweetly there. I never saw a death more calm and peaceful. For him we cannot weep, but for ourselves we cannot help weeping, for we feel that the hand of God, in his removal, rests very heavily and very sorely upon us. He was my brother —my intimate friend—my beloved associate. With him I preached and prayed and took sweet counsel; with him I

ate and drank and took all my recreations; with him I com-
muned in Christian intercourse and fellowship. We leaned
upon each other; we cheered and comforted each other in
all the dark days through which we were called to pass together; and do you wonder that I feel bereft? Pray for
me, that in this the darkest hour my faith fail not. We
buried our dear brother on Monday, in the little graveyard
to the east of the village church.

But you are waiting to know our errand to Bashkollah.
On last Saturday night a messenger arrived from Gawar,
bringing the *sad* news that Tamo had been arrested by five
soldiers while going to a neighboring village, carried to
Dizza, and there charged again by the modir with the murder of the Turkish soldier. Six hundred and twenty tomans
(twelve hundred and forty dollars) were demanded as the
only condition of his release, and he was sent as a prisoner
to Bashkollah. We immediately forwarded a messenger
post-haste to Tabreez, to Mr. Stevens, H. B. M. consul, for
letters to the pasha at Bashkollah. These we received, and
are now on our way to secure, if possible, the poor prisoner's release.

MEMIKAN, Oct. 12.

When we reached Bashkollah, we found, much to our
surprise, that Tamo had been released. We had an interview with the pasha, but could learn of him nothing more
than that Tamo had been charged with forcing some Koords
to work for him without pay in building a house. He said
he reproved him for it and sent him home. We knew that
Tamo's seizure was the work of his enemies, and that it was
effected by false and foul charges; and we took occasion to
give the pasha a brief history of all that had taken place
since our coming to reside in Koordistan. He professed
entire ignorance of everything that had taken place—even
Tamo's long imprisonment. When we reached here we

learned that the modir, instigated by the bishop and two
or three others, had actually made out charges against Tamo, that he had built a house this summer by compelling
the villagers around to furnish him workmen; and upon
the strength of this charge the pasha sent and had Tamo
arrested.

AN ARAB SHEIK,

The pasha kept Tamo a prisoner five days, making him
work in the day-time, and at night hanging a heavy chain
about his neck. A noted sheik, residing near Bashkollah,

and Mecro Bey, a famous old Koordish chief, interceded
with the pasha in behalf of the prisoner. But we incline
to think Tamo's own defence, stating, as he did, his relations to us, and asserting his innocence, had more influence
on the pasha's mind than the interference of the friends
who espoused his cause.

I am now alone. The country is in a disturbed state.
One of the most noted of the old Koordish chiefs is in rebellion against the government. Large parties of Koordish
horsemen, in the employ of the government, passed our village last evening and to-day, going toward Kharnatha, the
village of the rebel chief, to intercept his flight into the
mountains. These are troublous times, but our God is with
us, and it brings complete relief to confide all unhesitatingly
to him; for he has said that he shall be kept in perfect peace
whose mind is stayed on him, and I know he will do it.

October 18.—The pasha has come. Order and quiet pre-
vail. The rebel submits. I called on the pasha yesterday.

Mr. Rhea accompanied Mrs. Crane to Oroomiah. She
was destined to a second bereavement in the death of her
first-born and only child, a fine little boy, more than a year
old, at a Koordish encampment where the missionary party
halted for the night. Even the savage Koords were touched
with sympathy, and tried to hush to silence their wild shepherd dogs on learning that the little one was in a dying
state. Though thus doubly bereaved, the widowed Christian found support in her God.

Mr. Rhea soon wrote to me from Gawar, October 18,
1854: "I reached here from Bashkollah two weeks ago
yesterday. The next morning Mr. Breath went to Oroomiah. Very sad feelings filled my heart for several days
after I was left here alone, as I walked through our deserted
rooms, visited the grave of my dear Brother Crane, and as

15 *

everything around me recalled the pleasant scenes of the last two years, and reminded me painfully of my sad loss.

"But I have not been alone. Jesus has been with me and has been teaching me some of the simplest lessons of faith and filial confidence. Oh, how we should prize and be grateful for that holy discipline, be it what it may, which only brings us nearer to him, which teaches us what it is to believe, to commit all without solicitude and in cheerful confidence into the hands of Him who has said: 'Lo, I am with you always!' Faith is the highest and most blessed form of knowledge; but how often doubts mingle with our faith and make it powerless! In true faith, especially with reference to God's promises, there is not the shadow of a doubt, and thus it amounts to absolute knowledge. When truly exercised it must bring into the soul that calm, sweet peace which passeth all understanding. O Lord, *increase our faith!*"

Thus we close in Mr. Rhea's experience a chapter of bitterness. The sweetness of its bitter flavored all his future life.

CHAPTER XIII.

MARRIAGE—THE SACRED UNION.

BEFORE leaving America Mr. Rhea had chosen single life, in full belief that thus he could most glorify God. He had a most refined and tender regard for all true women. He was not insensible to their charms; yet was not then, as afterward, fully aware of the height and breadth and depth of woman's most unselfish devotion, both to the husband and children, to whom she gladly gives her life, and to the humblest for whom Christ her Saviour died. He wrote to me at Mosul, two years and a half before this time: "Because I might prefer to spend the first years of my missionary life, and *probably all of them, unmarried,*" etc. He had not then seen Miss Harris. The writer may of her very confidently say with Wordsworth:

> "I saw her upon nearer view,
> A spirit, yet a woman too!
> Her household motions light and free,
> And steps of virgin liberty;
> A countenance in which did meet
> Sweet records—promises as sweet;
> A creature, not too bright or good
> For human nature's daily food.
> A perfect woman, nobly planned,
> To warn, to comfort and command
> And yet a spirit still, and bright
> With something of an angel light."

Deaths of tender women for Christ's sake are often

charged as sin by those who bring no such charge against deaths of young men upon ten thousand battle-fields, not always for Christ's sake. For Christ some would even dare to die, and our Bible does not read, "we *men*," but "*we* ought to lay down our lives for the brethren." It is idle to forbid. As long as there are sinners to die for, tender and delicate women will live and die for Christ.

But Mr. Rhea need no longer discuss the wisdom of inviting the gentle and refined to such trials. God had led forth to Persia one every way worthy of him.

"Mr. Rhea was now the sole occupant of the remote mission station in Koordistan," says Dr. Perkins, "but the Lord had provided for him a most estimable help-meet, Miss Martha Ann Harris, a congenial spirit, every way worthy of his heart and his hand, who had been two years at Oroomiah as the teacher of the children of our mission, in which sphere she greatly excelled, and had early won the hearts of all her pupils and their parents. They were married at Mount Seir (October 31, 1854), and in a few days went to their lonely and self-denying home in Koordistan."

Many letters written to her shortly before his marriage lie before me. I extract a few pictures, as much to give the eye and heart of Mr. Rhea as the scenes described:

"*July* 28.—Brother Cochran and myself have just returned from Ishtazin. Left early, reached the valley by ten. All the people had gone to their pasture-grounds. After resting we went up to make them a visit. Our road much of the way was charming, shaded often by the walnut, the oak and mulberry. As we slowly wound up the mountain the evening breeze wafted the fragrance of mountain flowers and herbs familiar and homelike. We enjoyed much the prospect of the valley; gladly turned our mules and for a few moments feasted our eyes upon the mountain forests in deep green foliage, the little fields of golden grain, and silvery streams peeping out from among them; and above all those hoary pyramids rising in lofty, solemn grandeur. Crossing the pass, we were soon at the town. I counted in all seventy of the little huts which form the summer residences of the people of Ishtazin. They are built of stone, some five feet high, circular in shape, and sticks are placed to form roofs like a dome, closely covered over with grass, making a cool and pleasant shade. In front of each hut is a little enclosure which serves as a yard. Within this little compass all the domestic affairs are attended to. How simple and how rude this summer life! In the hut where we stopped I counted some fifteen or twenty earthen vessels of various sizes, several bags of cheese were in process of making, large pots of milk were boiling, a tray filled with fresh corn hoe-cakes, a lamb just slaughtered and hung overhead. This was all that was to be seen in the summer-house of a mountain Nestorian, the hut of the first family in Jeloo.

These high pasture-grounds are the Saratogas of Koordistan. Here all classes repair during the summer heat for health and recreation. They gladly welcome the return of the season when they may leave their hot ravines and climb up to the green slopes of the mountains, breathe the fine bracing air and drink the cold snow-water. We spent a very happy evening. Forty of the chief men of Jeloo gathered around us evening and morning, and listened most attentively. I never more enjoyed holding up Christ as the only Saviour of poor lost sinners—a salvation for all, without money and without price. We endeavored to be as faithful and pointed as possible in showing the hollowness of those hopes on which we knew they were resting.

We descended "a wild ravine below Barbarra. After winding down the bank of the foam-dashing river, the road

M

sometimes cut out of the cliff hanging over it two or three
hundred feet, we suddenly turn to the right, and find ourselves in a narrow defile ten yards wide and walled in by
perpendicular rocks several hundred feet in height. This
defile is two miles in length and is on the highway to Jeloo
and Bass. It was quite dark when we returned weary to
Mar Ogloo's house, but not too weary to point the little
company who had gathered round us to the Lamb of God."

Again in August, he writes: "Another day has flown
—so we say—but where has it gone? We speak as if it
had fled, but it has done its work, and is now become a
component part of an eternal existence. It has gone up to
the great white throne and opened the books, and, with an
iron pen, written its record. Oh how solemn is life! and
how strange too! May it be our highest aim to live in
sight of God, and the cross, and the judgment, and the New
Jerusalem, and the everburning lake, and eternity. Then
life would be true and earnest and divine. A life true to
God, true to our fellow-men, and to the high behests of conscience, and to all the divinely inspired and noble feelings
of the heart—how beautiful! how sublime! how powerful!
Such an one need not go out of himself for sympathy and
support. I say out of himself, for I suppose God to be
within him, dwelling in the innermost temple of his soul.
Do you need sympathy, or can you live without it? I know
full well you appreciate it, but does it add much to your
quiet and satisfaction of mind to know, in any important
step you have taken, that you have the sympathy and approval of others? or, having taken that step in the fear of
God, and with a distinct reference to his glory, do you in
that consciousness find complete rest, and feel indifferent as
to the opinion of others? Oh it is a great thing to live
among men and yet above them—to be ever pouring forth
fresh tides of sympathy, but ever drawing from a fountain

deep within—even God in all the fullness and blessedness of his perfections.

August 4.—I have just returned from our evening service. We seldom have fewer than five or six strangers present, and often twenty. I felt, as I went to deliver the message God gave me, that I must deliver it, feeling that perhaps at that very hour it would be sealed to the awakening and conversion of some soul. When I returned to my room, I found myself sitting down to pen a line to you, forgetting that something all-important had been left undone, *i. e.*, commending the truth spoken and those who heard it to God, earnestly imploring his Spirit this night to wield the sword of Divine truth to pierce the hard heart. Oh, what a blessing to get rid of formalism! this doing God's service mechanically and professionally!

August 6.—This morning my heart was heavily burdened for poor, perishing souls. The bishop, Mar Eshoo, was at our table, and in depicting to him the piteous condition of these poor wandering sheep, and pressing upon him his responsibility, my own sympathies were very tenderly drawn out; my heart bled; I felt the almost crushing weight of responsibility.

This morning there were sixty present at our service, and during some parts of the discourse more than ordinary feeling.

In the many precious opportunities we have of meeting the people this summer so frequently and in such large numbers, our hearts are greatly cheered and comforted.

This evening ten persons from Jeloo were present. While Deacon Tamo was preaching, he asked an old man with snowy beard, "Do you know what it is to be born again?" He said, "No; I know nothing about it." After Tamo explained to him in simple manner, he said, "Now I understand it; but we are all going to hell. There is no hope for us!" *How favored I am to be permitted to live in these dark lands! Of all men I ought to be the happiest*, thus to have the privilege of breaking the bread of life to those who otherwise would certainly die in their sins!

August 15.—I have just attended a prayer-meeting with the native brethren, and found it very refreshing to my spirit. The thought presented was, every man a brother, be his character what it may. I find that it is only when I think of these poor men about me as my brothers, and these poor women as my sisters, that I can at all approach to that love and sympathy for them and that readiness to lay down my life for them, for which I earnestly long. It is written, "Covet earnestly the best gifts," and I think this is one of the very choicest of all; I do long for it. To be successful I must have it. It is the very soul and life of the missionary spirit. What is all our brothering and sistering if there is no heart-work about it? It is a sham. How beautiful is simple truth, an inward life of feeling and sympathy corresponding with all our outward expressions! I want no man to "brother" me with his lips who does not do it in his life, and I will try to do the same. "Brother" belongs to the race. How easy to speak it; how hard to act it out! A class-leader once said, "*Brother Jones, you are a liar!*"

You have a large share of the gentle, genial sympathies of our nature, and to these gentle sympathies I commit my poor people, and I charge you rebuke in me for their sakes the first risings of an unkind, uncharitable, censorious spirit. When abused, when ridiculed, when reproached, these poor people shall look to us, their sympathizing advocates, and we will put the best construction truth will justify, and with the mantle of charity cover all their imperfections.

Tuesday, August 29.—Oh, through what scenes have we

passed! Before this the sad intelligence has reached Oroomiah, and you weep with us. I say sad—not sad for our dear brother (Mr. Crane), who we believe has been these two days in the immediate presence and blessed society of our Lord Jesus, but sad for our stricken sister. It is sad to me. I think it is the heaviest stroke by far that ever fell upon me.

. . . I must not conceal the fact that some of the happiest hours I ever enjoyed I have spent during these days of my loneliness. I have been able to confide all in the hands of our dear Lord Jesus, to believe his precious promises; and I have at all times enjoyed great peace. I cannot now tell you all I have felt and all I have enjoyed. I fear lest my heart should be led to turn too much in upon itself, and thus lose its sight of the Lord; I have given myself to him. The consecration has been entire. I have given my own will and my own private preferences. I am then to live in a waiting posture; simply to know the will of the Father. Each returning hour and moment brings the events of his providence, and in those events we shall know his will concerning us.

On his way to rescue Tamo, at Khosrawa, in Persia, September 28, 1854, he saw one who had talked in person with Henry Martyn (that name so precious in all the churches): "We went over to Khosrawa yesterday afternoon. Visited Mar Zaiya. I was struck with the European cast of his countenance and his intelligence. He had just returned from Tabreez. I inquired about Henry Martyn, and we were highly entertained with his account of the visit Mr. Martyn made him. He was with him some six days, talked Latin and visited the antiquities in this region. He spoke of him as very learned and a charming man; and when he told how he talked Latin the old man could hardly contain himself. He spoke also of a visit he had from Wolfe,

16

but added: 'Wolfe, chin, chin, Shedana' (Wolfe has no sense)."

While at Oola, he gives the following faithful picture of his quarters. Oriental travelers can sympathize with him: "Perhaps you would like to know just how we are situated here. The room is very large, high and airy. One corner is spread with felts. This we occupy. A huge flour-bin stands in another. In a third, a stack of beds, and in the centre is our baggage. Still the great room seems to beg for something more to relieve its airy emptiness. We have any quantity of cats and chickens around, who seem to be perfectly at home. At very early dawn a famous old herald of the day rises from one corner not far from our beds, flaps his wings and goes off in a strain anything but melodious. This he repeats from time to time, until he has convinced us that it is certainly daylight, and time to rise."

Mr. Rhea gives the following description of his building experience in Gawar, not unlike that of Layard in his difficulties with the Arabs at Nineveh:

My building affords me almost endless amusement as well as annoyance. Think of a Yankee undertaking to work half a dozen lazy, good-for-nothing Koords. Poor creatures, they are still immortal men—who have only learned well how to light and smoke a pipe.

I wake up early—call for the head mason—Oshana, where are your men? Not come. Sun an hour high—send for them—they come, dragging their sluggish limbs along—then follows a quarrel about wages. Sun gets two hours high. At last fairly at work, at least going through the motions. Next morning, no Koords! Send for them—won't come or must have more wages. The head mason, Oshana, an expensive man on my hands—sinking money fast. We must have workmen, so we bargain to give them their food. We get started again—eight lusty Koords—

one gone to the spring for water, stays an hour—another is picking in the ground with a would-be mattock that makes one nervous to look at—another, pretending to dig, is down on his knees and for a few moments he tears up the earth tremendously—and looking around with infinite self-complacency—he most audaciously and coolly *sits down to smoke!* Another brings stone from a distance of ten steps, slowly plodding along, his hands behind him supporting the stone on his back; reaching the place he tosses it off, and then stands five minutes apparently in mute astonishment at his herculean efforts.

Oshana, the mason, having never worked Koords before, is all in a stew—calling to this one "Hurra" (go,) and to that one "Wena" (come,) which is about the extent of his Koordish vocabulary, and it were almost as well if he had not that—for at first he gave the rogues the impression that he knew more, until he began to scold and found himself brought to a stand, the butt of their rude jokes and ridicule. So things go, at least so it was at first; but we are getting them "broke in."

This afternoon one of the sly fellows came to my room at nearly sundown, and as a special favor asked permission to go to another village. In a few moments he returned and asked for his wages. I sent him to Oshana, who pays them. This he knew very well; and at the very time he was asking *me* he was holding and rubbing between his fingers the keran which Oshana had just before given him for his work!

It is amusing to see Oshana distribute their wages at evening. He stands off some distance, and with a consequential air and miserably-broken Koordish, reckons with them and tosses each a keran. Each examines his piece most carefully, probably the first that some of them had ever received, and if it is a little smooth, of course it won't

go, and back he tosses it to Oshana, and then a chatter.
But this is no sooner adjusted than another finds himself
in possession of a recently-coined piece, and it shines so
brightly that he thinks it must be lead, and then down it
goes at Oshana's feet, and then another jabbering! Oshana,
with broken tongue, somehow generally comes off victor.
This is the way we build a home in Koordistan.

Thus was the house built. But the following letter
shows that a house built for one family is often occupied
by another. He wrote to me at Mosul, October 18: It
is my present plan to spend the coming winter here. Mr.
Crane, before his death, had almost completed two upper
rooms which he intended to occupy with his family this
winter, and we had put up an upper room last summer.
These three I am now having plastered and whitened.
We also have two lower rooms, and two store-rooms. With
these one family can be quite comfortable. We have had
to burn native fuel hitherto, but I am hoping to get wood
enough for one stove at least.

I am trying to make our home as comfortable and inviting as may be, in this wild region; but after all the
chief joy of my dwelling I hope to bring from Oroomiah.
It is my plan now to be married this autumn, and yet God
may order otherwise. He has been teaching me not to
have any plans of my own; but to wait, day by day, and
moment by moment, the developments of his providence,
and then choose what evidently seems to be his will for my
own also.

November 10, 1854, Mr. and Mrs. Rhea reached their
new home. The fact was thus announced to Mr. Coan:
"Can I tell you my dear brother, with what feelings we
took possession this evening of our new home, and consecrated it at our family altar? We would invite our Lord

to be our first and ever-abiding guest. He is ready to come in."

They were soon gratified by a visit from their tried friends, Dr. Wright and Dr. Perkins. The latter says: "I soon visited them to tender to them my congratulations, and cheer them in view of the long and dreary winter before them. Their humble quarters were now much improved by the addition of small upper rooms, which relieved them from the annoyance of smoke and some of the ungrateful odors of the adjoining dwellings of the rude village." "Mrs. Rhea entered zealously upon the discharge of every duty devolving upon her," says Dr. Wright. "She regarded it as a leading duty to make her husband a pleasant and inviting home, that nothing might be wanting which conduced to his health and happiness. Her success in this respect was complete. Everything about her house was orderly, and, though plain, in good taste; and all she did was done in a quiet, noiseless way, as though costing very little effort. For one so intellectual, so fond of books and study, it was a marvel, to some of us, that she could be such a model for a housekeeper. Her character was *complete*.

"It was the last of November when Mr. Perkins and myself made them their first visit from friends abroad. A more pleasant, a more happy home, no one could desire; the very abode of peace, the pilgrim's resting-place in this vale of tears. In our musings when seated in those cheerful upper rooms, we often asked ourselves, 'Is this Gawar? Is this Memikan, that place of vermin and filth?'"

Dr. Perkins proceeds: "On Sabbath evening, the night before my departure for Oroomiah, Mr. Rhea invited me to walk with him in the twilight. The theme which he soon introduced, and on which we conversed at length, was, the grand secret of holy living and gaining a meetness for

16 *

heaven.   This theme was neither new nor unusual; it was
the study of Mr. Rhea's life, and few mortals of any age
have made more successful progress in the study, as was
patent in his daily walk.   It was about this time that he
wrote his touching colloquy between the Christian and his
Saviour."

The writer of this memoir makes no apology for intro-
ducing this colloquy at this point; for, Reader, this book
desires your sanctification—will utterly fail of its object
with *you* if it does not leave you no longer dreaming, but
intensely active to be more holy.   Surely no reader can
sympathize at all with the manner and spirit with which
this book has thus far been written, without perceiving that
its primary aim is not to entertain or instruct with regard
to the rich and glowing East, not even to give a history of
the mission field and work, so much as to give insight into
Mr. Rhea's soul; not so much for Mr. Rhea's soul's sake
as for that soul's connection with Christ's wide family.
Mr. Rhea's life is nothing if it be not God's trumpet-call
to the future high stand-point of the Church of Christ.

If Mr. Rhea be the peer of holy David Brainerd, as holy
as the sainted Martyn, or possibly a freer, larger, more
Christlike soul than either of those radiant men, we will
approach him as to a burning bush—burning with varied
experience and trials—not to behold the bush, but Christ in
the bush.   Having been privileged to look into Mr. Rhea's
soul as very few have as yet had opportunity to look, the
writer would pronounce this colloquy remarkable, in being,
not the mere fanciful creation of intellect, but a reality.   It is
the life and spirit of his own soul.

THE SACRED UNION.

I. IN THEE, THOU IN ME.

Jesus.—Behold, I stand at the door and knock.   If any

man hear my voice and open the door, I will come in to him, and will sup with him and he with me. To-day I would be an abiding guest in thy house. In its retirement and privacy thou shalt find me. I must know thee and be known of thee inwardly, in Spirit and in Power, else I cannot be known savingly.

Disciple.—O Jesus, thy words of grace and comfort fall upon my ears like strains of heavenly music. What condescending gentleness and meekness! Come in, thou beloved and adorable One. Dost thou invite me to the embraces of thy love? Art thou ready to fold me in thy bosom and to give me the rest for which my tossed and troubled heart has so long panted? I welcome thee. I adore thee in silence. In quietness of spirit I wait upon thee. Speak, Lord, for thy servant heareth.

Jesus.—I am the Life, and I come to make thee a partaker of that Life. I come by gentle whispers and secret longings. These will test thee, if indeed thou longest to enjoy my abiding Presence.

Disciple.—O Jesus, if I should listen to some of the deep cravings of my spirit, especially during the hours of my supplications, I would say that, of all things, my soul panteth for this Blessed Presence; but when I watch the inward movements of my thoughts, after and during the intervals of my devotions, I see so much of apparent indifference and foolish wanderings of heart and lips, that I tremble for the sincerity of my prayers.

Jesus.—The past I can forgive and I can forget. Oh let this sink deep into thy heart: I can forgive and I can forget. I come to thee once more. Art thou willing to welcome me to be no longer a transient guest, but an ever-abiding Presence? I have often come to thee. Thou hast to some extent known me, but as yet thy life has been only intermittent pulsations. The ever-flowing fountain has not been opened within thee. My interviews have been transient ones. Thou hast not yet attained unto the true life. Thou sayest thou dost welcome me. Perhaps thou dost welcome my light, and love, and joy, and peace; but dost thou welcome my cross? Wilt thou be a cross-bearing Christian? Art thou willing to follow me without the camp? Art thou willing to resign to my inward guidance thy whole being, so that thy will shall be swallowed up in mine? Thou must lose all that thou callest thy life, if thou wouldest find me the life everlasting. The old life of sin must be cut out, if the new life is engrafted. Ponder well what thou now doest. Count the whole cost. It is nothing less than the death of self, that I may become all in all to thee. For this art thou ready?

Disciple.—O Jesus, what shall I respond? Tremblingly my heart says, I am ready for the last sacrifice, if I might but experience this blessed union with thee. I hear thy voice; I open the door. Thou art my Life, my Light, my Love, my Joy, my Peace, my Sacrifice, my Lamb, my Great High Priest, my Wisdom, my Righteousness, my Sanctification, my Rod, my Staff, my Guide, my Portion, my Song, my Refuge, my Rock, my Strong Tower, my Shield, my Wealth, my Gold Refined, my Pearl, my Hid Treasure, my White Raiment, my Balm of Gilead, my Physician, my White Stone, my Hidden Manna, my New Jerusalem, my Eternal Home. My Beloved is mine and I am his.

THE SORROWING CONFESSION.

Disciple.—O Lord, I think above all thing else my soul mourns these frequent slidings of my feet, these strayings away from beneath thy gentle wing, and I long for that constant spirit for which thy servant David prayed.

Jesus.—Draw near in confidence, and tell me all thy heart's sorrows.

Disciple.—O Jesus, there have been times when I have doubted thy power to grant a full salvation, so sad have been some of my wanderings from thee. Some days I go with light and joyous step, chanting gently to myself thy praise, and sweetly assuring my heart of thy love, and feeling inwardly thy fond embraces. Sometimes at early dawn I renew my covenant vows, lay all upon thine altar, and enter into rest; when, ere one fleeting hour is past, some hasty word, some impatient look or idle thought embitters all that day, and I seem to hear the rustling wings of the departing· Spirit. Or, if not so, I have seen the Sun of all my joys sinking slowly away, and felt the cold chills creeping about my heart, and I, a helpless thing, seemed unable even to cry for help. O Lord, why is it thus with me?

Jesus.—There may be reasons more than one. Thou didst once pride thyself too much upon thy soft and humble walking with me. Thine eyes were turned from me, thy Sun, to my reflected beams upon thy heart; and as thou didst begin to glory in them thy Sun went down; thy heart grew dark and chill. Then thou didst learn that thy light was borrowed, and that thou must ever run thy race looking unto Jesus. But oftener, far, the secret cause of thy wanderings was thy failure to watch and pray, and thou didst enter into temptation.

Disciple.—Yea, Lord, I know that I must watch and pray, but why didst thou not help me to watch and pray unceasingly?

Jesus.—Had I not watched and prayed within thee, long since thou wast lost. All the watchings thou hast done were from the strivings of my ever-wakeful Spirit. How oft hast thou not heard my gentle whispers when nearing in an hour of levity a fearful brink! How often have the messengers of my love, a voice of warning like a trumpet-tongue from my holy Word, or a solemn thought, or a

petition inbreathed among thy formal prayers, startled thee
into new life! Think of the ten thousand forms in which
I have whispered to thy soul, and then canst thou say that
all the watching thou hast done is from thyself, and not
from me? Perhaps thou wilt ask why I did not put forth
my power to keep thy feet from ever sliding? But, remember, I keep thee through thine own prayers and watchings. Thou wilt only learn to watch and pray when thou
knowest that thou must watch or die. Know, once for all,
thou must strive, work out thy salvation with fear and
trembling, take the kingdom by violence. *These* must
ring in thine ears until thou sing the song of victory, struggling, watching, praying; thou wilt never be so perfect
here as that thou canst for one moment lay thine armor
down. By my almighty power I can keep thee sinless.
But this is not the method of Holy Growth, Discipline and
Conquest. I will bring thee to unceasing vigilance, but in
such a way as that it shall not be something out of thee,
but the habit of thy inmost soul. The angels ceased to
watch, and fell. Remember thy discipline is for eternity.
I have never left thee until thou didst first leave me. Thou
hast yet to learn that my Spirit is a most gentle spirit, most
easily grieved away; and before I knit thee to myself as
the branch to the Vine, and take up my constant indwelling
within thee, and fill the temple of thy soul with my glory,
thou must learn to count my presence as the hid treasure,
the one precious pearl, for which thou art willing to sell all
that thou hast.

Disciple.—O Lord, would that I might remember all the
lessons of thy love! My waiting eyes are unto thee. I
wait in silence for the gracious words which fall from thy
lips. Evermore give me this bread.

THE UNSEEN PRESENCE.

Surely the Lord was in this place, and I knew it not.

Disciple.—I have long sought to be filled with thy Holy Spirit, as thou hast commanded me to be; but still thou withholdest from me this most precious gift.

Jesus.—Speak not too hastily. Whence those long and unwearied seekings? Canst thou seek for the Spirit without the Spirit?

Disciple.—Yea, Lord, I know that without thee I can do nothing; and for those inward hungerings and thirstings I adore the riches of thy grace; and yet, O Lord, I have not that Baptism and Unction for which my soul above all things longeth.

Jesus.—Thou hast all that it was best for thee to have; but, remember, the Spirit's workings are ever various and with unerring wisdom. Hast thou not felt yearnings for some precious soul? Then was thy prayer answered. Hast thou not been led to loathe thyself? Those inward kindlings of penitence were answers to thy prayers for the Spirit. Hast thou not felt thy heart bruised and broken, leading thee to walk softly and tremblingly before the Lord? Hast thou not felt an unwonted watchfulness, lest thou shouldest grieve him whom thy soul loveth? Hast thou not felt the keen reproofs of conscience for what once it slept over, and never spoke out? Hast thou not been often startled by a still small voice, saying, This is the way, walk ye in it? Hast thou not felt thy compassions yearning toward the widow and fatherless, the poor and hungry, the naked and oppressed? All these were the gifts of the Spirit, and should have been to thee the sweet tokens of his indwelling presence, and that thy prayers have come up a memorial before God.

Disciple.—O Lord, with shamefacedness I fall down before thee, and acknowledge all my unbelief. How often hast thou been with me, and I knew it not!

Jesus.—Thou receivedst all for which thou hast prayed, the baptism and unction of the precious Comforter, but not in the form in which thou didst expect. Thou hast been waiting often for high joys, great illuminations, sensible comforts, but, remember, *these* are gifts which, in my sovereignty, I bestow upon those who are so humble as not to be inflated by them. I ever give thee what is best for thee. Wilt thou not now trust me?

Disciple.—Yea, Lord, I will now walk in simplicity of spirit, as a little child, knowing that thou doest ever what is best. I see that I have prescribed to thee, instead of humbly and patiently waiting for thee. Instead of welcoming the bread, the staff of life, I have longed for the oil and wine, those spiritual dainties which in wisdom thou hast withheld from me.

THE GREAT CONDITION.

If thou canst only believe.

Disciple.—Most gracious Lord, I desire above all things else that thou wilt come and make thine abode with me, that thou wilt dwell in me and walk in me, that I may walk with thee, even as Enoch walked with thee, cheered by this testimony, that he pleased God.

Jesus.—And to this I will assuredly bring thee, if thou wilt look to me only. This life for which thou longest is the Life of God, and the most resplendent glory of his creatures. But it is made up of holy habits to which thou must be trained, until thou shalt be changed into the image of the Lord.

Disciple.—Adorable Lord! my heart leaps within me even at the distant prospect of this angelic life; and yet, when I look within my faith staggers.

Jesus.—If thou canst only believe, all things are possible for thee. If thou canst only believe that I love thee with a love whose depths eternity alone can explore, and with an ardor that burned unto death ; if thou canst only believe that I am nearer to thee than thou art to thyself, and long to fill thee with the fullness of my light, and life and joy and love; and if thou wilt most humbly wait upon me, and look only to me, all thy spiritual longings shall be satisfied.

Disciple.—Even so, come, Lord Jesus.

By this far-off Mississippi I have just opened a small rosewood writing-desk. On the metal of its lid is graven "Mary and Julia." It was a father's gift to his dear motherless children. From many neatly filed and tied and labeled little letter-packets written in delicate handwriting, sacredly kept as they were carefully put away by one who rests opposite Nineveh on the banks of the Tigris, I have selected one package which holds letter after letter labeled "Miss Harris." Please accept permission to read a few lines of the first, directed to New York city, as a sample of the warm affection that breathed through all, only ever growing purer and more refined. It runs:

"Constantinople, *April* 10, 1852.

"My Dear Julia: Will you not pardon me for calling you Julia? for I love the name and the one whose name it is. From this Eastern world I send greeting. From my windows I look upon the land which is soon, I trust, to become your home and mine. I often, very often, think of *you*. Why should I not? It was happiness to meet you in New York.* There are some hearts so warm that we cannot but love them; and to meet and receive sympathy

---

* Miss Harris was the sister of the eminent Dr. Harris, of the New York Board of Health.

from such a heart brings the joy we feel when, after dark and stormy days, the sun shines out and the birds begin to sing. And not only do I remember you as one who brought a ray of sunshine to my soul, but my sister says that you taught her to be cheerful. May your own path be full of light for the joy you have given us!"

That path did shine more and more, and is now passing on and shining on in perfect day. But when Mr. Rhea next wrote from Gawar, having now a home, it will be seen that he felt some promptings of soul to extend a very cordial invitation in sympathy with that friendship. November 27, 1854, he says: "We are now quite settled in our new home, and shall be happy to see you and Mrs. Marsh whenever you can visit us. If my wife should go through Koordistan to see you in Amidiah, will not Mrs. M. accompany her back? But it is yet a long time until next summer, and we know not what the intervening months may bring forth." Mrs. M., with her husband and Dr. Lobdell, had made, in October, a visit to Amidiah, the farthest point ever reached by a lady from the Mosul side of the mountains. They were examining in reference to a summer health-retreat for the Mosul station, which might be at the same time a field for labor among the mountain Nestorians.

Mr. Rhea most intensely sympathized with all efforts to give the gospel to the tribes of Western Koordistan. For this he assisted the seminary at Seir most efficiently in raising up native helpers. He gathered a small boarding-school about him at Gawar, partly from that plain, but very largely from the still more rugged districts beyond.

The winter, long and dreary as it was, Mr. and Mrs. Rhea passed in Gawar in solitude. Mrs. Rhea was deeply interested in all the plans and labors of her husband, and in many cases of perplexity was able to aid by her judgment and counsels. She not only managed the arduous and often perplexing domestic department of the boarding-school, but performed an important service in giving instruction. She won the hearts of the rude pupils, and they looked up to her as a mother. She was indefatigable in her efforts for the temporal and spiritual good of the women of the village. She won their confidence and love, and they often sought her advice and instruction. She frequented their humble dwellings, weeping and rejoicing with them. She also diligently improved her own mind, indulging her taste for reading when not directly engaged in usefulness for others; and having joined her husband in the study of Hebrew, she this winter read with him the book of Genesis in the original. No one could bear, uninjured, the death-like, winter solitude of Gawar without large internal resources; but as both Mr. and Mrs. Rhea most happily possessed these, the winter passed pleasantly and usefully away.

CHAPTER XIV.

DURING THE CRIMEAN AND PERSIAN WARS—DRIVEN FROM THE MOUNTAINS.

IN a single battle of the great Russian and Turkish war more souls entered eternity than all the missionaries who have died for five hundred years. Honor to the brave! Let them win earthly applause. Those who came out of sieges, battles, pestilence, and, from Kars and Crimea, returned safely to Sardinia, England, France, *they* had the honor of the nations. But did not the angels look down as approvingly upon those who, throughout the Crimean and Persian wars, held the missionary front in Koordistan? Was the hero of Kars or the Malakoff more heroic than the solitary lady amid the Koords and snows of Gawar?

General Williams in those days sent an officer, a Pole, in hot haste from Kars to check a great Koordish rebellion on the Tigris. Russia was not only besieging, but intriguing against him, and he must meet Russia at a distance. Persia was long trembling on the edge of plunging into the red war sea for Russia. Her Moslem followers of Ali are drilled to hate with bitter intensity Turkish followers of the Ommiades, the murderers of Ali.* Almost drawn into the Crimean war, Persia actually engaged in war with England; but, fortunately, not till after the very sudden and unexpected peace arranged by Alexander and Napoleon.

The wild tribes of Koordistan sensitively sympathized with these agitations. It was a question whether some of

---

* The two sects into which the Mahommedans are divided.

196

their hot and trembling mountains might not belch lava and run down with liquid fire. Reports of Koordish warriors massing for storm rolled in, long reverberations through the Koordish mountains. The alert movement of General Williams from Kars, in sending an officer to negotiate with Yez Deen Shir, was none too quick. The Turks removed the powerful young chief from Jezirah, and made him a state prisoner at Mosul. He used to visit us at Mosul to while away his time, and had savagely informed us that he would "like to kill every Jew, Yezidee and Christian," politely adding, "except yourselves, my friends, and drink their blood!" The Turks, in straits of war, trusted him to raise soldiers among the Koords. Koords flocked to his standard, not simply five thousand, but enough to lead him to defy the Turks. He rebelled, held Jezirah for several months, took and held all the fastnesses where the Tigris for fifty miles cuts through mountain-clefts grander than the Highlands of the Hudson. Before putting to death the pasha of Seert, he ignominiously rode him upon a donkey with face to the tail, making him carry puppies. The atrocities committed by him upon the Christians of Jebal Tour sent shuddering through the mountains.

While scenes of blood were enacting on the great highway from Bagdad to Constantinople, Mr. Rhea, one hundred miles farther east, was occupying apparently the most exposed point of all. Mohammed Agha, near him, was trying to get up a Russian party and proceed to the Russian camp, in avowed rebellion. We all knew something of the treachous character of the Koords. A number of our missionaries had been robbed by them. I had undergone that process twice and Mr. Cochran once in the neighborhood of Gawar.

During these months, Mr. and Mrs. Rhea nobly labored on and trusted God. Alluding to Yez Deen Shir, then in

17 *

possession of Jezirah and all that region, including the field of our native missionaries in Botan, Mr. Rhea wrote to me:

January 23, 1855.—How much we have to be grateful for! Our homes might have been desolated, but God has kept us as the apple of his eye. How his great presence is round about us, and from his infinite heart streams of love and mercy are ever gushing out, and *we see him not!* How many hours of each day pass off, and how few warm, hearty, loving thoughts go up to that great Being, at the faintest conception of whose Eternity and Immensity our feeble intellects reel and stagger; and before the unsullied glory of whose purity and holiness our poor hearts quail and sink within us! There are times when I have unutterable longings of soul to *know* that great Being who made me and sent his Son to redeem me.

We may tell over and over again his glorious perfections, and become most skillful adepts in what we call theology, but after all how little genuine heart-knowledge! At this point we can only confess our utter impotence, and fall down at the feet of our Immanuel, remembering the words that he used while he was yet with us, "No man knoweth the Father save the Son, and he to whom the Son will reveal *him.*"

I thank you for your kind congratulations. Every day and every hour I congratulate myself when I think of my happy home and the dear partner God has given to travel with me, sweetly and lovingly, until we get at last home, safe home. The gift of Christ-loving wife, what a precious boon when contemplated in connection with our pilgrimage heavenward!

Often he sings of his comforts. Do winter winds sweep like gales at sea, he thanks God for daily mercies within, and mentions most gratefully that his wood holds out like widows' oil, "not half gone, and the coldest weather over!"

Do wild, passionate boys, fresh caught, and yet as unbroken as their own mountain goats, and helpers more im-
perfect even than we ourselves, try him, and does hot
Eshoo blaze into ungoverned passion, he thinks of his own
sins, mourns and prays, and looks for perfect peace to the
sinless heaven. When in late April, with still four feet
depth of snow, the winds whirl the drifts in tempest, he
hears in the wintry wail another requiem for his brother
Crane, sleeping under the pure snow; and when the mild
days at length come, and nature looks spring-like, he says:
"The birds fill the air with songs of joy that the winter is
passed, and we sing with them."

In his pilgrimage he often bursts out in such thoughts as
these: "How purely must our life, if life at all, be a life
of faith! How often do we travel at night, or at least in
dusk of evening, or in mist and fog! Not so with all!
To favorites the King reveals court secrets; grants frequent
and refreshing interviews. And yet I think he will none
the less love those who, without those more extraordinary
manifestations do still meekly take up their daily cross and
follow after the suffering Saviour in darkness.

"Oh, how full our world is of crosses! Our path is
planted with them. And all are mercifully given that the
spirit of self, in all its countless forms, may be put to death
over and over again, until we can say, 'I am crucified with
Christ, nevertheless I live; yet not *I, Christ liveth in me*—
the very life of the lovely Jesus reproduced and reacted
in and through me! Blessed life! Thrice blessed—if only
we might attain unto it! *I fear in this age too much stress,
relatively, is laid upon the* FIRST STEP, *the conversion, and not
enough upon the* GROWTH, *the struggles and the victory.*'"

His tender heart sympathizes most keenly not only with
missionaries and native helpers and brethren, but also with
the wandering and lost. By simple mountain villager he sits

down, feeling kind interest in his heart-story, in his domestic troubles, his poverty, his taxes, his funeral grief, disappointed hope, or joy of coming bridal.

Now and then, amid the more momentous issues of the soul, the excited state of the Koords attracts his attention.

April 3, 1855, he writes: Our plain for some days has been in feverish excitement in consequence of movements of Mohammed Agha. The pasha gave him a handsome present to keep him in good humor. For the last month he has been using his newly-acquired power in a way to excite the jealousy if not alarm of the Turks. Accompanied by two or three hundred men, he left his village for pleasure. When near Bashkollah the pasha sent for him. He offered to come with his little army. The pasha wished only a private interview. He avoided the snare, and bade the pasha defiance. The pasha gathered up his cannon and went after the rebel. We long to hear that Mohammed Agha is in chains, and on his way to Stamboul. We feel anxious to learn the result, which may concern the safety of our residence.

May 8.—Things are getting into a lawless state. Koordish·chiefs riding on the plain, exacting at pleasure from the poor Christians, and the word in everybody's mouth, "The Turks are used up." The Koordish chiefs say, "The English will certainly get the country, but until then let us have a good time." I see nothing doing to restore order; and unless the Turks bestir themselves, this region will be beyond their control. We had a visit from Chellabi Agha (a Koordish chief) yesterday. He has always been friendly, and pledges his two hundred men for our defence if necessary. We do not fear molestation. We trust the Lord will permit us to remain.

May 29.—He writes to his parents: I am studying Koordish. I am every day brought in contact with

KOORDISH WOMEN AT THE SPRING.

Koords; and for our protection and security here it is important that I know their language. But my chief design in making myself familiar with their language is that I may preach to them Christ crucified. If my poor life is spared, this I confidently hope to do. They too are immortal, and many among them numbered doubtless among God's elect ones to be gathered from the four winds of heaven. Oh, what a privilege to be the instrument of bringing a wild and savage Koord to the feet of the Lord Jesus! What sacrifices may we not gladly welcome to be thus honored. I do not think it will be a difficult language to acquire. Being a corruption of the Persian, it belongs to the great Germanic family, and is a distant relation of the English; it does not sound so strange as the Syriac did to me at first.

About two weeks ago we had some pleasant arrivals in Gawar. First, two of our good brethren from Oroomiah, Stoddard and Cochran, the only American faces we had seen since last fall. If you had been housed for five months and had not seen the face of a friend, nor heard the sweet sounds of your native tongue in the prayers and converse of a missionary brother or sister, would you not welcome them with joy to your home? Imagine then the happy hours we spent with these good brethren during the few days they sojourned under our roof. But we had another arrival, and I can assure you it was a very pleasant one—the box—the long looked-for box from my home. It had been on the road almost a year, but it came at last unharmed. We opened it with great joy, because it looked like home, and it and all that was in it came through precious hands and spoke tenderly of the love of kind friends. With peculiar emotions we took up one by one the articles which your own hands had handled and packed away. We thought of the dear friends who had contributed them, and thanked them in our hearts. The last thing I opened was the little box containing what we now call our household treasures. As I looked upon those dear faces, I wept. So natural were they that I wondered we could not speak one with another. I seemed, as it were, transported in a dream into your presence, but by some strange ordering our tongues were holden. Long, long did I gaze upon the faces so familiar.

In August, 1855, Mr. and Mrs. Rhea left the mountains and spent five weeks in Oroomiah, attending the Annual Mission Meeting, and enjoyed the delights of social and religious communion with cherished friends in Persia. From Oroomiah he wrote to me (September 1): "I still feel the loss of Brother Crane; perhaps in nothing more than in those frequent and free conversations on experimental godliness, the way to live nearer to God. How often have I thus been revived and stirred up to press with greater diligence toward the mark! Yesterday I was reminded of these golden privileges by an hour's pleasant converse with Mr. Stoddard on holy things. Do you not think it an important means of grace? Do we make enough of it? The command, *Exhort one another daily*, has a meaning.

"I long to drink deeper from the fountain of life. I desire that love, and joy, and peace, and spiritual-mindedness, and love for souls, all the Christian graces, may become *habits*. If I could *keep up* the struggles I have some days, the spirit of prayer and watching, and feeding upon the word, and strong faith in Jesus, I think I should make rapid progress, but I mourn a want of steadiness in waging an *unceasing* warfare. To make progress in religious things we must make it *the great every-day business*. Be assured, my dear brother, I shall always most gladly suffer the word of exhortation from your kind pen."

After spending five delightful weeks in Persia, constantly preaching in the villages, and constantly enjoying spiritual intercourse with refined and sympathizing friends, Mr. Rhea left his wife there for six weeks, and with Mr. Breath entered the mountains. During that long and arduous tour, in which they visited fifty villages, we had the rare delight of welcoming them for a stay of less than five days in Mosul.

From Serpil he writes September 19 : Mar Shimon, the Nestorian Patriarch, yesterday was welcomed to the valley with the roar of guns, martial music and the presence of a large and enthusiastic gathering. The Koords, Resh Agha and Chellabi Agha, with their armed men from Gawar, had arranged themselves on the mountain slope, and just as Mar Shimon emerged from the ravine they gave him a grand salute, which was responded to by the Jeloo troops accompanying the patriarch. You can imagine such a volley of musketry reverberating through these wild ravines as somewhat grand. The patriarch gave us a very civil reception ; he said, " My body is faint, my soul is sick. The last age spoken of by our Saviour has come when kingdom should rise against kingdom."

From Bass, September 22 : More than one hundred have gone from this district to join the patriarch, who was almost on the point of resuming independence. Still we have good congregations. Oh that the Lord would give the hearing ear ! Deacon Tamo enters into the work with all his heart, and preaches with great acceptance.

We all enjoy the journey greatly. Walking down the mountains so relieves me of the fatigue of riding that, at night, I can sit till 10 or 11 o'clock preaching and talking. A number are waiting for medicine. Oh that they would seek the Great Physician ! Blessed be God, there is balm in Gilead ! It is the greatest delight of my heart to lead

18

my dying fellow-men to our tender-hearted and compassion-
ate Saviour. The patriarch became very angry with the
remaining helpers, reviled them, and would not suffer them
to come near him. He said he would take a mule from
Eshoo and Shlemon for reading in our school last winter,
and if they went again he would take another.

From Gawar, November 22, 1855, he alludes to this tour:
I am very happy in writing to you once more from my dear
home. We came up from Oroomiah about ten days ago.
I was detained there by a week's illness. We had a safe
and prosperous journey from Mosul homeward, and reached
Oroomiah fifteen days after leaving you. I never enjoyed
a tour more. May the Lord of the harvest watch over the
scattered seed, that not a grain be lost! There were times
when, as we sowed, we wept.

Again in their mountain home, alone but cheerful and
earnest, Mr. and Mrs. Rhea labored for the souls around
them. Yet was it a winter of trials. One of their female
pupils, a bright Nestorian girl, was carried off by a son of
the Koordish chief, greatly to the grief of the missionaries;
the war between Great Britain and Persia necessitated the
removal of powerful friends in the British embassy; Turks
and Koords were menacing each other in Gawar; Mrs.
Rhea's father was instantly killed (in America) by being
run over by a railway car; lawless Koords were plundering
the Christians of the plain. But, with the thermometer at
20°, 30°, 36° below zero, our heroic friends long maintained
their position, and stood, trusting only in God, witnesses
for Jesus Christ.

Mr. and Mrs. Rhea were for months in lively expectation
of welcoming a physician to cheer them in their solitude,
relieve them in their sickness and strengthen them in their
work. But they were doomed to sore disappointment. The

physician, who started from America, mysteriously turned back from Liverpool; and, during the last days of autumn, Dr. Wright and Dr. Perkins hastened to Gawar to solace them under the trying intelligence, and cheer them in the prospect of another lonely winter. They both heroically and submissively bore that saddening disappointment, and were happy and hopeful in their missionary work.

During the previous year the Turkish government had withdrawn all its garrisons from Central Koordistan to reinforce its armies in the Crimean war. Those wild regions were now left entirely to the mercy of savage Koords. Disorders and robbery and murders became frequent and frightful, and sad forebodings to the solitary missionary and his wife were earnestly pressed upon their attention by the Nestorians. It was even rumored that the malevolent patriarch, Mar Shimon, was attempting to instigate a bloody Koordish chief to murder the missionary and seize his wife for his harem. That evil-minded man was certainly not above pursuing such a policy. But they held nobly on in their missionary work, unchecked and undaunted, till midwinter, when fresh outbreaks and the accumulating snows admonished them that they would soon be absolutely imprisoned by that barrier, whatever might come upon them, and they deemed it prudent to retreat to Oroomiah. Their journey was one of great hardship, performed much of the way on foot, over lofty mountains, which were then all but impassable for footmen, and entirely so for beasts of burden.

Dr. Wright vividly sketches the journey: "They started, trusting in God. It was near the last of January. The first day Mrs. Rhea was able to ride, and for a while also the second day. But on the mountain separating Gawar from Oroomiah the snows were too deep for the horses to carry their riders. Our friends were obliged to walk, and that, too, in deep snow. For several hours that day, indeed till they had nearly reached the village of Basan, situated on the declivity of the mountain on the Oroomiah side, Mrs. Rhea was unable to mount her horse. We marvel that her strength did not fail, and that she did not fall exhausted at the roadside. An unseen Hand upheld her. They reached us unharmed. After a few days' rest they went out on a tour in the villages."

They were gladly welcomed at Oroomiah, for their friends had passed anxious days and nights thinking of their perilous situation.

Mr. Rhea engaged with his accustomed ardor in missionary labors at Oroomiah, and wherever he circulated and preached in the villages the Spirit of the Lord accompanied his message, while he "so spake" that many believed.

I should perhaps sooner have stated, in regard to Mr. Rhea's remarkable powers as a preacher, that he was himself so unconscious of possessing them that often, at the close of a service in which he had thrilled and deeply moved his audience, he betrayed a painful apprehension of failure, conceiving, with the least imaginable reason, that he had only been "beating the air." In this matter, as in others, he had, in an eminent degree, the modesty of genius. On one occasion, when he was on a visit to Oroomiah, as he returned to his room, at the close of a service at which he had preached with great pungency, he said, "I have failed, as usual, to make any impression;" while some of the Nestorians who had listened to him were heard to say, as they left the place of worship, "How he made our hearts sweat!" an Oriental figure expressive of deep emotion.

CHAPTER XV.

GOOD soldiers sometimes retreat, but, as every point of earth belongs to the Captain of our Salvation, soldiers of the cross can never in soul abandon their field. From that lonely grave of Mr. Crane, Mr. Rhea heard a call, not as Joseph's taking oath, "Ye shall surely bear up my bones to the promised land," but rather, "Gawar is promised land; hasten, brother, bring the promise up to my grave." In May, 1856, a degree of order having been restored to the mountains, they hastened to resume their post.

June 11th, to his parents: You will rejoice with us that, after an absence of four months, we are once more in our own mountain home. Those Koordish chiefs who kept the country in a constant turmoil during the last winter, bidding the Turks defiance, killing their pasha and then returning to crush with iron heel the poor Christians, are now, some skulking in the mountain fastnesses, some have already gone in irons as state prisoners, and those who have not yet been seized, or who have not yet fled, are waiting every hour in anxious suspense. The chief rebel, Mohammed Agha, whose lawless movements drove us in the dead of winter from our home, has not yet been seized, but two hundred Turks are after him, and will doubtless take him ere long. The Turkish troops returned here six weeks ago, accompanied by Shir Bey, from Diarbekir. He is still here with his 1500 ruffian soldiers, quartered upon the villages, like locust swarms, devouring everything. Though he did a good service in aiding the Turks to crush the rebel Koords, his exactions have been cruelly oppressive.

What a miserable government this is, especially in remote provinces! This Koordish chief is entitled to rations from the government, but the pasha sends him here with his hungry horde, and gives him full license to revile, curse, beat and plunder the poor Christians, devour their flocks and empty their dairies and granaries. The Turk is no longer worthy to rule. He will make the fairest promises to the English and French governments; still, in practical fulfillment, the poor Christians suffer greatly, especially in the remote sections of the Empire. A more corrupt set of officials cannot be found than these Turks.

Coming up from Oroomiah, after I reached the plain of Gawar, I had a little adventure. I called on the authorities at Dizza, who treated me very kindly. I heard then that their ally, Shir Bey, was in the plain, but not on my road. As I approached the village of Muskhoodawa, I saw two flags planted on the roofs of the mud-huts, and observed large numbers of armed Koordish soldiers standing around. We got down to let our horses rest and eat a few moments, and I sat down in the shade talking with a Turk. I had not been there long when a Nestorian came running to me and said: "They have thrown off your baggage and seized your mules." I went at once, and sure enough they were throwing off my baggage. I remonstrated with the Koord who superintended the operation, and told my Nestorian to put on what had been thrown off. At this the Koord, who I afterward learned was brother of the chief, struck my attendant two blows over his head with a stick which he held in his hand. The blood spouted out and streamed down over his face. I demanded of him why he thus insulted me. He said I was a Russian spy; no such character as I could pass without being arrested. I told him I was a resident, showed him where my house was, and told him that I had lived there five years, had been absent a few months and was returning to my home. He would not hear to this.

I directed my man to go at once to the authorities in Dizza and state what had occurred. The Koords understood my meaning and seized him. I then told them I would go. No, they would not consent to that. Being in the hands of three or four hundred armed ruffians, I saw resistance was in vain. I then demanded that he would send a man to Dizza to the authorities, who knew me well. He consented, and, for the time being we were put under guard. It was then about ten o'clock. The Turk who was there invited me to his house to remain till the soldier who was sent to Dizza returned.

It was not long before the chief sent for me. He evidently began to relent for abusing my Nestorian. He had coffee brought, and wished to get dinner for me, but I declined. Pretty soon the head man of the village, a Nestorian, came in and whispered in my ear that if I would give the chief a small present he would let me off. This suggestion was repeated time and again, and the more as the soldier delayed returning from Dizza. After a while a fat, pompous old Koord came in puffing and blowing, and said he had been keeping a most vigilant guard upon my baggage, and if it had not been for his unremitting efforts it would have been plundered by the crowd. I replied that I had no concern about my mules and baggage, as I would hold the chief responsible, and that I should remain indefinitely before I would buy myself off. It was approaching sundown. I had waited five hours to hear from Dizza, not more than three miles distant. I observed a Koord going up to the chief and whispering for some time in his ear; that Koord

had been fumbling about my saddle-bags on my horse, and
had noticed some papers. I was certainly a Russian spy,
for my saddle-bags were full of papers. In prying around
he also detected a small bag of money. He informed the
chief, and asked permission to appropriate it; but the chief
refused. At last the soldier arrived, and brought word that
I had been here for five years, and should not be interrupted or in any way molested. The chief then said, "You
have come welcome—go in peace."

This is just the reply which I wanted. I took my leave.
Quite a number of suitors for presents gathered around me
as I was mounting my horse—one, because he had so nobly
defended my baggage; another, because he had made me a
cup of coffee; another, because he had gone to the authorities on my business; another, because he had struck up
some doleful notes on a cracked tambourine for my entertainment, and called it music. I referred them one and all
to the chief, who, of right, ought to pay the cost.

One plan, we note, among others employed by Mr. Rhea
for preaching Christ, was to offer to passing travelers a guest-
room. In July he mentions that five or six hundred had
received his hospitality and heard glad tidings.

From his journal of September, 1856: *Monday*, 22.—In
the morning, while in the mountain, had a delightful sense
of God's love shed abroad in my heart; longed for that
perfect love which casts out all fear. All nature seemed
vocal with the love of God. Thought I should retain
through the day those pantings of heart after God, but
failed. Were the love of God all-absorbing, nothing would
divert me; it would be with great difficulty that I could
detach my thoughts from him to think of earth.

Wednesday, 24.—Began the day with earnest desire to
walk with God. Do not remember to have spoken an idle

or thoughtless word. Had frequent thoughts of God in the midst of my employments. Nothing but grace enables me to get the victory over any, even the least, besetting sin. Felt sensibly God's restraining grace when tempted to idle and censorious conversation. Conversed with a poor man from Bilignai.

Thursday, 25.—Read and conversed in Turkish. Enabled to maintain, for the most part, a spirit of watchfulness; to remember God and seek his blessing upon my different employments. At different times through the day enabled to say, "Abba, Father." Felt all through the day deep longings after that fullness of love which will make all obedience sweet—that perfect love which shall cast out all fear. Hope to attain it by the grace of God. Determined to strive for it with all my powers. That love is salvation—is heaven. I see no reason why I may not, through rich grace in Christ, love God with all my heart. That I do not, is of all things the most unreasonable and the most unpardonable. If I do not, I cannot be fully assured that I am a child of God. God is a jealous God. He demands all my heart. O Lord, help me to give it to thee without any reserve.

Friday, 26.—Read and talked Turkish. Less watchful and prayerful than on the preceding days.

Saturday, 27.—A morning of sorrow, remorse, and, I trust, of contrition. Suddenly overcome by an easily-besetting sin. Felt deeply humbled, ashamed to meet my offended Saviour and tell him all, and still felt that I could not stay away from him. Found some relief in pleading the promise, "If any man sin, we have an advocate with the Father." Did not have the calm enjoyment of some preceding days; the reason obvious; hard to get back on the old ground of acceptance and assurance. Prepared for the Sabbath services. Talked Turkish in the afternoon. The thought of having the approving smile of God, of pleasing him in all my deportment, a delightful one in the evening. Oh, if to-day's experience could make me henceforth go softly, with a bowed and bruised spirit, it would not be in vain that I was left to fall.

Sabbath, 28.—Read to-day the chapter on holy living in Hodge's "Way of Life." If there is anything in this world that I desire it is perfect holiness, which is perfect love. This is salvation, redemption.

Early in October, Mr. and Mrs. Rhea visited the districts of Ishtazin, Bass, T'khoma, Tal and Diss. No lady had ever penetrated those wild and rugged regions, except the near district of Ishtazin. We have a glimpse of a part of it in a letter from Mr. Rhea:

GAWAR, *Nov.* 6, 1856.

You may be interested to hear something of a tour made recently by Martha and myself to the interior of Koordistan. I had been twice through those wild regions, over the most frightful and dangerous roads, and I made up my mind never to take my wife farther into the mountains. She, however, has felt very anxious to penetrate where an American lady had never before ventured, and meet the mountain Nestorian women in their own homes. I knew that such a tour would involve no little risk. We set out on Thursday, October 2.

You may like to know something of our mode of traveling. We had six mules; on two of them Martha and myself were mounted, on two others, Deacon Tamo and Guergis, our Nestorian servant; and on the others were our tent and a large pair of Russian saddle-bags, large enough to carry our bedding, some provisions and cooking utensils.

Our village lies just under Jeloo, the highest mountain in Koordistan, supposed to rise sixteen thousand feet above

the sea, and nearly nine thousand above the plain of Gawar.
We began at once to ascend this lofty range. We crossed
it in a comparatively low gap, and the ascent is quite easy.

TENTS FOR THE TOUR IN KOORDISTAN.

As we wound up the mountain the plain of Gawar spread
out beautiful behind us, and the snowy tops of Jeloo rose
grandly in front. The descent was not very trying for
some distance. M. rode on her mule until we came to a
cool spring gushing out from under some old walnuts.
There we halted and lunched.

But now came the tug of war. Far, far down we saw
the little fields and trees of the village, which we were to
reach that night. We were on the brink of a frightful
gorge. Here M. dismounted, the idea of riding being out
of the question. To have gone down over that precipitous
stairway would have been a greater feat than Putnam's
gallop. For an hour and a half M. walked, holding on to
my hand the most of the time. Once at the bottom, and
looking back to find our zigzag road, it seemed impossible
to trace it among the crags and along the almost perpendicular face of the mountain.

We had not been on the road more than an hour and a
half when a messenger came after us post-haste, saying that

Miss Fiske and Messrs. Stoddard and Cochran were on their way to join us in our tour, and would reach our village the next day. We were somewhat perplexed for a few moments to know what to do; but finally, since it would be very difficult, if not impossible, for them to find mules in Gawar, we concluded to go on to Ishtazin and send our mules back to bring them over on Saturday.

We reached Ishtazin in good season, and it was but a few moments before our little green tent was pitched and the tea-kettle singing upon the blazing fire. The family of our old friend, Mar Ogloo, the pipemaker, were very attentive in their efforts to provide us with milk and carrots, which was all that could be furnished in the way of eatables.

Saturday, October 4.—Our friends joined us about the middle of the afternoon. We welcomed with joy such good company for the rest of our journey.

Sabbath, October 5.—Early on Sabbath morning we scattered among the villages of the district to proclaim the glad tidings. M., Mr. Stoddard and myself went up to Serpil. M. rode, and Mr. S. and myself went on foot, the distance being only about an hour. We were pained to see such entire disregard of the Sabbath. Nearly all the men were away at work. A little company listened, though not without rudeness, to the gospel of grace and love. Martha sat under a walnut, and many women came and sat down by her. No lady from our number had ever visited that village before. We have a helper stationed there, but as yet do not see much change for the better among its wild, rude inhabitants.

We came back to our tent after dinner, and, being joined by Mr. Cochran and Deacon Tamo, I visited the villages in the opposite direction; thus all the five villages of the valley were once more invited to Christ. Many, however, were too busily engaged in worldly matters to give heed to eternal interests. Why should they? Their priests tell them "All is safe—they need pay no attention to these strange doctrines"—and they willingly sleep on.

Monday, October 6.—We were up bright and early, pulled down our tent, and were in our saddles by eight o'clock. Immediately after leaving the village our road led through a narrow defile, and on either side the cliffs, like colossal towers, rose apparently a thousand feet above us. Sometimes our road was cut from solid rock, four or five feet wide, and many feet above the roaring stream below. At such places the ladies always dismounted, as a slip of the mule's foot might dash animal and rider upon the rocks below. All at once, by a sudden turn, we found ourselves ushered into a very narrow gorge between lofty, perpendicular rocks. We did not emerge for a half hour. It seemed as if the sun had never sent a cheering beam into that deep, dark ravine. We were five hours in reaching the top of the mountain, from which we looked down upon the beautiful village of Zeir. There it lay with its terraced fields and houses one above the other, on the face of the mount. There was the village church, and an old dilapidated castle, where a brave chief, in the days of Nestorian independence, had defied the invading Koords.

We had now a long, steep descent. We all dismounted and went down at a brisk walk. Many of the Zeir people had stopped at our house during the summer, taken a meal and heard the gospel, and were quite friendly. They gathered in large numbers about our tent. We held a religious service after getting our tent pitched, the men gathering on one side of the tent and the women on the other. After supper we went up to the old malik, or chief's, house.

The malik listened attentively to Tamo as he preached

19

Christ, and salvation by free grace alone. He at length interrupted him, saying, "We have a head (Mar Shimon), and just as he says we will do."

MISSIONARY LADY AND MOUNTAIN NESTORIAN WOMEN.

This was popish infallibility strong enough. Tamo replied that this matter of religion and the soul's salvation was personal between every man and his God, and Mar Shimon had no right to interfere in any way, except to teach the sinner how he might find pardon from an offended God.

To this the malik did not reply. We spent a very pleasant time upon the roof, Messrs. Cochran and Stoddard addressing the people after Tamo had closed his remarks.

When we reached the tent it was near nine o'clock. We found a large company of women, Miss Fiske and M. in their midst, telling them of Him who so loved us that he gave himself for us. We know not but on that night the heart of some Lydia may have been opened to welcome Christ.*

One night they were roused by distressed bleatings, and, looking out from their tent, saw a bear moving along upon a high wall to get at his victim. He was soon, however, driven away by the mountaineers.

Dr. Wright says:

Though the effort was too great to be repeated, taxing strength of muscle and nerve to the utmost, Mrs. Rhea was glad that she made the tour. She saw much of the field to which she and her husband were devoted; she visited the helpers in their homes, and could better sympathize with and pray for them; she spoke the words of life to many perishing females; she was made to realize more than ever how inviting her Gawar home was in contrast with the more rugged and inaccessible parts beyond. Government and order had been partially restored, and our friends were greatly encouraged in their work. The Holy Spirit appeared to be sealing some souls for eternal life.

November 3.—How are the Turks behaving on your side? Here there is but one long, loud cry of oppression and wrong. I was preaching in the villages yesterday. In one, the night before, at a late hour, twelve Turkish soldiers entered a house, seized two women, dragged them from their beds, put them on horseback, and were making off, they crying piteously. The husband of one was gagged and beaten. The villagers succeeded in rescuing one, but the other was taken off to Dizza. They say she has become a

---

* The reader interested in the Nestorian people and work will find much that will please and instruct him in *Woman and her Saviour in Persia*. It is issued by Messrs. Gould & Lincoln, of Boston, to whom we are under obligations for aid in illustrating this book. *Dr. Grant and the Mountain Nestorians*, published by the same firm, is another work of interest bearing upon this field and people.

Musselman; and what Nestorian woman would not when a prisoner in the hands of Turkish soldiers?

Again was the Nestorian mission afflicted, deeply afflicted and bereaved, by the death of the Rev. David Tappan Stoddard, a man of saintly life, fine culture and high usefulness. His death deeply impressed Mr. Rhea. February 3, 1857, he says:

How hard to realize that our dear Brother Stoddard is no longer with you; that we are never to see him again there or here! He will have no more to do with earth, unless it be as a ministering spirit to the heirs of salvation. In spirit I see the face which had struck so many as a peculiarly heavenly one. It is my daily, almost hourly prayer that the death of Mr. Stoddard may leave an abiding savor of heaven, and of Christ, and of divine things upon all our hearts and deportment, upon all our native brethren and upon our entire work. I find myself often lost amid musings and pleasant recollections of him. I can truly say that all the influence he ever exerted over me was for Christ, heaven and eternity. He was the first missionary I knew personally; and my first impressions of missionary character could not have been happier. Oh, that I might be quickened by his life and death to more ardent hungerings after holiness and a deeper devotion to Christ's service! *

In March he writes to myself:

We have good news, the very best we could have from Oroomiah. The Spirit is breathing light and love into some hearts. I wept when I heard of it—for joy, that sinners are penitent; for grief, that I have never yet, to my knowledge, had a seal of my ministry. Pray for me, dear brother—for this little company of youth under our roof. I

* The memoir of this man of God, prepared by Rev. Joseph P. Thompson, D. D., is published by the American Tract Society, Boston.

do long to see them *in Christ;* but oh I am so fearful they will go away unimpressed, unsaved!

The following is characteristic: Dear brother, I hope you will never be so naughty again as to send one of my letters to America or anywhere else. I tried to find a thick sheet of paper, so that the appeal to your pocket would prevent it, but did not succeed.

Of Harriet Stoddard, who soon followed her father, he writes to Mr. Coan, April 6, 1857: Our Mosul friends would like to know everything about dear Harriet's sickness and death. How wonderful the grace of Jesus, that can inspire the most timid of his lambs with a courage that quails not before the dread presence of the king of terrors! The tender and sensitive nature, shrinking back from everything of a frightful character, now meets death unappalled. The little child with firm step approaches the brink of the stormy river, laughs at its surging billows, plunges into its breakers, sinks and rises, sings amid the buffetings of the waves, until at length on the far-distant shore is seen the little victor, calm, serene, exultant, standing amid bands of shining angels, who pour upon her their welcomes and congratulations, and unite with her in songs of victory. May we meet death as calmly and sweetly as dear Harriet. The battle is fought, the victory won. Oh sometimes how I envy those who have got safely over the swelling tide!

April 27.—He measures six feet of snow—treasures for Persia—to melt and flow down upon its plains.

Late in May a small band was gathered, the first in Koordistan for several hundred years, to observe the Lord's supper with anything like proper solemnity and decorum. Shortly afterward, June 4, 1857, he kept a private holy day. He then, entering upon the care of this little mountain church *anew,* solemnly gave himself wholly to God. His

19 *

journal is resumed, and reads: *June* 4.—A solemn day! Oh that its impressions may not be as the morning cloud and early dew! In the morning felt deeply dissatisfied with myself as I saw how far removed I was from that high standard of holiness held up in God's holy Word. At noon read the chapter in Hodge's "Way of Life" on Holy Living. In the afternoon retired, and spent near three hours on the mountain. I went to meet with my Saviour, to tell him of all my wanderings and backslidings, to mourn over my many sins, to seek his free forgiving love and solemnly to dedicate myself to his service. Blessed be his holy name! he was pleased to meet with me in that lonely spot, to give me in some measure a contrite and broken heart, to enable me to renew my vows to be wholly his. How sweet it was to pour out my soul before him in penitential grief, to feel the joy of forgiveness and acceptance, to cry "Abba, Father!" to say, "I am wholly thine for ever!" Yea, I was enabled to believe that he did receive the unworthy offering. I was deeply humbled when I remembered how often I had thus laid myself upon his altar, and after a time again served sin and self, and my earnest entreaty was that now he would work a deep and powerful work of grace in my heart; that he would deeply regenerate my nature and evermore keep me from falling into sin. Jesus can and will save me from every sin if I only abide in him. Oh, Divine Redeemer, thou knowest that I am utter weakness. My only hope is in thy almighty power and the riches of thy grace.

June 8, 1857.—We had a visit from Brother Cochran three weeks ago, and you cannot imagine with what joy we welcomed him *after an interval of five months*, during which we had not seen the face of missionary brother or sister, nor heard the dear accents of our mother tongue save from each other's lips. We had a delightful visit and a deeply interesting communion season—the first when our Nestorian brethren united with us, of whom, on this occasion, there were eleven. He mentions Deacon Tamo and others, and adds: There are four others for whom we have a pretty good hope, but we thought best for them to run a while longer, that they themselves and we may be better satisfied that they are truly in Christ Jesus. Before celebrating the Lord's Supper the Nestorian communicants rose and entered into a solemn covenant, taking upon them the vows of God and the obligations of a holy life. It was a deeply affecting scene to our hearts. Oh may it be the beginning of good things in Koordistan! We have a weekly prayer-meeting, when our lay brethren take part in the devotions.

God had given his servant the great desire of his heart in the removal of rubbish of idolatrous forms and empty ceremonies, and the establishment in the mountains of a church founded on the Rock which cannot be moved. Had his life accomplished no more, it were well spent. We conclude this account by giving the last record we can find from his journal for more than four years to come:

June 10.—Enjoyed for some days sweet peace. Enabled to say continually, Abba, Father, and often to renew my covenant vows. To-day had many anxious, perplexing thoughts about our native helpers—wages, employment, etc. I wish to be strictly conscientious in everything, and to imbue them with the same spirit. If every thought was in subjection to the obedience of Christ, I should not indulge these anxious thoughts, often so dispiriting. Oh how manifest that I am not yet made perfect in love! "Lo, I am with you always" has often brought sweet repose to my bosom, and I have been emboldened by the unspeakably precious promise to lay all my affairs before Jesus, and in my loneliness here, having no one to consult with, to seek his guidance and direction. Yes, it is my privilege to speak freely with Jesus, my Elder

Brother, and I believe he will always make the path of duty plain.

That path led him to Oroomiah for a few delightful weeks, including two weeks spent with Dr. Wright in a missionary excursion to Bashkollah and Van, and afterward into untold sorrow.

KOORDISH SHEPHERD OF THE MOUNTAINS, IN HIS STIFF FELT COAT.

CHAPTER XVI.

AT THE GATE OF HEAVEN.

GOD has hallowed the mountain-tops. Many he has reserved for angels; some spotless with undefiled snow, some melting and flowing down, altars with ever-burning fire, into which angels may pass and ascend in his presence.

Other mountains tolerate the foot of man. God has chosen these lower mountains for sanctuaries of most privileged intercourse—Moriahs, Sinais and Horebs, Hors and Nebos, Olivets and Tabors. The Beloved Son has selected them for his beatitudes, sermon and prayers, for his transfiguration, crucifixion and ascension. If, then, our Lord and Master say, "Get *thee* up into this mountain," thrice blessed art thou if taught by the Comforter implicitly to obey.

Three times God had called Mr. Rhea and his wife unexpectedly from the delights of that Persian circle to go alone into the mountains. Three times they had obeyed; and now a still greater test of faith was in store for them.

"Enjoying excellent health," says Dr. Wright, "Mrs. Rhea had often expressed the idea that her husband's days might be few, and she be left a widow. The main object of her visit to Oroomiah had been to cheer and comfort the bereaved. She came an angel of mercy, so sweet in temper and spirit, her soul so possessed of eternal realities, her large, speaking, dark eye so beaming with sympathy and compassion. The death of Mr. Stoddard and Harriet had led her to drink deeper of the wells of salvation. She had

225

taken a higher stand in divine things. This appeared in her gentle, holy walk with God, in her earnest pleas at the throne of grace."

In August, 1857, Mr. Rhea wrote to me: We were absent from our home nearly six weeks. More than two weeks were taken up by our trip to Bashkollah and Van. It had been more than a year since we had visited our good friends in Oroomiah, and you can imagine with what keen relish we enjoyed it. We are happy to be once more in our own home and engaged in our work. We confidently expected to hear, by this post, that an associate was appointed for us, but we have been disappointed again; and from the tenor of letters received from the Missionary House, we can hardly expect to have associates for the coming winter. Well! just as the Master pleases. The mountains are dearer to him than to us. I think that my strongest desires are not personal, but that we may be able to carry forward more vigorously the work of evangelizing the mountains.

The following touching allusion in the same letter shows that in the most heroic the spirit indeed is willing, but the flesh is weak: "I accidentally found Martha crying to-day, after our mail came, and I half suspect this matter of associates was at the bottom of it. These long, lonely winters are rather trying for her; and, though she has a remarkable fund of happy contentedness in her disposition, there are times when the prospect of another winter without an associate is rather too much for her. Still, when the time comes to be shut in again, I have no doubt she will be as happy and contented as any one of her missionary sisters."

Within a month he wrote the following letter to his parents:

GAWAR, *September* 17, 1857.

I send you heavy tidings to-day. My dear Martha sleeps

in death; but I cannot doubt that she still lives in heaven with Jesus—a glorified spirit—a companion of angels—perfectly blessed. She sunk sweetly in the arms of Jesus yesterday, September 16, at six o'clock P. M., after a most painful illness of many days.

Oh that I were by your side to weep with you—to have you comfort me! Near where I sit, my dearest earthly treasure, my earthly all, lies clothed in the habiliments of death. I am as a man struck dumb. I ask, Is it a dream? I go and lift the covering, and there lies my darling one, cold and pale in death. Sweet face! so calm, so serene! No more agonizing—no more suffering—thou hast found "thy long-sought rest."

During her long and intense suffering she manifested the sweetest spirit of patience and resignation. Not one murmuring word escaped her lips; not a cloud intervened between her and her Saviour. A bright light from his blessed face seemed ever beaming down upon her soul. Peace passing all understanding took possession of her heart from the first.

We left Oroomiah Wednesday, July 22. On Thursday morning, just as we were mounting our horses, Martha was taken with a severe pain, which passed off, but returned the next day. We went on by easy stages, reaching our home safely. The same pain occasionally returned. But on Thursday evening, August 20, so intense was the pain that the perspiration was bursting from every pore. Gradually, however, its severity subsided. Immediately after the last attack I sent for Dr. Wright; he, accompanied by Miss Rice, reached us the following Friday. He was surprised to find her so well. I talked with Dr. Wright particularly about her case, and the result was such as to relieve my mind of all anxiety. As he was needed in Oroomiah, he returned on Monday. At three o'clock a violent paroxysm came on. The pain was intense for several hours, and followed by great prostration.

I sent for Dr. Wright about an hour after she was taken. He reached us the Saturday following, having ridden that day sixty-five miles. On Monday, just after breakfast, another attack came on, surpassing all previous ones in violence. It seemed as if her sufferings were unendurable.

Monday night, when I asked her, "Is Jesus near, Martha?" she replied, "Oh yes, so near! Whenever my severe pain comes on, then Jesus comes and helps me to bear it. Jesus will not leave me." Seeing me weeping, she stretched out her hand and wiped away the falling tear, saying, " He will take care of you ; do not look so sad."

She uttered many short, fervent, affecting petitions, such as, "Jesus, come wash me from all my sins ; make me wholly thine." "Oh, what a sinner I have been! but Jesus is a great Saviour; he is so near, so lovely! I wonder why I never saw him so before. Earth fades away; this world is nothing. I know there is nothing in me, and do not tell others what I say, for they will think me holier than I am ; but it is all of Christ. It would be so easy to die now—to sink into the arms of Jesus !"

On Tuesday morning she asked what the doctor had said about her case. I replied, he spoke of it as critical, but still hopefully. She then said, " Well, dear, I am rather glad. The thought of death is very pleasant. I have had no fear from the first. It seems as if it would help me to bear my pains to think of a speedy release; still it is not because I suffer that I wish to die. I want to see Jesus and lie at his feet." Seeing me affected, she said, "You know, dear, I love you, but we must love Jesus first. It will not be long until we all meet. O eternity! eternity! how short will these moments appear then !"

On Tuesday night she prayed, "O Jesus, remember thy

sufferings, and, if it is possible, lessen mine; but not my will but thine be done." Again: "Oh, could any one bear it better than I? Perhaps so; but Jesus groaned, being in agony." Speaking of heaven: "Oh, that home! No more sin, nor sorrow, nor restlessness!"

I asked her once if she had any doubt. She replied, "No; none at all. I do not know why Jesus comforts such a poor sinner as I have been. All is bright, and calm, and peaceful. Not because of anything in me; all is of Jesus. He knows I could not bear my sufferings if he did not come near me! When I am easier, then I do not think so much of being happy as to see if indeed my feet are on the Rock. Then it is no matter about joy; that will come just as my Saviour pleases; but when I am suffering it relieves me, soothes me, to talk of Jesus and the joy he gives me. Then I think more of being happy, and Jesus gives me joy."

Once she asked Dr. Wright, "How long do you think I could live and suffer so?" To his reply that he did not know certainly, but not long, she said, "My sufferings will end. What if they were eternal?"

I do not think there could be a richer exhibition of the power of Divine grace to sustain and cheer the suffering saint while racked with agonizing pains. Oh, if I could only forget how she looked when those pangs were upon her; but God has taken her where there shall be no more pain. Oh, how tenderly she won upon our love by her gratitude and her anxiety lest some one of us should get sick by waiting upon her.

The last book which we read together, about two weeks before her death, was the Memoir of Richard Williams of the Patagonian mission, illustrating in a wonderful manner the power of the love of Jesus to fill the heart with joy unspeakable and full of glory amidst scenes of deepest distress. She alluded more than once to it during her illness, and I doubt not it had its influence in kindling into so bright a flame her love to Jesus.

On Monday morning, September 14, her first words to me were: "Oh, what sweet thoughts I had of Jesus. I am so afraid I shall lose the sweetness of his name if I get well; but he can help me so that I shall love its savor even amid the busy cares of life."

Again: "For many days, when I was feeling a little better, I was satisfied to come back and live; if I might grow in grace every day it might be as well to live as to die; but oh it would be sweet to die and be with Jesus, and never sin any more. You will not think that I do not love you."

"I want my brothers and sisters to know that I never had a wish that I had not come to the Nestorians. I rejoice that I could labor for them a little while."

During the day, when able to converse, her words were full of heaven and her heart of tenderness for friends present and absent. The night was one of pain and restlessness. Tuesday she spoke little, being for two hours racked with agony.

Wednesday morning she was beyond all hope of recovery. All day long I sat by her, fanning her. She wished me where she could see me when she opened her eyes. 'There I sat and prayed hour after hour. I took my Bible; opening it, my eyes fell upon the words, "And when he would no longer be persuaded, we ceased, saying, The will of the Lord be done." It flashed upon my mind that I had been hoping against hope; that I was trying to persuade the Lord, but he would not be persuaded.

Once, in the forenoon, I asked her, "Martha, is Jesus near?" She promptly replied, "Oh yes!" and as often as I asked her, this was her reply. I asked her if she could

join in a soft, gentle prayer? She said, "I am too faint;
I can only pray a word or two at a time." Opening her
eyes once, she looked steadily at me and said, "Thank
Jesus that he does not leave me." All day the native
women were coming taking a last look, and passing out, sobbing bitterly.

It was now evident that our dear one was struggling with
death. Seeing me weep, she beckoned me to bend over her.
She threw her arms around my neck and tenderly embraced
me. This was her last farewell. As I bent over her to
catch her words, seeing the tears streaming from my eyes,
she quickly put her hand to her eyes and motioned as if
she would have me dry them. Not long after, she said,
"My thoughts are very clear, but I cannot express them."
Her hearing was perfect until about the last, and when her
power of speech failed, by a nod of the head or gentle pressure of the hand she could say, "Jesus is near!"

The last rays of the setting sun were touching the tops of
the mountain. The curtain blew aside and the fading
light fell upon her face; she opened her eyes, looked at me a
moment—a few more gentle breaths, and she was in heaven.

Thus sweetly passed away my dear Martha. How near
heaven seemed at that moment! I had followed her even
to the gates. She passed in—I stood without, weeping.
Oh, how I did long to pass in with her. What raptures
filled her bosom when for the first time her eyes fell upon
the glorious person of her Redeemer! What a change!
One moment gasping, dying—the next crowned with glory,
honor, immortality and eternal life! We had lived all
alone nearly three years. In each other we had found a
joy and a solace that made us forget our lonely situation.
Our hearts were one. Hand in hand we walked together,
seldom dreaming of a day of bereavement. It seemed as
if one could not exist without the other. No words can tell

you of my loss. God only knows. A heart more tender in its love, nobler in all its feelings, never beat. Her love to me was the purest and most ardent, and her dear hands were ever engaged in some way to make my home happy. Pray much for your bereaved and deeply-stricken son. None but Jesus can help me in this hour. All day Thursday our home was filled with weeping; many scores of the poor women and children, with their husbands and brothers, and with them many Koords, came to look at her calm and sweet face. Many wept as if their hearts would break. They had lost a friend — one who was ever going about among them to do them good. On Friday, at twelve o'clock, I followed the remains of my beloved wife to the grave. Religious services were held in the village church —it was crowded to overflowing. Dr. Wright addressed the people very tenderly. At the grave Deacon Tamo again addressed the people, and prayed in a touching manner for the stricken husband and the far-off kindred, and the precious remains were committed to the bosom of the earth. She sleeps in the little enclosure on the hill by the village church, just under the little willow which I brought from Oroomiah and planted, that it might cast its shade upon the sacred spot.

Says Dr. Perkins: "This was a very unexpected and crushing blow to Mr. Rhea; but he was supported under it. Nor was he left friendless in that sorrowful visitation. Miss Rice tenderly nursed his suffering wife during the last weeks of her sickness; and Dr. Wright, 'the beloved physician,' was there during the last few days. Mrs. Stoddard and myself were hastening to them, in the apprehension of a fatal termination of the disease, when we were met by a messenger, midway, who announced to us Mrs. Rhea's death. The shock of these mournful tidings but quickened our pace; yet the grave had just closed over the remains of that beloved missionary sister when we reached the desolate dwelling.

"Missionary duties required Dr. Wright and myself to hasten back to Oroomiah, while Mrs. Stoddard and Miss Rice lingered a week or two, to comfort and assist Mr. Rhea, who then returned with them.

"The self-denials, the trials and the sore bereavements which had so thickly beset Mr. Rhea's path during the more than six years of his missionary life and labors in Koordistan were far enough from diminishing his interest in that arduous field. God had given him very precious fruits of his toils there, though baptized in tears; and the two missionary graves on the hill in the Memikan church-yard were strong magnets to bind him the more firmly to the mountain work. His missionary brethren at Oroomiah, however, deemed it quite inexpedient for him to pass the following winter at his post alone. By their urgent advice he concluded to itinerate and journey through the mountains to Mosul, and spend the winter with the missionaries at that station."

Mr. Rhea wrote:

GAWAR, *September* 25, 1857.

DEAR BROTHER MARSH: When you were writing to me, September 16, my dear wife was just on the verge of heaven. She sunk sweetly in the arms of Jesus at six P. M. Oh, my dear brother, I have no words to tell you of my grief, my sorrow, my bereavement! When I look long at myself, or my desolate home, or the objects that are every moment calling up so vividly the dear departed, I feel that I have no strength to drink the cup which God has given me. I know you will pray for me. Having been so near heaven, how near ought I henceforth to live! I never needed your prayers so much as now, and I know you will ask from Jesus all needed grace for me.

20 *

October 26.—I am often able, in the midst of tears and the bleeding of a deeply wounded heart, to look up and say, "Thou art mine and I am thine for ever;" but not always. Oh pray for me that I may enjoy the uninterrupted light of his countenance; for there are times when all around me seems very dark. But I will trust him. The cup which my Father gives me I will drink.

You have drunk the cup of sorrow, but not so deeply. Oh may God spare you this! I think you would drink it with a sweeter spirit of resignation. But he knows I have never murmured. I have fallen at his feet and in silence poured out there my tears of grief—I trust of contrition—but no murmuring word has ever escaped my lips. I hope I shall be able to say, It was good for me to be afflicted; but as yet I dare not. I know the deep treachery of my heart. For many days after the loved one of my heart was buried out of my sight I was overwhelmed and crushed to the earth. I was bewildered. But I remembered that no chastening for *the present* seemeth to be joyous; nevertheless, *afterward* it yieldeth the peaceable fruit of righteousness unto them which are exercised thereby.

My home is desolate. Every object wears a bereaved look. I shrink away from this deep loneliness—from the objects which are every moment bringing the dear departed so vividly before me, and still I cling to them. I long to remain here, and still I fear the effects of a long winter of solitude. Every object that my eye lights upon only suggests the greatness of my loss, and when I walk abroad I am not able to divert my thoughts; for there is not a path which her feet had not trodden with me, nor a flower her hand had not culled, nor a scene of beauty or sublimity which we had not enjoyed together. I often find it too much for me to visit the hallowed spot where she sleeps. Oh it seemed cruel to lay that loved form in the ground and heap the earth upon it! But I will not think of that. I will think of her as clad in the white robes of her Redeemer's righteousness, and with the golden harp singing and celebrating his wondrous love. I will think of her as free from pain and sin—as standing at the portals of glory and beckoning me to come up higher. I will think of that blessed day when, as she said, "We will fall together at the feet of Jesus!"

But I beg pardon. I did not intend to intrude my grief upon you.

I accompanied Mrs. Stoddard and Miss Rice to Oroomiah, and spent a few days with the kind friends there. I felt strengthened by their prayers and sympathies. My friends seemed very unwilling that I should pass the winter here alone. The idea of spending the winter in Oroomiah would be a very pleasant one if I should follow mere selfish inclinations. While Oroomiah is well supplied, the poor mountains are without shepherds. In the providence of God I am the only one directly responsible for looking after these lost sheep. How can I withdraw from them.

Seeing, however, that the friends in Oroomiah felt so strongly about my remaining here alone, I proposed to them to spend the winter upon the other side of the mountains—a part of the time in Mosul, and touring in Amidiah, Botan, and in fact among Nestorian villages wherever they could be found in that region and reached in the winter season. This struck them favorably. It has seemed to me that by going over to your side I should still be identified with my own field, and would be able to do far more for the mountain Nestorians than if in Oroomiah or Gawar. I have felt, too, that I must see our helpers in T'khoma, and, if possible, give the work an impulse there by opening schools. If suitable young men can be obtained, it is my plan to plant two helpers in Amidiah.

My home, though desolate, is dear—of all others the dearest place. But after this fall of snow it seems clear that it is best for me to go on the other side of the mountains. I went a short distance with Brother Cochran (on his return). We were an hour and a half going to a village twenty minutes distant. I suppose he told you what a fall of snow we had on the twenty-first and twenty-second of this month (October)—three and one-half feet! Half, at least, of the harvest in Gawar is under the snow. Hundreds will probably go down to Oroomiah, and also to the plains west of the mountains. This little village will be half depopulated. If I desired to keep our boarding-school open, it would be impossible to buy the necessary provisions.

I shall leave Gawar probably next week. It is uncertain when I may reach Mosul. I hope ere this you have greeted your associates. We have sympathized with you in your loneliness and in the heavy burdens resting upon you. We now wish to rejoice with you. Oh, that your little band might long be an unbroken one! If they have come, I wish with all my heart to welcome them.

The very day that Mr. Rhea wrote this long letter to me—extracts from which only are given above—October 26, 1857, I started from Mosul to welcome those associates from America in Diarbekir, and with them form plans for our Assyrian mission. We left Diarbekir November 17, 1857; Dr. and Mrs. Haskell and myself upon one raft of inflated goat-skins, and Mr. and Mrs. Williams on the other, with our necessary raftsmen and attendants, to float down the Tigris. It was like a week's pleasure-excursion, with grand scenery for two hundred and ninety miles. We reached Mosul November 25. Before another month Mr. Rhea had completed his mountain tour. Meantime the whole party remained our guests, for before Mr. Williams could move into his house Mrs. Williams was taken ill, and grew worse and worse, and still worse, and when Mr. Rhea arrived her case was alarming. He came a welcome angel.

KELLEK, OR RAFT OF INFLATED GOAT-SKINS, ON THE TIGRIS.

I extract from his letter after his arrival:

MOSUL, *Dec.* 19, 1857.

MY DEAR FATHER: . . . I am now a homeless wanderer. Be it so, if I may only keep my face continually set toward the gate of that city which hath foundations whose builder and maker is God!

I had a most toilsome journey through the mountains owing to the lateness of the season. I came very near being shut in by the deep snows and made a prisoner in one of the mountain valleys. I lingered just as long as I could, preaching the precious gospel to large and attentive audiences. I expect to go up in a few days to Amidiah (seventy miles), and may open a school there. If not, I shall spend the winter in traveling among the Nestorian villages on this side of the mountains.

I found our friends in Mosul in affliction. Mrs. Williams is dangerously ill. The Lord grant her healing mercies.

How joyous the meeting, when, on November 25th, the

new-comers, safe and well, sat down with us, a Mosul mission band of seven adults and five children! How sad, on Christmas day, after its long hours of light had passed away, and as toward midnight we gathered about the bedside of our Sister Williams, just a moment after the spirit had taken its flight! A month to a day, and how reversed the picture! How sad, sad, sad! Yet it was Christmas day, and some of the same angels who sang to the shepherds came and bore with song a forgiven spirit up to Him whose birth they sang.

Mr. Rhea writes again to his parents:

MOSUL, *Dec.* 28, 1857.

Can you imagine a more distressing case of affliction? Oh, what mean these strokes so thick and fast upon God's missionary servants in this part of the world? We are as one large family. We feel toward each other, I think sometimes, even more tenderly than toward our kindred in the flesh, and it seems as if there was always a death in the family. We are scarcely recovered from one stroke until another falls upon our broken band. What does God intend by these strange dealings? Does he intend by thus thinning and wasting our ranks to drive us from the field of labor to which we thought we heard his voice bidding us go and preach his gospel? It seems very dark, very dark indeed; but still it is our Father's doing, and he doeth all things well. We will trust him in the dark.

Mr. Rhea did not linger idly with us in Mosul. From our comparatively mild climate again he plunged back into winter snows; from our city of safety and comfort into the danger of strange mountain roads, wild Koords, Yezidees (devil-worshipers) and mountain Nestorians; from our little American colony, to solitary service for Christ. He wrote to me five letters during that month of January, and they show him going from village to village, starting a school at Deira near Amidiah, and everywhere preaching the word.

No one who has not been over the ground can imagine the endurance of hardness and the self-denial involved. In those mountain huts he writes, " in haste, by a dying light;" but often utters such thoughts as these:

" The idea of a complete redemption from sin is at times most ravishing; but that day seems so far distant. Why these longings for purity and holiness if they are never to be realized on earth? Why is Jesus called a Redeemer if he does not save from the power of sin in this life? The question of personal holiness is yet to stir the heart of the Church to its depth; there is no question about which I feel so much perplexed, and none upon which I long so much for light."

On the Sabbath his servant gathered the Tall people from Amidiah market. " These, with the T'khoma people and a few Nestorians from this town, almost filled the room. The mountaineers are rather wild, and it reminded me of some of the boys' meetings in New York, but they soon became quiet and gave very good attention throughout the service. Such opportunities for making known the precious love of Christ do much to relieve my loneliness here, and comfort me amid those desolate feelings which will sometimes storm my soul and threaten to swallow me up."

January 26.—He writes us from Shermin, speaks of his path disappearing in falling snow, of his horse with snow up to his knees ploughing through it " manfully" and " opening a path for the mules," of coming unexpectedly upon a Moslem village where no dog barked, and found a village of Sofees " so holy that they had banished all the dog tribe," yet he read to his well-pleased Sofee host the Sermon on the Mount. He asks at one time, " What Nestorian village did not Dr. Grant find?" yet himself preached the gospel on that tour in one a missionary had never visited before. At Usyan, where he found forty families, three priests and ten deacons, he "spent a delightful Sabbath." "It was the first Sabbath in my new year, the thirty-first of my life, and I shall always remember it as one of the happiest. Oh shall I meet any of those precious souls in heaven? After leaving the village, two young men—deacons—came after me, saying they wished to read in the school at Deira."

Of a Sabbath in Bebadi he writes: "The air seemed as balmy as spring and I sat out on the roof for several hours. I had an audience of fifty persons; among them a number of women. I tried to point them to the Lamb of God that taketh away the sin of the world. It was a tender theme, and many were melted to tears. The people of Bebadi seem very teachable."

In February, 1858, he called upon us in Mosul, and I joined him for three weeks in a tour toward Amidiah, and then to Jebal Tour, above Jezireh, on the Tigris. We went into the mountains till the snows absolutely barred our farther progress. An idea of some of the roads may be formed by attempting to ride on a stone wall with snow breast-deep on either side, and often no path visible. Every night we found audiences. Our quarters were as wretched, with smoke, cattle under the same roof and fleas, as can well be imagined; but the work was blessed.

At one time, near Azakh, where my Arabic took the place of his modern Syriac, we found a swollen torrent, from melting snows, where usually no water runs, and it bore Rover, with me on his back, down full two rods; but fortunately, by God's blessing, I kept his head up stream, and he was not thrown down; and the noble animal (a true Arab) bore me through safely.

In all that tour I saw the life and work of Mr. Rhea with new admiration for his tact and power, and I trust with new sympathy for his self-denying and Christ-like spirit. No difficulty or hardship deterred him. His body seemed far enough from Paradise, but his soul hourly waiting at heaven's gate.

KOORDISH CASTLE OF KOSH AB, MAHMOODIYAH.

CHAPTER XVII.

ALONG THE TIGRIS—OVER TO PERSIA—BACK TO AMI-DIAH—AGAIN TO PERSIA.

NO missionary to Persia, not even Dr. Grant, ever searched out the whole Nestorian field both in Persia and Turkey, so thoroughly visiting again and again every nook and corner, as did Mr Rhea. His trials as well as his joys directed him to this great work. Everywhere he bore the Bible and other works of the press in Oroomiah, and located, directed and encouraged the native helpers.

The outline of a fruitful year is given at the head of this chapter. Let us enjoy the filling up from Mr. Rhea's own pen:

To Mr. Coan, April 13, from Mosul: Three weeks ago, as Mr. Williams and I were walking on the banks of the Tigris, we saw two black objects slowly descending the river, Watching them, our curiosity was increased when we found they had houses on them, and it was not long till we were satisfied that they were the rafts containing our Diarbekir friends. A few moments more and they landed, and we were exchanging happy greetings. The party consisted of Mr. and Mrs. Walker and little Freddie, three months old, Dr. and Mrs. Nutting and Annie Nutting, and Mr. and Mrs. Knapp.

Mrs. Walker was sister of Mrs. Williams, who on Christmas day left us lamenting, and now the living of our little band wept and rejoiced together.

With the opening spring Mr. Rhea started on his return to Gawar, accompanying some of the families of the Eastern

Turkey mission a few days up the river Tigris on their return to their respective homes in old Assyria, and administering essentially to their relief and comfort in the case of a sick one of the traveling company. The Rev. Mr. Knapp, then on his way to Bitlis, says: " On our four days' journey from Mosul to Jezireh my wife became disabled, and had to be borne for upward of forty miles on a litter carried by eight Jews. As I knew not their language, I had to depend upon Mr. Rhea to guide us through that desert with those obstinate men. He endeared himself exceedingly to our hearts by the wonderful degree of patience he exhibited during those two trying days. Well do we remember how often those weary litter-bearers ruthlessly thrust the litter, with its agonized burden, upon the ground, positively refusing to bear it another inch. Our patient friend would again and again rally them by putting his own shoulder to the heavy burden, and thus showing them an example of kind endurance in hours of severe fatigue. The strength of our attachment to him grew stronger in proportion to the severity of our distress. He did not desert us. When at length all danger was passed and we were forced to part with him, we shed tears of gratitude as we watched his form receding among the rugged mountains, the scene of his missionary labors. An own brother, or even a parent, could not have shown us greater sympathy than did he during those anxious days."

He left them just where Xenophon left the Tigris. A few days later Mr. Rhea wrote to me from those mountains:

SHAKH, *April* 28, 1858.

I parted from our good friends where the road turned up to Mar Yohanan. I am seated to-night where we were seated together more than four years ago—in the churchyard. I have had a very attentive congregation of thirty persons. I have been much pleased with the young bishop,

Mar Yoseph. He seems to be quite studious, desirous of acquiring a knowledge of the Scriptures and of teaching his people. How much I would give if I could only induce him to spend a winter or two in Oroomiah! I do hope the Lord will fully enlighten him and make him a great blessing to Botan. The prospect improves; the school numbers thirteen, besides six young men who read with Ishak on the Sabbath. I would hope with trembling that Yohanan and Tamo are new men in Christ Jesus. They appear well, and have suffered much for Christ's sake. Ishak is a precious jewel. I bless God for such a light in Botan."

Those who do not despise the day of small things will know how such testimony from Brother Rhea refreshed my heart. When alone, during my first year at Mosul, I had taken the responsibility of sending Ishak, then a lad, over to Persia to be educated. He had been hopefully converted there. Often from Mosul I had visited the Botan field. Just after Bishop Yoseph, not then of age, had been made a bishop, I found him one day in that churchyard at Shakh, alone, with a little manuscript book, to which he was adding proof-texts against Protestants. Deacon Eremia and myself talked and prayed with him, rejoicing that for any purpose he was studying the word of God. Still later, after Mr. Rhea's visit, the bishop and Ishak were so desirous of communing with our little church in Mosul that they came the long journey to Mosul, were examined and joined us in celebrating the dying love of Christ. Both have since witnessed a good profession. Mr. Rhea adds: "I now set my face toward Amidiah."

From Dayree, Amidiah, May 8, 1858, he alludes to the robbery of his muleteer: "He came well enough until within two hours of the town of Amidiah, when he stopped with a caravan in a kind of cave. About dusk a band of armed men, about ten in number, rushed suddenly into the cave, or rather under a great overhanging rock, at once bound the eyes of all the men of the caravan and tied their hands behind them. They emptied my traveling-bags of their contents, and took away the most valuable part of my wardrobe and a number of valuable books, with a number of articles of my attendants, amounting in value to about one hundred and seventy-five dollars. The men who attacked were Koords. Wandering parties are abroad; the bolder, as they are soon to return to their high pasture-grounds near Gawar. Selim Agha is a famous robber." In the list of lost articles, that of books is worthy of note: "two large account-books, in which all my accounts are kept; one Life of Martyn; one McCosh on the Divine Government; one Septuagint; one Hebrew Bible, written through in notes, meanings of words—and had probably spent a year of time upon it, and valued it highly."

After futile efforts to secure his lost books, priceless from association, he proceeded into the great mountains and passed through T'khoma, delaying there with favorable opportunity to preach. He toiled on through the mountains by T'khoma and Julamerk, and, June 11, he writes to me again from Gawar: I reached my home May 12. We feel anxious to hear how you made that long journey to Mardin, and how the ladies and little folks endured its toils. I spent some very pleasant days in Dayree in the shade of those fine old walnuts, though the cause of my detention was not the most agreeable. I was trying to find the thieves who plundered my brave muleteer, your old friend Mentor. Guergis jokingly said to him at Tel Keif, "They will stop you on the way." Seizing his dagger, he replied, somewhat indignantly, "Then why have I stuck this in my belt?" Poor fellow! How crestfallen he was when I met him! He looked as if he had been sick a

21 *

twelvemonth, so hardly had his great fright worn upon him. I suppose you can see the brave old Falstaff, and picture to yourself how he would deport himself among the thieves. He acknowledged that he told the Koords to take his load (a good haul, too), if only they would let him go.

I came up yesterday from Oroomiah. The other day I rode down from Seir, and Brother Cochran in his carriage, with his wife and five little chicks all dressed in white, came driving up and singing, "There is a happy land." It really seemed as if one of the chariots from above had come down.

God willing, I go down again in three weeks, to be there at the departure of our friends for America. I look forward to it as a very sad day. I would gladly escape it. How often I long for your joyous soul! Partings try me sorely. I can't bear them. I do not think enough of the glorious meetings just beyond. And is it not a very precious hope that we shall all one day be gathered in our Father's house? A brief moment, as the apostle would say—just a brief moment—and then the eternal weight of glory!

But shall I ever get home? I may prove a castaway. That always seemed to me one of the saddest words in the New Testament. A castaway! Plain old Saxon! How touching! how solemn!

I sit in our dining-room and look out upon the plain—a scene of rare loveliness; but Martha is not with me, and my heart is too heavy to enjoy it alone. I thought if I could only keep busy I should forget my loneliness; but there does not seem a moment when I am not conscious that my heart has been crushed and emptied of all but the sometimes trembling hope that God is my God and I am his child. I find myself continually thinking that dear Martha is sitting in our little bed-room, just where she always sat, and still I know it is not so; and I strangely go to the door and look in, and then chide myself.

I do long and pray that these quiet days may be richly blessed to me. Martha's grave is a very dear spot. Oh it was such a relief, after my long absence, to bow there and pour out my soul before Him who smote me!

GAWAR, *July* 25, 1858.

I reached my home yesterday from Oroomiah, the only object of my journey there being to bid farewell to Father Perkins, our good Sisters Stoddard and Fisk, and our young friends Lucy, Katy and Sarah. They left us Thursday, July 15. It was a sad day in our circle—a sad day to many Nestorian hearts. At an early hour the courts were filled with hundreds of Nestorian friends, men and women, who had come from all parts of the plain and from distant villages.

Just at noon all the mission sat down to dinner at Mr. Coan's. It was rather a flow of tears than a "flow of soul." Dinner over, Mr. Breath made a few very appropriate remarks on the one hundred and twentieth Psalm; then kneeling down, he led our devotions as we all bore our departing friends with swelling hearts into the arms of Infinite Love.

We then proceeded to the chapel, now overflowing with Nestorians, to have with them a parting word, a parting prayer. Mr. Perkins, much overcome and in a very affecting manner, took leave of the bishops, priests, helpers and all assembled. Tears flowed freely. Probably there was no dry eye in that large assembly.

The party started at once—the ladies in Mr. Cochran's wagon, to go as far as Gavalan, the girls in cajavas, the rest on horseback. A large crowd followed on for two miles, with many words of sympathy and invoking many prayers upon their departing friends. They halted a few minutes to give the Nestorians an opportunity of again saying farewell.

Mr. Cochran and myself accompanied the party as far as Salmas, spent the Sabbath with them, and took leave early Monday morning.

Dr. Perkins says: "Mr. Rhea proceeded to Oroomiah just in time to see me on the eve of my departure for America, in July, 1858. He then submitted to me for inspection a few sheets of a commentary which he had commenced on the Gospel of Matthew. I have hardly seen it surpassed in all the desirable attributes of a concise, rich and finished commentary. He now possessed the rarest and highest qualifications for every department of missionary labor. He was learned in ancient and Oriental lore, a writer of the finest style, prompt and efficient as a man of business, and a prince among preachers.

"Mr. Rhea kindly accompanied the departing band three days on our journey, and spent the Sabbath with us at the last Nestorian village, in Salmas. How sweet was our communion, during those last days, in the expectation that our next meeting would be in heaven, though the fact proved otherwise!"

The name of Eshoo, the brother of Tamo, will be remembered. To Dr. Perkins Mr. Rhea wrote: "You will be pained to hear of the death of our good old father Eshoo. He fell asleep—as I trust—in Jesus last Friday morning. His disease was bilious fever. I never saw any one so violently attacked. As he took his bed he remarked, 'I have no fear of death, not the least.' He spoke of his strong confidence in the Saviour and the good hope of salvation he had through grace. During his lucid intervals he was continually praying, not so much for health, as for grace, pardon, sanctification and meetness for heaven. Once he said to me, 'Perhaps I shall see Khanum;' another time he said, 'Let me ascend and see my Saviour, and Guergis and Khanum ("lady," i. e., Mrs. Rhea.) It was remarked by all that he seemed to be rapidly growing ripe for heaven this summer. I never witnessed such a scene of lamentation as we had the night of his death. I never saw Deacon Tamo give himself up so entirely to grief. The plaintive elegies which he sang impromptu as he hung upon the lifeless remains were very affecting.

"I feel very much as if I had lost a father. There was no Nestorian toward whom I felt a deeper attachment. There was a simplicity and artlessness, a depth of tenderness and kindliness in his natural character, but more than all he loved the Saviour with an unusual depth and warmth of affection."

He soon passed through the mountains again as far as to Amidiah. He there met the archbishop of the Jacobite Church, banished from Mosul, to whom in his distress he rendered some assistance.

October 26.—Having made the long return journey to Persia, he writes to Dr. Perkins from "Mt. Seir, Persia: Yesterday a thrill of joy ran through every heart here. What a flood of letters! Thank you, thank you for all your kind letters to me. I was already in debt. How delightful the privilege of canceling such debts! I unite with you first in thanksgivings for all that love and mercy which went before and accompanied you and the dear sisters and children every step of your way." And so he goes on charmingly. We cannot omit an extract as to the reason of his visit to Persia: "I came down to consult with the brethren about my location for the winter. We hear that Mr. Ambrose has actually sailed, but he will probably not reach us until after the middle of November. The mission meet this afternoon. I offer my services to go to Amidiah and labor this winter to be joined by Mr. Ambrose early in the spring."

October 29, from Gawar: I wrote you a hurried note from Amidiah. I then confidently hoped to spend the winter there; but my brethren, while they feel the great importance of occupying that post, do not consent to my being there alone. My heart-trouble seems to grow upon me. Dr. Wright thinks it best for me to spend the winter quietly in Oroomiah, and derive what benefit there is to be had from his counsel and aid.

I felt disappointed in not being able to carry out my plan; but if it is the will of the Master that I remain in Oroomiah this winter, I must be contented to do so. The society of those dear friends will be very pleasant and cheering to me after having been so much alone in the mountains.

Under the same date Mr. Rhea wrote to us, hoping that we had returned safely to Mosul from Mardin, two hundred miles north-west.

Friends in Hartford, her birth-place, had presented to Mrs. Marsh a superior melodeon. It had crossed Atlantic and Mediterranean safely to Smyrna, then by steamer safely to Scanderoon, thence through Aleppo, across the Euphrates, past Abraham's birth-place, and by the Tigris at Diarbekir. It had come out of the gates of Diarbekir, and was approaching Mardin. Its eight thousand miles of sea and land were safely completed to its very last stage. It had only once more to be lifted on to a mule's back to reach its expectant mistress in Mardin. When the melodeon should have appeared there, the muleteer entered and placed a bag down with about a bushel of screws, hinges, rods, and the lock and key. His brother, left in charge while he tended the mules, had probably lain down smoking; and, at any rate, when he returned from his mules he found his brother asleep and the box burning up! This will explain Mr. Rhea's allusions in the following letter to us:

" Very many thanks, and I hope this letter will find you and dear Wallie well and happy in your old home, none the less dear after your toilsome journeys and unsettled summer life. It was a great undertaking, that of yours, and if you are really home again, all safe, I shall join you in thanksgiving. How much seed you must have sown in that virgin soil! How many prayers you offered that the Lord would give the increase! And he will. Your sojourn there, I firmly believe, will be one day ascertained to be the instrumentality which God used to gather some of his jewels from the city of Mardin—perhaps some of those poor women. I have come to the conclusion that the world is not to be converted by telegraphs and steam and plenipotentiaries and pills, but by *prayer*. And oh how little, and how feebly and faithlessly and miserably we have prayed! Who of us can lay his hand upon his heart and say, I have prayed as I ought for my own soul, my servants, the dying about me? Oh sometimes I think I ought to spend whole days, and often too, in prayer for those for whom I am directly responsible! Has not the fallow ground at many a point been broken up in these lands? and why should not the great awakening extend even unto us?

" Thank you, Mrs. Marsh, for the beautiful hymns to which you called my attention. I shall always hereafter associate them with your name, and sing them with a new interest. I always feel sad when I think of the ignoble end to which your melodeon came. Just to think of that beautiful rosewood crackling in the flames, and all those mellifluous susceptibilities and capabilities ending in smoke! Mine stands mute and sorrowful in our little bedroom, more than almost everything else speaking to my heart of dear Martha. Oh, shall I ever sing with her the new song in heaven?"

December 9, 1858, he writes to me: I left Gawar upon

the arrival of your messenger from Mosul, and am now pleasantly situated at Seir (near Oroomiah), in the family of Mr. Cochran, the only family now at Seir. What changes since the last winter I spent here! My work will be aiding Brother Cochran in the seminary during the week, preaching in the villages of Baradost on the Sabbath. I am happy to announce the arrival of my associate, Mr. Ambrose, a capital man for the mountain field.

About this time, in a letter to Dr. Perkins, he mentions that he had recently spent three weeks in Gawar, and that he had not strength to teach two hours in the seminary, and was obliged to take but one. He also experienced for a few days so much trouble with his head that he feared he might have to throw up study entirely for a time. He was at work upon the Minor Prophets and Romans, and in his commentary had reached the twenty-seventh chapter of Matthew. The year (1858) closes with the earnest thought, "We work for coming ages;" and the winter months of the new year, 1859, find him longing for a revival, and believing in "a higher life soon *to be poured through* the nations."

March 24, 1859, from Seir, he says: Probably before I hear from you again I shall have taken leave of my missionary field and be on my way to America. You are aware that I have been for some years troubled with a cardiac difficulty. It has increased upon me; and what I had hoped was merely temporary and likely to yield to remedies employed here, now threatens to be organic in its character. Dr. Wright feels perfectly clear that I ought to leave for America at once and seek the best medical aid. This was quite unexpected to me; but I have no doubt it is best for me to follow his advice, though by no means sanguine as to any aid I may obtain.

We have many indications of good on the plain—revivals

at some points. I have just heard from Tamo at Memikan of considerable religious interest there. He reports fourteen who have come out on the Lord's side. Our work has never seemed more prosperous.

I hope I may find some relief in America and be permitted to resume my labors in the mountains. Even if I should find none, and still had the prospect of living a few years, I should much prefer to spend them on missionary ground.

If this messenger delays, I fear I may not hear from you before leaving. I shall always thank God that I was permitted to meet with your dear circle and enjoy so many pleasant hours with them; and I wish to assure you, my dear brother and sister, of the tender gratitude I shall always feel toward you for your sympathy and love while I was with you bereaved and sorrowing. Than yours the memory of no missionary brother and sister is more precious and dear to my heart; and I hope that our correspondence, which on your part has been so delightful for nearly eight years, will continue until the end.

Of his work at this time in Persia Dr. Perkins says: His labors (teaching in the male seminary and preaching in the villages) were much needed and very useful. His exegetical lectures on the Minor Prophets, delivered in the seminary that winter, appear substantially in his admirable notes, in Syriac, on those prophets as afterward published.

During this winter symptoms of disease became so serious in Mr. Rhea that our physician urged his immediate return to America as holding out the best and perhaps the only hope of recovery. He left the mission in April, 1859, a little more than eight years after first leaving his native land—eventful years of as unwearying toil, marked success, manifold self-denials, sacrifices and trials, and as rapid

22

growth, as are often crowded into that period of a missionary's life.

Mr. Rhea returned to America by way of England, and
was in London at the time of the spring anniversaries, where
he deeply interested some of the audiences by his thrilling
missionary addresses.

BEDOUIN SHEIK AND WIFE, ON DROMEDARY.

CHAPTER XVIII.

VISIT TO AMERICA.

MR. RHEA had spent eight years absent from favored America. The first three were mainly solitary. Then followed three blessed years of home life in a strange land, succeeded in contrast by two years the more inexpressibly lonely and desolate, crowded with privations and dangers and utmost self-denial, of arduous journeys in the highest and wildest regions inhabited by man. Now, by order of his beloved physician—who himself spent twenty-four years without return—he was on the way to America.

Few lingering in civilized lands can know the greatness of the change from the minaret and crescent to the steeple and cross—the mingled emotions of one returning under such circumstances. What a return from a land without a stage-coach, or steamer, or car, or gaslight, or native newspaper, or jury, to earth's highest civilization! from Moslem intolerance and grinding oppression to well-ordered freedom! from stagnation to life! from ages before the flood to the present day! in short, from Persia to London, New York! from Koordistan to Tennessee! How the heart leaped and thrilled! Well that it had the interval of a long journey by sea and land to allow it to anticipate varied possibilities and probabilities and grow calm.

On reaching Boston, in July, 1859, his health had become quite restored by the effect of his journey and voyage, and his whole appearance was so ruddy and hale that it was difficult to conceive of him as having been an invalid—a not uncommon nor undesirable experience of returned mis-

255

sionaries, though sometimes embarrassing to them, as exacting ones in the churches (not, as a rule, the largest con-
tributors) *must* know wherefore their missionaries have left
their field.

"At last he came to us in Tennessee," says an earnest
friend, "already improved in health, much changed by the
long, laborious years, so that no one could have said that
the dignified, entertaining traveler, whom some one
called a Persian patriarch, with his sun-browned face and
great, handsome beard, reaching half-way down his vest,
was identical with the blushing, modest youth that we had
known, though he was modest still and gentle as a woman.

"A few days after his arrival in Tennessee he came to
Jonesboro' to visit his aunt, Mrs. Luckey. The first day, in
taking a walk with Judge Luckey to see the changes and
improvements in his absence, he noticed a new brick house
and inquired, "Whose house is that?" Judge Luckey replied, "Dr. Cunningham's; and, by the way, Mrs. Cunningham was Mrs. Foster, of Knoxville memory. Would you
like to see her? Let us call." How our hearts burned
within us when we heard that Judge Luckey had brought
Mr. Rhea! It seemed a great thing. Missionaries in
Tennessee are not like missionaries in Massachusetts—an
every-day sight. We gazed upon him with wonder. We
took him by the hand, and looked into his eyes, and heard
him speak; a live missionary, for long years a resident of
the wild Koordish mountains in the heart of Asia, come
back to us! He seemed almost like a being of another
sphere, too; not that the savage associations of those sin-
darkened fastnesses had eclipsed any of the pure light of
his character, but the contrary. One might have thought
that he had spent the intervening years in some fine school
of morals and of manners, so pleasing and winning was his
address, so gentle and refined his tones and language.

" After that, he preached for us several times to the unspeakable delight of all who listened. After the first sermon, one good old lady remarked to another as they passed out of church, 'Did you ever hear such a preacher? What a pity he should waste himself upon the heathen !'

" During the winter following his return a gracious season of revival was enjoyed in the Jonesboro' church, and in a passing visit from Mr. Rhea some most solemn and thrilling sermons were preached, which greatly added to the awakening. The impression he made in the pulpit and out of it was that of a man of God whose conversation was in heaven. When he spoke upon the themes nearest his heart, such as union with Christ and holy living, his eye lit up with a softened fire, his features glowed and his brow radiated light, so that his countenance, thus animated and beaming, was an impressive sight to behold. I doubt not that many, if not all, that have heard him preach have noticed this peculiar radiance of his features—a rare and holy light. His voice was deep and full and rich, a fine bass in singing. His manner in the pulpit was without the slightest affectation, very animated, but very simple. He commanded attention and held it. It was impossible not to listen."

We return to Dr. Perkins' charming reminiscences: " Mr. Rhea remained in America about one year; a year as crowded and eventful as any one that he had spent on missionary ground. His influence and incessant labors among the churches were of the happiest kind, and made a very deep and lasting impression, particularly in Tennessee, his native State, where the subject of missions was less common but not less welcome than in New England.

" Early after his reaching America the kind hand of the Lord led our brother to the acquaintance of Miss Sarah Jane Foster of Jonesboro', Tennessee, the lady who is now

22 *   R

his deeply-stricken widow, and whom he had known in childhood. Of her eminent fitness for the missionary work, and not less eminent fitness to bless the home of such a man, we dare not trust ourselves to speak as our feelings would prompt, for she is still among the living. I may be pardoned, however, in hazarding the remark that few unions are formed in this world where tastes are more congenial or affection more deep and abiding."

Much correspondence evincing Mr. Rhea's deep spirituality during this American visit must be omitted, as has been much of former years, lest our volume be unduly large. Brief hints alone can be given.

January 23, 1860.—Having started northward, he mentions at Marion, Tennessee, 'a kind welcome, union congregations of Presbyterians and Methodists, an extra meeting to hear more about Persia on Monday, cordial grasps of his hand and Christian sympathy.

He next dates from Washington City, January 25, 1860.— Mentions cordial welcome from the representatives of his State in Congress—Nelson and Maynard—alludes to the eloquence of Corwin and failure of Keitt; heard Jefferson Davis speaking dryly in the Senate Chamber, and was introduced to some Christians in Congress.

He next writes from New York, January 27, 1860: I came directly to Dr. H——'s, and met a warm greeting. Here I am perfectly at home, and were you with me would be completely happy. Life is a constant self-sacrifice. "If any man will come after me, let him deny himself!" He whose we are, to whom we have unitedly and with whole-hearted devotion consecrated our entire being, demands an entire self-renunciation. This is his right—our will completely merged in his. This done, there are opened up in the soul depths of peace and blessedness unspeakable. We give all and take all. We get far more of earth and earthly good than otherwise, even the hundred-fold. Will he not with Him freely give us all things?

He speaks with delight of a call from Mr. Cobb, afterward missionary to Persia:

"And who do you think came in while we were talking? Father Perkins! He looks remarkably well; preaches here to-morrow; thinks he may be able to go out with us. Isn't that pleasant? but we may be disappointed, so we will not think about it too much."

"NEW YORK, *Jan.* 31, 1860.

"How I long for quiet repose far away from these rattling stages, jingling car-bells and the noise of a hard, money-loving, money-making world! But there are pure and noble hearts, thousands of them, in this great city, whose lives of humble effort in self-denying love for the poor and sorrowing send up a rich and precious incense to the Master. Oh, I long to forget myself! I want a heart beating in sympathy with every human heart. I want to throw the mantle of charity over the frailties of every fellow-man and love them, for there is something to love in every one."

The following letters will give some idea of the whirling, crowded life which missionaries are often obliged to lead in America:

"PALMER, MASS., *Saturday, Feb.* 4, 1860.

"While waiting for the train I am writing with a pencil an inch long, my hat for a table, and plenty of folks around. Left New York at 8 A. M., reached Amherst at 4; was met at the depôt by my Brother Brainerd. How glad we both were! I found Father Perkins at Palmer. We were to be guests of Professor Tyler, so we went whirling there in Mr. Thompson's sleigh. Went over Wednesday night and saw how my brothers were situated. Called at Professor Hitchcock's. What an interesting old couple, so very cordial and kind! I did not tell you what a good man Professor Tyler is, and what a warm-hearted, earnest missionary wife he has. But all at Amherst and South Hadley are missionary."

We learn from Dr. Perkins that while in America Mr. Rhea attended the ordination of the Rev. A. L. Thompson, of Amherst, Massachusetts, who had been designated to the Nestorian mission. The marriage of Mr. and Mrs. Thompson was solemnized in the church of East Amherst at the close of the ordaining services. Mr. Rhea, not sure that he would be able to be present, had declined a prominent part in the exercises, but on his arrival he was requested to make the concluding prayer. Few who heard that melting prayer will ever lose the impressions of it. No part of the services was more touching and thrilling. In the rush of memories of the past and foreshadowings of the future, after commending the consecrated pair to God in other relations, he feelingly said, "And when they are called to part, for part they must," etc., an allusion that brought tears to many eyes, and was almost a prophetic foreboding, as the sorrowful sequel proved; for in about seven months from that time, and within two months after reaching his field, Mr. Thompson was suddenly cut down in the buoyancy of his youth, leaving his still more youthful and not less joyous bride in the deep shadows of widowhood.

Mr. Rhea writes from Amherst, Massachusetts, February 4, 1860: "I am driven to death, trying to do in five days what should not be done in less than ten. This morning I was scribbling a note on my hat in a railway car, and now, at ten and a half, Saturday night, shall I resume the thread which the whirl of the engine snapped in two? Thursday dined with the council which had been examining Mr. Thompson. Made some pleasant acquaintances among the

New England clergy. After dinner the church in East Amherst was packed—forty-six from Mount Holyoke. Dr. McEwen, pastor of Miss Wood, at Enfield, preached the sermon, perfectly delighted at the idea of his church sending out a missionary. Dr. Stearns offered the ordaining prayer, Mr. Woodward, the pastor, gave the charge, Dr. Perkins the right hand of fellowship. All these services were ably performed, deeply interesting, and listened to by a deeply sympathetic assembly. Then followed another scene—the youthful missionaries stood in the aisle; there was deep stillness; holy vows were assumed, and they were pronounced man and wife; then followed the missionary hymn, and services were closed by prayer by the younger Persian brother."

Thursday night he preached at the college, "Lengthen thy cords, strengthen thy stakes," etc. He also was desired to preach on the Sabbath, February 5, 1860, and says: "Rose under deep depression of spirits. How shall I get through the labor of the day! It was trying to preach before the president and faculty and three hundred students, but I tried to remember that there was One present, and but One whom I should fear—for whose approval or disapproval I should at all care. I had freedom. At half-past one preached missionary sermon in East Amherst; dined with Dr. Belden; took tea with President Stearns, and, as it was monthly concert, addressed the students for forty minutes on missions. Never spoke with more freedom extempore; began with much trembling, but was wonderfully carried through.

Let us be instant in prayer. My life is too prayerless. How unfavorable is this running to and fro for the cultivation of the heart! I can hardly find time for prayer and reading the Bible, but I must find time. How weary I am of visiting! Not that I do not meet some of the most lovely

Christian spirits in the world, but I long for quiet; I long to have time to think on my own ways, to talk with Him whom our souls love.

I went to my brothers' room, sat a while with them, prayed with them. They are good brothers; love me much; have taken a good stand as to scholarship and moral character; both, I trust, Christians. How much I love them! How I long to be more with them!

Of a visit to Mount Holyoke, riding over in a sleigh with his brothers: "Miss Fiske met me at the door;—went into her room; there we sat and chatted most pleasantly. How I shrunk back from having three hundred pairs of eyes fixed on me as I entered the dining-hall! Chatted away till five, then drove down to Smith's Ferry, over the river, took cars, and was in Westfield by seven P. M. Spent the evening at Mrs. Stocking's, the night at Mrs. Perkins'. Returned Saturday to Amherst." From Amherst he proceeded to Boston, and writes from "Albany, February 9, 1860. Reached Boston, Monday at four; five minutes at mission rooms; just time to get to Andover depôt; reached Andover at seven; guest of Prof. Shedd; saw Lucy and Katy Wright, and gave them the kisses which I brought nearly ten months ago from their dear parents.

"Tuesday morning heard Prof. Park lecture. Went out and spent the night with Dr. Anderson. He and Mrs. A. are patriarchal, and I love them.

"Dr. Anderson and I talked over our mountain Nestorians. The Prudential Committee are very desirous that I, with Messrs. Cobb and Ambrose, begin the new station at Amidiah, on the score of my 'extensive experience' in that region. The time for our sailing will probably be the last of June. With a nice house in Amidiah, associates so refined, hearts so loving, and a work so angelic to do for our Master, we shall, or ought to, be the happiest of mortals.

I long to be there. I think of you more and more as a brave-hearted woman, able to meet any emergency. In giving your life for a dying world, you have made the purest and noblest disposition of it which is possible. Let our standard be simply Christ. I love to ask myself continually, If Christ were here, how would he act? and then try to act just as gently, kindly, nobly, truly, independently as he would.

"I spent nearly all day yesterday helping Mr. and Mrs. Thompson buy their India-rubber clothes, saddles, etc., etc. I left Boston at three, reached Albany at eleven P. M."

"HOMER, N. Y., *February* 11, 1860.

"I left Albany accompanied by Dr. H.; traveled all night; reached Syracuse at five, and Homer at half-past ten A. M. I have been forcibly reminded of my winter home in the mountains. Oh, how it blew yesterday! How cutting these northern blasts! How they bite and sting! For some days my lungs were sore, a thing unusual with me; now relieved.

"I had some sad hours to-night on the way from Albany. Once I bent forward and, resting my head on the car-seat before me, wept bitterly over past unfaithfulness—infinite unworthiness. It seemed as if I must yet pass through deeper and deeper waters before I reach those peaceful shores. Oh that I could feel His presence every moment, and that his Spirit would guide my every thought, my every written and spoken word!

"We will put our hands into the hands of Jesus, and we will beg him to guide and shield and love us unto the end. Are we not his? And if we have followed him afar off, and wounded him, will he cast us off for ever? Can he not again embrace us, forgive, and heal, and cleanse us? I long to know that you are kept in perfect peace, stayed on him. Oh, he is unspeakably lovely! How can we follow him *afar off!*"

And now Mr. Rhea moves again to his own sunny South; breezes soften, skies brighten, spring appears. March 1 finds him in the country at Union, Tennessee, making a temperance address.

ROGERSVILLE, TENN., *March* 22, 1860.

Preached last night to a large and attentive congregation. Pray that the seed sown may spring up unto everlasting life. Reached Russellville at nine—pleasant ride. Left there at noon. Oh what a ride in that hack, sixteen miles; five hours of jolting, worse than a camel's back by far, and worse than all it must be repeated! Am to preach to-night.

If my Master will only give me his smiles it is sweet to labor for him. How great my wants! and yet there is not one thing I need he cannot and will not give me. What a precious assurance—able to do exceeding abundantly above all we can ask or think! I believe it. I embrace the promise—it is mine—but my great difficulty is not unbelief—it is spiritual numbness—deadness. Oh I pant for a new, fresh divine life! Will not Jesus give it to me?

BLOUNTSVILLE, *April* 19.

To-morrow I start for Cold Spring with father—spend the night with Colonel McClellan. I shall be glad when it is over. There is a publicity—an ostentation—what shall I call it?—a kind of parade about missions and missionaries from which I shrink. I wish to go along gently and un-obtrusively—to take the lowest place and do my Master's work. I am often addressed as if I were doing some great thing. It pains me—for often it requires more grace to live to God in small things than in great—as much to be perfectly kind, gentle, patient, forbearing, charitable, prompt, punctual, forgiving in the little sphere of the family circle, as to enter upon some great undertaking. It is harder to rule one's own spirit, keep down its pride, and envy, and vanity, and anger, and censoriousness, and indolence, and malice, and rule it into all the sweet and loving and Christlike tempers, than to take a city.

April 24.—We had a good visit at Cold Spring, the finest portion of our country—staid old citizens—good Presbyterian stock. I preached Saturday and Sabbath mornings; on missions in the evening; also preached yesterday morning.

When I reached the depôt I found no one there to bring me home; and I set out courageously on foot, met the buggy and Uncle Jerry (colored). This was a relief. There were kisses waiting me at home—mother and four sisters. We spent the evening around the fireside, all quiet, pleasant, each one seeming to enjoy him and herself. If our Father please, it will not be long until you will be with us and one of us. I rehearsed my travels, John his. We ate candy and chatted on.

Mr. Rhea and Miss S. J. Foster were married in the Jonesboro' church, Thursday evening, April 26, 1860.

"Mr. Rhea's delightful home," says Mrs. Rhea, "with father and mother, five brothers and four sisters, was twenty miles above Jonesboro', a little off the railroad. The day after our wedding I entered it for the first time. That abode of filial love seemed to me a little type of heaven. In my own lone orphanage I had never known such a genial domestic atmosphere, a home of so many diverse members, and yet such union and concord. The father, like faithful Abraham, of whom God said, 'I know him, that he will command his children and his household after him;' the mother, ruling by gentleness; and the brothers and sisters, each looking, not on his own, but the things of

23

others, in honor preferring one another; and, as it seemed
to me, putting brother Samuel, the eldest, at the head and
in the centre, as the one whom all delighted to honor,
and whom, by common consent, they all loved first and
best.

"I pass over the scenes of parting from our two dear
homes—the agony, the weeping. There are some who
think that missionaries have less feeling than other people,
and that *they* could never endure the separation. It is not
easy to flesh and blood. Even the Saviour did not prove
it easy, or wish it to be easy, when he declared, Whosoever
loveth father or mother more than me is not worthy of me.

"I pass over many last visits and farewell words from
Southern circles and at the North, especially at my *Alma
Mater*, Mount Holyoke Female Seminary.

"The last Sabbath we spent in our native land was at
Andover, where our large party received a formal charge
from Dr. Anderson in the chapel of the Theological Seminary. The last night we passed at Dr. Anderson's house
in Roxbury, where we enjoyed delightful intercourse with
that good man and his good wife.

"We sailed from Boston in the *Smyrniote*, July 3, 1860."

CHAPTER XIX.

RETURN TO PERSIA.

THE morning of July 2, 1860, found on the deck of the barque *Smyrniote* a large reinforcement for the Nestorian mission. The company consisted of Mr. and Mrs. Rhea, Mr. and Mrs. Labaree, Mr. and Mrs. Cobb, and Dr. Young; besides Mr. and Mrs. Burbank, destined to the Eastern Turkey mission.

Mr. Rhea was recognized by common consent as the leader of that well-selected band. It is not easy to overestimate the importance of the influence which such a leader exerts on his younger brethren and sisters on their way to the field. The value of such a missionary model and guide as Mr. Rhea—who came as near the beau-ideal of both as ever did a mortal—in smoothing the roughness of the way and happily initiating the inexperienced to Oriental scenes and circumstances, will never cease to be remembered by every individual who accompanied him.

Just before sailing Mr. Rhea had written from Mount Holyoke to Dr. Perkins:

"Those bitter farewells over, I turn my eyes longingly toward my own chosen home and work, though I know no smooth seas nor flowery paths await me: a life of labor, trials and conflicts till the summons comes."

Mrs. Rhea adds: "In a few hours we were all wretchedly sea-sick, and continued more or less so; not entirely because our passage was a rough one, but because of the smell of bilge-water, mixed with the leakage of rum-barrels in the hold, which continued day and night. . We were nineteen days from Boston to Gibraltar, and thirty-one from Gibraltar to Smyrna. Our voyage through the Mediterranean was specially tedious, from calms and adverse winds. Mr. Rhea was nauseated all the time, and ate almost nothing from Boston to Smyrna. Yet he was patient and good-natured, and ready for every good word and work. Several hours of each day he devoted to biblical study, committing the Psalms of David and many sweet hymns to memory, which he would repeat to me as we walked the deck. He also read Bushnell's Nature and the Supernatural, Tayler Lewis' Divine and Human in the Scriptures, McCosh's Typical Forms and Special Ends in Creation and Intuitions of the Mind, The Elohim Revealed, Tennyson's Idyls, Reviews of the Classics and Geographical References, and other books, besides teaching a class in Syriac, which we all began to learn at sea. And through all those days I can bear witness to the earnest cravings of his soul, described in Matt. v. 6: Blessed are they which do hunger and thirst after righteousness.

"When our ship touched the land at Smyrna, the first news we heard was of the horrible massacres in Mount Lebanon."

That was a terrible welcome! Many thousands in the "goodly mountain" and at Damascus butchered in cold blood! Writing from Constantinople, Mr. Rhea alludes to some slight retribution: "The news from Syria yesterday was startling. Ahmed, Pasha of Damascus, one of the greatest pashas of the Empire, with a number of the wealthiest and most influential men of Damascus, who were the instigators of the late massacre, were shot down like dogs in the public square! French troops were in Beyroot; but the French general, a determined man, went up to Damascus and demanded it. Some expect an uprising of the Moslems; I think the Turk, stunned by such events, will fold his hands and bow to his inevitable fate. We take the Austrian steamer."

Mrs. Rhea proceeds: "Such was our greeting on the Asiatic coast, the rude continent in which our future lots were cast. In Constantinople we were detained a month. We were the guests of Dr. and Mrs. Dwight, then in the Bebek Seminary, now Robert College. We also visited in the families of Drs. Goodell, Schauffler, Riggs, and Messrs. E. and I. Bliss and Washburn. What happy days! What princes of the chosen tribes those reverend men seemed to our admiring eyes! Their manners most refined and courteous, yet transparently simple and childlike, every one; their hands full of work, their heads full of learning and experience, the elder crowned with gray hairs and covered with honor. Yet all their hearts as fresh and kind and overflowing as we ought to expect great, ripened hearts to be, that had so long held and dispensed the love of Christ. After we had passed a social hour, singing with the genial-hearted Dr. Goodell, one evening, he turned to me and said in his own animated and peculiar way, 'Do all you can to cheer up your good husband; keep him singing! You and he, in your Persian home, and we here, will go singing on till the Master calls, and then we will go singing home, and sing together there perhaps these very songs!' Oh blessed thought, that we shall sing together there! We who have *so loved* to sing together here!

"A very pleasant incident connected with our stay in Constantinople was the meeting with old friends and Tennessee acquaintances in the family of Colonel Williams, our United States Minister. We greatly enjoyed their cordial hospitality and kindness to us personally, and all the more highly on account of the very excellent repute of our American representative among all parties, and their special

23 *

friendly and social relations to the families of the missionaries, who were usually invited to spend a day every fortnight at Colonel Williams' house. At last, after many days
of pleasant waiting, we took our leave for the regions beyond."

Mrs. Rhea affords us views of the latter part of her
tedious four months' journey from America:

"A prosperous voyage of three days in a fine steamer,
brought us to Trebizond, on the Black Sea,* September 24.
The first night there, when I turned back the clothes of the
bed which I had spread on the floor of an unfurnished room
of the mission-house, I quickly dropped them again and
started back, for there was a scorpion! I gathered myself
trembling into my camp-chair, and waited for Mr. Rhea.
It was a long time; and when he came how sad he looked!
The Armenian pastor, Baron Hagop, had just given the
gentlemen Oroomiah letters announcing the death of Mr.
Thompson! What a shock this gave us! This solemn call
came home to our hearts. Thus our long land-journey began in gloom and sorrow. *Why* was he taken, so young, so
promising, just entering on his work?

"The first Sabbath out of Trebizond, as we kept holy
time in solemn worship, and our sanctuary was the little
tent, Mr. Rhea read to us from the Sacred Scriptures about
the great I AM, the sovereign God who ruleth among the
armies of heaven and the inhabitants of earth, and whose
thoughts are not as our thoughts, nor his ways as our ways;
whose resources are boundless, whose work is infinite, whose
plans are irreversible, whose chosen spheres of labor, of usefulness and of honor for his faithful and beloved servants
may be far wider than we can measure, and higher than we
can reach; and we were comforted to think that even the
untimely death of our young associate did not prove any
thwarting of God's eternal plan, either in regard to that in-

* See illustration on page 39.

dividual laborer or to our precious work—more precious still to Him who died for its accomplishment.

"Mr. Rhea was our leader on the way. The land-journey from Trebizond to Oroomiah is performed on horseback. We had only caravan animals, and a sorry set they were. We also had one pair of cajavas (panniers) in which two ladies rode by turns. The horse of one gentleman, or another, of our party, used to come down to the ground about every day, and all of us got over the mountain only by dint of patience and hard driving. Two Nestorians, returning from Constantinople to Oroomiah, helped about the tents, meals, etc. Mr. Rhea made ready in Boston some boxes, with separate compartments for plates, knives and forks, and cups and saucers, flour, sugar, salt, tea and coffee, kettles, frying-pan, etc., etc. We had two tents, which we made into four sleeping-rooms, by curtaining. Mr. Rhea slept with his watch under his head and matches near. Soon after three o'clock A. M. he would call from the tent for the mulcteers to begin to feed their horses and the Nestorians to make fire for breakfast. Then a busy scene ensued. We would all get up and dress as fast as we could, fold the bed-clothes, roll up the beds, pack them into large bags, which were carried outside the tents to afford us breakfast room within. Then the table-cloth was spread on the carpet and the tin plates rattled down, and soon we were seated around on the tent floor, with keen appetites and grateful hearts. We could get milk and eggs, and occasionally chickens, and the traveling-chests afforded the rest.

"After breakfast, enlivened by much cheerful conversation, the dishes were carried off to be washed, and Mr. Rhea drew out his pocket Bible, reading a daily portion, followed by a hymn, for we were all singers, and a prayer, in which we craved the blessing and protection of our great Leader through the dangers and exposures of the day.

"Then the lunch was prepared, the dishes counted and packed and adjusted, while everybody dashed about here and there in the din of Babel. Muleteers, stubborn, lazy, unaccommodating, never ready to start and never willing to hurry, cursing and swearing, reviling and beating their woebegone horses and grumbling about the loads; while we, very uncomfortable and impatient to get off, with riding-skirts dragging in the wet grass, are walking about, leading our horses, watching them lest they fight, and trying to guard loose articles from the thievish villagers, who by this time, accompanied by yelping dogs of every description, have gathered around in giggling, gaping crowds to look at us and steal whatever they can find.

"At last, however, the cajavas lead the way, and we are off, greeted perhaps by the rising sun, or glad if we can even a little anticipate his ardent beams. The scenery for a few days from Trebizond is mountainous and very fine; afterward monotonous. We pine for trees, but only a few, with willows here and there upon the water-courses, appear. We should pass the filthy, half-subterranean villages without suspecting their existence, were they not pointed out by Mr. Rhea or announced by the wolfish dogs."

At the foot of a mountain range between Trebizond and Ararat stands the city of Erzeroom, the chief city on the route to Persia, to which reference will also be found in Mr. Rhea's first journey to Persia, p. 41. To Christians it has the additional interest arising from its occupation as a station by the missionaries of the American Board. It stands on the verge of a large and beautiful plain, near one of the streams which unite to form the Euphrates; and though this plain lies six thousand feet above the sea-level, from it the eye looks up to higher peaks that stand crowned with never-melting snow. Commanding the main thoroughfare to Persia, it was once a fortified city of im-

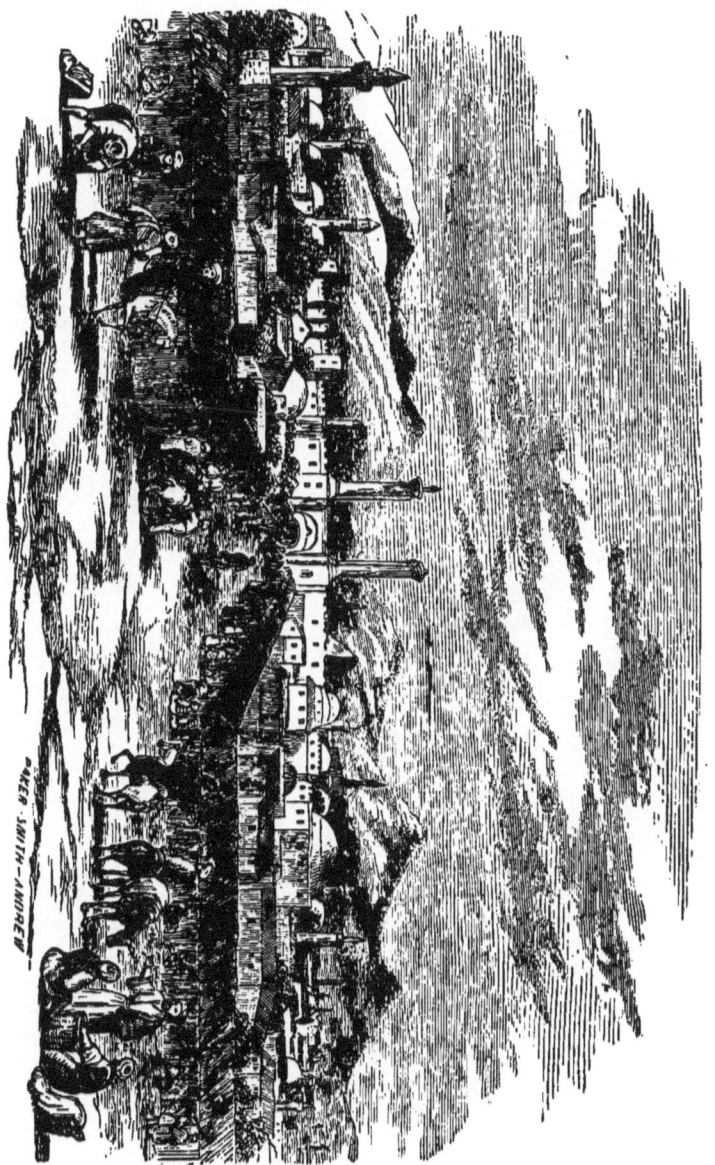

FREETOWN.

BAKER SMITH ANDREW

S

portance, and the old walls still stand in part, though the
city has outgrown its ancient limits and barriers. Like
other Eastern cities, though fair without it is filthy within,
yet a place of deep interest as a centre of trade and influence. It has a population of sixty thousand.

"I rode mostly in the cajavas," says Mrs. Rhea, "chang-
ing to the saddle when tired. A lady or some heavy box
balanced me on the other side. Mr. Rhea was generally
near, looking out safe paths for the cajava horse, where
the road was narrow, steep or rough; and with this protection I could feel safe and easy enough to cushion my weary
head on a pillow and sleep, though helplessly boxed up
and tied on the back of a stumbling horse.

"Much of the time we dreaded Koords. When we entered a narrow mountain pass, or turned a sudden corner,

MOUNT ARARAT.

or saw dark objects over a hill, or met horsemen, we would
think they were upon us. Mr. Rhea's calm trust in the

protecting Hand that led us through those wild and dangerous regions did much to comfort and reassure us, and through that guiding Power we were safely kept."

The following allusions to Ararat will please all who delight to think of that famous mountain whose name is indelibly associated with the ark and flood.

"We are now encamped on the great plain of Moolah Sooleiman, and Mount Ararat is in sight, lifting a snowy, dazzling cone above the distant mountains, very beautiful indeed aside from its sublime associations. Passed shrubs in brilliant autumn colors, an orchard of real apple trees, brooks very clear, the bottoms lined with pebbles in gay mosaics.

" *October* 13.—Got up very early, thinking to have an early start; but had to wait. It was a glorious sunrise over Ararat, the soft, purple twilight of the hills becoming pink, and then resplendent with golden hues, and finally all dazzling in the full light of the mighty sun."

That evening the gentlemen bathed in the Euphrates. They passed the Sabbath there at the poorest and meanest village they had seen. On Sabbath morning villagers gathered at the tent door, talked with Mr. Rhea, and received some Bibles. Afterward he preached in Syriac to the men.

October 16.—They passed an imposing Armenian structure, contrasting strikingly with the mean huts, its "corner-stone said to have been laid by St. Gregory fifteen hundred years ago!"

They met a Koordish dignitary, his attendants with long spears on fine horses, now and then one dashing out off the road, scouring in a cloud of dust over the plain, galloping like the wind, with incredible speed. It was beautiful indeed. The chief was very distinguishable by his grand air and scarlet robe and jewels. As we passed, the head horseman of our party, without knowing it, dropped from his saddle a bag containing valuables worth forty or fifty dollars. After an hour it was missed, to his utter consternation. With tears and entreaties Mr. Rhea and Babillo were prevailed on to return while we pursued our journey and pitched camp at Drodeen.

Before night Mr. Rhea returned successful. They came upon the Koords just beyond the Three Churches. The Koordish chief commanded restoration. The finder denied having seen the bundle, but finally brought it out, to the great joy of the chevadar, who presented a pistol to the Koordish chief, and returned along the road singing, where he had before gone weeping and mourning.

October 18.—The company reached the dividing line between Turkey and Persia. They formed and passed the line all abreast, with joyful and grateful feelings singing a hymn of praise to God.

October 22.—They came upon a beautiful village; fenced orchards; apricots and other fruit trees in regular rows; sycamores, willows and English walnuts in abundance; fields of castor oil bean and cotton; a higher civilization bursting upon them like a glimpse of the trees and gardens of Paradise.

October 23.—Crossed a plain white with salt. A neighboring mountain glistened with salt embattlements. Another singular range had oblique-striped strata, brown and red. On passing the boundary we were interested in the improvement of the scenery and houses, and in the people, the latter looking more cleanly and intelligent. When Mr. Rhea pointed out to us Nestorian villages on the plain of Salmas, our journey seemed near its end. But they must first learn the blessings of free America by a little despotic experience. Our boxes, containing household articles and clothing—all we possessed—being unjustly detained by the custom-house officials at Khoy, who refused to give them

24

up to a servant, Mr. Rhea was obliged to return after them in person.

The journal continues: "So I am left alone. Came in sight of the Lake of Oroomiah. Above it hangs a beautiful rainbow." The next day they reached Gavalan, and, by hard riding till several hours after midnight, Mr. Rhea rejoined them, the boxes still detained at Khoy. "At Gavalan we were greeted by many demonstrations of affection by the people for whose sakes we had left our native land. The next day, October 25, riding in the rain, we met, about noon, Mr. Coan and Mr. Shedd coming to greet us. The sight cheered us, and fresh horses made the last half of that day's journey the most pleasant of all.

"After the hardships and exposures of the journey the mission-houses seemed like a paradise. Every little comfort was a luxury unspeakable. Mr. Breath, Mr. Coan, Mr. Shedd and Miss Rice, and the pupils of the Female Seminary occupy mud houses, which, with the mud printing establishment and chapel, face upon a court partly paved and partly of grass, with sycamore trees whitebarked and very tall. The houses have flat roofs; the mud floors are carpeted. The houses look not at all like anything in America, but the rooms seem pleasant and homelike. We were very cordially welcomed and hospitably entertained."

Thus the new-comers found entrance to Persia, and Mr. Rhea returned to his blessed labors for Christ.

TRAVELING IN PERSIA IN THE CAJAVAH.

CHAPTER XX.

M R. AND MRS. RHEA, with their companions, reached Oroomiah October 25, 1860. Death had made one vacant place in the mission in the removal of Mr. Thompson while this reinforcement was on the way; and this, with the impaired health of several others, and the exigencies of the work in Persia, soon determined the location of Mr. Rhea at Oroomiah as his future residence, rather than in Koordistan. After a day or two of resting with associates, who, as well as the natives, seemed delighted at his return, Mr. Rhea started for Tabreez to get orders from the consul to recover the boxes. In his absence Mrs. Rhea began housekeeping in Dr. Perkins' house at Seir, with Mr. and Mrs. Labaree for boarders. While the good wife is busy and waiting, and, at a glance from her window at Mount Seir, taking in the plain and the city and Oroomiah Lake and the many mountains, some near Tabreez, seventy or eighty miles away, yet hardly ever out of sight in that clear air, Mr. Rhea is writing the following letter:

TABREEZ, PERSIA, *Nov.* 4, 1860.

MY DEAR PARENTS: You will be surprised to see that I am again so soon many miles from my home. I had hardly been in Oroomiah a week when it was thought best that I should come to Tabreez to the English consul, to endeavor to get his aid in rescuing our boxes from the clutches of the custom-house officers.

I am spending the Sabbath with Nicholas, an Armenian,

who many years ago was in the families of our missionaries. I had prayers with the family this morning in Syriac. Other than this I have attended no public service for the worship of God; in fact, there has been no other in this city of one hundred thousand inhabitants. They are in the blindness and bigotry of Mohammedanism, which still reigns with unbroken sway in all this Empire. It has been my privilege to pray for this city; and that is all I can do. When will the sound of the church-going bell break upon the death-like stillness which hangs over it? When will multitudes throng these streets on their way to the courts of the Most High? I think of you to-day—our dear church and pastor, your songs of praise, your holy worship, all your privileges. Why has the Sun of righteousness risen upon you in such beauty and glory, and all so dark here? Ah, my heart bleeds and my eyes weep, and I ask, Why do his chariot wheels delay his glorious coming? Pray for me that I may be found in my lot at my post, faithful at his coming, and that I may so watch for souls that I may give my account with joy and not with grief. What a difference between this place and the plain of Oroomiah! Here all is silent as the grave; no spiritual movement, no inquiry about the soul and its deathless interests. There, in more than thirty villages, Christ is preached, and in every village there are witnesses to the power of the gospel to sanctify and save.

I can't express to you my great joy in being restored to my work. Not that it was joy to leave you, for it was a bitter cup, but I am thankful for all God's tender care of me and my dear wife and my companions in travel over a wide and stormy sea, and our land-journey with its many exposures and dangers, and that I am once more where I humbly hope his providence designed me to be. I preached my first sermon last Sabbath; text, " Is the Lord among us or not?" It was an affecting occasion to me, and I was enabled to speak with great freedom, considering that I had not preached in Syriac for a year and a half. How much I suffered in America from my inability to preach extempore! Here I have not the slightest difficulty.

Afternoon.—Since writing I have had a short service in Syriac; one of my congregation, a Nestorian woman, who lives with the consul; there were also three poor men, who, with sixty other Nestorians returning from Russia, where they had spent the summer harvesting, were robbed a few days ago of all their earnings in a Mohammedan village on the way. I talked to them of the treasure hid in the field. Oh that they might find it!

"He soon returned," says Mrs. Rhea, "bringing the boxes and a present for me, a Persian carpet from Tabreez."

Just here let us give place to one who doubtless often took his position on that flowery carpet.

Mr. Labaree says: "My first winter in Persia was spent in Mr. Rhea's family. Very many were the delightful conversations we had together on spiritual themes, in all of which he took high ground and advanced views. His was not a faith that was satisfied with touching simply the outside of gospel truths, and especially of practical Christian doctrine, but it penetrated to the inner core, devoutly appropriating to his own spiritual wants their purest riches. This faith enabled him to accept unhesitatingly many forms of truth at which another might stumble. Reason was too slow for him on many subjects, and not so satisfactory as a simple faith in the plain, pregnant statement of God's word, even when he could not follow with a logical argument. He used to say that he had little confidence in *reasoning* with an infidel; unless there was some faith at the start, arguments were of small account. His faith in Christ as a loving and personal Saviour was only equaled by the intensity and purity of his consecration to him. He was very fond of conversation in which the character of the Divine Redeemer or his relation to his followers was the subject; always ready to turn from the most distracting and absorbing cares to these serene themes as those most natural to him. Nor was there anything of affectation in his religious conversation. However simple a remark he might make, his manner of utterance showed that it came from his heart, his earnestness and fervor forbidding it to seem trite.

"His faith was not merely characteristic of his modes of Christian believing, but was equally fervid with reference to his whole missionary life and work. He had great confidence in the power and success of the gospel. He never hesitated to sow beside all waters from any misgivings as to the hardness and unfruitfulness of the soil. He was ready to preach the gospel to every class and to every nationality, however unpromising the case might seem to human view.

"One bleak winter day we were caught in a terrible storm as we were on our way up to Seir, and with difficulty managed to reach a Musselman village, where we obtained shelter till the storm was over. During the most of our stay he was engaged in an earnest religious conversation with the head of the house, who was only an ordinary peasant. The fanatical intolerance of Mohammedanism in Persia naturally discourages the missionary from much serious labor with the bigoted followers of the false prophet, but it did not deter him from preaching salvation by Christ only, nor from hopefulness as to the results of such labor.

"I remember at one of our annual meetings, when the question of missionary labor for Mohammedans was under discussion, and those who preceded him had taken the ground that no special efforts were called for, and none practicable. Mr. Rhea led off very warmly in opposition, urging more attention to the acquisition of the Turkish language on the part of the missionaries, that they might be able to preach the gospel to Musselmans at every opportunity, adding, with emphasis, with the full design of converting their souls. There will be no toleration, he continued, until it is called for; and we must have faith that there will be converts here in Persia. In the spirit of this sentiment, in his subsequent intercourse with Mohammedans, which became very considerable, he was always forward to introduce religious conversation, with great tact and prudence, leading them to the most disastrous admissions respecting their own religion, when he would in contrast exhibit the more rational grounds of Christian belief.

"Few men had a happier faculty for such kind of missionary labor than had Mr. Rhea. His conversational powers were of a superior order. He possessed an elasticity of mind and a fluency of speech that gave freshness and charm to all he said, whatever the subject he touched."

We left Mrs. Rhea at Seir, only having to lift her eye at her front windows to see a semicircle with a radius of seventy miles from her centre. She had just received her carpet, and her husband was safe at home again. She proceeds:

"We were soon settled at our winter routine; Mr. Rhea assisting Mr. Cochran in the Seminary and preaching in the villages; the new-comers busy, of course, learning the language. Oh, what hard work it was!—how dark and unget-at-able! The sounds of those letters, the deep guttural *khaite*; the sharp, wiry, twanging *tate*; the broad, swallowing *kope*, especially! And then the genders for everything! The nouns declined and the verbs conjugated, with peculiar terminations all through for gender! We expected, of course, to commit words to memory, but who had ever counted the cost of those jaw-breaking and throat-splitting letters? And who had ever expected to learn two languages—one for men and boys and another for women and girls? I remember once making a set speech to the washerwoman, which I had studied out and *knew* was correct, but afterward, my teacher, who was present, said to me, 'You talk as if to a man, and the verb you used means "to wash" the hands and the face, and the dishes and so forth. We have another verb for washing clothes.' No wonder, then, at the blank stare in the washerwoman's face! But the more discouraged I grew the more hopeful was Mr. Rhea. He would laugh and say, We give a year for learning the language, but you will be preaching in six months.

"One day in the spring, Sarra, my teacher, asked me if I would not consent to let the women, in the afternoon, come to a prayer-meeting. I was very much frightened at such a prospect, but finally assented if she would sit very near to me and help me. They came. We began with a familiar song of Zion, then a short chapter and a few simple remarks which I had gone over and over with my teacher at the morning lessons, then prayers from Sarra and another good Christian woman, and I said, 'We have finished;' and the women rose quietly and solemnly and 'poured their peace' and went away, while I looked after them anxiously, to see if any knowing winks should betray their suspicions that an Uzziah had offered strange fire at the altar. The French say, 'It is the first step that costs,' so that was a relief. The next morning Mr. Rhea took occasion to come in during my lesson and ask Sarra, archly, Did the women understand Khanum preaching? She said, 'Yes.' So, little by little, as the Nestorians say, my tongue opened."

"Mr. Rhea's fluent command of the language was wonderful. One of our new missionary ladies, in her zeal to learn the Syriac well, inquired of her teacher where she could find

the best model of its pure and elegant use. The prompt
answer was, Rhea Sahib. In pronouncing the language,
while he bestowed a correct notice upon all the strange
aspirations and gutturals, he was able to do it without making them conspicuous, as many of us have to do if we do
them any justice."

That these remarks of a loving wife are not overdrawn,
the Editor of these papers has abundant proof in the testimony written, and in his possession now, from representatives
of the entire Nestorian people and from his fellow-missionaries. The following description of his abundant labors
and his fitness for them is from the clear and able pen of
Dr. Perkins, to which we have been so often indebted:

"The sudden death by cholera of Mr. Breath—then the
Nestor of the mission in the field—the year following Mr.
Rhea's return, brought a paramount responsibility upon
him, for which he was now remarkably well qualified. The
bare enumeration of his missionary duties will show that
his labors were henceforth alike manifold and onerous.

"He was the *postmaster* of the mission. He was *treasurer*
of the mission, a heavy charge, where accounts must be
kept with scores of helpers, as well as with members of the
mission and with neighboring missions, in different curren-
cies, ever varying and uncertain, besides the full semi-annual
returns to be made to the treasurer of the American Board.
After the return of Mr. Cobb to America, Mr. Rhea took
charge of the *Mission Press*, editing our monthly paper and
furnishing other matter for the printers till my return to
the field in 1862, when he shared those labors with me.
He had charge of the *Mohammedan Department*, which
means the transaction of business with the Musselman
authorities, proper attention to Mohammedan visitors, to
whom much religious truth may be imparted on such occasions, and specially the post of *days-man* between the poor,

suffering Nestorians and their numerous and cruelly oppressive masters, a position often of great difficulty and
perplexity.

"The trials and anxieties, the sleepless nights and toilsome
days which this last-named task sometimes involves, may be
learned by reference to an affecting sketch (hereafter to be
given,) of a very trying case of the abduction of a Nestorian
girl, with the purpose of compelling her to profess herself
a Mohammedan and marry the wretch who stole her away.
Such tragic cases are not of unfrequent occurrence; and the
constant rush of oppressed and outraged Nestorians to the
missionary, to whom they look as their protector, in the absence of all others to care for them, imposes a burden which
it requires the shoulders of a Hercules long to sustain.   Mr.
Rhea's warmly sympathetic heart never allowed him to
spare aught of sleep or strength or personal safety, if
by the sacrifice he could bring relief to the humblest
sufferer.

"He had charge also of the *Armenian Department* of our
work, which, though in its incipient stage, required not a
little care and correspondence, particularly as the helpers
at the out-stations in Salmas were frequently and greatly
annoyed by their persecuting enemies.

"Last, not least, Mr. Rhea was a most indefatigable
preacher—constantly to the Nestorians in modern Syriac,
and often in Turkish to the Armenians.   His sermons were
always fresh and well elaborated, as though he had devoted
most of his time to their preparation, while we marveled
how he could find time thus to prepare a single sermon.
With all his other pressing avocations, he ever regarded the
preaching of the word as the missionary's prime and paramount work.   He was "a prince" among preachers, and no
more moderate term would properly characterize him, while
this fails to impart an adequate idea of the rare unction and

the moving and overcoming power of the matter and the delivery of his sermons.

"Added to all the active duties of Mr. Rhea were his hours of close study of languages and of the Scriptures, and his preparation of commentaries, which, it must be acknowledged, he was to a large extent obliged to redeem from midnight silence, while others were hushed in repose.

"No other missionary ever in our field," says Dr. Perkins, "has possessed a better knowledge of modern Syriac or spoken it so well. No other member of our mission has ever become so familiar with every portion of our field and every department of our work. There is not a district, or hardly one, of the Nestorian country which he has not at some time occupied or superintended, and not a branch of our labors in which he has not personally engaged. And I hardly need add that whatever he put his hand to was sure to be well done, with a zest, skill and success peculiar to himself. His intimate acquaintance with all the dialects of the people, acquired by his familiarity with every portion of the field, and his experience in applying the language to all the various purposes of conversation, teaching, preaching, translation and preparation of commentaries, imparted a scope and finish to his use of it which no other missionary here has ever possessed.

"His acquisitions in other languages of these countries besides the Syriac, as Turkish, Koordish and Persian, were also very considerable. He had for several months previous to his death been perfecting his knowledge of Turkish preparatory to the great work of translating the Bible into that language, which is spoken by uncounted millions all the way from Hungary to India, and into the Central and Eastern dialects of which the Scriptures have never been translated. He had just commenced this great work, which was peculiarly congenial to his tastes, and engaged in it with an interest, ardor and ability that characterized all his labors, and which could hardly have failed of success."

Such was Mr. Rhea essentially during the five years that succeeded his return to Persia. His character had taken its ripe, symmetrical shape as a goodly tree planted by the rivers of waters, its boughs spreading out year by year with a longer reach and more bountiful amplitude of leaf and fruit. He glorified the Father by bearing much fruit.

While his brethren, yet grateful to God for his life of mingled beauty and strength, rejoice in his support and shade, let us devote the next chapters to considering the exciting influences under which God was developing in him so much fitness for present admiration and future glory. They will exhibit his Christlike efforts to succor the needy and distressed from famine and oppression, and the heavenly atmosphere of his happy home.

CHAPTER XXI.

HELP FOR THE OPPRESSED.

ONE woe that never passes from the Christlike heart in a Mohammedan land is to be constantly lacerated in its sympathies. How long, O Lord? is the ceaseless cry.

Where there is no consul, as was the case in the Northwest Province of Persia, the creation by a mission of a Mohammedan Department seemed of imperative necessity. While Mr. Rhea had charge of this department, his powers were taxed to the utmost. If missionaries and consuls, with all the vast shadow of European and American protection behind them, are yet sometimes greatly outraged, even massacred, what are the daily deaths of unending oppression which wear out the poor Nestorians, away from the eyes of the nations, in the savage recesses of Koordistan and Persia!

As a part of his duty Mr. Rhea drew up the following statement which illustrates the facts we mention:

A Statement with Reference to the Nestorian Christians of Persia (not including the larger numbers in Koordistan).

1. They number about 25,000.

2. The mass of them are in their own villages, and not mixed with other nationalities.

3. The large majority of the villages are owned or favored by a very few powerful khans.

4. The Nestorian Christians in their present condition differ but little from serfs. They are attached to the soil to all intents and purposes. When a village is bought or

sold, the rayats go with it, and they can't remove from one village to another to escape the oppressions of their masters. If they do they are almost invariably brought back.

5. With few exceptions the Christians are peasants, and cultivate the soil. Formerly, in farming the lands of their masters, they were permitted to furnish the seed and receive two-thirds of the fruit of their labors; but of late years the masters furnish the seed grain, and the rayats after furnishing all the labor both of men and teams, receive one-third of the products.

6. The Nestorians are kept down in a state of serfdom, because there are so many restrictions and barriers to entering any other employment. They are regarded as ceremonially unclean. Frequently, respectable Nestorians— in some cases ecclesiatics—have been cruelly beaten in the streets because they happened to touch a Mohammedan. With one or two exceptions they have never attempted to have shops in the bazaars. Their touch is pollution to a Mohammedan, and everything in the shape of milk, curds, butter, cheese, fruit coming through their hands is defiled.

7. They are helpless in the hands of their Mohammedan masters. The lands which they have been accustomed for ages to plough for bread may be taken at any time and turned into vineyards by their masters, and the water belonging to the village, and necessary to the irrigation of the lands, may be, and often is, sold to other villages. The masters may exact from the rayats any amount of labor or any number of ploughs. They cannot legally exact more than two days' labor a year, and one plough from each house; but they often take ten laborers and as many ploughs in the busiest season of the year. Hence the rayats are at the caprice of men for the most part all-

powerful, avaricious and oppressive; and there is hardly a limit to their extortions and the extortions of their mohassils, moobasheers, darogas and their own servants, in the shape of forced labor, and exorbitant presents at their feasts, marriages and other occasions.

8. Of late years the sanctity of the home and family relation of the poor Nestorian has become more and more defenceless. Masters, their sons and servants, can enter the houses of the peasants, to any extent decoy, allure, or force the female members of the family; and, being miserably poor, the offer of new clothing and a comfortable living is often a greater temptation than they can bear. Within two years more than twenty-five females have been thus abducted, some willingly and others forcibly. There were cases in which little girls fourteen years of age were thus carried away; and when, afterward, they were brought to our premises, and with their broken-hearted parents declared their unwillingness to become Musselmans, they were still forced to do so. Some of these cases were represented to the sardar at Tabreez, but there was no redress. When a girl has been carried off, whether enticed or forced, she is kept closely confined for several days—in some cases violated—and then brought to the governor's—occasionally to our premises—surrounded by a crowd of Musselmans, to declare whether she is a Christian or not.

9. The testimony of Christians is not received in courts of justice.

10. In cases of the murder of Christians there is seldom any redress obtained. There are murderers of Nestorians every day walking the streets who have never been punished in any form.

That Mr. Rhea most tenderly sympathized with the people in regard to whose sad earthly lot he wrote the preceding statement, is gratefully testified by the Nestorian whose

25 *

words helped to comfort the widow in her affliction. Mrs. Rhea records, in her brief sketch:

"Yesterday I had a little call from Priest N'weya of Nazee. He said to me with tears, 'When your husband died I lost a father, and my village lost a father. When he came to us he generally would spend the night; and next morning, rising early, we would take a walk, first toward the brook and then into the grove, he talking pleasantly and earnestly about the Christian life and about a pastor's duties until we got to some quiet spot, where we would kneel down and pray. And now,' he added, with deep emotion, 'when I walk there I remember him and those seasons of Christian communion, and every tree and stone and mound is a "heap of witnesses" to me and a monument to him. When we walked through the village and he beheld the poor, the destitute and the naked, he was quickly moved to pity, and would turn to me and say, "Give such an one a suit of clothes, and I will pay for it;" and often thus from his bounty I have warmed and clothed the naked, even from head to foot.' And then turning to Benjamin, a poor, palsied cripple, destitute of this world's goods, but rich, we trust, in the kingdom of faith, he added: 'He was always ready to contribute to the necessities of this needy brother. If he did not come for several monthly concerts to the city, he would inquire for him and say, "How is the health of Benjamin? How is the health of his family?" and when I arose to leave he would put something hard, wrapped up in a paper, into my hand and say, "Give that to Benjamin."' I well remember Mr. Rhea's tender pity for this Benjamin, who seldom failed to ask and receive monthly aid from Mr. Rhea; and one monthly concert day, when we passed Benjamin in the yard, I said to my husband, 'There is your everlasting protégé, Benjamin, come again. Don't you get tired of him?' He said, gently,

'I try not to, for the Master's sake. I am sure he is one of Christ's poor.'

"The winter of 1862 was one of great scarcity and suffering in Oroomiah. Beggars abounded. Our yards were never free from them. They flocked about the stair-steps and doors, so that sometimes we could scarcely get in and out, and attacked us with doleful importunities whenever they could find us. Mr. Rhea gave and gave—white money and black—bread and clothes—until prudence demurred, and we began to feel it seriously. The more we investigated and tried to relieve the wretchedness and suffering from nakedness and famine, the more we were impressed with the magnitude and hopelessness of the task before us. Mr. Rhea said we must save for the poor and practice self-denial in every way we could; he should give up drinking coffee, and that I must buy and make no more. We had a struggle. I would not obey. I knew that his health required regular and simple though nutritious food; and the slight tonic effect of the breakfast cup of coffee had been so manifest in Mr. Rhea that I could not consent to banish this very moderate luxury from my Persian housekeeping. By and by generous gifts began to come from American and English Christians for the relief of the poverty-stricken around us. The funds we received were divided equally among the missionaries for distribution, so as to reach all parts of the field. Large quantities of the cheapest calico and strong cotton cloth were purchased wholesale from the bazaar and given out piece by piece and garment by garment for men, women and children and pinched and shivering babies, until the naked and famishing were clothed and fed, and widows' and orphans' hearts sang for joy.

The abuses to which the Nestorians are subjected is well illustrated in the following narration by Mr. Rhea :

THE STORY OF NERGIS.

On Thursday, at the dead hour of night, fifteen artillery-men, heavily armed, came into the village of Digga, just under the shadow of our city walls, rushed upon the roof and dragged from her bed the daughter of Baba, the chief man of the village, a girl fifteen years of age. Her cries for help aroused the villagers. They ran to her rescue, fought desperately with the ruffians, but were overpowered. Two of her uncles were severely wounded; one is now at the point of death. But all was in vain; though the poor girl herself made a desperate resistance, she soon had to yield under the blows of the soldiers. She was dragged by the tresses of her hair from the village, her cries imploring help being heard to the last. Before light the intelligence of her seizure was brought to our premises. Knowing her well, having often stopped at her house, and from her modest demeanor being satisfied that she was entirely innocent, that it was a most flagrant case of violence, and that without the promptest measures in a short time she would be made a victim of Moslem lust and fanaticism, I resolved to use all the strength and influence of our mission to save her.

I sent at once to Rejab Ali Khan, colonel of artillery, and stated the case. He promised that in two hours the girl and the guilty soldiers should be brought to our premises, and, if the facts were as above stated, the soldiers should be severely punished. In the mean time a very affecting scene took place in my room: the chief men of the Nestorians, bishops and priests, had gathered in; they seemed entirely broken down. Strong men wept, and smote upon their breasts; and especially when the bloody garments of the uncle, who had fought so nobly the night before to save his niece, were brought in, there was a gen-

eral outburst of sobbing and lamentation. The women
wailed, laid hold of my skirts and implored my help.

The two hours were up, and the girl was not brought.
I went to the Persian general and told him this matter must
not be protracted. It was the most flagrant case that had ever
happened here, and the greatest insult that had for many
years been offered to a people already in the deepest straits
of oppression. The girl must be forthcoming! He promised, with the most solemn oaths, that before sunset she
would be in the city on his premises, alleging she was in a
distant village. At sunset I went again. The girl had
been found, but had not been brought to the general's
premises. He had gathered in his moollahs, ready at the
first moment to pronounce the irrevocable sentence that
she was a Musselman, and espouse her. No one of Nergis' relatives had been permitted to see her. No one knew to
what she may have been subjected during the twenty hours
that had elapsed since her seizure. The general insisted
that she should be brought at once and questioned. I declined, apprehending that she may have been terrified, and
the matter was compromised by her removal from the
house of a fellow-soldier of Ferraj, her captor, to the house
of Buyuh Agha, a Musselman, but an old and tried friend
of Nergis' father.

I left the general, and after waiting until there was time
for her transfer, though it was ten o'clock at night, and she
was conveyed to a remote part of the city, I determined to
see her. Accompanied by Deacon Isaac and a number of
her friends, we went to Buyuh Agha's. We found poor
Nergis there, and heard from her own lips the story of her
seizure and her feelings of despair for many long hours, not
knowing that anything could be done for her. In the presence of all in the room—Nestorians and Mussulmans—she
made the strongest protestations of her fidelity to her own

religion, and declared her readiness to die rather than become a Mussulman. I returned home with a light heart. The poor Nestorians were overjoyed. We felt satisfied that Nergis would stand firm through the trying ordeal before her. Morning came. We heard that at midnight a party of moollahs had gone to the house where Nergis was, and spent hours in attempting to induce her to abjure her religion; but it was all in vain. The general had promised that at an early hour the girl should be brought, and if she made her confession that she was a Christian and had been violently carried off, she should be released and the soldiers severely punished. We went to his house, but the girl was not brought.

In the mean time Ferraj was brought out into the court, and the general went through the process of administering a mock bastinado. I remonstrated against this, knowing it was a trick to gain time, to make a favorable impression as to his impartiality, and to palliate the detestable course he was about to take in order to make a victim of the girl. The beating, such as it was, being over, still Nergis was not brought. I pressed the general; he said she should be brought at once to the house of a moollah living near by. We went there—the moollahs assembled—still Nergis was not brought. After waiting some time, I returned to the general and requested him to excuse me from waiting further, as I was satisfied it was not his intention to have her brought. Soon a man came in and said Buyuh Agha was demanding twenty tomans to let the girl leave his house, and that this was for the general. I turned to him and remonstrated against such an enormity. The Nestorians, however, made up the sum, and were ready to give it, not to secure Nergis' release, but only to have her brought before a moollah to say whether or not she was a Mussulman.

The general seemed ashamed and embarrassed that his

cupidity was brought out to the light, but he consented that the girl should be brought to the house of the moollah at once. It was announced that she was brought. The general accompanied us to his gate. We supposed he was going with us, but a letter was placed in his hands; he read it, and then excused himself from going farther. Instead of going just across the way to the house of the moollah, where I had gone in the morning, and who was quite a friend of Dr. Wright's, I found Nergis was to be brought to the house of Meerza Ali Akbar, the chief mooshtaheed—a grand old hypocrite, and full of venom toward the Christians.

He was the same man who last year forced a little Armenian girl to become a Mussulman, though she declared herself a Christian in the presence of a large number of Mussulmans. A large number of moollahs and seids were gathered in the room. I never saw a more perfect specimen of an old Pharisee; his great white turban, his sanctimonious mien, his eyes rolling heavenward, his measured and pompous utterances! He opened the conversation by saying, with great pomp of expression:

"It has been recently communicated to me that an individual had manifested her *choice* to become a Mussulman."

He was then interrupted, and instead of *choice*, he and all present were informed that she was violently dragged from her bed at midnight by a party of armed soldiers, and she was to be brought into his presence, so that he could from her own lips satisfy himself that this statement was not true.

He was brought to a stand. Then rolling his eyes and elongating his face to a painful extent, he laid his hand on a large red book, and said he had just been reading a conversation that took place between Jesus and the devil, the purport of which was that everything should be done with great *deliberation*.

He had no doubt made up this story for the occasion, and adapted it to the case in hand. He did not intend to question the girl then, but after a few days. I told him that if he would listen but five minutes to her story, he would be satisfied that it was a case of violence and a great outrage. I entreated him in the name of justice and humanity to release her; but no! "She was in an excited state of mind; she must be kept quiet; her friends were crowding around her." Then turning to the large crowd of Nestorians who had gathered in, intensely interested to see what was to be Nergis' fate, he waved his arm and said:

"Away with you; you have no place in this court. Go to your work. Away! away!"

His servants and some fierce seids who were around beat them from his court. I felt it was a time for apprehension. The market was close by, and a word from the arch-fanatic would have kindled a fire which would have swept the Christians away in its fury. Nergis was brought. As she passed through the yard her cries were heard: "I am a Christian! I am a Christian!"

I said to the moollah: "Don't you hear her? Can you doubt or hesitate to let her go?"

He was unwilling, and said she must remain in his house a few days, and then be questioned.

This was not assented to for a moment; for we knew, once in his hands, her fate was sealed. With great difficulty we got him to consent to let her choose where she would spend the night. He sent Kyâsin Agha to ask her. She said, "I want to go to the sahib's" (the missionary). The reply was, "That can't be." "Then let me go where I was—to Buyuh Agha's, my father's friend." This was assented to. Kyâsin Agha came in, and said to the moollah, in the presence of all the moollahs, " Why are you detaining her? Twenty times she declares she will never become a Mussulman."

Still the moollah refused to return her. He hoped yet to get thirty of the one hundred tomans that had been offered the general if he and the moollahs would carry the case through. He angrily remanded her back to Buyuh Agha's. I felt an unspeakable relief when I saw her pass out of the gate of the old bigot and under the protection of one who would defend her to the last; and I felt a greater relief when I got back home, with the large crowd of Nestorians, whom I could not keep from following me. I knew a spark would set on fire and kindle to a blaze the sleeping passions of Moslem fanaticism.

There was no time to be lost—Nergis must be got out of their hands. The case was stated to the vizier, acting governor during the prince's absence. He promised she should be brought in the evening. Evening came, but she was not produced. I went again to Rejab Ali Khan, and he promised that in one hour she should be brought. An hour and a half passed; but he had gone to the bath, and there was no evidence of the girl's being brought. I then sent him word that we would give him no further trouble, and that he would have to answer at Tabreez for the part he had played in this disgraceful affair. He sent two or three times afterward to exculpate himself, but I had no further intercourse with him.

I again went to the vizier's and requested a guard, knowing that as long as Rejab Ali Khan's men were prowling around there was no security for Nergis. In lieu of his failing to bring her to his court-town and investigate the case, he consented to give a guard and became security for her until morning.

In the morning the bishops and chief men gathered in the vizier's court and demanded the captive girl. But it

26

was evident the vizier too had been bribed. He put them
off—said he was afraid of the moollahs. The approach of
the prince-governor was announced. The Nestorians turned
out in large numbers to meet him; they held up the bloody
garment; women covered their heads with ashes and lifted
up their voices in lamentation. The prince promised to
send for her at once. In the evening, from the interview
held with him, it was evident he did not intend to release
her, but only involve the case more and more. He too was
bribed. He said, "She must come spend the night at his
house; his khanum would talk with her—he himself would
talk with her. In the morning the moollahs would be
assembled and the case disposed of." Word was at once
sent to Buyuh Agha not to give up the girl. Though the
prince is an old man, still, knowing his vile propensities, I
knew there would be no security for the girl in his house.
Officers were sent once and again, but Buyuh Agha evaded
them until, at midnight, everything being quiet, he conveyed Nergis away to another part of the city.

Having seen what the prince's intentions were, and de-
spairing of any redress in Oroomiah, at two o'clock the next
morning Deacon Isaac left for Tabreez, to lay the case before the English consul. Very early on Monday morning
the officers of the prince gathered around Buyuh Agha's
door and pressed him for the girl. For a time he was able
to evade them. While he was putting them off, in company
with the vizier, Meerza Nejef Ali, the chief of the Christians, and the bishops and prominent men who had gathered
in from the villages, I went to the court-room of the prince.
We did not intend the girl should be brought until the
moollahs were assembled also; but she was brought. The
vizier, though urged to hear her story, refused; she must
go into the harem. As I saw the poor girl pass in I feared
the worst. For three hours every effort was made to induce

her to become a Mussulman; she was threatened with beating and death; she was promised a village; strings of pearls were brought and held up before her.

She said, "I do not want your jewels; I have enough in my father's house. I do not fear your threats; kill me, disjoint me, cut me to pieces. I will never be a Mussulman; my burial shall be a Christian one; I will lie down in a Nestorian graveyard."

We waited for a number of hours, hoping the prince would come out of his harem; but he did not. He hoped the girl would come to terms. Finally old Meerza Ali Akbar writes a note to the prince; the prince sends it to his court-room; the mooshtaheed writes, informing the assembly of the new convert to Mohammedanism, says he has not interfered in the case, and requests that Meerza Nejef Ali, the chief of the Christians, come to his house to talk over the matter Meerza Nejef Ali bounced to his feet and cried out, "When has a new convert been made to Islam? The evidence is all the other way. Shall I go to the moollah? Let him come to me. Shall I remain here longer? Can I any more hold up my head when things are managed in this way?" He was in a towering passion for a moment, but the vizier and the prince did not let him leave. After an hour three of the principal moollahs were called in. With the prince, vizier and Meerza Nejef Ali they went into the harem. Again the noble girl passed the ordeal like a heroine. Undaunted, she declared her determination to die a Christian. The old moollahs came out shaking their heads and saying, "It won't do; *she* can never be made a Mussulman."

During the day frequent reports were brought that hundreds of Mussulmans were gathered about Meerza Ali Akbar's door, stirring him up to press the matter and force the girl to become a Mussulman. It was also reported that several times he threatened to give a sentence for the slaughter of the Christians. He ordered the stores to be closed and business to be suspended. Said he, "If such things are permitted, Mohammedanism is at an end." The prince, seeing, after the moollahs had been in, that he could not accomplish his object, sent the girl out of the inner court to the outer, where some Nestorian joiners were at work. The good joiners during the forenoon had frequently gone in, and, as they found opportunity, spoke words of comfort to Nergis, assuring her that, if she would only be patient, all would be well. Nergis sat down and ate bread with them. Her female relatives came in and saw her, and it seemed as if light was beginning to dawn. In the afternoon Nergis was committed into the hands of the Nestorian agent, Meerza Nejef Ali.

We supposed she was virtually released, and that she would be sent to our premises at nine o'clock in the evening. But the night passed, and she did not come. Early the next morning, much to our surprise, she was remanded to the court-room of the prince. The great mooshtaheed, with his moollahs, came in with quite a swell and parade. Nergis was called in, and again passed through the ordeal. But her words were few. She stepped forward, took hold of the moollah's skirt, and said, "What kind of a religion is this that you are attempting to compel me to embrace? Are you not ashamed thus to persecute me?" The grand old bigot hung his head, and the whole party were overwhelmed with mortification. The moollah rose to his feet, and striking the ground forcibly with his long cane, had the audacity to say that a number of Mussulmans had testified to him that they had heard from Nergis' lips that she was a Mussulman.

Said he, "There is no remedy. She must go to Tabreez,

and the case be investigated there. When such proceed-
ings are tolerated, Islam has gone by the board."

Unfortunately, just after this speech, as he went down the
steps, his foot slipped, and he sprawled in a very undig-
nified manner on the stairway, while his great white turban
rolled ignominiously in the dirt, greatly to his mortification,
but much to the enjoyment of the Nestorian bystanders.
Nergis was again sent back to Meerza Nejef Ali's for the
night. The only thing remaining now was to stipulate about
the present to be given to the prince to get her out. He
had not by any means darkly hinted that he must have his
present. Meerza Nejef Ali wrote to him in the evening
that he wished to commit Nergis to her friends. The reply
was that he must delay—there was fear from the moollahs.
Of course he only wished to increase his present. But before this reply was received Nergis hearing that they were
bargaining to get her release, took the matter into her own
hands, climbed over the wall and came to our house. A
boy soon came running in, and said, "They are beating
Khatoon" (Nergis' aunt). She, too, attempted to escape,
but failed, and the servants fell to beating her. Meerza
Nejef Ali was informed of what had taken place, and he
readily consented that Nergis should not be taken from our
house, and that Khatoon, her aunt, might go home. Thus
terminated this very trying case.

26 *   U

CHAPTER XXII.

HOME INFLUENCES.

IN connection with his condensed and vivid account of Mr. Rhea's abundant labors, Dr. Perkins suggests:

"The inquiry naturally arises, Why did he not sooner break down under such a burden of care, responsibility and toil? Primarily, I should say, his domestic bliss exerted on him a marvelous sustaining and rejuvenating influence. The faithful and joyous companion of his bosom was literally and emphatically 'the delight of his eyes,' while the beautiful olive plants that were springing up around his table contributed largely also to fill to the brim his cup of enjoyment. Often, indeed, the quiet of his meals was interrupted by the intrusion of suffering ones seeking bodily or spiritual relief, but he did not allow such intrusions seriously to impair the hallowed delights and duties of his *home*. He was almost uniformly well, strong and buoyant under his accumulated cares and labors.

"Sacred music also, of which he was rapturously fond, contributed materially to sustain him under the unwonted pressure of his missionary toils, especially as associated with that joy in the Lord and communion with Christ which were more habitual with him than with almost any other individual I have ever known. He also had a keen zest and an abiding delight in his missionary work, particularly in preaching the gospel, which seemed ever to exert on him a recuperating power.

"Mr. Rhea's moments of relaxation in his family were

always fruitful moments. The little prattlers upon his knee were entertained by some Scripture narrative told in his own inimitable style, and *Jesus* became the presiding genius of his dwelling in the minds and on the lips of those little ones, long before they could distinctly pronounce that 'sweetest name on earth or in heaven.'"

The first months of their residence in Persia, before Dr. Perkins' return, was in his house at Seir;* but December

---

* We can here appropriately introduce an illustration of the Seir mission-premises, with a brief sketch by the Rev. H. N. Cobb.

The name of Seir is inseparably associated with the history of the Nestorian mission. Residing for a large part of the year in Oroomiah, their early experience was one of great suffering—almost constant sickness and frequent deaths, especially of children. A retreat was absolutely necessary from the extreme heat of the city and the poisonous exhalations of the plain. A suitable spot for such a retreat was early found at Seir, a small village of perhaps a hundred inhabitants, about six miles west from the city, and at an elevation of one thousand feet above it, on the eastern slope of the mountain of the same name. The mission premises are represented in the cut annexed. A court surrounded by a high wall of mud and with circular towers of the same material at each corner form the enclosure; an arrangement made necessary by the danger of incursions from the thievish Koords. This court is divided in the middle by a continuous row of buildings of sun-dried brick and mud containing permanent residences for three families. The view from the roof is commanding and beautiful, embracing the broad plain dotted with villages; the city, almost hidden in the midst of the dense foliage of its gardens; the lake, and the mountains, encircling lake and plain on every hand.

Seir is also the seat of the Male Seminary. As such it has been the scene of most earnest and devoted labors on the part of those connected with the Seminary, and of precious and powerful revivals among the students. It is hardly too much to hope that Seir may one day be to the revived and reformed Nestorian Church what the famous school at Edessa was to their ancient Church.

Seir also has an interest, as proving, in its own history, the power of the gospel as taught in its school. Originally it was a village of

13, 1861, Mr. Rhea notes briefly: "Moved to the city; entered our new home." It was a consecrated residence, left
by Mr. Breath, recently gone to the house of many mansions, hallowed by his prayers and those of his poet-wife,
whose words of song have cheered many of our hearts.
Mr. Rhea adds: "Sarah and Annie rode down with
Mr. Coan. Daniel had moved all our effects with great
care. Spent the evening at Mr. Cobb's. Discussed Turkish with Doctor. Afternoon very stormy." Do you ask,
Who is Annie? Let the mother tell:

"The next summer after our arrival in Oroomiah our
mission was blessed by a visit from Dr. Dwight, of Constantinople, and Mr. Wheeler, of Kharput. Dr. Dwight had
recently buried his beloved wife, and the fine gold of his
Christian character, fresh from the purifying crucible of
such an affliction, showed lustrously. His gentle, chastened
manner and heavenly-mindedness, his affectionate kindness
and deep interest in our work, his encouraging comments
and his wise counsels, won the hearts of all and greatly
deepened our already-formed attachment to him. A month

highway robbers. Now it is believed that every family is represented
in the little community of believers. One who was once the leader
of the gang of robbers has been for many years a leading communi-
cant, a sort of elder and a trusted messenger of the mission.

And there attaches a sorrowful interest to Seir by reason of the
deaths that have occurred there and the graves of those devoted servants of God, or of their little ones, whose remains slumber peacefully
in the little cemetery on the mountain-side (seen on the right of the
picture). Stoddard, and Thompson, and Breath, and Wright, and
Rhea, and a company of little ones whose dust is dear to those who
laid them there—these all lie buried in that little cemetery. No one
can visit that spot,—no one can rightly think of it—and not feel that
it is hallowed, or without feeling how holy and precious the work is
in which and for which these laid down their lives or the lives of
those they loved.

MOUNT SEIR.

after his departure the Lord mercifully remembered us in the gift of a little daughter, whom we named after her two grandmothers and this beloved missionary-father, Annie Dwight. Our first-born saw the light at Seir, August 24, 1861. In the following years there were given to us two sons and another little daughter, as follows: Foster Audley, born in Oroomiah, January 24, 1863; Robert Leighton, May 13, 1864; Sophia Perkins, April 18, 1866."

The development of paternal feelings in Mr. Rhea seemed to add many cubits to his stature morally. These precious treasures, so beautiful and so perfect in his esteem, excited the liveliest gratitude toward the Giver; the relations of the heavenly Father toward us, his believing children, were more clearly discerned than ever before. In many ways it was a means of grace to Mr. Rhea to be a father. The immortal souls of the little beings committed to his care at once became the most sacred and responsible trust. If he loved and needed the mercy-seat before, how much more now! If the promise was precious and comprehensive before, how much more so now! "For the promise is unto you and to your children," Acts ii. 39. When he entered into covenant with Jehovah for his children in the holy ordinance of baptism, it was with the profoundest realization of the height and depth, the length and breadth of the temporal and eternal privileges involved, so far as a finite being can realize and appropriate them.

In Mr. Rhea's intercourse with his children, Annie particularly, who was old enough to receive religious impressions, the keystone of all his words was "the dear Jesus." Even the younger children, Foster and Robert, before they knew anything else in books, knew all their little hearts could hold of "the dear Jesus." Their father said if their young minds were preoccupied with Jesus and salvation through his death, they would not so easily fall into Satan's

snares. From the rich treasury of Scripture lore he drew
all his teachings for the children; all his stories, all his
evening entertainments, all his moral principles and all his
illustrations. It was the Alpha and Omega, the beginning
and the end, the ever fresh, ever relished, ever flowing fountain from which he daily caused their young lips to drink.
He most literally fulfilled the Mosaic precept (in Deut. vi.):
"Thou shalt love the Lord thy God with all thy heart and
with all thy soul and with all thy might; and these words
which I command thee this day shall be in thy heart, and
thou shalt teach them diligently unto thy children, and
shalt talk of them when thou sittest in thy house and when
thou walkest by thy way, and when thou liest down and
when thou risest up."

Every evening when the supper-table was cleared away,
the happiest hour of all the day, her father would sit in
his big chair, with Annie on his knee, and talk about Jesus,
always about Jesus! The same theme! It never wore out!
How he was born and lived and died, and *why!* Philosophers cannot exhaust the theme in its deep, eternal mysteries, and angels long to look into it; and yet *this* theme
the father constantly unfolded to that infant mind, and it
was understood. Oh, with what delight it was received!
how beautifully it was unfolded! And then, when the lesson was finished and the Book closed, the child, unsatisfied,
would beg a little song. What shall I sing, Annie? Sing
about Jesus! And he had made "a little song," a low,
sweet, gentle chant, beginning with the star of the wise men
and the shepherd's vision, and ending with the ascension of
the Son of Man in clouds to heaven. And then the little
one, filled full and satisfied, climbed down, and knelt and
prayed and kissed her father's lips, and said good-night.

"Mr. Rhea was the most loving of fathers as he was the
kindest of husbands. He always took upon himself the

heaviest part of the burden and care when the children were sick and in danger, watching them night after night when necessary, always ready to wake and rise to soothe their fears and supply their wants. He seemed to do these things as by an instinctive impulse; no one asked him to do them; but they were done before a duller ear could wake or a slower hand could reach. The burdens, cares, anxieties, watchings and labors that devolved upon him as a father were always borne patiently and without complaint, though sometimes they were very heavy.

Many times these traits were sorely put to the test. "When Annie was about a year old and very sick," writes Mrs. Rhea, "we were advised to carry her to the cooler regions of Tergawar. We performed the journey in the dark, stopping at midnight in a wild place to feed the horses and rest. We arrived at Nuebi about five o'clock in the morning. Annie grew gradually worse. We were in a tent, a very uncomfortable place for the tender invalid. At noon the heat of the sun was most intense and the glare blinding; and when the wind blew at all, clouds of dust accompanied it. But the nights were chilly; so that the changes of temperature in the course of twenty-four hours were very great. The natives came around us in crowds, curious and impertinent. Mr. Rhea always received them patiently and kindly, omitting no opportunities to speak to them of Christ, and not hesitating to dismiss them when he thought it necessary. Sometimes the Mussulman master of the village would make a visit of ceremony, when I had to vacate part of the tent and retire behind a curtain with my sick child, to whom the noise of conversation was very annoying.

"One day we had furious gusts of wind, which made the tent intolerable, and, indeed, dangerous, for it was almost carried bodily away. So we moved into a native house—a

27

wretched hovel near—first cleaning out one corner to spread
our carpet and the baby's bed. Immediately an onset was
made by innumerable fleas, and we were half devoured.
At the time of lighting the native ovens, the smoke came
in through the crevices in the mud walls and almost put
our eyes out. At best our little, close room was dark and
hot, and at midnight it began to rain, and poured in dirty
torrents through the sieve-like roof. I was in despair, but
not so Mr. Rhea; his patience was inexhaustible, and his
resources equal to all emergencies. He quickly threw a
rubber over the little bed, and went out to sweep the roof
and fill the cracks with mud. By day, by night, his place
was by the baby's bed. He did not seem to lose himself in
sleep a moment. We had written on Thursday to Oroomiah to have burial-clothes prepared in case they might
be needed, and to apprise our friends of our great sorrows.
The same night Mr. Cochran and Miss Crawford came to
us and stayed till Saturday morning, when we all started
home together. Although our child was in a dying state,
we thought we could bring her over the road even more
comfortably than we could keep her there, and so our
friends advised. Annie rode part of the time in cajavas
on a pillow in her nurse's arms, *but the most of the way her
father walked and carried her;* and so, traveling slowly and
carefully, we came safely and without harm to our home.
When our doctor saw Annie he thought she was dead.
But God was pleased in mercy to accept her parents'
broken-hearted submission; and in answer to her father's
prayers, perhaps, the stroke was stayed and our first-born
was spared."

In 1863 Mrs. Rhea writes to friends in Tennessee of great
comfort in the health and prattle of their children, while
their own patience was tried by the prolonged discomfort
and sometimes agony of ophthalmia.

The following letter, written August 11, 1863, discloses a great sorrow. Think of the eyes aching with ophthalmia, the dim, twilight-room, darkened in that Persian home, with "thick curtains and blue blankets," and the sad heart of Mr. Rhea inditing these tender words:

"And is my dear father dead? Did you stand around his dying bed? Did you close his eyes in death? Did you lay him down gently to rest, where more than twenty years ago he said to me, pointing to the spot, 'There they will lay me!' I remember well how my heart filled full and I turned away, wondering what would become of me if I should then lose such a father. But God spared me then that great sorrow and that great loss. Our deeply revered and beloved father continued to be to us a beautiful staff, on which our mother and we, each of us, leaned and felt that it was strong.

"We could not expect always to keep him who seemed so necessary to us. We could not expect to detain him from the home toward which for nearly fifty years he had been traveling, for which he had been ripening, and was now fully ripe. During how many years we have tremblingly looked upon the wasting of his earthly house? How we longed to believe that our dear father was not dying, when every day, for a number of years, death was doing its silent but true work. God strangely, but to us oh how mercifully, lengthened out that frail life, and seemed to endow father with an unnatural fortitude and energy, as if he would not die until he had done his work. Let us from hearts deeply grateful, though deeply bleeding, praise God that he so long heard our prayers and spared to us him in whom our earthly and spiritual well-being seemed bound up. Let us praise God for the inestimable gift of such a father, such a life, such an example, such a friend. One of my first thoughts was, 'What shall dear mother do?'

and then I was at a loss to know; but then I said, God's grace
will be all-sufficient.   Yes, dear mother, he will never leave
nor forsake you; he will be all and in all to you.   Dear
brothers and sisters, in spirit I want to kneel with you
around the grave of our deeply revered and now sainted
father, and vow in God's strength to take up his mantle and
walk in his footsteps until we shall meet him in heaven.
My heart is full, but my eyes will not permit me to write
more now."

"In the autumn of 1864," Mrs. Rhea tells us, "when we
reached Gavalan, returning from a tour to Salmas, our little Foster was taken very sick and had convulsions.   We
were exceedingly distressed and frightened.   We remained
there in the mission-house over the Sabbath, but resumed
our journey Monday, carrying the little sufferer in our arms,
in high fever most of the way, and doing all we could to
make him comfortable in the heat and dust of the road.
We reached home near evening the same day.   But the
city was very unhealthy at that time, and we felt obliged to
retreat to the mountain, where we had only two rough upper rooms and few comforts.   Foster's disease now assumed
the form of obstinate fever and ague, which also attacked
me and prostrated me completely.   At the same time
Annie was seized with the most violent ophthalmia in both
eyes.   The lids were so swollen and inflamed that she
could not open them, while scalding tears kept running
down her cheeks; temporarily blind, she went groping
about, not able to see, but pierced with frantic pains by
every sunbeam.   Our babe, Robert, too, fell sick and wilted
down under a consuming fever.

"Can I ever forget Mr. Rhea in those days?—his patience, his cheerfulness, his tenderness, his manly strength;
now sitting at my bedside bathing the throbbing temples,

amusing Foster, feeding or soothing him, weighing out and administering our medicines, carrying baby, rocking him, singing in soft tones, telling Annie about Jesus, while the patient child, charmed, would sit with upturned face, oblivious of her pain. Not an impatient word, look or act; no, not one; but instead a firm and quiet trust in God, whose providence had ordained for us such dark and suffering days.

"This way which he had of receiving adverse dealings from the Omnipotent Hand made him a happy Christian and a happy man in all the relations of this suffering life."

The third child of Mr. Rhea, named after the holy Archbishop Leighton, seemed designed of heaven to ripen the most heavenly graces in the heart of his father. He often called him "the little archbishop," and frequently said, "There is something so pure and holy about the child, I feel rebuked in his presence."

The child was extremely fond of his father, and had the gift of resting him when worn with cares. When, tired from his day's labor in the study, Mr. Rhea came in to supper, he would snatch Robert up from the floor, place him on his shoulder and gallop around the room, with Annie and Foster at his heels, and before many circuits the *weary, worried* look on his face and print of *"crow's feet"* on his brow would disappear. Seated at table with Robert at his elbow in the high chair, you could not have told that that happy, genial father had ever seen trouble and care. While the blessing was being asked Robert would "pray" too, little chubby hands over his eyes and rosebud lips murmuring musically.

So the child grew, increasing in loveliness and preciousness every day for one year and one week, and then he was smitten down suddenly in the richest bloom of health. He

27 *

had a few days of dreadful sickness, and then Jesus took him away.

The same week Mr. Rhea wrote the following letter to one similarly stricken :

 OROOMIAH, *May* 23, 1865.

DEAR BROTHER WILLIAMS: Your letter was sad and it found us sad. You wrote of your angel Willie, and our hearts bowed in sorrow, by faith responded; we too have an angel, Robert. You wrote of a desolate home; and when we went to our home in town, where Robert came up at every step and turn—came only in memory—we could not but exclaim, as a sense of our desolation came over us, "The child is not; and I—whither shall I go?"

We own a little green turf now. We laid him under it yesterday. And how beautiful he was in death! It was hard to believe it, but Annie even seemed fully to understand it, as she often repeated, "It is only his little body. Robert is in heaven with Jesus." It was hard to believe it and lay that beautiful clay in the bosom of its mother earth; but we asked for help to do it, and God helped us. We gently laid him down in faith of a glorious resurrection.

We never thought we should keep him—so we said; but now we know that we knew not what we were saying. We expected to keep him. It was a sad surprisal. He was very different from Annie and Foster. So beautiful, and perfectly gentle, with so much of strength, energy and seriousness in his character, that if an angel had come down to give us an example of angel infancy he would not have deported himself differently from little Robert.

Just five days he suffered from an obstinate dysentery. All was done for him that we knew how to do; but he was on his way home—we could not detain him—and at seven last Sabbath morning he fell asleep.

I thank the blessed Saviour that here on earth he called

a little child to him—that he took him up in his arms and put his hand on his head and blessed him.

It was hard to have him go alone—we not with him—through the dark valley; but the angels were around him and the arms of Jesus at the other end to welcome him. Could it be possible that their angels, which do always behold the face of their Father, should not have been despatched as a convoy to the gates of the heavenly city?

I have written two or three little funeral sermons for little children who have died here, intended, too, to comfort the bereaved; but I wonder at it now. It was presumption. I knew nothing of that sorrow. *I talked about it;* now it has become a part of me. The heart has found a new experience; sleeping sensibilities have been touched; a sealed fountain of tears has been opened; the tongue utters a new language of grief; and now, if I met a parent similarly bereaved, though I should not utter a word, my presence would be of more comfort to him than any utterance; he would know that I knew just what it was, and there would be a real sympathy—*fellow-feeling.*

Dear brother, the Lord in mercy comfort your deeply wounded spirit, build your waste places, light your candle, put a song in your mouth. I can only say, we are with you in your great sorrow, and we ask God to help you—and this is *all* we can do. Will you not ask God to help us and make the death and the new life of our little boy in heaven life to us as from the dead? We need all this, or God would not have sent it. God grant that you and I and yours and mine in heaven may talk more intelligently of these matters!

Your ever affectionate brother,   S. A. RHEA.

One other special preparation did Mr. Rhea need for the highest and purest life on earth and ripest fitness for heaven.

He was to lie helpless in body and spirit, expecting to be borne in by the angels for Christ's sake, and then be lifted up by them and brought back to active life yet a season longer before translation. The wife proceeds: "Mr. Rhea's health, though very wretched before his most propitious visit to America, was so improved and re-established by that voyage and journey that it was even robust, and not often broken during our married life. Though in that time his burdens and labors were immense, he bore them manfully. His enjoyment of life was evident. His trust in God was like a rock; his mind was almost habitually cheerful, kept in peace, because stayed on God.

"I have not many memories of him as an invalid, yet I have a few. Several times he had attacks of low fever, which kept him for a longer or shorter period confined. A few weeks after Dr. Wright's death he was thus prostrated. I was very much alarmed—not so much at any existing symptoms as at the tendency to settled and obstinate fever.

"I watched and tended him for six long weeks. It was a very tedious and exhausting sickness. He bore it patiently and uncomplainingly. Often during the long and weary hours of the night he would lie sleepless and watching, but restraining his restlessness and tossings lest I should be disturbed as I lay sleeping in snatches on a sofa near by.

"After the fever began to yield, Mr. Rhea's recovery was still very slow; but his convalescence was a delightful season to me. Mr. Coan kindly took us out for a short ride on pleasant mornings, and fresh air proved a fine tonic. When we returned I would read aloud to him a great deal from the Bible and such authors as Leighton and Howe. His mind was in such a heavenly state, it seemed almost like being with one who had beheld the King in his beauty, and had freshly returned from the land that is very far off. He told me he had had many vivid and most solemn impressions of the unseen world. God had come very near to him, and he had looked the king of terrors in the face. His feet had even reached the brink of the cold river, and he was ready to go over. Jesus was near, his presence real, his promises true, and his love most sweet and precious. 'And now,' he said, 'I grieve to leave those blessed communings and that nearness to the Saviour and come back to the weary world and sin again, and wander away from Him whom my soul loveth. It was easier to go than to return.'

"I said, tearfully, 'But, dear husband, how could you leave your wife and babes? What would become of us?' 'I was not grieved for you,' he said; 'I left you with Christ and the covenant promises.'"

"Many such words, solemn and heavenly, passed between us. I wish I could recall them all as he said them. It was comforting, later, to revive at least the impression I received from them of how a good man can die, passing serenely down the valley, leaning upon the arm of the Beloved, when, a few months afterward, he suddenly, and without warning or farewell, passed beyond the veil. This sickness was his death-warning. He received the call, 'Set your house in order, for you must die.' This was the messenger summoning the pilgrim from the land of Beulah to the presence of the King."

Yet he rose up from that sickness strong and well again, with much to do and suffer in the few remaining months before he could quite say, "I have fought the fight, I have kept the faith, I have finished my course."

We close this chapter on home influences with words thus accounted for: "Among the various gifts distributed to different members of the little missionary circle keeping Christmas with us December 25, 1863, the following lines in a sealed envelope came through the post-office, addressed to Mrs. Sarah Jane Rhea:

v

" And thinkest thou, my darling wife,
My Muse is dead, and withered all
The bloom and freshness of my love?
Have I no song for thee, whom God
Selected and brought to my side,
Enclosed thy hand, thy heart, thy life
In mine? Have I no song for thee,
Who for my sake forsook thine all
And sundered every tie, and gave
To me a love than which there ne'er
Was purer love nor love more true?
Thou'st cast a mantle over all
My frailties, and seen in me naught
But man complete—for perfect love.
Thou'st given a love with which I know
A spotless man would be content.
No song for thee, whose heart has been
Attuned to mine in harmony,
Whose every throb has echoed back
To mine sweetly, devotedly?
No song for thee?   When I look around
On cherub faces and behold
Our blended image penciled there—
Lineaments of our united souls?
All song's not written.   There's
A melody of soul, and
Sweeter than all the harmonies
Of wire, or tone of well-tuned lute
Or lyre,—our wedded life has been
A constant song! My heart has e'er
Thrilled in fond music to thy praise,
And found its sweetest rest in *thee.*
No song for thee! My Annie dear,
My noble boy shall sing a song
For thee; and well I know 'twill wake
Thy soul and make it bound away
In ecstasy of joy.

CHAPTER XXIII.

EVENING LABORS.

OFTEN, as busy day draws near its close, work is so pressing that thought can scarcely turn to home, waiting with welcome, and the eye takes no respite to study clouds that will add to the glory of sunset. So it was with Mr. Rhea's five years of oriental evening following the year of noon-feast in America and the eight years' morning of his Eastern life.

Already, in 1861, his journal becomes mere fragmentary hints for memory; and in 1862, like an oriental brook, it dries up and disappears in the thirsty earth.

Parts of the journal the American reader would readily understand, as: "Returned from Salmas, found little wife and baby well," "Quite fagged out," "Hormuzd fell from horse with Annie," "Deacon Tamo took supper with us." Other parts have marked Oriental flavors, as: "Call from Meerza Assad Ullah" (Prince Lion of God), "Visit from Haji Khan's sons," "Persian letter with Latif Bey," "Call from Meerza Saduk," "To Dizza, Badilabad and Charbash," "With Sarah to Goolipatâlikhan," "Turkish hymn," indicating a translation by him or original, is frequent; and some translations are named as, "How sweet the name of Jesus!" "There is a fountain," etc., "Jesus, lover of my soul." He notes communion at villages, or funeral, and sometimes that he preached in Syriac, English or Turkish; and several times "Read Persian newspapers" occurs, showing that no less than four Oriental languages, beside his

323

Hebrew and Greek of the Bible and his Latin and English, are attracting his most marked and successful attention. Gradually "Preached in Turkish" and "Read Persian" grew frequent. Among the latter entries we read, "The governor put on his khalat to-day—how earnestly sought for, how prized! Would that he would seek with equal earnestness the royal wedding-garment from the Great King." "Gave the sertib, Falootah Khan, a ride to Hyderloo." "Wrote to the governor and sent him a Persian Testament, with a mark on the passage relating to adultery." The following seem to be the last words of his journal: "Visited Shahany; talked with Oosta Babila about the contributions, schools, etc.; arranged for a Bible-class every Tuesday evening. Evening called on Dr. Young—quite poorly. Spent the evening on accounts. Persian."

That was December 14, 1862; and during the following three years he does not seem to have found time for a single entry.

His correspondence with Dr. Perkins becomes mutilated scraps, in which names of Persian khans, nobles and princes alternate with those of American battle-fields; and mention of Turkish and Syriac translations intertwines with allusions to village visits for Sabbath preaching, excursions to distant plains of Salmas and Tabreez or nearer mountains, and the care of Oriental printers and presswork in strange tongues.

In the *fragmentary notes* to Dr. Perkins we read passages like this: "Hajee Meerza Megif Ali has seized old Mar Yoseph; he is now at Mar Yohanan." "How soon all things save eternity and its tremendous realities will seem utterly insignificant! If a storm is brewing, we know God rides on the storm."

From the springs near Salmas he writes: "Valley below reported full of armed men. Chavaders have not dared to come. We keep a guard at night, but trust Him who neither slumbers nor sleeps."

Another commences: "General Hassan Ali Khan got hold of the Pictorial History of the War, and was so pleased that he requested a number of the copies to send to the king of Persia." Another note charges that the general, who was fond of the pictorial war history, "clandestinely, or at least very thoughtlessly, made away with three of Mr. Cochran's numbers." Strange hieroglyphics in another would be found only to be the Syriac chorus for the familiar "I do believe." The next note tells of Sanum's funeral, and how "last night," as death was near, she called in "friends, relatives and children, gave parting words, and while she had a voice to sing sang praises to Christ."

January 11, 1864.—To-day I have had six cases of oppression, some involving much property and very flagrant. Each one had to be listened to, his case investigated and planned for. How weary one's soul grows of living in these lands of oppression and violence! Clouds of mercy are gathering over our heads. Souls are crying out for eternal life.

The following mingles the ludicrous with eccentric in a Persian noble: "Have just been to see the prince's gay rooms; every variety of wall paper, intermixed with every variety of picture, papered on; many from London Illustrated News; for vacant spaces he desires *more;* I am making up a package of good, bad and indifferent, and if you would immortalize yourself on the prince's walls he will be happy to receive any contributions." Note after note is devoted to printers, and many to the oppressor of the Nestorians. The following is a characteristic note: "I will very gladly send Priest Oshana a copy of the notes on the minor prophets. I wish very much we could see a deeper earnestness in the study of God's word. I deeply feel my

28

great deficiency in the little done to furnish notes and comments to stimulate to that study. In this study I believe both minister and layman are thoroughly furnished and made perfect. I cling to this Book all the more now that it is subjected to such an ordeal by the great infidel critics. Would that it dwelt in us all more richly! I was thinking to-day, and with great sorrow, of the year gone by, in which so little time has been given to the *prayerful* study of God's word."

Persian dignitaries were a great care and annoyance; but God's servants often must stand before princes to plead for God's poor. "Haji Negif Ali," he writes to Dr. Perkins, "said yesterday that the prince had appointed Friday for his visit. He told me that General Boyook Khan also would go. Your table is likely to be full. Have attended to the *last sheet* of the hymn-book. They will strike it off to-morrow."

The following to Dr. P. is interesting: "We shall have occasion of complaint if you persist in your hermit life. The days are long, the morning air balmy, the evening breezes refreshing. Can't you ride down oftener and spend a day or a few hours of a day. Dr. Bushnell says it is good to air our piety in the world's atmosphere: I can assure you we have it down here. (Dr. P. was at Seir, one thousand feet above Oroomiah city, six miles off.) I do not believe Dr. Bushnell would covet to breathe it long at a time. The great problem of my life is to keep in decent humor—to keep cool, unchafed, unfretted; but I succeed most miserably. In the process of collecting a pittance from a printer, I had to flee into an inner room to-day. Well, it ought to be more of a comedy than a tragedy; I ought to *laugh*, scores of times, when I *scold*.

"Nejif Ali, I hear, spoke openly in opposition to us and our work. What a comfort that we have a tireless Protector who is Meerza Nejif Ali's Master, and that he cannot move a finger without his permission. How beautiful was the simplicity and childlikeness of Luther's faith in the midst of raging storms!"

We again quote from Dr. Perkins:

"There was something almost mysterious in the ardent attachment of Mr. Rhea to his friends and his devotion to their comfort and welfare. I dare not refer to his affection for his wife and children, farther than to say that it was a great deep, seldom ruffled on its surface and ever overflowing with an amplitude, sweetness and freshness which could not fail to make his home an earthly Eden.

"For his associates and their families his affection was only less ardent than for 'the delight of his eyes' and his own lovely children. When Dr. Wright was taken from us by death, his grief was quite too great for suppression, and as he entered 'the house of mourning,' he could not refrain from audible and almost convulsive weeping. I remember, too, on another occasion, when he called on the writer to administer comfort in the depth of his affliction, his emotions in like manner were quite beyond his control.

"To the widow and orphan children of an older missionary associate, who were in deep want in America, after their return to that goodly inheritance, I happen to know that he twice remitted money from his private funds; and for the infant son of his mountain associate, born several months after the devoted father died, he placed one hundred dollars in a savings'-bank, from the same private source.

"My heart yearns and my hand trembles as I record these facts, before probably unrecorded except as business transactions, from the thoughts that are stirred within me in regard to these two classes of sufferers—missionary widows and children. And the touching exclamation of a little orphan boy, thus commiserated (who had known the pinchings of hunger within a few rods of *Christian mansions of affluence*), when his elder brother enlisted to fight in the battles of his country, 'O Willie, don't go; if you do we shall certainly starve!' still rings in my ears, and will never cease to do so. Mr. Rhea had a heart to feel and a hand to relieve such sufferers.

"Very much in harmony with the noble and beautiful character of Mr. Rhea was his fine person and manly and commanding, yet ever modest mien. Of medium height, a fair complexion, a genial, expressive face, a rich blue eye and a highly intellectual brow, there was a *completeness* in his whole appearance which we seldom behold in a mortal.

"But I allude to his personal appearance especially to mark a single aspect of it which transcended all the rest in interest, viz.: the heavenly radiance that habitually, and sometimes almost supernaturally, lighted his countenance. This point is so well set forth in a letter from one* of his former associates, now in America, that I will quote a few lines in illustration of it: 'Did it ever occur to you how easy it is to realize Brother Rhea as in heaven? There lingers in my recollection a sort of glow his face had at times, which I always associated with Moses' face when he came down from communion with God. The lustre in our dear brother's face had the same origin, I doubt not, differing only in degree, and it is easy for me to think of his expression as being merely intensified and perpetuated.'

"The present families of our mission will certainly never forget his appearance and the impression he made at the last baptismal and communion service which we attended with him, just before he started for Tabreez. The celestial air his features wore, and the almost angelic strains in

* Dr. Young.

which he spoke and prayed, seemed to bear us up, not indeed to Sinai, but to the Mount of Transfiguration.

"Such was our missionary brother, culminating in all that is noblest and purest that we ever witness in a human being."

The following extract is from, I believe, his last letter to his beloved brother, Rev. Mr. Williams, of Mardin: "Have not the skies grown brighter across the water? They certainly seem so to me. They are certainly brighter for East Tennessee. I do not despair of the republic. I do not despair of the Lord Jesus Christ, to whom *all power* in heaven and earth is given. His divine thoughts have made all this stir. He is alive. His words still vibrate through our air, his thoughts still thrill human souls, his soul still pervades God's embattled hosts. The fact is, dear brother, the materialism of this age had almost dethroned God. There was no sign, no voice, no miracle, and consequently there never had been one. 'On a journey,' 'turned aside,' or 'asleep!' When suddenly his throne of judgment is set— a great guilty nation is arrested and brought to his bar, and bolts of divine vengeance flame against her. For one, I am entirely satisfied with the administration of the Lord of the whole earth; and with profoundest reverence I would bow to his will and say, *Let it be done*—come what may, *Let it be done!* I cannot understand many things about it, nor do I wish to, until he pleases to inform me.

"Just now the *Levant Herald* reports defeat in East Tennessee, but I do not believe it. How hard for men abroad to get any idea of the physical or moral dimensions of our great war!"

To a playful remark of a correspondent about the "wagon," "Oh you aristocratic folk! Riding in *carriages!*" he replies: "Just think of it! Poor Brother Abraham in South Africa trudging along in his ox-cart, at snail's pace,

28 *

'whoa-hawing' till so hoarse he can't preach, belaboring the dumb brutes until he has exhausted strength and patience—to see himself in the *Illustrated London News* in a gilded coach drawn by shining steeds, with liveried footmen, bounding over hill and dale, and all this with the money of the laboring poor!

"*How kingly you* do things up in Mardin! Riding on beautiful white asses! One so large, so strong, so comely, so gentle, so nicely gaited as to take your whole family on his capacious back; and not satisfied with such extravagance, a horse to boot—maybe a grand old Turcoman with his kingly tread, or the costly, blooded Arab with all his beauty and fleetness! Oh, you aristocratic folk!"

To Messrs. Coan and Shedd touring in the mountains of Koordistan, Mr. Rhea wrote: "Dear brethren, the glorious news of peace will make your heart beat high and strong. This Divine interposition in the affairs of our world will have to the Church and the nation all the force of a miracle. The war, its origin, prosecution, close and results, will form one of the most intensely thrilling chapters in the history of our race. God alone is great, and to him be all the glory.

"We are having a breezy time. One day the Charbash church is closed and our people shut out; another the straw rooms are rased to the ground by order of Nejif Ali, out of pure spite toward us; another day the Begler Bey's servants come and stop the school—finally the Begler Bey sends to have the school assemble again. Nejif Ali consents to the use of the church, and seeing he has burnt his finger by tearing down the straw rooms, begins to draw in and becomes decidedly soft; but his villainy consists in this putting on the most friendly airs when he is stabbing the deepest." The reader will be rejoiced to know that through Mr. Rhea's able representations sent to the capital of Persia this Haji Meerza Nejif Ali was deposed. Mr. Rhea must needs have interviews with other subtle Persians in higher position before the happy result.

The following letter gives some account of Persian wiles met by the wisdom of one taught from above. Mr. Rhea had left his home on a long journey with his family for Tabreez, and this very full letter, which we can only give in part, seems to be the last letter but one which he ever wrote. It was addressed to his brethren jointly, dated near Salmas, at

SAOORA, *August* 8, 1865.

DEAR BRETHREN: We had a beautiful moonlight ride out to Uzarlu. Some of the leading men, whom I at once recognized, came to the tent in the evening as we were pitching it. They reminded me that I had taken thirty tomans ($60) from them. I exhorted them to forsake for the future all such costly enterprises as filching American travelers' bags. They retired, but on their way from the tent, to Mrs. Rhea especially, gave an illustration of Oriental inborn propensity to thieving, by making away with her American bridle. We left early.

At Gavalan a passing remark tells the whole story of their spiritual interest. "We will attend preaching to-morrow—perhaps the sahib will interest himself in recovering our sheep." Yet several persons seem near the kingdom of heaven.

Up at four—off at six—going to Jemalava crossed track of a "sâlav." Old fruit trees remain standing several feet deep in sand and stone. That vineyard had flourished there scores of years, and yet in one night a sâlav came down and made a deposit which future geologists might say required several years. Old Nature has her freaks, which geology ought to provide for in its speculations.

We rode ten hours, reached Saoora at six. Mrs. R. and

I rode in advance and rested in the shade while the rest
came up. Ate pears in Khosrova. We found Khoshaba
and Elishwa under ban, prohibited from preaching, teaching or selling books.

Old faces soon appeared, full of cordial welcome as ever.
The nearest neighbor, a mukdoosy, (holy man because he
has visited Jerusalem) seems decidedly evangelical—brings
his family regularly to preaching and evening prayers.
Last Saturday they had a hail-storm which did great damage to the melon gardens. On Monday I passed vines cut
to pieces, literally riddled, scarcely a leaf appearing, while
the ground was covered with unripe melons, lying out naked
and forlorn-looking. A day or two before the storm, one
hundred and fifty tomans (three hundred dollars) were refused for some of the gardens. After it, the owners left
them, utterly ruined. Strong men wept like children,
rushed out frantic before the pelting storm, bared their
heads and rubbed their faces on the earth, imploring God
to have mercy. After all was over, visits of condolence
were made, as after the death of friends.

I saw the Naib this morning. He soon introduced his
"little book," with orders from headquarters. Spent some
time looking over them to refresh his memory; quietly put
them in his box and asked, "What is your view? I want
to hear all your orders read; if I can answer them to your
satisfaction, well; if not, wait a few days until I return from
Tabreez."

He said, "It is not worth while to read them; the sub-
stance is, first, American priests are not to reside in Salmas
or open a printing-office."

"I have not done either; but only come as a guest, spending a month or two."

"Well, let that go."

"No; but why have you threatened to send Khoshaba

off (the native Christian helper)? Is he prohibited? He is not an American, but a Persian subject. Have you any order to drive him out?"

Quite perplexed, he evidently had none. " Well, we'll pass on. You must print no books except such as Mahmed Rooli Khan endorses."

" His agent was in Oroomiah a year and a half and sanctioned the issues of our press; but, pray, what has that to do with your prohibiting Khoshaba from selling books? and especially the Torat and Anjil? (law and gospel—Old and New Testament). Where is your order for that?"

Again silenced, he passed on. " You must not proselyte."

" Prove that Khoshaba has proselyted any one."

" Then what is his business here?"

" Not to proselyte, but to instruct in the Scriptures and call men to repentance. What! do you say he is doing wrong to tell the Armenians their worship of images and of saints is contrary to the Anjil (gospel), and a sin? Is this proselyting? Let them remain Armenians, but forsake their errors—what you yourself know to be errors."

" Well, if he is not proselyting now, he intends to some time."

" When he does, then arrest him, if it is a violation of law."

" But the people don't want him here."

" Some do. This you acknowledge when you say you broke up his school. If he had a school, he certainly had some friends."

He wound up by saying, " It is not best to talk about this matter too much. We will arrange all this evening."

It was evident he was troubled at having gone beyond his orders.

Thursday morning.—The Naib called this morning. He wished to know what he should write to Tabreez: " Shall

I write that all the Armenians are opposed to Deacon Khoshaba ?"

"No. That would not be true; you know he has friends."

"Let them come and say they want him."

"They have been threatened, and fear."

He disclaimed ever having threatened them with fines and beating, which was untrue. I then said, "Give me a paper guaranteeing freedom from all molestation if they make such a statement, and the men are at the door ready to make it." He backed down, and soon took leave, saying he would write as he thought fit. He was made to understand that if he wrote falsely, all his intriguing for presents, the affair of the clock and transgression of orders, would be exposed. He was very civil, and evidently wished to avoid being complained of. He sent word by his servant to Khoshaba that if he would give him a watch he would write just as we wished.

Called at the governor's in the old city. He said the papers with regard to the house were entirely satisfactory.

The last letter he ever wrote was from Tabreez, August 19, 1865. He speaks of hospitable entertainments and a dissipated week; also of photographic rooms; of a friend religiously all afloat; thinking "the Christian religion almost as much as any other involved in difficulties. How one longs to be able to speak a word in season! None but God's omnipotent spirit can reach such a case. We were at Mr. Nicholson's on Tuesday. Spent the night. A number of Europeans were there to breakfast and spent the day. Everything done up in princely style.

"The order came down from Teheran (the Persian capital) that Nejif Ali's case should be investigated by a council in Tabreez. Nejif Ali begs off, requests to go to Oroomiah and have his case investigated there! Of course he knows no Nestorian *there* will dare to testify against him.*

" *Monday morning.*—We had an interesting day yesterday. About thirty were present at our services, nearly all Armenians. We had baptism of Eshoo's child and sermon and communion. All the services were in Turkish. Of course there is much to say about our missionary work here, for which there is not time at present. On the whole, there is ground for encouragement.

" We hope to get through our visit here this week, and early next week set out on our return. Still we do not wish to leave until we get our matters in a satisfactory state, if possible. The children's eyes are sore. Foster in a bad state. Our quarters, too, are not very comfortable for a family of little children, and we should like to leave as soon as we can. With much love to all our circle, I am, as ever, yours, very sincerely."

CHAPTER XXIV.

ALI SHAH.

THE village in Persia named Ali Shah, after Ali the murdered son-in-law of Mohammed, the fourth caliph, who is annually mourned in Persia, has a special claim upon our remembrance.

In the great Persian cities, during ten days of the Sacred Month, the whole population give themselves up to lamentations for their slaughtered imaums, Ali and his two sons, Hooseyn and Hassan. Men robe themselves in black and tear open their garments. Assembled at mosques and courts of great men, most eloquent mollahs harangue, and on high platforms actors represent the tragic scene. Once Mr. Rhea wrote: "To-day, as plaintive tones rehearsed the mournful events, the whole vast multitude of several thousands, with their princes and governor, and military men and high nobles, and men of all ranks, broke forth in the most violent fits of weeping and sobbing and smiting their breasts. When shall this wonderfully emotional nature of the Persians pay its homage, thrilled with the fact of a crucified Saviour, at the cross?"

We turn in explanation of our interest in Ali Shah to the sad letter of Mrs. Rhea, conveying to her own mother the story of her journey to and from Tabreez:

SEIR, PERSIA, *September* 11, 1865.

I wrote about two months ago, mentioning our anticipated visit to Tabreez. We started August 4, looking for

A PERSIAN JOURNEY, WITH CHILDREN IN BASKETS.

only sunshine and blessing, but the Lord had other things in store.

All the journey I made by the side of my dear husband, enjoying the most delightful conversation, and receiving, in his most tender care and love of me, proofs of an affection which has rendered my life like the unfolding of a rose gladdened by incessant sunshine.

Our horses carried us rapidly in advance of the party, which consisted of four loads, two muleteers, two Nestorian servants and our two children, riding in their baskets. It was our plan to ride on rapidly and then stop a little while to rest under some shade or near some stream until the loads came up. In this way, the whole journey was accomplished without fatigue.

We left home on Friday afternoon, arrived in Gavalan Saturday, about noon, where we spent the Sabbath and commemorated the Lord's Supper with the little church, and Mr. Rhea baptized the infant daughter of the priest, our Nestorian helper. The preparatory meetings held, one on Saturday evening, the other on Sabbath morning, with the members of the church, I shall never forget. Mr. Rhea's counsels were so heavenly, his manner so impressive, his words so solemn, so tender, so appropriate. Two young men, communicants, had been quarreling, and had raised their hands to strike, and been parted by some worldly spectators. How tender, how sorrowful his reproofs! saying only a few earnest, telling words, and leaving the application and condemnation to themselves. They were not slow to make it. They seemed broken down and humbled to the dust. After the communion the collection of the monthly concert was taken up, and established as a future rule of the little church by the affirmative vote of every member. The village of Gavalan has been in Mr. Rhea's care for several years, and he has felt the deepest interest in its spiritual welfare. On leaving it this time, he promised the helper there that, as he returned, he would stop several days for the purpose of evangelical labors.

After dinner on the Sabbath, though weary and needing rest, he walked over to Jemalava, a Nestorian village, one or two miles distant, and preached again.

Monday, we arrived at Sawoora, an Armenian village on the Salmas plain, where we have a Nestorian helper. Mr. Rhea enjoyed conversation and religious exercises here with all who came, and called upon the head man of the village and the governor of the province with reference to securing a more satisfactory recognition of our helper's residence and labors in Sawoora. He obtained a respectful hearing, and a promise that the helper should be unmolested. Thursday, we went to Pigajuk, where we met two girls, former pupils of the seminary, now married to Armenian merchants. We spent an hour in friendly and religious conversation, tea-drinking, etc., and then, after an evening ride, arrived at Yanshouly, where our tent had been pitched for us in advance, and where we found a carrier with our American mail.

Two more days brought us to Dizza Khalib, where we pitched our tent in a quiet garden for the Sabbath. How sweet the memories of that Sabbath! Several hours of the forenoon were spent in reading the Bible, religious conversation and prayer in the Turkish language with an Armenian whom we picked up on the way, with our Mussulman host and our servants. In the afternoon we had another long and deeply spiritual meeting with our own servants, reading several chapters in the Bible, with remarks and explanations, Mr. Rhea praying himself and calling upon each of them to pray.

We arrived in Tabreez August 15, Monday, and stopped at the house of Eshoo, our Nestorian bookseller and deacon.

For a week we were all well—Mr. Rhea full of business of every kind. We visited the European families, the bazaars, Eshoo's Bible depository, several Armenian preachers, the ancient Armenian church, graveyard and school. Mr. Rhea also had several earnest conversations with the English consul about the affairs of the Nestorians, etc., and made an official call upon the vizier, whom he saw alone by particular favor and talked with a great while, disabusing him of a score of slanderous and injurious reports about the work of the American missionaries in Persia, who, he assured the vizier, had no political designs, either present or future, but whose only business was to teach the precepts of the Old and New Testaments and the worship of one living and true God.

The vizier made himself extremely polite and accessible, and Mr. Rhea described his interview as entirely gratifying and satisfactory. On the first Sabbath after our arrival Mr. Rhea conducted the services of the communion, baptism of Deacon Eshoo's child, and preaching in Turkish before an audience of thirty-five persons, who listened with breathless attention and beaming eyes. The Spirit of the living God was in the midst, and the interest attending the services was something not of earth, but imparted from on high. It was so felt and recognized at the time, and solemnly remembered afterward. The same evening, in Deacon Eshoo's house, we had another solemn meeting; the subject was Eternity, on which the missionary's mind had been greatly absorbed for several weeks. His words were worthy of the theme.

In a few days afterward he was taken sick, and Annie also in a similar manner. They seemed to have taken cold in some fierce gale from the Caspian, such as is common there. They were both confined for a week with fever, but not alarmingly. I administered some simple medicines at first,

29 *

and afterward called in Dr. Yurist, a German. He came three times, prescribed large doses of quinine, and said that they would soon be well. He then bade us good-bye, as he was going to a distant village, and supposed that we should be in Oroomiah before he returned. Mr. Rhea grew better, walked over to the grounds of the consulate, and Thursday morning, August 31, rode half an hour out of town to call on the English consul.

We thought the air of Tabreez bad for us. Our confined quarters were certainly unwholesome, and, as we longed to get home, we planned to get out at once on our return journey, making it slowly and by the shortest possible stages. We started from Tabreez, Mr. Rhea on horseback. Once out of the close, dusty city, we encountered a refreshing breeze, which we both enjoyed.

We rode along rapidly and very comfortably to Myan, two hours from Tabreez, where we stopped in a caravansera. We gave our horses to a man in the stable-yard and went up stairs to a little upper room, where I persuaded Mr. R. to lie down on my shawl and rest.

By and by the loads came up, and after a cup of tea and bread we retired, but not to rest. Mr. Rhea was seized suddenly with the most excruciating pains in the abdomen. They came on in almost incessant paroxysms, so violent as to force the perspiration from every pore, drenching his clothes, and extorting groans expressive of intolerable agony. He obtained no rest, not even for a moment, through the night. Three times he was obliged to get up, and seemed so deathly sick with purging and vomiting that a horrible thought came to my mind—*Can this be cholera?*

During the night he would often lift up his soul in gentle tones to God in prayer for help, for relief, for submission. I listened in agony to hear if he should ask relief in death ; but he never did. He prayed as if he was leaning on the bosom of Jesus; and, assured of sympathy and love, was telling him all about it and committing his case to the great and good Physician. Once he said, with great earnestness, "Oh how sweet, how sweet the rest of heaven will be after all these afflictions!" Again he said, "The hand of the Lord is very heavy upon me." "Perhaps we never realize *how heavy* it is more than in personal affliction and strong pain." He had a long, sweet sleep in the forenoon, when I kept the flies off him and Annie. Our room was such an open place, and the Caspian breeze so fierce, and his perspiration so copious, that I did not venture to use any such remedies as baths or hot applications.

On Saturday morning I wished to send to Tabreez for a takhterawan (a chair borne by horses) and to return thither. But he did not consent, preferring rather to go on to Ali Shah, the next village, four hours distant toward Oroomiah. We had heard that we could find a comfortable room to rest in there for the Sabbath, good water to drink, and a takhterawan for our journey. The water of Myan was bitter, and no one but the inhabitants of the wretched place could drink it. We had brought a little water in a jug, but it lasted only till noon of Saturday.

Of his own accord Mr. Rhea told the servants to get out the horses, and we would try to go on to the next village. He made himself ready, and we started off near five o'clock Saturday afternoon. I little realized how ill he was, though, as we were mounting our horses, I noticed how pale and feeble he looked, and told him that he had changed in a night and a day. He did not seem to have the least apprehension of anything fatal in such a pain, nor did I. Daniel walked by the side of his horse, holding the bridle and rendering any little assistance he might ask. Mr. Rhea sat in the saddle, holding his umbrella till the sun grew low.

About half an hour from Myan we stopped to rest. He

said, smilingly, "Is it not too soon to rest?" We only stopped a few minutes, and Daniel and Guergis helped him on again.

Then we rode on and on, I watching him all the time, fearing and feeling that he was suffering, though unable to detect it by the expression of his patient features.

Not far from Myan I said, "Would you not like to return?" He shook his head a little and said, "I scarcely know what I want." Riding on, after another interval I said, "Have you any comfort?" He said, "Not much."

Occasionally I gave him a little wine to wet his lips. I seldom spoke, not wishing to tire him. After a while I said, "You do not ask to stop: would you not like to rest?" He replied, "The wear and tear of getting off and on is more than the good. There is no place here to lie down." It was a dreary place—an unmitigated desert. But I insisted on stopping a little; and Daniel helped him down, while I jumped off my horse, spread the shawl and received his dear head in my arms, sitting down by the side of the road.

He was very tired; panting, and breathing with difficulty; trembling, shaking and perspiring. His enunciation seemed a little difficult on account of the panting. I gave him a little wine and bathed his face with camphor. He did not lie quite still, seeming to be uncomfortable. I begged him to try to rest a little, and prayed little sentences of entreaty that God would comfort him and relieve his pain, and take us safely to the village.

By this time the muleteers, with the loads, had come up, and the chavadar called out in a commanding tone, "Why do you linger here? There is danger. Let us be going; the village is very near; rest there."

Mr. Rhea was on his feet before he had finished, and said, "Let us go." He went to his horse, taking the bridle from

Guergis' hand as if to mount. At the same time he told Guergis to ask the chavadar how far it was to the village.

Guergis looked in his face and burst into tears!

Mr. Rhea looked at him steadily, as if he did not understand his emotion. I told our Nestorian men, Daniel and Guergis, they must put the bedding on one of the loaded horses, arrange it as comfortably as possible for Mr. Rhea, and then place him upon it and hold him on. They did so, both walking by him.

I rode as near as possible to him, listening and leading his now empty horse.

Sometimes, as one side would be heavier or lighter, he would be called upon to move a little, which he did promptly and with an appearance of strength.

The motion of the horse extorted frequent though gentle groans of pain. He was very thirsty, and both the children were crying for water. Water there was none. At a previous brook he had tried to drink, but spit out the bitter water in disgust. The wine was better than nothing, but unsatisfactory.

At length the moon rose. The children now grew quiet. Daniel passed a rope around his back and over his shoulders, to keep him from shaking about on the horse; and, taking off his hat, protected his head with a flannel. He grew quiet, and I said, "He sleeps." So we rode on and on in the still night, no sounds except from the horses' feet or an occasional word about the precious load. Will the village never appear? They said it was very near. Oh, how long the way seemed!

My mind was very active, picturing that comfortable room where we should rest at Ali Shah; the refreshing water, the quiet rest, the soft bed for the dear invalid, the quick cup of tea, his sweet words, our subsequent journey home in the takhterawan, our safe arrival there. All this time my eyes were on him and my ears strained to catch a sound. How long he sleeps! How still he is!

And then I prayed to God! No one understood the language except the Hearer of prayer. I plead every promise and every ground of hope, and entreated with all my heart and soul that God would have mercy, help and comfort us, and restore my dear one to health. I was comforted. The fear of a dread calamity passed away. My mind was calm, and so strong to take care of him.

We hired a countryman passing along the road, so that three men were all the time engaged in making his position comfortable; and the two chavadars also rendered assistance when any adjustment or change was called for.

At length the weary, weary road was all passed. We reached the village, and stopped at a house where they said we could find a room. Daniel and I ran in to see it first, opened the windows and spread down the shawl and pillows where he could rest; then went back to the gate, and I charged the men not to let him exert himself at all, but to take him down like a little child and carry him carefully in. I ran forward then and got in through the window, which was low, opened my satchel and got out the wine and camphor, and spreading a pillow on my lap, received him in my arms.

Just as they deposited him in my arms he drew one long, deep sigh. I wet his lips, bathed his face, spoke to him, called his name, raised him up, kissed him and entreated him to speak. I chafed his soft, warm hands, felt his heart, felt his pulse, his temples, his neck, seeking everywhere for signs of life. In vain. He was dead!

But I did not believe it. I assured Daniel that he was not dead. It was impossible, without a look, a word, a sign! I knew it was not so, and begged him to say so too! Tears were my only answer.

I shed no tears for hours. I knew some dreadful thing had happened, some awful dream; but he was not quite dead yet. He would open his eyes, move or speak, or smile, and I would assure him of my undying love and kiss him good-bye and give him up to God. I was stunned. I was confused. It was *I* who was dead. My God had killed me with a sudden thunderbolt!

*   *   *   *   *   *   *   *

Daniel brought paper and ink, and said I must write two letters, and told me what to say. I obeyed mechanically. I wrote to the English consul in Tabreez, begging him to send me a coffin, ice, horses and men as speedily as possible. Then I wrote to the missionaries at Oroomiah, begging one of them to come and meet us and help us home.

I will not speak of that night as I watched at the door of my dead. The next day was the Sabbath; but not of rest to me. If he had died, I said, I might have borne it, for all must die; but to die *thus!* Such a death was agony.

At length the Divine Comforter directed my thoughts to the agonizing death of Jesus Christ. *He* had no comfortable room, no soft bed, no downy pillow, no sympathizing friend, no relieving hand near to administer any alleviation. He even begged for water to quench his dying fever, and they gave him vinegar to drink. That was too much for my stony heart; it melted and flowed down. I yielded myself to Him who gave his only and well-beloved Son so to die. I could not reproach God for the manner of my husband's cruel death when I saw how Jesus Christ had died.

I began to look for the coffin soon after noon of the Sabbath, desiring to hasten the precious remains to their resting-

place at Seir. The coffin did not come, and I waited on in
an agony of suspense till Monday noon.

The body was then closely enveloped in a white sheet
and India-rubber blanket, and placed in the coffin, surrounded by charcoal. The coffin was nailed up and sewed
into a woolen matting, and bound firmly to the pack-saddle.

I hoped to send it on rapidly, and follow as fast as we
could. Mr. Abbott wrote to me very kindly, and advised
me to return at once to Tabreez, and bury in the Armenian
graveyard outside the city. But I very earnestly desired
to lay the remains of my beloved husband among the people
for whom he had spent his life.

The first day we only traveled two hours, resting till after
dark. This was the less distressing to me because Annie
was very sick, and I should have feared for her tender life,
traveling in the hot sun. We rode all night, the children
in their baskets. Deacon Eshoo, from Tabreez, rode near
me on one side; Daniel, with the baskets, on the other.
Some distance ahead, accompanied by the faithful Nestorian Guergis and a chavadar, moved the coffin, on which
my eyes were ever fixed.

At dawn we stopped at a village. I supposed the coffin
would go on; but the chavadar said his horse was tired,
and it was impossible to induce him to move. The weather
was intensely hot.

At dark we started again on our funereal way. I found
the chavadars had turned aside from the lake road and
had taken a much longer route by the mountains. It made
me feel very sad. The wind blew very fiercely. We passed
several caravans of camels encamping.

This night passed like the first. What a road we went
over—so desolate, so drear! I had never seen anything so
desert, and could hardly believe I was passing the same
localities we had enjoyed so much three weeks before.

Wednesday morning at dawn we arrived at Yanshally. We did not wish to stop till an hour later, but the chavadars with great rudeness cast down the loads in the middle of the village in the street; so we threw ourselves on the ground exhausted, and took a little sleep. From Yanshally the precious remains had been brought on my own horse, which carried them the rest of the way. I earnestly begged the chavadars to let me go on with the coffin to Gavalan, promising them reward and rest there, but they were cruelly deaf to all entreaty. Eshoo and Guergis hired a man and took one of the chavadars, his horse and mine, and pressed on to Gavalan, while I was forced to remain in Cucurran with Daniel and the children till the next day.

At the watch-house on the mountain we were rudely assaulted by the soldiers, but were suffered to pass without actual violence.

Near Gavalan we met Mr. Coan, who took care of us with gentle kindness, speaking words of sympathy and comfort that were like sweet cordial to a heart overstrained and bursting. At the bridge, Mr. Labaree met us with the carriage, and Dr. Perkins and several kind Nestorians. We learned that the coffin had arrived early Thursday morning at Seir, and had been buried in a loving, Christian manner before noon.

When I went up to see the sacred spot, at sunset of Saturday, I had no words to express my sweet sense of gratification and appreciation. The mound was beautifully and symmetrically shaped, and sodded with green grass freshly sprinkled, and marked with a stone at the head and foot. It was beautiful and peaceful. God remember Dr. Perkins for the comfort of that sight!

30

CHAPTER XXV.

CLOSING SCENES.

ABOUT twenty-four hours after the first stunning intel-ligence was received, says Dr. Perkins, the corpse reached Mount Seir, borne in solemn stillness upon a horse. Brief funeral services were soon held by a company of sin-cere weepers, and the loved form was affectionately com-mitted to the grave.

Never was sorrow more deep and general among the sympathizing Nestorians than when the sad tidings went rapidly abroad; for no other man was ever more univer-sally beloved by the entire people. Very many among the Mohammedans also deeply lamented his death.

At eleven A. M. all that was mortal of that man of God so greatly beloved, reachéd the spot which his active feet had so often trod, beautiful upon the mountains as bringing good tidings; where his eloquent tongue, which had not inappropriately won for him the title of Chrysostom among the Nestorians, so often proclaimed to them the message of salvation. Devout men, among them several of his own faithful Nestorian helpers, were awaiting the sad solemnities, who, with their own hands, gladly prepared his hallowed resting-place, and then buried him, making over him *heartfelt* lamentation.

The time and manner of his summons, so mysterious, unexpected, so trying and crushing, were *chosen* of God in wisdom and love as those by which this beloved disciple could most effectually glorify God in his death, as he had

350

so long and so effectually done in his life. He had just left a heavenly savor at Tabreez, as in circumstances quite analogous did the sainted Henry Martyn a little before his death, when he had toiled but half as many years in the missionary field. Mr. Rhea had in like manner borne his last testimony for Christ in that dark city, seldom blessed with the presence of a missionary. And there he had put forth his last exertions with the Mohammedan authorities for our welfare and that of the suffering Nestorians.

It is the lot of few mortals to meet so trying an ordeal as that through which Mrs. Rhea was called to pass. The overwhelming shock of that sudden exit on the road, among strangers, in a dark land; the necessary preparations for bringing the precious remains over the long and wearisome journey of more than a hundred miles, the widow following them in a lonely caravan under a burning Persian sun, with her tender orphans on her hands, one of them sick, and the only earthly comforters near her the sympathizing Nestorian attendants. Oh, this was a trial too severe for flesh and blood to bear, save as grace, abounding grace, sustained her. She reached Mount Seir the day following the interment of the remains of her husband.

A massive block of snow-white gypsum, neatly polished, was soon placed over Mr. Rhea's grave by his widow, bearing the following inscriptions:

"REV. SAMUEL AUDLEY RHEA,
MISSIONARY TO THE NESTORIANS;
Born January 23, 1827; died September 2, 1865.
Present with the Lord."

On the reverse side the name, office and dates are the same, in modern Syriac, with the Scripture—
"He was not, for God took him."

Persian roses and blue violets are planted round the stone, and fill the air with fragrance.

His grave is often visited by loving and grateful Nestorians, as are others in that hallowed cemetery, to drop a tear of affectionate remembrance.

The same power of sustaining grace which supported the crushed widow under the first shock of her overwhelming bereavment, has wonderfully borne her up since she was led into the deep waters, comforting her in her sorrows, strengthening her in her arduous duties in the care of her three orphan children and her abundant labors in the Female Seminary, carrying her through scenes of sore trial and suffering, and shedding around her an atmosphere savoring so much of heaven that she has been to our mission, to our work and to the Nestorian people an angel of consolation, encouragement and hope, such as the furnace of affliction alone could give to us and to the cause of Christ on earth.

CHAPTER XXVI.

HIS CHARACTER.

WE append, from the many tributes to the memory of Mr. Rhea, a few fragments illustrative of different traits of his character. In them we find not merely reasons for placing him among the eminent of God's children, but suggestions for growth in the graces of a true Christian life on the part of others.

The venerable late Foreign Secretary of the American Board, Dr. Anderson, wrote to the afflicted widow: "I know not that I ever felt so painfully despondent as I did on Saturday last, after reading your own most touching narrative to your mother, which came to me unsealed from Constantinople, but which I remailed the same day. Unfitted for work, I went home; but as I was ascending the hill to my house I said, O Jesus, thou art infinite in wisdom, and therefore I believe that there is mercy in this event—that it is all merciful; and then a ray of light broke into my darkness. The blow was from our heavenly Father's hand. This we believe; the Lord help our unbelief."

WALKING WITH GOD.

Rev. Mr. Cobb having been forced to return to this country, thus mentions his impressions of Mr. Rhea: "I do not think the manner of his death mattered much to him. For he seemed to me, more than any man I ever knew, to have his conversation in heaven, and to be ready at any moment for translation thither. I can never forget through life,

and perhaps not through eternity, his constant longing after
greater purity of heart and conformity to Christ, nor the
oft-repeated expression of his conviction that perfect love
and perfect conformity ought to be attained.   I do think
that in him, more than in any one I ever knew, was exemplified my ideal of walking with God; and I shall ever
feel that some of the strongest impulses I have ever received in the divine life have been through him.   His noble
countenance and earnest words are almost as vividly present to me now as when I saw him in some of our little gath-
erings in Oroomiah, and heard him breathe out the aspirations of his soul after God and Christ and holiness."

HIS LOVE OF COUNTRY AND OF LIBERTY.

From the Rev. Mr. Shedd, of the mission to the mountain Nestorians:

Some of the finest traits of Mr. Rhea's character came
out in connection with the civil war in America.   The deep
personal love he bore to those near and dear to him in the
Southern armies gave a tenderness and solemnity to all his
words, and showed his adherence to the national cause to be
the result of self-sacrifice as really as his love of Christ.
His sympathy with the masses of the Southern people and
his admiration for their bravery, his sense of the magnitude
of the struggle, his grasp of the principles involved, and
his faith in the triumph of the government and the ultimate overthrow of the oligarchy of the South were remarkably strong and clear.   The Fourth of July, 1865, the last
before his death, was celebrated by our mission circle, and
all present well remember how much he contributed to the
interest of the occasion.   His gratitude that the war was
really over, and the right had gained the day, was poured
out in thanksgiving.   Especially we remember the tender,
enthusiastic admiration with which he spoke of our fallen

President, and the still deeper emotion with which he responded to the sentiment, "The loyal men of the South." He was excelled by few men in the beauty and eloquence of his addresses on such occasions, and his love of country was a sacred duty, second only to his love of God.

DR. PERKINS.

Of Mr. Rhea's love of country, Dr. Perkins says: "We should not do justice to the memory of Mr. Rhea were we not to allude to the depth and ardor of his patriotism. This was very conspicuous during the fearful war in America. He was from beginning to end a thorough-going Union man. Though a native of Tennessee, and though he loved the State of his birth with a devotion second to that of no other citizen, and though some of his dearest friends were drawn into the ranks of Secession, his attachment to the Union never wavered. And in the darkest periods of the war he was firm in the hope and belief of the ultimate success of the government; perhaps more so than any other member of our mission, and his joy in the final triumph of our arms amounted wellnigh to ecstasy.

"While we are bound to make this honest and honorable record, we should also state that, sore as was the trial and deep his grief in differing from his friends who were arrayed on the opposite side in the appalling conflict, he ever cherished the kindest feelings toward them, never applying to them a reproachful epithet nor impugning their motives, but regarding them as sadly mistaken on a momentous subject. And as such he could earnestly remonstrate with them and pray for them. But in regard to the plotters and leaders of the great rebellion, he could and did at the same time pray for their overthrow as heartily as ever the Psalmist prayed for the discomfiture of 'the enemies of the Lord and of David.'

"His full sympathy with the measures of President Lincoln, at the time, for the overthrow of slavery might seem strange were it not known that he had long been from principle a decided anti-slavery man. Perfectly free from the slightest tinge of that vituperative spirit that has animated too many earnest abolitionists, he was not a whit behind them in his deep sense of the evils of the 'stupendous wrong' of American slavery, or in his long-ing desire for its complete removal. I have never found a stronger sympathy on this subject in any missionary in Asia, and far less in some. Soon after he reached our field he incidentally mentioned to me the fact that his father had long before liberated his slaves, that they might join the colony in Liberia; 'and on that day,' said the young mis-sionary, 'my father took me to the stables and said to me, Sam, now you must take care of the horses.' This, of course, was the key that explained the whole subject of his interest in the freedom and welfare of the colored race.

"Mr. Rhea's views, well known to his brethren, seem now prophetic. In January, 1857, he wrote to his friend at Mosul: 'An all-wise, just and merciful God has permitted for the present the triumph of slavery. I delight to submit to his disposition of the matter without one murmur. He knows the wrongs of slavery. The blood shed in Kansas, I believe, is but the beginning of blood-shedding in con-nection with the accursed system. I have no idea that the exodus of three millions of slaves out of the house of their bondage can be effected without bloodshed. I know not what form it will take, but I believe it will come in terrible judgment on the heads of slaveholders. Were the majority of slaveholders, or any large proportion of them, Christian men, I should have hope that one day there would be a peaceable solution of this dark problem; but they are not.

The great majority, like hundreds and thousands at the North, love the ease and emoluments of slavery.' "

FROM THE MOUNTAIN POST.

From Gawar, Koordistan, the Rev. J. H. Shedd writes the following glowing tribute : " My acquaintance with Mr. Rhea began in New York city the morning myself and wife embarked for Persia. In the few hours of that bustling morning he quite won our hearts by his brotherly assistance and kindness. He left our side at the very last moment, and his farewell grasp was our final adieu to our native land. Fourteen months later, on the open plain of Oroomiah, in a drenching autumnal rain, I grasped his hand again. With others of our circle I had ridden out several miles to welcome him and his associates to Persia. The next five years we were often associated in missionary counsels and labors, and in social and religious intercourse. The final grasp of his fraternal hand was in July, 1865. The night previous we had spent in adjoining tents in Anbar, a village on the border of the plain of Oroomiah. In the morning we were to separate, myself and wife to resume our journey, and he and his family to remain for missionary labor in the village. He was looking toward Tabreez and we toward Koordistan for our summer labors. After united family prayers we started mountainward, and for an hour he accompanied us on our way. That hour's ride now rises before me. His countenance and dress, his words and gestures, his kind adieus and advice to the natives of our company, and his final farewell, all have the distinctness of a picture. We had talked much during the morning of our work and of vital missionary themes, and his last words related to our annual meeting, to be held after our summer's journeys and labors were over. In a mountain valley we parted, my own heart softened and

strengthened by the conversations of the morning and by
his tender adieu. Such partings on missionary ground have
the conscious uncertainty that *perhaps* our next meeting will
be in heaven.

"Before the summer's work was done, or the time for that
annual meeting came round, *he* was *there*. The news of his
passage to the skies reached us in Memikan, his home for the
first years of missionary life. My wife and several of the
village-women had just been to the graveyard upon the hill,
where rest the remains of Mr. Crane and Mr. Rhea's first
wife, 'Martha,' as the mountaineers affectionately call her.
As they returned, conversing of the departed, a messenger
from Oroomiah came up. A company of the villagers
gathered round, little thinking of the heavy tidings they
were to hear. When the sudden announcement was made,
'Mr. Rhea is dead,' the silent tears of some and the audible
grief of others paid, as no words could, their tribute to his
memory. All we could do to comfort them was to repeat
the record of Enoch, 'He walked with God and he was not,
for God took him.'

"The next day was communion Sabbath, and the occasion was especially solemn and hallowed to us all, as one
and another spoke of him who had labored so abundantly
for their souls, and so earnestly and beautifully pointed
them to the cross of Christ. Those villagers never can forget how holily and justly and unblamably he and his wife
behaved themselves among them. Those who are yet young
people can tell how kindness and gentleness won their child-
ish hearts; and those of maturer years verily believe there
never was a man so learned and wise, so full of mercy and
piety, as their own beloved missionary.

"As his successor in the mountain-field, I have heard
many unaffected tributes to his character and life, and especially to his self-denial and love of souls. Many of our

mountain preachers were first taught by him, and they never dwell upon his memory without deep emotion and en- thusiasm. In traveling in his footsteps I have often been struck with the interest and admiration for his character with which men have asked for that 'sahib' who first visited them with the word of life.

"In one district he spent a week, shut up by a storm, and the impression made upon the man in whose house he lodged never passed away. That man is now one of the most devoted Christians among the Nestorians, and one brother and two sons are hopefully pious. In a distant val- ley the people eagerly inquired for that blessed man, 'Kasha Samuel.' He there also had been snow-bound, and left a savor of piety and such seeds of life as can never perish. In a Papal village, after a long day's ride, he found a company of men utterly ignorant, but willing to listen. Instead of retiring, he spent nearly the whole night in unfolding to them the way of life. These are but illus- trations of his labors in the long and often perilous journeys he made in Koordistan.

"In those first years of his missionary life the sphere of his labors was not one to call out all his talents. But then and ever after his life illustrated one eminent missionary trait—viz., unceasing personal effort for the humble, the ig- norant and the lost.

"He showed us all what the missionary should be in his daily intercourse and tours. His faith and love of souls transformed the weary, rugged paths into ways of pleasant- ness, and made many a wild and selfish mountaineer to feel the beauty and power of the cross and the throbbings of his own and the Saviour's love to the lost.

"This entire consecration to the work of Christ was the commanding impression made by his life. No one could more truly say, 'I spend and am spent.' He loved to work;

and all the strength of his mind and body, and all the wealth of his affections and talents, were daily given to the blessed service of his Lord.

"In the five years of my acquaintance with him memory can recall no act or sentiment or manner that did not bear the stamp of a pure and noble character. In all social intercourse there was such richness and versatility of conversational power, combined with such scrupulous regard to the feelings of every one, that his company possessed a charm and left a Christlike fragrance. In his presence every unbecoming thought or act was silently rebuked, and the worst men for the time seemed inspired into something like sympathy with a higher life.

"To his politeness were joined such scholarly and linguistic attainments, and such a fund of general knowledge, as always gave weight to his words even before the proud Persian khans and princes.

"He had the eminent qualification of naturally and reverently turning every topic into a spiritual and practical channel. I doubt if any one, whether European traveler or Persian noble or Koordish chief, ever resented as an intrusion the subject of personal religion as introduced by him, and few indeed rose from an interview with him without having heard in some form his testimony for Christ.

"In him was an illustration of Christ's presence sought and realized in the midst of the most harassing cares. One day I remember on entering his room he was talking with the Mussulman Mirza over a very perplexing matter of injustice. The Mirza, Persian like, was full of futile compromises and expedients. At last Mr. Rhea turned round to him with great earnestness, saying, 'I could not endure this for a day except as I take counsel with Jesus, and ask him to help me and help the right, and I cannot understand how you can endure it without such a refuge and friend.'

The impression made upon the Mirza by such remarks is showed by his once saying, 'Mr. Rhea is full of beautiful preaching to us in the midst of all our business.'

"He exemplified the duty of rendering service to the Lord in every item and detail of life. When pressed down by cares and labors uncongenial to his tastes, I have seen him still apply himself—for instance to moneyed accounts or perplexing details of business—with such serenity, patience and fidelity as left no doubt that his heart was rendering service to the Lord."

THEOLOGICAL VIEWS AND STUDIOUS HABITS.

"In his theological views and opinions," says his companion, Mr. Coan, "he sympathized strongly with his father, who was of Scotch descent and a thorough Calvinist in the best sense of the word. He used to say, 'I am a high Calvinist.' The soul-humbling views held and taught by that wonderful Reformer exerted a marked influence in moulding his character. His views of sin, as seen in himself, were especially clear and pungent, and led to great self-abhorrence and exaltation of the free grace and sovereignty of God in Christ.

"As a scholar he was studious, thorough, patient, persevering and accurate, never resting satisfied short of truth. His tastes were philosophical and linguistic. Amid varied and distracting mission labors he maintained scholarly habits to a remarkable degree or he never could have left such a rich legacy to the Nestorians in beautiful hymns and commentaries on Matthew and the minor prophets. Nor could he have pursued his philological researches but for his persistency. His study was his home; but how often, for many, many consecutive days, was he obliged to sit up late at night if he would prosecute his studies and still be ready with copy for the printers! He wanted everything

to go from him finished.   During his first winter in Gawar
he read carefully the entire Hebrew Scriptures.

"His knowledge of the languages of Koordistan and
Persia had prepared him to enter with great zest upon
translating the Bible into Tartar Turkish; and his daily
recent habit was to carefully read his Greek Testament to
better fit himself for the great work.   His discourses to
Armenians in that Tartar Turkish were exceedingly chaste
and edifying.   His last public discourse was in that tongue
when at Tabreez.

"His love for and study of God's word were remarkable.
The Lord's secret was with him, and from concealed foun-
tains, which the multitude rarely deign to visit, he drew
living water, where men less imbued with the spirit of
Christ would find nothing.   His quick eye would detect
bright, beautiful gems which seemed to ravish his soul.
In our prayer-meetings, how ever varying and new and rich,
were the lights in which they were displayed.   How he delighted to hold up the sparkling jewels to our wondering
admiration!"

AS A PREACHER.

As a *preacher* he was a prince.   The glory and beauty
of his sermons was Christ.   He was enthusiastic, and his
enthusiasm was to win souls to Christ.   His evidently deep
conviction of the truth of what he uttered, his earnestness,
his burning eloquence swept all before him.   No wonder
efforts so strong were made to retain him in America, where
he might have adorned any pulpit!   Some have called him
a Chrysostom.   He had the flaming zeal of an Augustine.
A Boanerges, he was also a son of consolation.   How did
he throw his whole soul into his discourses, and every
muscle and fibre of his body seemed laid under contri-
bution, while speaking eye and clarion voice gave forth the
message of God to man!

CHAPTER XXVII.

VOICES OF THE NESTORIANS.

LET us give place, in the closing of our narrative, to the voices of the Nestorians of Persia and Koordistan with regard to him who laid down his life in serving them. Mrs. Rhea says of his bearing with them:

"Though Mr. Rhea could be a terror to evil-doers, fortunately this kind of work was not often called for. We oftener think of him in his connection with the natives as a gentle shepherd and bishop of souls. I have very delightful memories of going with him to villages, where, visiting the people in their houses and churches, he appeared to the finest advantage. How soon and how easily he would bring the conversation to a spiritual turn! The name of Christ seemed to sound more naturally from that 'golden tongue' than any other. Alas, with many worldly Christians it is like drawing eye-teeth to draw that name into the conversation! He never could be long in a village without getting a circle of children around him to repeat the Lord's Prayer, the commandments or Scripture questions, or to sing one of Zion's songs.

"Even poor and ignorant women and heedless young girls have said to me with tears, 'Such and such a sermon of Rhea Sahib's is ringing in my ears. I shall never forget it!' The winter after his death, one day when I had come home from school and was giving the children bread and cheese, in walked, to share our simple lunch, John, the former pastor of Geog Tapa, one of the

363

first converts to the truth and the brightest light among
the Nestorians—a flame of fire among them! His work
now is itinerating. He goes from village to village, from
church to church, rousing the backsliders and wakening
the impenitent by the most pointed and earnest personal
appeals in the pulpit; a revivalist of the Boanerges stamp,
doing a world of good, himself burning up with zeal that
acts contagiously upon his sympathetic people. He took a
seat and said earnestly:

"'I have come from Charbash. I bring glorious news
of the work of salvation. Your husband's labors are reap-
ing fruit, his prayers are being answered, his sermons are
pricking men's hearts and rousing their consciences; though
dead and buried, he lives and works among us still! This
work is the power of God! It is wonderful—strong men
weeping, inquiring what they must do to be saved; prayer-
meetings crowded; one hundred and fifty assembled this
morning; the women are awakened, the children are interested! It *is* the work of God! It is a glorious time! Mr.
Rhea's toils and prayers are seen and recognized, and they
are bearing fruit. He is dead, but God has not forgotten
them. His record is on high!'

"Such earnest words! Such beaming looks! Such speaking gestures! *Such news!* I thought of Mr. Rhea, of his
laborious and conscientious care of that village for years,
his anxieties, his labors, his prayers, his faith in God. And
now the answer and the fruit after he had gone to rest!
My heart melted and my eyes overflowed. How true is
God!

"One day last term I gave our dear pupils for their com-
position subject, 'Narratives of memorable days.' Sara,
of Geog Tapa, wrote thus: 'There is a memorable day of
last year which I can never forget. It was the holy Sabbath (such a date), and, as our custom is, we went up to the

house of God for worship. Rhea Sahib preached, and his text was the Prodigal son.' Then followed an analysis of the sermon in the order of its divisions, very well made out indeed for a Nestorian girl, showing how deeply it had impressed her mind and heart. 'When I came home,' she said, 'I went weeping to my prayer-closet; I was not at rest; neither did I find rest until, like the prodigal, as I hope, I arose and came to my Father!'

"Some of Mr. Rhea's sermons are now vividly remembered among this people by distinctive names which they have given them, as 'The Sabbath-day sermon,' 'The Bible sermon,' 'The Passover sermon,' 'The Publican sermon,' 'The Prodigal sermon,' 'The Lost sheep sermon,' 'The Heaven sermon,' 'The Women's sermon,' 'The Jerusalem sermon,' etc., etc."

The death of Mr. Rhea called out expressions on the part of his Nestorian pupils, hearers and associates that have a double interest. In their immediate relations to him they properly belong to his memoirs, but they fittingly crown the record of his life by showing that his labors were not in vain. When first met by American missionaries the Nestorians were as intellectually ignorant as they were morally benighted. What they now are may be inferred by the thoughtful after a perusal of extracts from a few of the tributes to the memory of their beloved guide. We give first a letter to Mrs. Rhea

FROM YOHANNAN,

A literary helper of Mr. and Mrs. Rhea, who was much with them.

OCTOBER 25, 1865.

MY DEAR, HONORED MOTHER:—Respecting that good and blessed father, resting from his toil, Mr. Rhea, be assured that this grievous chastisement of God which has

31 *

fallen upon you is not for you only, but is such for all our Nestorian people. It especially seems to me that God has crushed me in taking that honored father.

Truly, fresh before my eyes are his walk and his zeal, and his love and the spiritual feelings he habitually had in this world. His holy walk seemed to me a most humble one. When I reflected on that walk I obtained a spiritual frame from his blessed example. His zeal also was most evident. He longed to rouse every soul to his lost condition, and of every nation of whatever religion, Nestorian, Mohammedan or Jew. He had great love for every mortal, loving every one as an own son. As the pot that boils over the fire, so fervent was his love to every one; that love held forth an example for reconciliation to any who were at variance or alienated from each other. His spiritual feelings were also very ardent. When he spoke or preached, it was by the spirit holding forth the mystery of the gospel; as Moses spake from the mouth of God so spake this our blessed father. I can say of him as of Enoch, "He walked with God, and was not, for God took him."

May we walk in his footsteps, and be spiritual kindred with him in the kingdom of our Father in heaven.

Dear mother in Christ, please excuse me. Being sick, I could not write to you immediately, and I came three times to condole with you, but you were not in the city. Be comforted.

FROM DEACON SIMON,

A former pupil of Mr. Rhea.

GAWAR, *October* 12, 1865.

To THE PATIENT IN TRIBULATION, MRS. RHEA, GREETING:—I have recently heard those tidings so bitter to the heart respecting Mr. Rhea, that blessed guide, the honored, the patient in every way, that prince of preachers, so loving

to our people and to every man; so just, so good, so meek,
suffering for the sake of Christ; so studious and thoughtful
for the weal and welfare of our people.

Of course we must grieve greatly under the chastisement
with which the Lord has visited us, for it is the bitterest
of all the chastisements that we have hitherto received.
This is the most severe rod of the Lord that he has laid
upon his afflicted people.

When the sorrowful news reached my ear in Dizza, it
filled my heart with sorrows as though coals of fire had
been laid upon it and burnt it to a crisp. Then I remembered two of his sermons which he preached at Seir. One
of them was last year at the last assembly. He preached
in the evening. The preachers (Nestorian) were all astonished. He made an impression on the people as if
God had come down into the assembly. The second was
on the prodigal son. On this he had five topics. I do
not believe it will ever leave my memory. I often think of
these sermons. I grieve that he has left us; that his voice
will no more fall upon our ears till our final meeting before
the feet of our dear Saviour.

I recall, too, when he accompanied us a little way when
we started for Gawar, he said, "Simon, are you sorry to be
separated from your family?" I said, "Of course, sir, a
man is sorry; but what alternative is there? We must
suffer for the sake of Christ." He encouraged me and
strengthened me for my journey, accompanying me a little
way.

Verily, how strange it is that such a man should so soon
taste the cup of death. When we witness such dreadful
events it is proper that we sorrow and pray to the Lord that
he may fill the aching void. If I thus recall him, how
much more do you! But there is one thing: the almighty
God of the covenant can comfort you. He has said, " I

will sustain you in all your afflictions," etc. Certainly by these promises you may be comforted and pass the time of your sojourning in the world till the Lord carry you to meet him in those upper mansions which Christ has prepared for those who love him. Since Christ willed that he go up to him and be free from a world of sorrow and toil, and free from the bands of sin, strive all you can to ascend to where there is no sorrow for ever. God cares for all the broken-hearted. May he heal the wounds he has inflicted, and give comfort and consolation, and support you so long as you are in the world, and be merciful to your little ones, a father to these orphans and the widow's God. Amen.

Farewell. From Simon, son of Joseph, of Goolpashin, who am in Gawar, in the village of Chandewar.

FROM DEACON TAMO,

An aged and very eloquent Nestorian preacher in Koordistan, who will be recalled as suffering so sorely at the hands of the Turks.

MEMIKAN, *September* 20, 1865.

MY DEAR SISTER, MRS. RHEA :—I, Deacon Tamo, must greatly sorrow for the death of my dear brother, Mr. Rhea, with whom for ten years I have journeyed to Amadiah, to Mosul, etc., and have dwelt with him here, and often engaged with him in the study of the holy Scriptures, and never for a day wearied of him.

When Mr. Rhea left us, and we knew that he would come no more to us, fresh sorrow arose in my heart as at the great meeting in the city, when I got up and said, "The door to the mountains is closed," and my heart was ready to abandon the ministry; such sorrow filled my heart for parting with that blessed man. And now how great is the bitter grief for the death of that holy man among his friends! Alas, I had hoped to see Mr. Rhea this year, but death forbids it!

It is true that a great leader has fallen from the earthly Church; but it is more true that a shining star has been added very near the sun, and there are tidings of great joy in the churches of heaven. What more can we say? The Lord gave and the Lord hath taken away; blessed be the name of the Lord. We have feasted on his instructions; we have seen his beautiful example. What then can we do or say for the assuaging of our grief? We can only long to have our portion and heritage with him. My dear sister, what grief you have! I hope that the Lord Jesus, with the same hand that smites and wounds, will also heal and comfort you. The Lord bless you and soothe your sorrowing heart.

LETTER OF CONDOLENCE FROM MARY,

A pupil of the Nestorian Female Seminary, to Mrs. Rhea.

OROOMIAH, *January 22, 1866.*

MY DEAR FRIEND, MRS. RHEA:—Great love and salutations of peace do I pour upon you, honored guide. For a little time I now desire to withdraw my thoughts from the world, which is vanity; from everything therein, to think of you, sweet lady, whose life has been made bitter by the Almighty. It is not you alone that tastes bitterness for that blessed father, Mr. Rhea; I also taste that bitterness with you. When I think of the great love which Mr. Rhea has shown for us, and when I recall his kind words to us; and, further, when I remember that we shall hear his sweet counsels to us no more, truly I cannot tell you how much my heart is weighed down with sorrow. Not for me only had he love, but for our whole nation, poor, fallen and down-trodden, crushed under the manifold oppressions of

Y

the Mohammedans. I remember how much care he used to take for all these things. Whoever came to him on these matters he sent not empty away nor unheeded, but would always exert himself for him.

Not only had he love for us in these things, but he had a yet more ardent desire to draw souls under the bleeding cross of our dear Saviour, to point the way of life to perishing ones, to show the strait gate unto pilgrims laden under the heavy burden of sin—the path leading onward to the blessed Zion—and to acquaint them with all the difficulties and dangers that would befall them on their pilgrimage.

We saw him ever longing for poor souls among all our people, that they might find salvation. And when he prevailed the tears would roll down his cheeks, made beautiful by the love of the dear Saviour. His words were like sharp arrows, piercing through the hearts of lost sinners, that were as hard as a flint. Truly, he was a watchful shepherd over the sheep that strayed far from the fold of Christ. He was ever wakeful for conversation with men about their souls, urging them to find Christ as their portion, their refuge and their salvation.

Verily this loss has not fallen upon you alone, not upon the band of the beloved missionaries alone, nor on our own family alone, but upon all our poor fallen nation; the crown of our people is cast down; the golden chain has fallen from the neck of our king; we are desolate and without a leader. Our nation is left an orphan, even like his own little orphans. His words have left an "aching void" in the hearts of his hearers. Truly the memory of him is more pleasant than anything else in the world. It is not possible for us to forget him—those among our people who have tasted his love—till our tongue shall be silent in the grave.

In a word, if we were to narrate everything of his walk,

paper would not suffice, even for the little that we know of him.

Truly, it is meet that we lament over the great breach that hath come upon us. We remain like the fowl, her wings clipped so that she cannot fly to make any shift for herself. Then, on every hand, whatever this empty world may promise, our refuge is to lean on our dear Lord and Saviour.

I would speak a little of myself. As I hope, about two years ago I committed my soul to the dear Saviour, who was offered up a sacrifice for me a poor sinner. I was bound fast in the fetters of sin, but w am I loosed from them all, as I hope, and bound unto him from whom may I never be loosed. One Sabbath we went to the house of prayer; Mr. Rhea preached a very delightful sermon on the subject of the prodigal son. It made a very deep impression on me; even unto the present time it affects me.

Truly, I have great affection for you, my beloved friend. Never are you forgotten by me, especially when I bow before our Father in heaven; and yet more when I see you crushed and bruised under the stripes of the soul.

Again, when I look on your family, left desolate, without guide and protector, truly my heart is very full. A very grievous chastening hath indeed fallen upon you. The hand of the Lord hath touched you. It hath borne from you your head. It hath taken the taste from your mouth. But though the Lord hath chastened you he can heal your broken heart. Moreover, for our profit he chastiseth us. We know not as he knoweth. Then let us lean upon the arm of the Lord.

Please remember me in your prayers, that I may advance in everything spiritual.

Now abide in peace.

From a sharer in your grief, Mary, daughter of Jacob, of the city, to Mrs. Rhea.

DEACON YONAN.

The following memorial address was delivered before the "General Assembly," at the annual meeting of the Nestorian laborers in the mission work, a few days after the death of Mr. Rhea, by Deacon Yonan. It is translated for us by Dr. Perkins, who says: "It was finely delivered, and left a profound impression on the audience; in itself, also, it is deeply interesting." We give it at length as a sample of Nestorian oratory:

"How are the mighty fallen!"

This is a question which oft arises in my mind in these days, and I think in the minds of all the members of our churches. When one turns his thoughts from the things of the world and contemplates the course of events and changes that have passed over us in the last two years, the providences of God appear very dark and marvelous. It seems as though the Lord had begun at his own house, and commenced the work of judgment there. When we survey in order these events, and walk through the ranks of our spiritual army, we see our chief and brave ones fallen, both in the circle of our missionary guides and of our own number. Those we most needed—the pillars of our churches—those of whom we have been wont to say, If this or that one were not, our work would go to ruin and no more move forward. Now the wonder is that these are the very ones who have been chosen. And we who remain, as we meditate on the work on earth, on the banner which they supported now fallen, on their homes and their families, widows and orphans; that some have returned to their native land

and some are in our midst to renew our grief, our heart cannot help groaning out, Oh how are the mighty fallen!

On yonder hillside sleep Mar Elias and the Melek, veteran soldiers in the service. A little this side of the river-bridge, on the plain, rises white the tomb of Deacon Joseph. In the narrow porch of the church of St. Mary rests Deacon Isaac. Priest Meerza sleeps in Saralân. And other distinguished individuals of our number have fallen here and there. Beyond the mountains of Koordistan Dr. Grant, the first-born of our martyrs, laid his head, and the wild Arabs walk around his dust. The snows and the tempests of Gawar sweep over the graves of Mr. Crane and the first Mrs. Rhea. The marked heroes of our age, Stocking, Stoddard, Breath, Thompson, Wright, with ladies, maidens and sweet infants, are on the mounds of our country, and the gentle breezes of our mountains breathe over their dust. And last of all, a bitter voice astounds us, like the thunder of heaven in a clear day, that the strong man, Samuel Rhea, has fallen on the desert of Ali Shâh! pouring perpetual anguish through the heart of his widow and unceasing grief through the circle of his associates; and the ranks and lines of the hosts of the Nestorians are convulsed by the shock. The soil of Persia never received to its bosom a mortal form superior to that of Mr. Rhea!

My friends, when we look at the usefulness of these brave and blessed men, and their needfulness to the work and to their poor families, we exclaim in astonishment, How are the mighty fallen! And I believe, too, that our hearts chill and our hands hang down, and hope dies within us. But this is our weakness, and it is not becoming. Why should we sorrow as those without hope? Though we are greatly afflicted and distressed by their fall, and their place is vacant in the ministry here, still to sit and sorrow only will be but to put far back the work which they bore upon

32

their shoulders and carried so nobly forward. Methinks that a work yet more necessary and important has fallen upon our hands, and demands of us to take courage and strengthen our hands that hang down for that work, and confirm our feeble knees and clothe ourselves with a double portion of their spirit. The cross they bore over plains and mountains, and through valleys and gorges, and through cities and villages, while they manfully performed their ministry, it is ours now to take up. Let the beautiful example of ancient Scotland energize us. It was, that their chiefs were wont to assemble and arouse their armies by a herald bearing a flaming and bloody cross, when the enemy invaded their country, or an emergency fell suddenly upon them. Their chief would slay a lamb and their priest make ready a cross from light wood and kindle it with fire, and dip its flaming head into the blood of the lamb and lift it on high, all smoking and dripping, while he exclaimed:

> "As this cross passes from man to man,
> The chief summons you to your clan;
> Blighted be the ear that does not listen,
> Palsied be the foot that does not hasten."

Then he delivered it to the faithful herald, who bore it speedily to the next village and passed it to the head man there, and only hastily pronounced the name of the place of the army's meeting. Whomsoever the cross reached, he held himself bound by solemn oaths and under fearful imprecations to send it on to the next village, until it thus passed rapidly through the country in a very short period. At the sight of it every man from sixteen to sixty must hasten to the place indicated. What a sight was that! The running herald of the bleeding, smoking cross—herald after herald seizing it—none letting it fall to the ground, and even if his lips parched and peeled from thirst, never stopping to drink water. He leaped over mountains; he darted across morasses; he speeded over plains, and tarried not till he reached his goal and accomplished his object, and the bleeding cross had passed through the domain, and its echo reached every man. Then every horse was equipped, and men hastened from the mountains and the valleys. The fisherman left his net; the smith his hammer and his anvil; the shepherd his flock; the husbandman his plough in mid-furrow; every man is ready for the service of his chief.

This work, my friends, rests upon us. The heralds gone before us have thus fulfilled their ministry; and we are bound by solemn vows and fearful covenants not to let the cross fall to the ground.

Reflect a little on the example of Mr. Rhea. With what courage and zeal he took up the cross and bore it speedily through the mountains of Koordistan; through cities and villages and provinces, inviting men to cleave to the banner of salvation! With what diligence and earnestness he toiled till he fell in this service! Oh that he were now in our assembly! How much we miss him! What a weight of sorrow is mingled with our joy! But since he has gone, and cannot be with us, how suitable that we now meditate on his example and character, and take his track and follow in his footsteps.

The affecting circumstances of his death you have heard from Mr. Coan, and you will read them in the "*Rays of Light*" for this month, from the pen of Mr. Perkins. I shall therefore not recount them here; but I will mention briefly some of the prominent traits of his character.

1. One conspicuous trait in his character was his *zeal*. Few are they who have exercised zeal like his in service for the poor Nestorians, both in spiritual things and for their temporal welfare. You remember with what de-

votion and ardor he passed a portion of his life in the village of Memikan, there, alone in the snows and tempests of Gawar, proclaiming the gospel to lost souls. I once made a visit thither. I saw his location, his toil, his patience, his zeal, and I said in my heart, Verily he is a brave man. And you remember his wearisome journeys among the rugged mountains of Koordistan; his zeal for the bleeding cross bore him on among them, traveling much of the way on foot to fulfill his heraldship.

What zeal he evinced also for the temporal well-being of our people! What sighs did he draw when he saw our oppressions! As one might say, he burned up with zeal and spent himself all he could to bring us relief. With what zeal and ardor did he engage last year from early morning till late at night for ten successive days, not having time and rest even to eat his bread, that he might rescue a poor girl from the hands of her Mohammedan kidnappers! Great was his wearisome toil for us, which must never be forgotten. Let us now show our gratitude to him in kindness to his widowed lady, now in the midst of us, by sharing her sorrow and comforting her who has lost so dear and precious a husband (she will find him in heaven); as much as in you lies, all ye Nestorians, show to her respect and kindness, and let us all try to copy his example of zeal in service for his Master, seeing that his toils have not been in vain.

2. Do you remember with what *ardor he preached?* His countenance glowed like the countenance of an angel. The truths that proceeded from his lips were watered and sown by the Holy Ghost. What a loss we sustain; that his place cannot be filled; that we have lost those pungent sermons, and shall hear them no more! Would that their impression might not be wiped out from our hearts. His voice, his words, his countenance, his action in the pulpit

and the instructions of his sermons, all so blended and so drew out the heart as to constitute Mr. Rhea chief among preachers.   He preached as though the truths he uttered were not intended to display his wisdom or were for others only; he himself was awake to their importance, and was deeply impressed by them; and with longing ardor and earnestness of soul he sought to rouse those also who heard him to their importance.   One of the great sorrows that he bore about with him was the lack of the outpouring of the Holy Spirit.   For the last year and a half that I have been more acquainted with him and have written letters for him to various places (as his amanuensis) which were under his supervision, this was the great subject to which he sought to rouse his helpers—our need of the Holy Spirit to be poured out upon our assemblies.   To one of them he wrote, "Oh how I should rejoice to hear that there is a revival there!"

3. His *humility*.   Though he was a man of wise counsel, the like to whom there was none among us, he still was not deaf in his wisdom.   He condescended to take counsel and inquire of men much below him, both in regard to the work of the Lord and on worldly subjects, accounting himself as a fellow-laborer and not as chief and lord of the heritage. The helpers who were under his supervision remember that for the welfare of the work of the Lord he would ask them, What do you think, priest or deacon?   Which course is most advisable?   What do you counsel?   If you see that my advice is not best, do as you judge preferable, no matter for my opinion.   Thus he impressed them with the idea that they also had responsibilities, and were not merely to lean on the counsel of others.   He was very meek, condescending to seek out and converse with individuals about their souls.   He would go out and sit in the dusty streets of the villages and mingle with men in their conversation, and

32 *

gradually turn it to spiritual things.   Once I recall, a company was sitting in the street and conversing; he from his
room heard their voices and came down and sat with them,
and mixed in their talk and little by little turned it to the
salvation of the soul, and so discreetly and feelingly conversed with them that men very hardened and their hearts
filled with the matter of their worldly deliverance, sighed
out, "It is true; till we go to Christ there is no relief
for us."

4. Mr. Rhea was a *peace-maker*.   When he saw divisions
in the church and Christians alienated from each other, or
Nestorians at variance, clique against clique, or individual
against individual, he was in deep sorrow, and would use
all his skill and ability to restore peace between them; and
he sorrowed that our nation was not united.   He would say
very often, Until this people strive together in love, in counsel, in union, there is no relief for it.   He tried all he could
to promote peace.   He accounted this nation *his own nation*.
When he spoke of the business of the church or worldly
things, he identified himself with the people, and used the
terms *we* and *ours*.   In a word, he was *one with us*, and
shared in our joys and our sorrows.

5. Again, Mr. Rhea was a very *just man*, and *without
partiality*.   I have heard differing parties of Nestorians
speak of him.   When they had a case that could not be
settled by any others, they would wind up by saying, "Let
us go to Mr. Rhea and Deacon Isaac; whatever they say
we will accept."   The Nestorians were so well acquainted
with these two blessed men, and so assured that they were
strictly just in their decisions and possessed a keen per-
ception to discern and a sound judgment, that they readily
committed to them their final and lasting settlements.
They were both wonderful men in their keen insight and
strict justice.   Their thoughts were law not only for mem-

bers of the church, but also for all Nestorians in general; those outside of the church also responding to their decisions.

6. Mr. Rhea *could not be imposed upon.* He was so wise and discriminating that he instantly saw through a matter. However much the guilty and faulty betook themselves to flattering words and (seeing that Mr. Rhea returned no hard words) supposed they had accomplished their purpose, in conclusion, in one short answer, they would see that Mr. Rhea was not moved from the right; that he stood firm; that he was not to be jostled, but was stayed like a rock in its place. Those who went to him thus learned that they must do and say nothing aside from the truth; for their artifice could have no influence whatever on him.

7. His *nobleness.* Mr. Rhea was very noble. There is something in the disposition and bearing and acts and mien and conversation of men that marks them as low and ignoble, or places them in the higher grade of humanity. The noble traits are found in no man more than they existed in Mr. Rhea. We know not who were his parents or what his pedigree in the Anglo-Saxon race. The missionaries understand that better. But for myself, from the traits I have seen in him, when I compare him with the kind of distinction of nobility in Eastern lands, he seems to me a man of truly noble origin. If this is also the kind of nobility that exists in the West, I err not when I say that Mr. Rhea was a nobleman of the human race.

8. Again, Mr. Rhea was *very courteous.* Though a nobleman by nature and gifted with the highest endowments, yet he was so courteous that he made himself noble indeed. For the most distinguished mark of nobility is to be *courteous.* The ignoble we distinguish by this, that when he rises to high rank or is superior in gifts, he is lofty and uncourteous. But Mr. Rhea, though a missionary guide and a

man of exalted endowments, was yet one of the most *courteous;* so much so, that those who went to him, as one might say, an awe of diffidence fell upon them, and they exerted themselves and took all possible care not to return his courtesy with impropriety.

My friends, in all his traits of character, taken as a whole, he was a *complete* man. Few are they who have left behind them a memory so fragrant. Great is our cause for sorrow in his loss; that one so good, a preacher so powerful, a guide so gentle and wise, in the height of his strength has left us. He may be even more missed in the dimished band of his associates. Let them rest assured that their Nestorian friends·share with them in their sorrows. As the representative of this assembly, and in its behalf, I tender to you our condolence; and to the dear widowed lady, may God comfort and support her in her affliction, and may he sanctify this mournful providence to the benefit of us all.

What can we more say? The Lord hath done it; and who can stay his hand? Though it seems such a loss to us, he knows what is best. Let us then be resigned to his will. Mr. Rhea has now rested from his toils. Sorrow and mourning remain only for us, his friends on earth. Would that there might be in this assembly Elishas on whom his mantle shall rest, and they be heralds of that cross which he so heroically bore and in whose service he fell.

Near the monument of his father, in the village grave-yard at Blountville, Tennessee, has risen a monument with this inscription:

OUR MISSIONARY DEAD

WHO SLEEP IN

PERSIA.

SAMUEL A. RHEA,

Died at Ali Shah, Persia,

Sept. 2, 1865.

AGED 38 YEARS.

" Present with the Lord."

HIS SON

ROBERT LEIGHTON,

Died at Oroomiah, Persia,

May 21, 1865.

AGED 1 YEAR.

" To die is gain."